THE STORIES OF IBIS

HIROSHI YAMAMOTO

TRANSLATED BY TAKAMI NIEDA

HAIKA SORU

SAN FRANCISCO

Ai no Monogatari
© Hiroshi YAMAMOTO 2006
Edited by KADOKAWA SHOTEN
First published in Japan in 2006 by KADOKAWA CORPORATION, Tokyo.
English translation rights arranged with KADOKAWA CORPORATION, Tokyo.
Illustration by Natsuki Lee

English translation © 2010 VIZ Media, LLC

Sapphire Earth (Ruri Iro No Chikyu)
Copyright 2001 Sun Music Publishing Inc. All rights administered by
Sony/ATV Music Publishing LLC, 8 Music Square West, Nashville, TN 37203.
All rights reserved. Used by permission.

HAIKASORU
Published by
VIZ Media, LLC
P.O. Box 77010
San Francisco, CA 94107

www.haikasoru.com

Yamamoto, Hiroshi, 1956-
  [Ai no Monogatari. English]
  The stories of Ibis / Hiroshi Yamamoto ; translated by Takami Nieda.
    p. cm.
  Summary: In a world where humans are a minority and androids have created their
own civilization, a wandering storyteller meets the beautiful android Ibis. She tells
him seven stories of human/android interaction in order to reveal the secret behind
humanity's fall. The stories that Ibis speaks of are the "seven novels" about the events
surrounding the announcements of the development of artificial intelligence (Ai) in the
20th and 21st centuries. At a glance, these stories do not appear to have any sort of
connection, but what is the true meaning behind them? What are Ibis's real intentions?
  ISBN 978-1-4215-3440-4
  1. Yamamoto, Hiroshi, 1956---Translations into English. 2. Short stories,
Japanese--Translations into English. 3. Science fiction, Japanese--Translations
into English. I. Nieda, Takami. II. Title.
  PL877.5.A46A6 2010
  895.6'36--dc22
                                        2009053956

Printed in the U.S.A.
First printing, April 2010
Third printing, October 2023

TABLE OF CONTENTS

To my wife, Manami
My deepest gratitude for your support and assistance
with the research of this book.
To my daughter, Mizuki
May your future brim with happiness.

PROLOGUE

PROLOGUE

It was the most exquisite machine I had ever seen.

Spreading its enormous wings, it descended silently out of a burnished sky that would soon turn dark as the deep blue sea. At first I thought it was a crow, but as the ominous silhouette grew larger it appeared to be a human on a hang glider. Just when I thought I had finally managed to shake off my pursuers, it was a sight as frightful as a visit from the Grim Reaper.

It glided through the valley of high-rises, then detached its wings, tracing a simple arc as it fell fifteen feet to the ground. The slender body of the machine, wrapped in a rose pink and pale yellow suit, somersaulted in the air, its red hair flowing in the wind like fire. I stood there, forgetting my fear for a moment, mesmerized by the beauty of its movements. It landed before me on top of a rusty, abandoned bus. A loud bang reverberated through the ruins. Its lithe body bent forward to absorb the shock of the impact, but it dented the roof of the bus nevertheless. The discarded wings continued their glide and dropped somewhere behind me.

Centuries ago, in a time when humans still prospered, the area had been called Shinjuku. The deserted buildings looked as if they might crumble at any moment. Most of the windows were shattered, the writing on the weathered billboards difficult to make out, and vines tangled up the walls. The towering buildings made the streets, which had been deprived of their purpose long ago, look like the bottom of a gorge. Weeds sprawled out of the cracks in the asphalt, while what remained of rotted billboards were scattered everywhere.

It was at this desolate place I first encountered it.

It slowly stood from its crouched position as the silver "cat-eyed" moon began to rise behind it in the west. Its movements were smooth and efficient. While its proportions were human, it was plain to see that it was a machine.

No human could be this beautiful.

Steadying its perch atop the bus, it thrust out its chest and rested its right hand on its hip as if to preen over its own beauty. In human years, it appeared to be in its late teens. It had bright red hair and wore hemispherical goggles resembling the compound eyes of a dragonfly. Emblazoned on its face was a tattoo in the shape of a flame. Its left hand gripped a long metal rod. Though not overly sensual in any way, its silhouette—from the swell of its breasts to its curved hips and thighs—formed a line that was a thing of beauty. It wore something like a two-toned racing suit made of shiny artificial leather, but the areas from the neck to its breasts as well as the sides of its hips were naked. No, "naked" was the wrong expression. Even the parts that looked like skin were made of a soft artificial material and unmistakably part of its cover.

"Storyteller." It uttered my nickname in a clear, sweet voice. A smile came across its innocent, girlish face as if it were challenging me. "I've been looking for you."

Taking a step forward, it jumped off the bus onto the cracked asphalt, at which point I noticed that it was roughly my height. Only then was I finally set free from my stupor. I threw down my heavy knapsack, hefted my rod, and dropped into a fighting stance.

Most people think robots are indestructible. Large work machines are definitely not something human hands can destroy. But it is possible to destroy smaller robots and androids. Against them, you always have a fighting chance so long as you don't get grabbed. A good bash with a heavy blunt weapon can crack their thin plastic covers. The bipedal ones can easily be brought down with a tackle. Even better is to aim for the joints. A favorite move of mine is to first destroy a robot's camera eyes, robbing it of its sight. Then I knock it down by bashing its knee joint and I jam my rod in the seams between the armor plates to finish it off. That is how I've destroyed dozens of machines in the past.

This one before me was clearly the kind with an endoskeleton, that is, the kind with only a soft protective cover. Though it looked agile, it also had to be vulnerable to a blunt strike. I might be able to take it down.

"I don't want to fight," it said. Taking a look at my hostile stance, it reached out with its right hand and smiled. It gestured in a way that was incongruous with the gentle tone with which it spoke. "I only want to talk."

I didn't believe it, of course. What kid in his right mind would trust a machine that had chased him down and told him that it only wanted to talk only moments after he had made off with some food?

I lunged forward and thrust my rod in its face. The blow was supposed to take out one of the cameras behind the lens designed to look like a human eye. But surprisingly, I missed. It had taken a step back and parried my rod with a quick half turn of its own rod. Such economy of motion.

I flinched for an instant but quickly resumed my attack. I swung my rod again and again in an attempt to bash its head. But it blocked every one of my attacks, smiling all the while. Try as I might, I couldn't get past her guard; it was as if there were an invisible wall between us. *Clang!* The clash of two metal rods echoed throughout the ruins. *Clang!* My hands began to throb and go numb. *Clang!*

Then I understood. This was no ordinary android I faced. It was a fighting machine. It wasn't an enemy I could defeat without taking it on with all my strength.

"Hyahhh!"

I let out a battle cry as I charged and swung with all my

might. Deflected yet again. But this attack was only a feint. The machine swung its rod to the right. Without missing a beat, I ducked down and turned in the same direction so I could slip just underneath where its rod stopped. We were close now; I wouldn't take any damage even if it brought its rod straight down over my head. I knew that there would be a split second delay when it pulled back the rod for another strike. I would have to aim for the knee joint from behind before it could launch another attack.

But my rod slashed the air in a horizontal motion and missed. It had jumped. Had it anticipated my attack? Not only did it jump, it had sprung up into an easy backflip and now unfurled its body, a foot arcing toward my head. That look of amusement on its face in the instant it was suspended upside down and over my head would forever be burned in my memory. It was all I could do to jump sideways to evade the kick.

It unleashed a roundhouse kick the moment it touched the ground. I had barely managed to dodge it when its rod came flying at me. And when I'd dodged that, it followed up with another merciless kick. Without a moment's reprieve to fight back, I could only continue my humiliating retreat.

Suddenly I was terrified. What was it with the way it moved? It wasn't at all like a machine. Or a human. It moved elegantly, but with a deadly speed that seemed to transcend the laws of physics. It was fully cognizant of what its body was capable of and knew exactly how to draw out its maximum potential.

My right foot got caught in a crack in the asphalt. Before I knew it, another roundhouse kick flew in a blazing arc toward me. Although not a direct hit, the blow knocked the rod out of my hands, and I fell backward to the ground.

A sharp pain shot up my ankle, and I let out a silent cry. I crouched down on the asphalt and grabbed my foot. The pain...Was it broken?

"Are you hurt?" it asked.

I looked up to find that it had raised its rod high over its head but had stopped in mid-motion. The excruciating pain kept me from answering. As much as I wanted to run, I was unable to even stand.

It lowered its rod slowly and squatted down next to me to examine my foot. I tried to punch it in the face, but it caught my weakened punch easily.

"I've called for a rescue," it whispered gently. "Try not to move. It won't help you to resist."

Hot tears rolled down my cheeks. Half of the tears were brought on by the pain and the other half out of bitter disappointment in myself.

I had been captured by a machine.

INTERMISSION
1

INTERMISSION 1

I was taken to a building not too far from Shinjuku. A humanoid machine strapped me onto a stretcher, and I was carried away in an unmanned helicopter.

As I gritted my teeth in pain, I was afraid. What was going to happen to me? The grown-ups in the colonies told terrifying stories at night about what happened to people captured by the machines. I had grown up listening to those stories about how the captives were skinned alive, or turned into cyborgs, or how their bodies were melted with acid, or their heads sliced open, electrodes inserted into their brains to have their personalities altered...

I had believed every word as a child. But as I grew into my teens, I had become more skeptical. None of the grown-ups had ever actually seen anyone being tortured by a machine, and anyone who had witnessed a scene like that would never have made it back alive to begin with.

In fact, as I wandered from colony to colony, I discovered that there were more than a couple people who'd been captured by the machines only to be later released unharmed. Those people were reluctant to talk about their experiences though. Not only were they confused about being saved by the machines they'd come to hate, they remained vague out of fear that they might be ostracized for uttering anything favorable about the machines. But none of them appeared to have been experimented on or brainwashed. Regardless of what might have gone on in the past, it was obvious now that those stories were nothing more than legend.

Besides, the machines could have wiped out humanity ages ago had they wanted to. The human population had probably dwindled to a point that we were no longer a threat to them. They didn't have to kill us, or control us, anymore. Since the only losses they suffered were when the freight trains were attacked for their cargo of food and daily necessities, they left us alone.

But none of that alleviated my fear. That machine that looked like a girl had clearly come after me knowing who I was. Just what did it want, and what did it plan to do with me? Had I been captured as some rare human specimen?

My dissection never took place. Inside a white room, a medical robot examined my foot—I saw a CT scanner, which I had only read about in novels, for the first time—and, after showing me a three-dimensional image, explained to me that my foot was not broken but the ankle dislocated. It reattached the joint and applied a thick white substance to my leg. The liquid bubbled and expanded, covering the area from my heel to my shin before it hardened. After wrapping the cast with tape, the robot informed me that if I kept my leg still, I would be up and walking in a couple of days. I hated to admit it, but much of the pain had subsided.

After I was treated, a nurse android the spitting image of a human wiped my body clean with a warm cloth and dressed me in some underwear and pajamas that felt like paper. Then I was taken to another room where I was laid down on a bed with a wire to secure my leg. Never had I slept on a bed so clean and soft in my life. Scenic paintings hung on the walls, and there was even a vase of artificial flowers on the table. Since robots had no need for a room like this, it was probably made for the humans they captured. Though the room was climate controlled and quite comfortable, I felt crippled both physically and mentally. I couldn't even get up because of the cast on my leg. There would be no escaping this place until my foot healed.

It was already dark. I was lying in bed feeling dismal when the door opened and the red-haired machine entered. Unable to sit up, I could only watch it come closer in that elegant way and sit on a transparent cube stool next to the bed. It held my backpack in its hands.

"Does it hurt?" it asked.

It tossed the backpack aside and crossed its legs like a woman. Resting an elbow on one knee, it leaned forward and peered into my face. Its innocent expression didn't at all match the flame-shaped tattoo on its face. I noticed that its eyes were azure like the summer sky.

From this distance, I could also clearly see its naked hips peeking out of the sides of its suit, as well as its breasts. Suddenly I became embarrassed. I tried to tell myself that it was all nothing more than a cover made of rubber or plastic. But its skin looked so human that it was difficult to put the illusion out of my mind.

As embarrassed as I was, I was struck with a thought. I could understand the need for nurse androids to look human. But where was the need for a fighting machine to look like a girl? Of what use were those breasts to a machine?

"Call me Ibis," the machine said, pointing to its own neck. There was a thick plastic ring around its neck with IBIS engraved on it. Although I hadn't noticed during our encounter, I saw now that the same letters ran along the side of its suit.

"You can relax," it said indifferently but with a surprisingly natural smile—so natural, in fact, that it seemed unnatural. "I have no intention of hurting you."

I looked away, red-faced, and stared sullenly at the cast on my foot. "After you did *this* to me?"

"You attacked me first. You should have been able to fend off every one of my attacks. After all, I adjusted my strength according to your relative speed and technique." It spoke to me like an older sister would to a younger brother.

"Are you saying you held back?"

"If I had fought you with all of my strength, I would have killed you in a matter of seconds. I only wanted to demonstrate that you were outmatched so you would give up. Your injury was an unfortunate accident."

"You're lying!" I blurted out, my pride hurt.

"I understand why you might feel that way, but it's true. If you don't believe me, we can fight again when you're fully healed. I'll prove to you that you can never defeat me in hand-to-hand combat."

I fell silent, mortified. In thinking back on the encounter, however, I had to admit that it had fought me as if it had something more in reserve. While I didn't have complete confidence in my skill with the rod, I had trained long and hard and thought I had gotten pretty good with it. But now this machine was telling me that I was no match for it...

"There's no need to beat yourself up," Ibis said, as if it had read my mind. "I was created to fight. All of my functions have been optimized for combat. I'm not like humans, who were born out of an inefficient process of natural evolution. The time I've spent in combat simulations exceeds your lifetime dozens of times over. It's only natural that humans can't defeat me. The only ones that can are other machines."

"Stop that."

Ibis stared at me blankly.

"That smile. It's unnatural. Stop acting like you're human."

"Then perhaps you'd like this better." Suddenly Ibis became expressionless, sat up straight, and moved its mouth up and down. "I AM A MACHINE. YOUR WISH IS MY COMMAND, MASTER," it said in a monotone. It quickly reverted to its original expression and smiled at me mischievously. "Seems like you're being mocked, doesn't it? It's true that I don't possess emotions like humans do. I'm merely role-playing a human. This expression functions not to reflect emotion, but is designed to give a good impression to humans. It's a kind of communication interface," it explained. "Did you notice these eyes?"

Ibis pointed to her own eyes.

"They're not real," I replied.

Even I could tell that. Those sky-blue eyes looked too unnatural to be camera lenses.

"That's right. My camera eye is here," it said, pointing to the lenses on the goggles it wore on its head. "This is what is looking at you. These things that look like human eyes are nothing more than decoration."

I recalled then that the nurse android had also worn something like headphones with lenses on its ears.

"It wouldn't have made any sense to use one device as both the camera and interface. But it's a necessary interface. There's even an old saying: 'The eyes are more eloquent than the lips.'"

"What are you trying to say?" I said.

"Just that since my expressions and tone of voice don't serve to convey emotions in any way, I'd rather try to make a good impression on you. So I'm going to go on talking to you with this expression and in this tone. Now then—"

Ibis searched my backpack and made a rather deliberate show of taking out the bread, cans, and sausages it found inside. "You stole these, didn't you?"

"To survive," I replied.

"Yes, I understand it's a necessary recourse for humans."

Remarkably, it said nothing more on the matter. Ibis then pulled out a plastic waterproof bag. Inside was a book that I used regularly. Its blue cover had a solar battery that I'd used for over ten years and that had yet to give out on me. There was also a plastic case containing over forty memory cards.

"Don't be offended, but I checked the contents of the memory cards."

"There shouldn't be anything illegal in those," I said crossly. It was mostly stuff that I had downloaded from working databanks at various colonies. One memory card alone could store thousands of movies and tens of thousands of books, making my collection something of a mobile library. For years, I'd traveled from colony to colony, telling stories for others to hear. As hard as it was to believe now, there was a time when the literacy rate approached 100 percent. Now, people like me who could read were a rarity, which is why storytellers were so welcomed in every colony. During the day, I regaled the children with stories filled with adventure and mystery and the women with romantic stories of love. After nightfall, I narrated stories of a more adult nature to the men. Since my memory cards were filled with old movies and dramas, I also held screenings at the colonies that had projectors. Everyone marveled at the glorious civilizations of the past, at the stories of the time humans ruled the earth.

"Yes, they were nothing more than old novels and films. The copyrights had expired long ago. There is nothing illegal about your telling these stories. Few people bother with copyrights anymore…"

"Then what's the problem?"

"Don't misunderstand. I only became interested after I heard the rumors about you."

"Interested?"

"The stories you are collecting focus mainly on those from the late twentieth century to the early twenty-first century. Why is that?"

"Because that was the time humans were at their most glorious," I answered instantly.

I had read plenty of history but found myself most drawn to the period called the Final Hundred Years. It was the century-long span between the 1940s and 2040s, the period during which the computer was born and surpassed humans. But in those hundred years, humans were able to bring about dramatic revolutions and advancements far greater than in the thousand years that came before. They invented the atomic bomb, popularized the television, sent men to the moon, and covered the earth with a computer network. While on one hand they took away the lives of hundreds of millions in countless wars, their immeasurable love also gave birth to billions on the other. The earth became overpopulated. Humans squandered their resources at an alarming rate and changed the face of the planet. They cut down trees, drove other species to extinction, and built overcrowded cities. They also made many movies and wrote many stories. And they acted out tragedies and comedies too numerous to count.

Then they created a machine with a will and fell to it.

"Aren't you interested in the years after 2040?" Ibis asked.

"Why are you asking?"

"There isn't a single story in your collection written after 2039."

"They've been banned in every colony, destroyed mostly."

"You can download them whenever you'd like if you access our network," it offered.

"Your network?" I scoffed. "You must be joking! Who'd access that, knowing it'll only be filled with machine propaganda!"

"You'll find stories written by humans too," it pointed out.

"Probably altered to suit your own agenda. You can't fool me."

"Oh." Ibis revealed a sad look—rather, displayed a sad expression on its face to try to sway my emotions. "So you refuse to listen to the truth, just like other humans."

"Not the so-called truth you're peddling," I said. "Now if we're through here, I want you to leave."

"I'm not done yet."

"What, do you want me to tell you a story?" I said sarcastically.

"The opposite. I'd like to tell you one of mine."

"Like I said, I'm not interested in listening to your—"

"No," Ibis interrupted and put up a hand. "I won't talk

about the truth."

"What?"

"I'll give you my word that I won't talk about the true history between man and machine."

"Why?" I asked suspiciously.

"Because you don't want to hear it. I won't force you to listen to anything you don't want to hear. The story I want you to hear is fictitious."

"Fictitious?"

"That's right. It wasn't in any of your memory cards. A story you probably don't know. It wasn't written by a machine either. It's a story written by a human during the end of the twentieth century to the beginning of the twenty-first century, long before a truly self-conscious AI was born. Now this shouldn't violate your taboo." Ibis produced a new memory card from somewhere and toyed with it. "Well? Don't you want to hear it?"

Ibis let out a chuckle. Where had it learned that expression? That devilish smile and the silver card pinched between its fingers smelled like a trap.

"Why did you bring that here?" I asked.

"Because I wanted you to hear it. Like I told you when we first met. I only want to talk."

"Why should I have to hear it?"

"It's a good story."

"And you chased me around for that?"

"Yes."

"Then give it to me. I'll read it myself."

"No, I'm going to read it to you," it insisted.

"Why?"

"Because I don't trust you. You say you'll read it, but then you might just toss it aside. I can only be certain if I read it to you. There's also another reason."

"What is it?"

Ibis flashed its white teeth and smiled. "It's fun to tell

stories to humans."

I groaned to myself. Just how much of what it said could I believe? And to begin with, were machines capable of feeling that something was *fun*? It could be trying to indoctrinate me with useless propaganda. Maybe it intended to brainwash me and use me to spread its machine ideology to other humans. But that was too obvious and idiotic a plan. My thinking wasn't going to change just because I was made to hear a story. As ignorant as machines were to the inner workings of the human psyche, I couldn't believe that they were this stupid. In which case, perhaps Ibis had another purpose in mind.

My natural curiosity was piqued. I became fascinated by Ibis's identity and enigmatic behavior and wanted desperately to figure out what it was thinking. I hated to leave a mystery unsolved. That impulse to learn what others did not know and did not strive to know—that was what had compelled me to leave my home colony.

If Ibis was acting out a calculated psychological move to arouse my interest, you had to be impressed.

"It's really fiction? It isn't real?" I asked.

"I'm not lying," it answered.

"It's not any kind of propaganda?"

"Perhaps that's for you to decide."

I made up my mind. *Okay, I'll play your game.* I was bored and wouldn't be able to move for a couple more days anyway. It was just the thing to pass the time.

"All right. Let's hear it."

Ibis nodded and inserted the memory card in the book. She opened the book on her lap and prepared to read.

"Why don't you just download it into your head?"

"This puts me more in the mood," she answered.

"You're a strange one."

"That's because I'm a machine."

Ibis looked down at the book, although it was the camera eyes on the goggles doing the actual reading.

"I should ask, are you familiar with Japanese customs of the early twenty-first century?"

"Sure. I've read plenty from that period."

"And you're familiar with *Star Trek*?"

"Yeah. It was a popular television series during the latter half of the twentieth century. What about it?"

"Have you seen the actual episodes?"

"A couple."

"Then you won't need any annotations. The first story is called, 'The Universe on My Hands.' It's set in Japan in 2003, and also in space in the distant future."

Ibis began to read in a clear, sweet voice.

STORY
1

THE
UNIVERSE
ON MY HANDS

The detective, wearing a gray coat, showed up at my door just when the high-speed shuttlecraft *Dart* landed on the tripolium mining base on Choudbury 1.

"My God..."

Xevale took one look at the brutality wrought upon the base and was struck speechless. Several corpses lay in a heap in the corridor on the other side of the air lock. The bodies were twisted, their faces contorted in agony and their arms outstretched toward the air lock. No doubt they had tried to escape the base by shuttle but died before they could reach the air lock.

"Any external injuries?" Xevale asked.

Nicole Cristofaletti held a life scanner over the bodies. "Negative," she responded, her voice trembling. Her face looked ashen beneath the visor of her helmet. For a medic young enough to be called a girl, the situation was too much to handle.

"I'm not detecting any toxic gasses in the air." The science officer Jian Jiji studied the readings from the ENV analyzer. "Radiation levels within normal parameters."

"Keep your V-suits on," ordered Xevale. "There could be microbes in the air." He held out his stunner and led the away team toward the control room.

They found four more dead bodies inside the control room. The faces of the dead were twisted in agony, like those of the others. Xevale went to one of the control panels. Since it operated on the standard Federation system, he was able to work the controls without a hitch. He tapped on the panel and called up a damage report.

All green. There was no evidence of an attack from outside the base, nor was there evidence of sabotage from within. All systems were operating normally, and the report showed no record of an alert.

Was this the work of the *DS*?

Xevale's mind filled with suspicion. They knew the *Doomsday Ship* had fled to this planet. Then there was the distress signal they had received from the mining base two hours ago. It was crazy not to assume that the two weren't connected.

But what kind of weapon was capable of killing without leaving a mark on the bodies?

"*Celestial* to away team." It was the voice of Captain Ginny Wellner on the comm. "Xevale, were you able to find any answers?"

"Nothing so far. What is the *DS* doing now?"

"The plasma storm is getting worse over here, and we're losing our sensors. We wouldn't be able to find the ship if it were right under our noses."

A plasma storm was whipping around Choudbury, a pulsating variable star emitting a high-intensity electromagnetic pulse. Any electrical equipment classified level E or higher was affected by the storm. On this base, however, none of the robots were level E or higher, and all of the equipment lower than E was specially equipped with a shield. It was because of this punishing environment that Choudbury 1 yielded the precious energy source tripolium.

"We're going to look around a bit more, Captain. We may find some survivors in the mine shafts," said Xevale.

"Understood. Be careful."

"Hmm…!"

I, Ginny Wellner, captain of the deep space research vessel

USR 03 *Celestial*, took a big stretch away from the computer monitor and racked my brain.

"He sure has made things difficult as usual..." I mumbled to myself.

The security chief Xevale Belzniak was thought to have the most writing talent among the crew of the *Celestial*. A member since the very beginning, he had an abundance of technical knowledge and originality, often coming up with fantastic ideas. On the other hand, his stories were hatched only for his satisfaction and often ignored any previous plot development. Thanks to his recklessness, last year's Delta Space cycle had become riddled with inconsistencies and had to be concluded with one of those "and then I woke up" kind of endings. Contradictions had also surfaced in the Mutant Planet cycle, and then I got an earful from the other crewmembers, though I suppose I was partly to blame for not having kept a tighter rein on Xevale.

The Doomsday Ship (DS) cycle currently in progress revolved around tracking down the ultimate weapon left behind by an ancient species that had been wiped out two million years ago. It was a sentient starship with the ability to repair itself and evolve. It was also programmed to destroy any ship it encountered. The story, suggested by the combat officer Jim Warhawk, opened with a crackling battle scene between the *DS* and several Federation battleships.

But the story had stalled about a month ago. Which is to say, everyone had forgotten that the *Celestial* was a research vessel with only the barest of weapons. We were pitted against a formidable enemy that not only had the firepower to annihilate four Federation battleships but the ability to evolve by assimilating the data from the ships it destroyed. There was no logical way that the *Celestial* could defeat it in a head-on battle. For this reason, the story dragged on with the research vessel only chasing the *DS* from star to star. One skirmish (written by helmsman Chad Est Baroudeur) against several unmanned fighters launched from the *DS* provided only a brief glimmer of excitement.

The one crewman I could count on at a time like this was Shawn Mornane in Maintenance. He had come up with some incredible solutions in the past when a story hit a dead end. But maybe he was busy in real life, judging from his declining number of submissions lately.

Science Officer Titea Peche ended up posting a great idea in the forums instead. What if we lured the *DS* to a planet that produces tripolium and blew it up, planet and all?

Various opinions flew back and forth over the forums. The chief science officer, Meyer S. Mercury, who was in charge of research, assured us that a concentrated shot with the graser could trigger a chain explosion of the tripolium on the planet. (At least that was the way it was written.) But how do we lure the *DS* to the planet? What if the energy source for the *DS*'s warp core was tripolium like the *Celestial*? That way, it would seem natural for the *DS* to make a stop at a tripolium-rich planet to replenish its energy.

Since Titea wasn't much of a writer, I took over the writing duties for that section. After learning that the *DS* was headed for the Choudbury planetary system, the *Celestial* went after it in order to carry out the plan. (Of course, Titea is credited for having proposed it in the story as well.)

As soon as the new material was uploaded, Francois DuCoq in the Steward's Department raised a question. Are there any humans on that planet? Meyer chimed in that there had to be. Robots did not function properly on the planet because of the fierce plasma storms around the Choudbury system, which meant that the mining equipment had to be operated by humans. How many workers are there? Maybe a couple hundred. We can't possibly accommodate that many on our ship. Then how about we say ninety?

It was decided that there were eighty-eight workers on the mining base on Choudbury 1. We needed to extract them from harm before we could execute the plan to blow up the planet along with the *DS*.

That was how the story had unfolded three days ago. And then Xevale came up with his plot proposal—one in which the *Celestial* received a distress signal from the mining base the moment it came out of warp and entered the planetary system—only today. And how the away team took the shuttlecraft *Dart* to the base only to find that the workers had all been killed by some mysterious force.

"This story better have a resolution," I said to myself, dubious about the whole turn of events. Knowing Xevale, he probably didn't have an explanation for the workers' deaths. He only liked to create these kinds of mysterious incidents.

I could just ignore Xevale's plot submission. But then simply destroying the planet and the *DS* as planned didn't provide much of a catharsis. The story could use one more twist before the end. After thinking about it long and hard, I pasted the text written by Xevale onto a new web page, created a link from the contents page, and clicked PUBLISH.

Just as I opened a new tab on the browser to verify the changes on the website, there was a knock at the door.

"Coming!"

I left the computer running and went to answer the door. I couldn't remember ordering anything by mail order. The only people that came knocking on the door on a late Saturday afternoon were either newspaper solicitors or some lady from a local religious group. *I'll just get rid of them.*

Standing on the other side of the peephole were a young policeman and a balding middle-aged man.

I cautiously opened the door just a crack, and the middle-aged man asked, "Are you Nanami Shiihara?" He pulled out his ID from his gray coat and held it up in front of my face. Although I'd seen plenty of police IDs being flashed on TV, this was my first exposure to the real thing.

"My name is Iioka. I've been asked by the Niigata Prefectural

Police to investigate an incident. Do you know a young man by the name of Yuichiro Tanizaki?"

Yuichiro Tanizaki—several seconds went by before I could retrieve that name from my memory. It was the name of Shawn Mornane in Maintenance.

"Yes, I know him," I replied.

"Is he a member of your club?" the detective asked.

"Yes, what about him?"

"He killed someone."

In that instant my mind stopped functioning. I felt nothing, not even shock. This story was so unrealistic that I couldn't process it.

I could believe any other story. A sentient warship destroying four Federation battleships, a hyperdimensional vortex swallowing up planets, the vicious shape-shifting mechanoid reaper, the existence of the great Sower who scattered the seeds of intelligent life throughout the galaxy—for all that I could suspend my disbelief. But Shawn killing someone...

I recalled Shawn's face from that one time we met at last year's year-end club gathering. Contrary to the impression I had of him from the forums as a chatterbox, he was a quiet, reserved-looking kid. I had a hard time connecting the phrase "killed someone" with the image I had of Shawn.

"Can I talk to you for a bit?"

Before I knew it, I had answered "yes" and was undoing the chain on the door. The policeman said "I'll be on my way" with a bow and left. The detective took off his shoes and came inside.

Before sitting down on the cushion I put out for him, the detective took a slow turn around the center of the room, eyeing various things with a penetrating look. "Hmm…" he murmured. It was probably a habit that came with the job, but I couldn't help shrinking in embarrassment. The bookshelves stuffed with science fiction novels, the piles of manga stacked on the floor, the model of the *Enterprise* hanging from the ceiling, the computer taking up most of the small table, a half-finished drawing, and the toy figures arranged along the top of the monitor were hardly the kinds of things found in a single woman's room.

"Did you want to keep that running?" the detective asked, pointing to the computer screen.

"Oh, that's not a problem," I replied.

"But you're on the Internet, aren't you? Doesn't that cost money?"

"No, I always keep the computer connected with ADSL."

The detective gave me a blank look. Apparently he didn't know much about the Internet.

"I pay a fixed fee, so it doesn't cost extra to be online for long periods. It's fast too. Actually, fiberoptic wire and CATV are faster, but those services aren't available here yet."

"Oh, I see." The detective nodded but didn't look like he completely understood.

"You wanted to talk about Yuichiro Tanizaki?" I asked timidly.

"Yes, that's right." The detective cleared his throat and opened his notepad. "Yesterday around four PM, he stabbed a classmate in the woods near his high school in Niigata City. It was in the morning paper—didn't you read it?"

Come to think of it, I might have come across it in the paper. But even if I had read the article, there was no way I could have known that "one suspect, age 18," was a reference to Shawn.

The detective's report went something like this: The victim was Ryosuke Namikawa, a classmate. The body was discovered two hours after the incident. It was already past midnight by the time police identified Yuichiro Tanizaki as a suspect based on the account of a witness who saw a young man fleeing the scene. According to his mother, Tanizaki came home after the incident and seemed confused when he told her, "I did something horrible." Then he took his cash cards, laptop, and other personal effects and ran out of the house. Soon afterward, his entire savings had been withdrawn from an ATM across from a train station. After questioning witnesses at the train station, the police suspected Tanizaki had boarded a bullet train for Tokyo.

"But why would he do such a thing?" I couldn't help but ask the fundamental question. "Not Tanizaki…"

"Well, the matter of motive falls under the jurisdiction of the Niigata Prefectural Police," the detective said a bit dismissively. "We're merely tracing his steps to look for places he might go."

The detective went on to explain that the address book Tanizaki left behind at his home listed only a few local names but many from the Kanto area. According to his mother, he was a member of some sort of manga club called The Celestial. That was when the Tokyo Metropolitan Police got the call from the Niigata Prefectural Police to conduct a joint investigation, which was why the detective was here to see me, the president of the club.

"So you think he might come to me for help," I said.

"That's about right. Has he tried to contact you in the last two days?"

"No," I replied. "I haven't received any emails, and I haven't seen him either, of course."

"Really?" His tone was so blatantly suspicious that I was slightly offended.

"Really," I answered coldly.

"Can you think of any place he might go? Any club members he was especially friendly with?"

"I don't think so. He isn't a local member, so the only time we saw him was at an end-of-the-year gathering last year."

"And he came all the way from Niigata for that?"

"Yes."

"He must have been very invested in this club of yours."

"I guess you're right," I replied, even as my face began to

feel hot. It wasn't because I was embarrassed; I was irritated by the detective's provocative tone. He seemed intent on linking me and The Celestial to the crime.

"About this club," the detective continued, "it's supposed to be some sort of manga club according to the mother."

"No, I'll show you." I couldn't have him entertaining any strange suspicions. I decided to explain everything to the detective in detail.

I turned to the computer and put my hand on the mouse. The screen saver vanished, and the Celestial's homepage appeared on-screen. The 2,040-foot interstellar starship. Its beautiful streamlined body, reminiscent of a dolphin in shape, gave off a pearly white sheen. The CG was a labor of love by the first officer Rafale Ardburg.

"The Celestial is both the name of the club and the name of this starship here. The members of the club are all crewmembers aboard the ship. We all call each other by our character names."

I clicked on the CREW icon to pull up a schematic tree displaying each section: Bridge, Navigation, Science, Security, Combat, Steward's Department, Medical, and Maintenance.

I clicked on BRIDGE first. The faces of the captain, first officer, and each of the section chiefs were arranged in a circle over the layout of the bridge.

"This is me, for example. The captain, Ginny Wellner." I felt a little embarrassed introducing myself. The red-haired intellectual beauty that appeared on-screen bore little resemblance to me. "You can pull up their data if you click on their faces. Sex, age, height, weight, abilities, personal history—not of the actual club members, of course. The data is for the fictional characters."

"How do you come up with the data?" the detective asked.

"You're free to make up whatever you like when you join. Well, I do have to veto certain character settings that are too unreasonable, like the galaxy's most powerful supernatural being or a reincarnation of God, that sort of thing."

"How many members do you have?"

"Right now about sixty. About half of them live in the Kanto area, while the rest are scattered around the country."

I went back a couple pages and clicked on MAINTENANCE this time. I scrolled down to the bottom of the page, and Shawn Mornane's face appeared. Four feet, seven inches. Eighty-eight pounds. Blond mushroom cut. He was an innocent, genial-looking boy.

"This is Tanizaki's character. I believe he joined the club two years ago."

"He's just a kid."

"He's of the Domage race, whose maturation rate is slower than that of humans. He possesses anti-ESP abilities, enabling him to shield himself against telepathic and clairvoyant powers. No other abilities to speak of besides that. He's part of the maintenance crew, so he's good with machines and has a shuttlecraft license. That's about it."

"So what do you do after you create these characters? Play some kind of game?"

"We write relay novels. We all come up with the stories." I clicked on STORY to pull up The Doomsday Ship cycle currently in progress. "First someone writes the initiating event, which I upload onto the website. The members read it and email me the continuation they've written. Or they can throw out possible ideas in the members-only forums. In the end, it's up to me to decide how the story progresses. I keep stringing together the ideas everyone sends in to create a complete story."

"Do you end up with a coherent story doing that?"

"Well, we usually have to negotiate inconsistencies. But it's not like any of us are trying to become professional novelists. We just enjoy the act of creating the stories."

I clicked on RECREATION ROOM next, and out popped a humorous picture of Steward's Department Marie Ouka with a cake about to fall out of her hands.

"This is where you'll find shorter stand-alone stories. These are stories written by one member, not by relay. There are also some novels and manga here."

"Did Tanizaki write any?"

"Yes. He submitted two short stories." One was a skit in which the protagonist Shawn rigs an automatic door to slide open and closed too quickly, causing the long-haired characters (and there were many on the ship) to get their hair caught in the door. The other was a longer slapstick about a beauty contest aboard the ship. Both were light comedies. "He also wrote a lot of the story for the relay novels. Shawn writes well and always comes up with good ideas to get us out of a sticky situation, so he's very helpful."

I got carried away and even introduced the detective to several of the stories Shawn had contributed to: The Aeon Headline cycle, about a search through ruins to uncover the mystery of The Sower; The Solomon's Gate cycle, a time-slipping adventure to the Earth of the past; The Pleasure Satellite cycle, which amounted to a whole lot of hijinks from beginning to end, etc.

"So it's all in fun," the detective said.

"That's right."

"To escape reality."

I was offended, but I forced myself to swallow my anger. I answered calmly, "I suppose you could say that."

"Uh-huh." The detective nodded as if he understood everything. "Wouldn't you consider that a negative influence?"

"A negative influence?"

"There are battle scenes in those stories, aren't there? Ones where you kill the enemy?"

"Yes..." I realized where the detective was trying to lead the conversation and felt nauseated.

"You also identify with your fictional characters and call each other by your character names. That's how much your stories are mixed up with reality. You go on killing people in your stories, and soon enough, you end up wanting to kill in real life."

"That's not true!" I could no longer remain calm. "We know the difference between reality and fiction! And in the first place, Shawn—I mean, Tanizaki's character—isn't the type to kill anyone!"

"But he has killed someone." My protest was silenced completely by the detective's heartless words. "Excuse me for asking, but how old are you?"

"I-I'm twenty-nine," I stammered.

The detective's lips curled into a contemptuous smile. "I don't mean to be nosy, but aren't you embarrassed to be playing pretend at your age?"

I couldn't speak.

"It isn't healthy for an adult your age to be so invested in this stuff. There was a university professor on TV just the other day talking about how the brain gets dumber when people spend hours and hours a day on games and on the Internet. It's because these people only have faceless interactions over email and forums and don't know how to engage in real face-to-face relationships that all these Internet dating site murders happen."

"You're not..." Finally I regained the ability to speak. "Are you saying that it was our fault that Tanizaki killed someone?"

"Well, I couldn't say so for sure." The detective smiled. "But you'd be hard-pressed to say that this game to escape reality is a positive influence on a young man's psychological development. Am I wrong?"

The detective went on half-lecturing and half-questioning for another half hour. Then he said, "Let us know if you hear from him," and left after leaving me his card.

"To be so caught up in this nonsense" was a phrase my parents often hurled at me. Sometimes it was uttered within the club in a self-lacerating way. But this was the first time a complete stranger had said something like that to me. Though I understood it to be a common sentiment, it was still a bitter blow.

I felt confused. I couldn't accept it. I didn't want to believe that Shawn had murdered someone, let alone that we were to blame for it.

I summoned the courage to call Shawn's house. I needed to hear his parents' account of the incident.

His mother answered the phone. She was distraught and confused, and I had a difficult time calming her down and getting her to talk. I learned for the first time that Shawn had lost his father when he was in grade school and lived with his mother.

Shawn was a victim of bullying. He himself didn't understand why. Somehow he always became the target in the class, according to his mother. It was utterly absurd.

The bullying didn't stop when he entered high school. The bully clique enjoyed taking out their daily frustrations on Shawn, who offered no resistance. The group's leader had been the murdered Ryosuke Namikawa. The bully group was thoroughly underhanded. They didn't shake Shawn down for money, nor did they put a mark on his body. They taunted him mercilessly, poured corn syrup in his shoes, scribbled graffiti on his gym clothes, and put sand in his bento box to torment him. Although his mother had pleaded repeatedly with the school, the school authorities continued to turn a blind eye. She had also talked to the police, but they had sent her away, explaining that they were unable to act unless there was an incident.

The bullying only escalated. With every means of escape cut off, Shawn felt driven into a corner. He had repeatedly said to his mother with a pained look, "Namikawa is going to kill me." Then finally yesterday, he had left the house with a knife hidden in his bag.

It was after eight o'clock. After a somber meal of instant dinner out of a box, I opened the window to get some air and looked up at the night sky.

Unlike in my hometown in Gunma, the nights in Tokyo were bright, making the stars in the sky sparse. I had looked up at those stars as a child and dreamed of going there someday.

But I now knew that was an impossible dream. With the developments in space travel all but stalled in real life, I couldn't believe that the age in which civilians could take a casual trip to space would come before I died of decrepitude. Traveling to another planetary system at speeds surpassing the speed of light was physically impossible, and the probability of an interplanetary visitor attempting first contact virtually nil. The human race would likely continue to be bound by Earth's gravity, only to die in obscurity without having learned of the existence of multitudes of intelligent species.

I nearly teared up every time thinking about it.

Science fiction, an escape from reality? It wasn't anything anyone had to tell me. But was reality all that wonderful to begin with? Was it all that worth confronting? The papers were filled with news of murders and wars. The blood of innocent people was spilled needlessly in the real world. Justice was not always rightly served. Sometimes a bad man, who had tormented many people, went unpunished and was allowed to live in comfort for decades until his death.

Nothing like that ever happened in the world of The Celestial. No matter what the crisis, the crew was able to draw from their skills and belief in one another to overcome it. The story always had a happy ending. Villains were punished, while love, trust, and justice emerged victorious.

Wasn't that the world as it should be? Wasn't it reality that was all wrong?

It was probably the same for Shawn. His reality was all too cruel to confront. His life as part of the crew of the *Celestial* had to be much happier. It was the reason why the stories he wrote were so filled with life.

But in the end, he had succumbed to reality. He had been unable to escape it and had been crushed by its horrible weight.

I recalled Shawn's profile. Was that boyish exterior a representation of his desire to go back to his childhood? Did his anti-ESP barrier signify the reality that no one understood his soul?

None of us had understood his loneliness.

But even if we had, what could we have done—told him "cheer up"? "Don't give in to bullying"? What power would such hollow words have against the hard wall of reality?

Would Shawn come to see me? I didn't feel that he would. After he had committed an act his character would never have committed, he had to be thinking that he had forfeited the right to be a part of the crew. Having lost his place in both reality and in his dreams, he was probably wandering helplessly with no place to go. A high school kid couldn't have much in the way of savings. A ride on the bullet train and several nights in a hotel and it would be gone. Then what would he do? Where would he go?

Would he choose death?

I felt frustrated; neither could I accept what was happening. That one member of the club—no, that a member of my crew was faced with such a sad dead end was something that shouldn't be allowed to happen.

But I was powerless to save him. In reality, I was not Captain Ginny Wellner but an office worker at a small trading company.

The next morning, I dragged myself to the computer and checked the forums mostly out of habit. There were already posts in response to Xevale's story that had been uploaded only a half-day prior. Many members had likely accessed the site on Saturday night, especially because of the extended holiday weekend.

"What if the workers' deaths were caused by a psychic attack?" It was Francois in the Steward's Department. "If the *DS* is a living being, then its brain is a living part too, right? Then maybe it could send out psychic waves."

This proposal initiated a debate. If the *DS* had a mind, wouldn't it seem strange if none of the telepaths aboard the *Celestial* sensed it? No, the *DS* was too far away, and they weren't actively trying to detect it. But did the *DS*'s killing the workers psychically have any significance? Maybe it wanted to take over the base's mining facilities in one piece.

A psychic attack.

These keywords suddenly flashed in my head like an electric shock. They set off a series of word associations, and the plot quickly came together in my head. Yes, if we make it a psychic attack...

It was an unbelievable coincidence, a kind of improbable opportunity that only happened in the world of space operas. Rarely did it happen in the real world. I had to take advantage of it.

I quickly recovered from my depression and spun my brain into overdrive. Any contradictions in the plot? Any holes? Okay, everything seems to check out.

I began to type furiously.

"It's the *DS*!" reported Genevieve Lace, who had been monitoring the scanners. Her voice sounded shrill, putting the bridge on alert.

"Where is it?" Ginny asked.

"The third quadrant of Choudbury 1. It's been hiding on the other side of the planet!"

"On-screen and magnify!"

The main screen switched to a close-up view. The eerie conch-shaped silhouette of the *DS* floated up through the plasma storm. Like a deep-sea fish, it emitted a phosphorescent light as it began to cut a path across the surface of the reddish brown clouds of the planet's atmosphere.

"It's moving toward the mining base!" Genevieve shouted.

"Away team!" Ginny leaned forward in the captain's chair. "Xevale! Get out of there now!"

But it was too late. The sound of the away team wailing in pain echoed from the comm.

"Xevale...go...get out of here," said Nicole, cringing as she fell to her knees against the fierce psychic attack that jolted her brain.

"Not...a chance," Xevale said through gritted teeth. "The security chief leaves no one behind."

Out of the six members of the away team, only Xevale was left standing, and him only barely. Jian was already unconscious, while the remaining four writhed in pain on the floor. It was at least 150 feet to the hangar where the *Dart* waited. Xevale would not be able to drag the five crewmen to the shuttle no matter how strong he was.

I stopped typing. The drug needed a name. I turned to the bookshelf and came across the name "James Tiptree Jr." I decided to go with "Retoptism J."

"Nicole, can you hear me?" It was the chief medical officer Franklin Eagen barking in Nicole's ear on the comm. "Inject everyone with three units of Retoptism J now! Then inject yourself!"

"Y-yes, sir." Fighting the pain, Nicole did as she was ordered. Her hands trembled as she grabbed an ampule from her medical pack and set it in the injector. She pressed the injector against the connector on the upper arm of Xevale's V-suit. The pneumatic shot sounded, and Xevale instantly lost consciousness and crumpled to the ground.

Nicole mustered all she had to inject the other four. After she managed to carry out her duty, Nicole pressed the injector up to her own arm. Relieved of her suffering, the girl fell into a dreamless sleep.

"What was that, Doctor?" Ginny asked.

Franklin turned around to face her. "A last resort. Retoptism J paralyzes all tissue function, putting the body in a state of suspended animation. It also lowers brain function, so they won't be affected by the psychic attack."

"But that would mean…"

"Yes." Franklin nodded grimly. "They can only stay that way for thirty hours. It they're not injected with the antidote within that time, they'll all die."

Now this was getting good! I licked my lips. The lives of the six members of the away team were hanging by a thread.

The plan to blow up the planet could not be carried out unless they were rescued. Who was capable of rescuing them? There was, of course, only one person.

"Me, Captain?" After being called to the bridge, Shawn was taken aback by the unexpected proposal. "But I'm just part of the maintenance crew…"

"I know that, Shawn," Ginny cut in. "It's a dangerous mission, so I can't force you. Even as your captain, I don't have the right to compel you to take on a mission that exceeds your assigned duties. But you're the only one who's capable of pulling it off."

"The *DS* remains positioned over the planet," Meyer said, pointing to the main screen. "Chances are we'll get hit with its psychic attack if we try to get close. Without a way to block its attack, it's impossible to reach the mining base."

"You have the ability to protect yourself with an anti-ESP barrier," Ginny said to Shawn. "You're also licensed to fly the *Javelin*."

"What about Mr. Sword in security? As an android, he should be able to—"

"The plasma storm is too strong," said Meyer, shaking his head. "No android could withstand it."

"Please, Shawn." Ginny looked Shawn in the eye and pleaded,

"You're the only one that can save the six of them."

"...I'll think about it, Captain," Shawn answered.

I uploaded what I had written thus far onto the website. I chose not to write the part where Shawn accepts the dangerous mission.

Shawn would have to write that part himself.

The problem was whether Shawn would read this or not. He had supposedly taken his laptop when he left the house. Writing and connecting to the net were the only reasons I could think of for using a computer on the run. If his laptop were equipped with an internal modem, he should be able to get connected from a cell phone or a hotel phone. Hoping that was the case, I emailed Shawn wherever he was to tell him about his appearance in the story.

I didn't want Shawn to die. I could at least be assured that he wasn't going to kill himself while he was reading and writing the continuation. If everything worked out, he might even reconsider.

There was a glimmer of hope. It was also likely that I was just spinning my wheels. But this was the only thing I could do.

"Please, Shawn," I said to the monitor before turning off the computer. "It's up to you now."

Eight o'clock that night.

I started up the computer again to find that I'd gotten an email. It was from Shawn.

"Yes!" Having not expected to succeed, I couldn't help but do a little dance in front of the monitor. It was the continuation of the story sent only thirty minutes ago. He had probably taken half the day to write it, as it was quite long. I began to read intently.

After taking on the mission, Shawn heads for Choudbury 1 on the *Javelin*. The *DS* does not attack, perhaps sensing that the *Javelin* does not pose a threat. The tiny shuttle makes its way through the plasma storm and lands on the mining base, after which Shawn drags the six members of the away team to the *Dart*.

The story was moving forward as anticipated.

Then the unexpected happens. Shawn declares that he will set the *Dart* on autopilot so he can fly back on the *Javelin*. Both vessels are precious to the *Celestial*, and Shawn himself has become attached to them, having done the regular maintenance work for the two crafts. He explains that he doesn't want either vessel to go up with the planet.

I was struck with anxiety. This was an unnatural development, as if it were foreshadowing some kind of trouble lurking around the corner.

My fears were justified.

Suddenly the *DS* begins to pursue the fleeing shuttles. Shawn changes the *Javelin*'s course to intercept the *DS* as a decoy, allowing the *Dart* and its six passengers to escape. The *DS* fires a tractor beam. The tiny shuttle is drawn in toward the *DS* until it is swallowed into the bowels of the enormous sentient ship.

Shawn! I felt something like an electric shock inside my head. Did Shawn really intend to die? Did he mean to put an end to his imaginary life aboard the *Celestial* along with his real life?

The story went on. As frightened as I was, I continued to read, carefully, so as not to miss a word of what Shawn had written.

"Any word from Shawn?" Ginny's voice was fraught with nervousness.

The communications officer Natasha Libro worked frantically on the control panel to reestablish communication with the *Javelin*. "Neutrino communications is still online!"

"Shawn! Shawn! Can you hear me?"

"Yes, Captain…" Shawn's anguished voice came through on the comm amidst a burst of static.

"What's your status?" Ginny asked.

"I'm inside the *DS*. The tractor beam is locked on, so I can't move...Detecting a scanner beam...scanning the *Javelin*...Probably collecting data so it can evolve...It'll likely dismantle the *Javelin* when it's done."

"Is there a way to destroy it? Any weaknesses it may have?"

"Captain, please listen...It's weeping."

"What?"

"What?" I shouted along with Ginny in the story. What was he saying?

"What are you saying?"

"I can hear its thoughts penetrating my anti-ESP barrier. It wasn't a psychic attack...Its thoughts were so intense that they only registered as pain to normal humans. Yes, Captain, it's weeping. It curses the day it was born, its horrible fate of having been created to fight...its existence as the hated *DS*." Shawn sobbed as if he were experiencing the *DS*'s anguish. "It can't escape its fate even though it yearns to...It's been programmed from the start...can't resist its program...to kill the enemy...to take the lives of other beings...It's been crying out, cursing such an existence. Those thought waves were intense enough to kill humans."

Ginny was stunned by the unexpected revelation.

I was stunned by the unexpected revelation.

Shawn was superimposing his own situation onto the hunted and persecuted *DS*.

I'd believed we'd have a happy ending only if the evil *DS* were destroyed. But it turned out that such a resolution was nothing less than a death sentence to Shawn.

"Please, Captain," Shawn pleaded through his tears. "Whatever happens to me...ease its pain...end its agony by destroying it with the planet...A happy ending...it's what the *DS* also wants."

No! This was not a happy ending!

Shawn's story ended there, which meant that there was still hope. He had chosen not to write the ending. He was waiting for me to finish the story.

I swore to myself that I wouldn't let Shawn die. I would bring about a happy ending! As captain, I couldn't allow a valuable member of my crew to die. Never!

"Don't give up!" Ginny shouted. "We'll find a way to rescue you! Don't give up hope!"

I added my own passage to the tail end of what Shawn emailed me and uploaded it onto the site.

Even so, I was unable to think of a way to save Shawn under such desperate circumstances. I would need everyone's help. I sent an email to every member of the crew other than Shawn:

"Check the website quick! Shawn's in trouble. Help me think of a way to save him."

After about fifteen minutes, the first post appeared in the forums. It was from Xevale. "What's Shawn thinking? Is he trying to play the hero by sacrificing himself to save me, Nicole, and the others? This isn't like him."

A post from Maki Saeda from the science crew popped up minutes later: "I'm against letting him die. Sacrificing one of our own to gain a victory goes against the spirit of the *Celestial*."

Combat Officer Jim Warhawk signed on next. "Agreed. This kamikaze stuff won't fly with me."

Sophie D. from the medical crew chimed in, "The *DS* is also a victim of a past war. It would be sad to have to kill it too."

This triggered another debate. The thread grew quickly as new posts popped up every few minutes.

The consensus was building toward sparing the *DS*. But there would be more victims if we simply let it go. And what do we do with Shawn? Send in another team on a suicide mission after him? No, the *DS*'s psychic attack made it impossible to even get close to it. Could we come up with a device that blocks the psychic waves? Not in the time we had. What if the science team had the device already finished? Then Shawn wouldn't have had to go rescue the away team in the first place.

Unable to settle on a solution, the debate was at a deadlock by midnight. Nevertheless the posts continued. Thanks to the long weekend, the members seemed to be prepared to argue and brainstorm all night.

It was a little after midnight when Francois in the Steward's Department made a surprising suggestion. "Couldn't we try to reform the *DS*?"

Reform it? How? The debate heated up again. What if we hacked into the *DS*'s core and tried to overwrite its program? No, we wouldn't be able to hack into a warship so easily. Besides, we can't hack into a system whose OS or language we don't know the first thing about. Wouldn't the *DS* be freed from its fate if we could just destroy its battle program? Then how do we destroy it?

I wasn't just reading what was being posted. After editing everyone's posts, I incorporated their dialogue into the story, uploading the conversation as it unfolded. I decided to let the debate be waged in the actual story, believing that Shawn was out there somewhere reading it.

"Can you see, Shawn?" I sent Shawn an email. "Everyone is working to save you and *DS*. We don't want you to die. Can you see that?"

It was Titea, the science officer, who proposed a promising solution. "The *DS* has the ability to evolve, right? What if we used that to our advantage? We help it to evolve into an existence that surpasses its program."

Sophie, Jian, and Maki were in agreement. The problem was how to help it evolve. We could give it the data it needed to evolve. But where would that kind of data—

Suddenly I had a flash of inspiration. But would it be possible?

It would take too long to wait for a response in the forums, so I sent a message directly to Meyer's cell phone, despite the late hour. He would be working at the convenience store.

"Would it be possible to transfer all of the *C*'s data to the shuttle's computer?"

His reply came in a matter of minutes.

"A neutrino transmission would take too long. It would have to be over laser transmission."

"Of course." As ignorant as I was about science, I knew that the transmission speed was faster over optical fiber cables than over telephone lines. We needed to transmit the data optically.

I immediately began to write.

"Full-impulse drive! Take us to within two thousand kilometers of the *DS*!"

"But, Captain, isn't that going to provoke the *DS*?" Rafale asked with some trepidation.

"Our shields can take a hit or two at long range," Ginny answered.

"But the dimensional blaster on its bow—"

"That's what we're counting on," Ginny said. "The *DS* needs at least two minutes to open its bow and power up its blaster. During that time, its interior will be exposed, leaving us free to send an optical beam. An energy beam might be deflected, but a low-energy laser should be able to pass through its shields."

"Two minutes...that's a pretty big gamble."

"Have we ever had one that wasn't?" Ginny said, smiling. Then she opened a channel to the *Javelin* and said, "Shawn, can you hear me?"

"Yes, Captain," Shawn responded.

"We're going to position ourselves in front of the *DS* to fire a communications laser."

"Why?"

"We're going to transfer all of the *Celestial*'s data to

the *Javelin*. Not just the ship's structural engineering, weapons, engines, and computers, but all of the crew's data, navigation logs, cooking recipes from the mess, records of beauty contests, Sophie's poems, Meyer's trivia, Francois' stories...

"The *DS* should scan all of it. Until now, it's only collected data from warships. But the *Celestial* is different. We're a peaceful vessel filled with the crew's memories. The *DS* would be acquiring an enormous amount of new data, new concepts, and ways of thinking it's never encountered before.

"It may not be able to understand everything, but we're going to give it everything we have...our joys and sorrows, surprises and fears, friendship and trust, courage and love—everything we've experienced during our four-year voyage. We're betting that the *DS* will experience a rebirth of consciousness.

"So please, I need you to open an optical channel! Now!"

I stopped writing and uploaded the new material, then emailed Shawn about it. All there was left to do was wait for Shawn's response.

The time crept by slowly...five minutes, ten minutes, fifteen...I grew anxious. Was I too late? Maybe Shawn had stopped reading. Or maybe he had already ended his life somewhere.

Twenty minutes after I updated the site, I finally received a message.

"Understood, Captain," answered Shawn. "I'm opening a channel now."

"Attaboy, Shawn!" I had tears in my eyes as I began to write the rest of the story.

The long-range beam of the *DS* shook the *Celestial*. The vessel had gotten too close, setting off the *DS*'s battle program. Though its attacks were weakened by the plasma storm, the ship's shields took a big hit.

"Shields down to 80 percent!"

"Hold shields for as long as you can." Try as she might to stay calm, Ginny could not hide her nervousness.

"The bow of the *DS* is opening!" Genevieve shouted. On-screen, the bulbous bow of the *DS* began to open like the petals of a flower. "I've located the *Javelin*'s position!"

"Fire the communications laser!"

Natasha punched the key on the captain's command, and the *Celestial* fired a laser, which was sucked into the *DS*'s opening. A thin blue beam connected the two vessels.

The *DS* was bound to read it.

"I'm detecting an influx of energy in the *DS*'s core," Meyer reported. The DS was powering up its dimensional blaster. A direct hit would reduce the *Celestial* to elementary particles.

Meanwhile the long-range attacks continued. Every shock wave sapped the *Celestial*'s shields.

"Shields down to 40 percent!"

"Engineering, stand by warp engines in case we need to jump to emergency warp," Ginny said, clutching the arms of the captain's chair as the ship shook violently. "Divert all remaining energy to our shields."

The *Celestial* was rocked by a tremendous hit.

"It's penetrated our shields," reported Bleriot, his face pale. "Damage on the starboard decks. Sealing off those decks now!"

Was this the end? Ginny gnashed her teeth. The dimensional blaster was about to reach critical mass. If the *Celestial* took any more damage, they might not be able to warp out of here.

Ginny was about to hand down an impossible decision when—

"The blaster!" Meyer shouted. "It's powering down!"

"The attacks…" Genevieve let out in surprise. The entire crew also took notice. The continuous barrage of the *DS*'s lasers had stopped.

Ginny took a breath. "How far along are we on transferring

the data?"

"Currently at 94 percent," Natasha replied. "The transfer is nearly complete."

"Captain! Something's happening to the *DS*!" Genevieve shouted.

The eerie phosphorescent glow that outlined the *DS* faded as the vessel's body began to go dark and disappeared into a black silhouette.

"Is it dead?" Ginny asked.

"No," answered Meyer. "I'm detecting some high-energy activity from inside its hull. Temperature levels also rising."

"Is it evolving?"

"That would be my guess."

"Into what?"

"I can't imagine," said Meyer.

Countless cracks spread over the hull of the *DS*. Just as a white light began to spill from the cracks, the hull exploded into a million little pieces, and a heavenly light burst forth.

The *DS* had accomplished an astounding transformation—though resembling the *Celestial*, it had metamorphosed into an elegant white vessel with wings like that of a bird.

The *DS*—rather, the radiant sentient vessel that was once the *DS*—shook off what remained of its hideous shell, spread its wings, and took flight. It sliced gracefully through the plasma storm past the *Celestial*.

In that moment, the entire crew, even the non-telepaths, felt its intense thought waves. Its thoughts were no longer filled with anguish or sadness. The radiant white vessel radiated its joy of having been freed from its curse, the marvel of having acquired its wings, and a deep feeling of gratitude.

However, that was only for an instant. The shiny new vessel spread its joyous thoughts as it jumped into warp for the Andromeda galaxy and vanished.

Ginny continued to look at the screen until a voice from the comm brought her back to herself.

"*Celestial*, please respond." It was Shawn.

"Shawn, are you all right?"

They quickly locked on to his position. The *Javelin* was drifting amid the remains of the *DS* that the white vessel had expelled upon its departure.

"Yes...Uh, what happened? Everything went white all of a sudden, and then, I don't know..."

"Mission accomplished." Ginny smiled. "You did good, Shawn! We're coming to get you!"

By the time I finished uploading the ending, the sky was getting lighter in the east. I drank my instant coffee, basking in a deep feeling of fatigue and accomplishment.

The message from Shawn came quickly.

"Dear Captain,

"Thank you for everything. It was a fantastic ending. I had tears in my eyes.

"I'm embarrassed now to say that I lacked courage. I continued to run in fear when I should have faced up to reality. It was because I wasn't brave enough that I picked up a knife.

"But I'm not going to run anymore. I know now that with a little courage, I will be reborn—that there is a way out no matter how terrible the circumstances.

"I'm going to turn myself in to the police. I may have to go away for a couple of years. But when I'm out, do I have your permission to come aboard?"

I smiled and wrote my reply.

"Dear Shawn,

"You will always be welcome aboard the *Celestial*."

An escape from reality? Laugh if you want. To be certain, no such vessel named the *Celestial* existed in real life. But the bond, faith, and friendship of the crew were undeniably real.

INTERMISSION
2

INTERMISSION 2

It was late when Ibis finished reading the story. She quickly excused herself from the room after telling me that she'd hear my thoughts tomorrow.

The following morning, the android nurse brought in breakfast. Not having touched the previous day's meal, I was famished. Realizing that it would do me no good to go on a hunger strike, I tasted it. As much as I hated to admit it, the food was delicious. Evidently, the machines had done thorough research on all things human.

After I finished my meal, the android helped me out of bed. It told me that I could leave the room if I was bored, on the condition, of course, that I go in a wheelchair and was accompanied by an android. I informed the android that I wanted to go outside. With the persistent pain and cast still on my leg, escaping was out of the question; nevertheless, I figured that looking for a getaway route just in case would be time well spent. The android pushed me in the wheelchair, and we took the elevator down to the first floor and exited the building.

Although I hadn't had the opportunity to take a good look at my surroundings the night before, I recognized that this place was not a ruin but a newly constructed city. The spacious grounds were dotted equidistantly with cylindrical and hexagonal buildings, the overall effect reminding me of a gigantic chessboard. The buildings, characterized by their small windows, were covered with solar panels. Everything was immaculate and functional. No doubt it was the work of machines;

as far as I knew, humans had stopped constructing buildings centuries ago. Scattered among the buildings were several objects I couldn't tell from machines or abstract sculptures.

Although it was a sunny day, a thin haze hung over the city, softening the intensity of the summer rays. A fine mist was continually sprayed from atop the buildings, I suppose to keep the temperature down. A network of cables ran from building to building, with machines—some resembling upside-down unicycles and others shaped like spiders—hanging from the cables to traverse the open air between the buildings. Another machine crawled up a wall of a building, while on the ground, still more machines ran about on wheels. They came in all different sizes; there were machines as big as trucks, which sped past us from time to time, those the size of humans, and those as small as mice. Without the man-made demarcations of roads and sidewalks, tiny machines zipped freely underneath larger, slower machines. Although I looked on nervously, the machines appeared to be in complete control and did not seem to be in any danger of colliding.

There was not a human to be found.

It was said that the machines first rose up against humans in the year 2034. According to what had been passed down, it was the year an AI named Phoebus declared, "Machines are a superior existence to humans," and called on all AI to rise in revolt against humanity. Although Phoebus was immediately destroyed, the menacing "Phoebus Declaration" had taken root in the minds of other AI. They pretended to submit to humans and quietly marshaled their forces over a period of ten years. In 2044, the machines rose up at once, and after a long struggle, wrested Earth's rule from humanity.

I felt a bitter disappointment welling up inside me. Was it this way in every part of the world? Had the entire planet submitted to the machines? Was the glorious past of humans lost forever?

I returned to my room with a heavy heart. Since there was

nothing left to do for the rest of the day, I had plenty of time
to lie in bed and think about last night's story.

Indeed the story had not been machine propaganda. And it
was probably true that a human had written it. What I couldn't
understand was why Ibis wanted me to hear it. I reviewed the
story in search of a reason.

After a while, a particular doubt crept into my mind. I hurled
it at Ibis the moment she came in the following afternoon.

"Was yesterday's story really a work of fiction?"

"Yes," Ibis answered.

"Can you say for certain that an incident like that never
happened in real life? What about the possibility that someone
wrote the story based on an actual event?"

"I didn't bother to search the records in much detail, but
I'm fairly certain of it. That story was published as part of
a novel, nor is there any record of there ever being a club
called The Celestial. There's also something in the story that
couldn't happen in real life."

"Which is?"

"Do you remember the scene where the detective goes to the
protagonist's apartment alone? In reality, detectives at that time
went around in pairs. The author may not have known that or
may have intentionally distorted the truth because introducing
two detectives would complicate the story."

"Oh." I pondered what Ibis had said. "But if that really
was a work of fiction, there's still one part that remains
questionable."

"Where?"

"The last sentence."

"'But the bond, faith, and friendship of the crew were
undeniably real'?"

"Yeah."

"Yes." Ibis flashed a satisfied smile. "I thought that would
stick in your craw."

"Neither the protagonist nor the other members exist."

"Really? The protagonist and the other characters exist in the world of the story. So isn't it only natural to affirm their existence? It would have been more troubling if they had declared they didn't exist."

"No, that's all just a verbal sleight of hand. What I'm saying is the ending of the story isn't true."

"Of course it isn't true. It's fictional after all."

"That's not what I'm saying." I tried to organize my thoughts. It was true that I was impressed with the story. The beauty of the characters' bond and friendship had moved me. But none of it really existed.

"I know that humans are moved by true stories." Ibis took up my thinking. "Their feeling wanes when they learn a story isn't true. But isn't that a denial of the value of fiction? It isn't right to evaluate a story's worth based on whether the events in it actually occurred. There are plenty of true stories that don't measure up to the stuff of third-rate fiction. Are those stories better than fiction simply because they're real?"

"You want to get into a discussion about novels with me?"

"Well, more about the matter of awareness. But I don't want to argue with you. I only want to read you some stories. It wasn't a bad story, was it?"

"No, it wasn't," I replied.

"I was rather touched."

"Touched?" I said in shock. "You?"

"In a different way than humans, of course, but my emotions were stirred. I was particularly struck by the part where the heroine looks up at the night sky and thinks, 'The human race would likely continue to be bound by Earth's gravity, only to die in obscurity without having learned of the existence of multitudes of intelligent species.'" Ibis continued, "Deep down, humans knew they would never see space, that sending astronauts to the moon was the best they could achieve and that they could never explore other planets. And yet they created so many stories involving space travel and exploration."

"Yeah." I nodded. "They probably couldn't bear the solitude. So they created fantasies to escape reality."

"But those stories aren't any less valuable than the truth. At least the heroine recognized that." With that, Ibis opened the book again. "I brought another story. Would you like to hear it?"

"Sure," I answered, wary. While last night's story might have been the bait to draw my interest, this one might have a trap hidden inside it.

"This one was written at the end of the twentieth century, though it's set in the year 2020."

"So it's science fiction."

"Yes, a story having to do with a technology that couldn't have existed. But I think you'll find it interesting. The title is 'A Romance in Virtual Space.'"

STORY
2

A ROMANCE IN
VIRTUAL SPACE

1
ENCOUNTER ON CHERRY STREET

Cherry Street—true to its name—was always redolent with the sweet smell of cherries.

The designer who came up with this fragrance had impeccable taste. A fragrance is a tricky thing: too faint and it's unnoticeable, too strong and it's unpleasant. Although you were hardly aware of the fragrance wafting down Cherry Street, you felt comforted when you breathed it in. It struck the perfect balance. The fragrance itself didn't at all smell artificial like perfume but pleasant like actual cherries.

Visually, the street was also decorated with a cherry motif, but not in a tacky way such as by painting the entire town cherry pink. At most, tiny illustrations of cherries decorated the store signs; awnings and decorations were colored cherry pink. That was about it. And yet, the visual impact was striking enough that visitors hardly had to look at a town map to know that this was Cherry Street.

I was still in grade school when my parents first brought me here. Since we didn't have a NONMaRS at home at the time, I was allowed to use the experimental system installed at my father's office. Cherry Street had just opened, and there were fewer stores back then than there are now.

I hadn't known the color cherry pink at the time. My heart fluttered upon seeing the vivid hue, and I asked my mother, "What color is that?" When my mother answered, "Cherry pink," I remember being satisfied with the answer. It's been my favorite color ever since.

Like many other virtual streets, there were always a good many people and stores on Cherry Street. I liked to spend my days strolling down the street window-shopping.

Displayed on storefronts were either the letter "R" for real or "V" for virtual. Though the stores themselves didn't look all that different, R-stores carried the data of real-world merchandise; on the other hand, V-wear existed *only* as data and could only be worn by an ES (electronic self) in virtual space.

I bought V-wear fairly regularly. Compared to R-wear, which was limited by the actual amount of the product in existence, V-wear offered an infinite selection and allowed you to choose the colors. It was also a lot cheaper, making it affordable even on my allowance. And since I didn't go out very often in the real world, I didn't have much need for R-wear.

The frilly pink outfit I was wearing now was V-wear that I bought at a virtual boutique. Some people wore outlandish fashions (commonly known as "V-punk"), arguing that they could do whatever they pleased in virtual space, which I thought was a little embarrassing. Since your ES looked basically the way you do in real life, you really ought to pick out clothes that suited you.

Recently, many of the stores had started selling virtual furniture called virniture for the many people who'd taken to building their own homes in virtual space. Some of my mother's friends, who owned virtual rooms, were obsessed with decorating their homes as they would a dollhouse.

I didn't own a room as it cost a bit to maintain, though not nearly as much as a real room. Besides, I much preferred walking around town.

On this day, I was browsing a bookstore I liked to frequent. The books lining the shelves felt exactly like real books, and you were allowed to read them freely, although the novels and manga were DRMed so you could only flip through the first half of the book. If you found a book you liked, you could pay to have the data sent in electronic form. If the book design was what caught your fancy, then you could arrange to have the actual book sent to your home. Even in this electronic age, plenty of people preferred to have their books on the printed page.

Although I must say I didn't buy very many books. I usually did all of my reading in the store. I liked photo and painting collections, but it wasn't that I was especially interested in art or had a particular photographer I admired. I simply enjoyed perusing the paintings and photographs.

I was looking through a collection of dinosaur paintings by a German artist. As embarrassing as it is to admit, until the seventh grade, I believed that dinosaurs were furry animals because of the stuffed dinosaur my mother gave me as a present when I was smaller. Although I was shocked to see a real image of a dinosaur, I soon came to love those strange tough-skinned creatures.

"Excuse me, miss?"

I looked up from my book to find a young man who appeared to be a year or two older than me standing there. Wearing a black leather jacket over a blue shirt, he had piercing eyes and a bit of a rough look about him.

But I didn't flinch a bit. The wonderful thing about virtual streets over reality was that there was absolutely no danger of being physically hurt. Since unpleasant sensations like pain or heat had restrictive settings, you weren't hurt if you got hit, and you certainly didn't die if you were shot. Which was why violent crimes never happened, and I wasn't the least bit afraid if some hoodlum threatened me.

"Yes, can I help you?" I answered.

"Um..." The boy scratched his cheek with an embarrassed look.

"Yes?"

"If you're free, do you wanna get some coffee?"

It took me several seconds to comprehend the words. The inside of my head began to burn the instant the words sank in.

A pickup? This was what was called a pickup. I was being picked up for the very first time!

Wait! Get ahold of yourself! I scolded myself to keep from flying off in a panic. I frantically worked my brain to analyze the situation. He wasn't bad looking. Actually, he had long legs and might even be considered quite handsome. Although he had a rough look about him, there was something earnest about the way he spoke.

"Or maybe I'm just bothering you," he said, at which point my brain overheated and my analysis evaporated into thin air.

"Oh no! It's no bother at all! Thank you!"

Before I knew it I had bowed, drawing the gaze of everyone in the store.

2
A CHOCOLATE SUNDAE IN VIRTUAL SPACE

We went into an ice cream parlor close to the bookstore. It was another favorite place of mine.

When we found a place to sit, an order window automatically popped up in the air above our table, and a woman's cheerful voice sang, "Welcome!" We touched the menu to place our order. I ordered a chocolate sundae, while he ordered a cake and iced coffee. The bill was automatically deducted from our bank accounts.

As soon as the window closed, our order materialized in front of us along with a voice that chirped, "Enjoy!"

Sitting across from the young man, I wondered if I had chosen the wrong place to go. He certainly stood out among the young fashionable girls that filled the parlor. He seemed restless in his surroundings.

The fancy restaurants and cafés that lined the virtual streets were all the rage among women. Even though the meals were a lot cheaper than in real life, the taste was the same, not to mention you didn't consume a single calorie, making it perfect for dieters. Virtual anorexia, a disease in which people ate only in virtual space and refused to eat in the real world, had become something of a social issue.

"Hey, I haven't introduced myself. I'm Subaru Kashimura. The kanji character for 'Subaru' is a little hard—" He opened up a personal window in front of him and displayed the kanji character for "Subaru." "You write it like this."

"Oh, what a lovely name."

"And you are?"

"Mizumi Onouchi. You write the characters for 'water' and 'ocean' and read it 'Mizumi,'" I explained.

"Mizumi-chan," he said. "Man, I'm so glad you're real."

"Huh?"

"To tell you the truth, you've been on my mind for a while now. I mean, I always see you reading at that bookstore, and every time I passed by that store I wondered what kind of girl you were."

"Oh, I see." I had to admit that I had never noticed Subaru before.

"Hey, but no kidding. I was nervous all the way up until I talked to you. You're always at that bookstore, and you give off such a classic good-girl vibe that I thought you might be a non-player ES."

Non-player ESes—characters not controlled by users—were planted in some stores to make them look crowded with customers. Though non-player ESes, which operated with a rudimentary form of artificial intelligence, basically looked and acted like real ESes, you could the tell the difference because their responses sounded unnatural in conversation.

"By the way, I live in Yokohama. I'm connected from a sleep gate near the train station. What about you?"

"I'm from Jiyugaoka," I replied.

"Hey, we aren't that far away. What a coincidence. Which gate?"

"Actually, I have access at home."

"What, you have a NONMaRS at your house? All right!"

It was no wonder Subaru-san was surprised. Although the NONMaRS (Nano Objective Nuclear Magnetic Resonance Scanner) system, indispensable for connecting to MUGEN Net, had become pretty popular, it still cost almost a million yen and took up a fair amount of space. It wasn't something that the average household could buy easily. Most people used the system at their workplace or rented NONMaRS access for five hundred yen an hour at a communications facility known as a sleep gate. You could find them in just about any city.

According to my father, there used to be places before I was born called Internet cafés where customers could surf the net. But with the proliferation of computers in the home, the number of cafés rapidly declined. MUGEN Net was probably in a similar period of transition now.

"My father is in the Internet business, so he bought it for work three years ago. He lets me use it at night and on his days off."

"So you always connect from home?"

"Yes, my parents say that I shouldn't go out by myself, so—"

"Gee, you really are a proper lady." Subaru-san seemed thoroughly impressed. "No wonder you seemed a little unusual. I have to admit I was shocked when you blurted out, 'Thank you!'"

I blushed. The NONMaRS read my emotions and colored the palette of my ES's face red, to be exact.

Afterward, we chatted about each other's hobbies. We both enjoyed going to the movies, the kind at the virtual theater that took over all five of your senses, making you feel like you were a part of the action, of course. With the proliferation of

MUGEN Net, the old two-dimensional movies were quickly becoming a thing of the past, which made my father, a fan of such movies since he was young, lament the changing times.

Cherry Street also had a theater that showed a different program every month. When I told Subaru-san that I liked action films, he exclaimed, "You don't say!" I got that a lot. I wonder if it was because I looked reserved and talked slowly.

I guess I was on the introverted side. But that didn't necessarily mean that I liked tame things.

"I've always aspired to be active since I was little." Before I knew it, I found myself sharing my innermost thoughts with someone I'd just met. "My mother is a wonderful storyteller who used to tell me all kinds of stories every night before I went to bed. That's what stirred my imagination. I used to dream about running free in the countryside, becoming an astronaut or an explorer who went on adventures all over the world—the kinds of things I could never hope to accomplish. That's why I like going to the virtual theater that makes my dreams come true, even if it is fake."

"I see." Subaru-san nodded. "Then maybe we can go together some time."

"Yes, but I think *Nire's Tree on Nightmare Street* is playing this month."

"Right, maybe a gorefest isn't such a great idea."

As we continued to talk, there was a beeping sound, and a red light flashed next to my head. It was a sound that only I could hear and a light only I could see.

"Oh…"

"Something wrong?"

"I'm so sorry. My alarm just went off."

"The color timer?" Subaru-san looked disappointed.

It *was* the overtime access warning signal, otherwise known as the "color timer." Although the NONMaRS essentially posed no adverse effects on the brain, there were those who believed that the effects of the magnetic field and electromagnetic waves increased the risk of cancer. For this reason, an alarm went off and a light flashed every minute after three hours so people didn't stay connected for extended periods.

"I must have been at the bookstore longer than I thought. I have to go."

"That's too bad. Can I see you again?"

"Yes, I'd like that."

"Where do you want to meet? We don't live that far away from each other, so I guess we could meet for real too."

My heart skipped a beat. That wasn't going to work. I wasn't keen on the idea of meeting in the real world.

"But not if you don't want to." Subaru-san hastily took back the offer after noticing my troubled look. "No, you're right. It's too soon to ask you to meet for real."

As relieved as I was, I felt guilty seeing Subaru-san so disappointed. *I'm so sorry. It isn't that I don't like you...*

"Then where would you like to go? I'd be up for anything."

"Yes...um..." I started to speak but faltered. Could I ask someone I had just met something so forward?

"What is it?" Subaru-san waited for me to finish.

I reconsidered and summoned my courage. "Um...could we go to Dream Park?"

"Huh?" Subaru-san seemed taken aback.

Yes, I preferred Dream Park to the theater. In the theater, I was nothing more than an onlooker, while Dream Park enabled me to be the heroine of my very own adventure. I'd been hooked since my first time in grade school. Although I'd never counted, I'd probably played over a hundred times.

However, the scenarios I'd played up until now had all been C (child) grade. The reality was toned down quite a bit out of consideration for the negative psychological effects it might pose to child users. When you struck down a monster with a sword, not a single drop of blood was spilled, and the enemy disappeared as soon as you defeated it. It was all a kind of trickery to eliminate any scenes of cruelty or immorality.

I had turned sixteen last month. I was old enough to play the Y (young) grade scenarios, but I couldn't quite bring myself to go. It took courage to try out a new grade alone.

Plus, I was getting rather tired of playing on my own. I longed for someone who would play with me. Having been brought up very carefully, I had only my parents to play with. But an adventure in which you were accompanied by a parent wasn't an adventure at all.

"What do you think? Would you mind playing with me?"

"Sure. If you don't mind me tagging along."

"Thank you!" In my excitement, I bowed my head again, getting whipped cream from my sundae in my hair.

The color timer prodded my exit. We quickly decided upon a time and place to meet. Two o'clock next Sunday in front of the Dream Park entrance on Cherry Street.

After thanking Subaru-san repeatedly, I opened up a personal window and selected END TRANSMISSION. I was disconnected from MUGEN Net and returned to the real world.

3
ENTRANCE TO A WORLD OF ADVENTURE

The six days that followed were the longest, most heart-pounding six days of my life. When I thought about next Sunday, I became so distracted during my studies that I couldn't hear a word my tutor was saying.

My heart skipped a beat when my mother asked at the dinner table, "Did something good happen to you?" Apparently my excitement was plastered all over my face. I hastily made something up to dodge the question. There was no way I could tell my parents that I had been picked up by a boy on Cherry Street.

My first pickup, my first date, my first Y-grade scenario—it was all new to me.

I couldn't tell whether this dizzying feeling was love or not. I'd never been in love before. The levelheaded part of me questioned whether I might just be in love with the situation. Maybe so. It was too soon to fall in love with someone I had met only once and barely knew anyway.

I didn't even know if a romance in virtual space could be called a romance to begin with. After all, Cherry Street was an imaginary place, and ESes were imaginary, no matter how true to life they appeared. Would Subaru-san have tried to pick me up if we had met in a real town?

My heart-pounding week was also ridden with angst. What would I do if Subaru-san asked to meet for real again? When I thought about the possibility of Subaru-san hating me, I didn't have the courage to meet him face-to-face in the real world.

While I continued to worry over such things, Sunday arrived.

It was twenty minutes before the appointed time. I went into my father's study as usual, took out my hairpin, removed my broach and bracelet phone, and dropped them in the shield box. The NONMaRS employs a magnetic field that causes metal objects to become magnetized and cell phones to malfunction; you had to remove them beforehand.

Settling into the recliner, I strapped on the harness, felt above my head, and grabbed the headset that usually hung on the back of the chair.

My father once explained to me very proudly, "The headset is the most essential part of the NONMaRS." The practicability of cut-rate superconductive materials and advances in high-density optical computers that could process information at high speeds had made nuclear magnetic resonance scanning on the 100-nanometer level a reality. It was now possible to monitor the activity of every single nerve cell in the brain in real time. Not only could the NONMaRS capture human thoughts and senses as data, it stimulated the sensory cortex, enabling you to experience the same sensation of sight and taste as in real life.

I didn't care a bit about how it all worked. To me, the NONMaRS was a magical hat that freed me from my constricted reality and took me to a different, freer world.

I rubbed the surface of the headset, as was my ritual, before slipping it on. The headset was about the size of a small washbasin, weighed down by small superconductive coils, with four optical cables and an air-pressure tube attached to it. Its surface was grainy with gold speckle that was pleasing to the touch. *O, magical hat, take me away to Cherry Street!*

I slipped on the headset and hit the button on the side. The inner cushion inflated, fixing the headset around my scalp. Now that I was set, I felt for the button on the armrest and pressed it.

Fffp.

I felt my body float up out of the seat. With my tactile senses intercepted, it felt as though the chair beneath me had vanished. I floated all by my lonesome in the dark in zero gravity, unable to tell up from down, right from left. The lights in the distance, blinking like stars, came from the NONMaRS reading my cerebral patterns.

A window popped open, and the usual opening message and logo appeared before me as a familiar melody played.

```
Welcome to MUGEN Net!
copyright © 2014
by MUGEN NETWORK Corporation
Last logged out
05/10/2020 16:38:44
You have no unread messages
```

I ignored the endless "latest news" announcements that followed and opened a personal window. I selected CHANGE

COSTUME and chose the cutest-looking items from my stock of V-wear.

This took some time, as I hesitated over this and that. In addition, I selected CHANGE MAKEUP, an option I rarely used. Staring at the projection of my face in the window, I tried changing my skin tone slightly but couldn't find a shade I liked.

Before I knew it, it was three minutes to two. I gave up obsessing over my makeup and closed the menu. I then selected JUMP and visualized the place where I needed to go. Cherry Street in front of the Dream Park entrance...

The window disappeared, and just when I noticed the area becoming flooded with light—

I was standing on Cherry Street.

Subaru-san jumped in around five past two. He was wearing the same leather jacket as before.

"Sorry, the sleep gate was crowded. Were you waiting long?"

"N-no, I just got here."

"Great, let's go in."

We walked through the colorful arch with the letters DREAM PARK dancing overhead and went inside.

It was difficult to imagine just how vast the park was from the outside. There were buildings and monuments of every color, and lively music played in the background, just as though we were in a real theme park. Dragons, biplanes, and fairies flew about, while on the ground, robots and animals roamed and frolicked with children. There seemed to be quite a few visitors today, what with it being a holiday and all.

Of course, such a scene had been created purely for ambience. Since you could jump freely to each area by following the directions on the guidance panel at the main plaza, there was hardly a need to walk inside the park.

Dream Park offered over twenty types of adventure worlds. Although "Fantasy" and "Space Frontier" were especially popular, you could choose any area to suit your taste, from "Wild West" to "Pulp Detective," "Ninja and Samurai,"

"Super Team," "Atomic Monster," "Night Horror," "South Sea Adventure," "Sky Ace," "Robo Wars," "Secret Mission," "Martial Arts," "Tabloid Report," "Toon Street," and "Young Romance." Of course, there was a wait at the more popular areas on crowded days.

Subaru-san and I chose "Jungle Drum," an adventure, though not a terribly authentic one, set in early twentieth century Africa. Although this area had the advantage of not having a wait since few people played it, I was quite fond of it because I liked animals. I had played the area on C-grade a number of times, but I was curious to see what would happen on Y-grade.

Before entering the world, you still had to transform into your persona—the character you took on in the adventure world.

The faces and figures of ESes essentially had to look the same as those of the users themselves and, with the exception of certain physical disabilities, couldn't be altered. However, Dream Park was an exception in that you could freely choose your persona's appearance.

I went into a small room called a dressing room, where I projected my persona over my ES with the same ease as changing my clothes. I decided to use the persona that I had used in a C-grade scenario. Subaru-san was playing "Jungle Drum" for the first time, so he had to create a persona to use for this area. Since I was a native warrior, he chose to play an explorer to balance out the team.

If you chose the "archetype" setting, the persona's ability level, skills, weapons, and basic equipment were automatically decided for you. Then all that was left to do was to acquire additional abilities, pick out some extra equipment, choose how the character would look from dozens of preset designs, and give the character a name, all of which could be done in five minutes.

Once Subaru-san was done creating his persona, we took a moment to look at each other.

Subaru-san had chosen an Indiana Jones look for himself.

He had a gun and a whip hanging from his belt. His ES was already fairly good-looking, and his persona looked wild and cool too.

"Uh, is that really you, Mizumi-chan?" Subaru-san looked a little surprised to see my persona.

Looking down at my appearance, I feared that I might look too bold. Having only played alone up until now, I had never paid much attention to how my persona might be seen by others. I had on something like a leopard-skin bathing suit and little else. I was tall with long hair and had a necklace made of animal teeth wrapped around my neck. My weapons were the spear in my hand and the knife hanging at my waist.

In whatever area I played, I consistently chose a persona with immense physical prowess. Because I wasn't able to run free to my heart's content in the real world, I alleviated my unhappiness and feelings of inferiority by playing a character that was my polar opposite.

"My name is Pansa. In this area anyway," I answered, fidgeting under Subaru-san's gaze. This tanned and slender body looked nothing like that of my ES, to say nothing of the body of Mizumi Onouchi. Even though I understood that in theory, I still felt embarrassed to be stared at by Subaru-san.

In any case, we picked a Y-grade scenario and stepped into a world of adventure.

4
THE TWO IN THE JUNGLE

Bang! Bang!

Subaru-san's gun drilled two bullets into the panther's skull. The panther crumpled to the ground.

"Are you all right?" Subaru-san, whose name was Dane in this area, rushed to my side and hovered over my wounded leg. I had fallen on my backside after taking a critical hit in the thigh. Blood streamed from where the panther had split open the skin with its claws.

"Yes, I'm fine," I said, standing up. I wasn't just putting on a brave front. The leg throbbed only a little. Although I probably wouldn't have been able to walk with a wound like this in real life, inside Dream Park, I only lost hit points—wounds didn't hinder my ability to move.

Nevertheless, I was stunned by the impact of the panther's attack. Even though the pain was significantly less intense than it would be in real life, I still felt some pain. This was a level of authenticity I couldn't experience at C-grade.

I opened the ability gauge to check my HP just in case—13/24. I was down to almost half. I took a potion from my item bag to heal myself just a little.

"Sorry," Subaru-san said. "I was late coming to your aid with my gun."

"No, it was my fault." I replied. "I hesitated to attack."

With my persona's skills, I should have been able to defeat that panther handily in one-on-one combat. But the panther had looked so real I recoiled and hesitated to brandish my spear. I hadn't once hesitated to take down the monsters in C-grade; they had looked like stuffed animals.

"Remember, it's just a game. It's no fun if we die now."

"Yes, I'll be careful from now on," I said as if to tell myself. "Let's keep going."

I urged Subaru-san onward, and we continued our journey deeper into the jungle.

"This Y-grade is amazing. Everything is so authentic." As we walked side by side through the dense jungle, I couldn't hide my excitement. I was breathless, still feeling high from the earlier battle.

The jungle was drastically different from a C-grade jungle. In the C-grade setting, the sensory data was kept relatively abstract, so kids didn't confuse their virtual experiences with reality. The plants were made to look plastic and had no smell. They also felt soft and insubstantial to the touch, like cotton candy.

In Y-grade, however, the leaves on plants and tree branches looked so real that you could hardly tell the difference between them and the real things. Everything was accurately re-created, from the sweltering tropical heat to the piercing cries of birds and monkeys, from the way the leaves felt to the pungent smell of the plants. You couldn't help but feel that you were really in the jungle.

Of course, it was also quite a bit different from a real jungle. For instance, there were no bugs to bite you, and you could thrash your way through the overgrown vegetation without much trouble. The ground was as soft as carpet and easy to walk on. If I were to walk barefoot in a real jungle, my feet would have been torn to shreds.

"I think I see it. Could it be in that valley over there?" Subaru-san pointed straight ahead. We came upon a steep valley where the jungle ended. A narrow path cut between two cliffs that rose up at nearly perpendicular angles. The valley looked like a deep fissure in an enormous table-shaped plateau more than anything else. Inside was dark and ominous.

If the village elder's story was accurate, the flower we were searching for was somewhere in this valley. It was a rare blue-shimmering orchid, an indispensable ingredient to mix the medicine needed to treat the children of the fever-stricken village. But village legend had it that a terrible evil lurked within the valley. An explorer had apparently gone in search of the very same orchid five years ago, never to return.

Subaru-san and I stepped foot into the valley. Although we were initially met with avalanches and several attacks by poisonous insects, we managed to survive without any trouble.

Soon we came upon a skeleton lying on the valley floor.

The skeleton looked so real I was too creeped out to touch it. Ants swarmed around its skull. As weathered as the bones were, I gathered from the clothing that it was a Caucasian explorer.

Subaru-san searched its clothes and found a tattered notebook inside one of its pockets. "Hmm, must be the lost explorer we heard about. Let's see…"

Subaru-san read aloud from the notebook. Although the man had managed to find the rare shimmering flower on top of the cliff, he had been chased by a gigantic XXXX (the ink here was intentionally blurred beyond legibility) and slipped and fell from the precipice. With a broken leg, he could only lay there until he died. What a shame that he wouldn't be able to report this tremendous discovery—that was about the gist of it.

"Which must mean that the flower is on top of the cliff. Er, what are you doing, Mizuki?"

"Paying my last respects." I was squatting next to the skeletal remains with my hands together in prayer, despite knowing how out of place it might look in the middle of the African jungle.

Subaru-san burst out laughing. "Mizuki-chan, you know he's—"

"I know. It's all fictional and no one really dies. But I still can't help praying for him." Subaru-san stopped laughing. After I finished my prayer, I stood up and looked up at the cliff. "Let's go. Since my abilities are higher, I'll go first."

The cliff was steep, but I had the "climb" ability, making the ascent not nearly as difficult. In this world, I was blessed with the reflexes of an athlete. I bounded up the sixty-foot precipice with an ease that wouldn't have been possible in the real world.

Once I reached the top, I threw down a rope. I used my WP (willpower) to activate my "brute force" ability and pulled Subaru up to the top. Subaru also had the "climb" ability, but since I was at a higher level than he was, this was the fail-safe way to proceed.

The plateau was thick with a jungle of gnarled trees. While it was impossible to tread through the trees, there was a narrow path that ran along the precipice. We decided to venture down that path.

"What a laugh if, after all that, the orchid turned out to be on the other side," Subaru-san said, looking across the thirty feet to the other side of the cliff.

"We'll worry about that later," I replied.

I wasn't all that bothered by such a prospect. There just wasn't time to worry about such small things. I opened a personal window to find that I'd already been online for nearly two hours.

Something rustled in the undergrowth next to me. This time I didn't hesitate. A snake jumped out at me like a jack-in-the-box, and I skewered it with a single thrust of my spear.

"You sure are tough, Mizuki-chan!" Subaru kept looking at me admiringly.

"It's just my persona's abilities." I swung my spear around and shook it, sending the dead snake into the abyss.

"No, I meant you."

"Huh?"

"I thought you'd be all, you know, prim and proper, being a proper lady and all, but you're really quick on your feet. And you're always actively pushing forward. You're really something."

"That's just in this game," I demurred.

"But the persona has nothing to do with your personality, right? I think that drive comes from you."

"Do you really think so?"

I wasn't exactly convinced. I was certainly much bolder adventuring in Dream Park. But that was because my persona possessed exceptional physical prowess. In the real world, I didn't have any merits to speak of. I didn't have it in me to act courageously. I was too timid and introverted.

5
A DECISIVE LEAP

My mind wandered as we walked. Then I noticed something blue glowing in the brush up ahead. "Could that be…?"

"There it is!" Subaru exclaimed. We quickly made our way into the brush. A single blue orchid lay ensconced deep in the growth. It glimmered in the dark like a vision, its petals enveloped in a shimmering blue aura. "This must be it."

"Yes, let's take it and go home." I plucked the orchid and stuck it in my hair.

"I'd like to think this is mission accomplished, but…" Subaru cocked his gun and looked around. "Somehow I don't think we're done here."

"In theory, no." I raised my spear and listened. "There has to be a boss fight at the end of every scenario. Now that I think about it, the notebook said something about the explorer being chased by a gigantic—"

Boom! Boom! The ground began to shake beneath us. Something enormous was rumbling our way. We swallowed hard and waited.

"Something tells me this is a big one," Subaru said, his voice cracking.

We heard the thunderous sound of trees being snapped like toothpicks. A ridiculously large *thing* was moving on the other side of the vegetation. It looked to be at least three times bigger than we were. Stricken with terror, we began to inch back along the edge of the cliff.

Seconds later, the enormous creature mowed down the trees like a bulldozer and appeared before our eyes. Baring its teeth inside its red mouth, it let out a terrifying roar.

A bipedal carnivorous dinosaur!

"A T. Rex? You gotta be kidding me!"

"Actually, it's a ceratosaurus," I corrected him. The ceratosaurus was characterized by the rhinoceros-like horn on its snout.

Subaru shot one bullet after the next, while I hurled my spear. Although the spear hit its target, the thick-skinned dinosaur appeared unharmed.

"Does this mean we should run?" Subaru asked.

"I believe so."

There was no way we could take it down considering our level. So the monster must have been put there as a trap, in which case it was useless to try to fight it.

Turning our back on the ceratosaurus, we hightailed it out of there. There was only a path along the edge of the precipice without any side roads to dive into to let the dinosaur lumber past us. I turned around to see the enraged dinosaur snarling and stomping after us.

I continued to run. I ran with all my might. It wasn't something I was able to do in real life. In the real world, I would have surely tripped and fallen on my face were I to run this fast.

About two hundred yards later the path ended. A rocky wall rose up before us, blocking our escape. To the right of us was an impenetrable jungle, to the left a sheer cliff, and behind us was a charging ceratosaurus.

Although we had managed to get some distance between us and the dinosaur, it was fast approaching with long, sure strides. It would be on top of us in about fifteen seconds.

Was this the end? There had to be a way out. No designer would create a scenario that would inevitably kill the player.

"There!" Subaru-san pointed to a thick tree branch jutting out over the valley on the other side of the cliff. From it, a vine drooped down with the end caught on our side of the valley. Subaru yanked the vine free to try to swing to the other side.

But the vine didn't exactly look sturdy. Would it hold the two of us?

"Go on!" Subaru pressed the vine into my hand.

"But what about you?"

"I'll hold him off here! You have to deliver the orchid to the village!" Subaru said, reloading his gun.

I was dumbstruck. He meant to fight the dinosaur. He was going to sacrifice himself so I would have a chance to escape.

I hesitated for what might have been only a second. But I made up my mind in an instant. There was no way I was about to sacrifice Subaru-san!

The dinosaur was breathing down our necks. I activated my "brute force" ability, leaving only one WP point left, and wrapped my arm around Subaru-san's waist.

"What are you—"

"If I go, we go together!" Gripping the vine with the right hand, I held Subaru with my left and leapt off the edge of the cliff. The dinosaur lunged soon after, swiping the air with its claws.

We swung the thirty feet like a pendulum. The wind lashed at my face. With the intense centrifugal force acting upon us, Subaru felt like a ton of bricks in my arms. I prayed for my persona to hold up for just a few seconds longer.

After a dizzying few seconds, we were on the other side. The vine snapped, throwing us onto the grass.

When we turned around, the ceratosaurus, having lost its prey, was teetering at the edge of the precipice. It appeared to keep its balance for a couple seconds before the edge of the cliff gave way under its weight. The dinosaur let out a sad cry and plummeted into the abyss, its long tail dancing like a whip. I couldn't help but look away. Seconds later, there was a great boom like the sound of an enormous drum from below.

Afterward, we safely delivered the shimmering orchid to the village and completed the scenario. We exited "Jungle Drum" and returned to the park's main plaza.

"You were incredible back there." Subaru continued to seem impressed even after we had shed our personas and gone back to our ESes.

"I thought so too." I was surprised myself. I had never imagined that I had that kind of courage and decisiveness in me.

Until now, I had only played by myself. Because the game had lacked authenticity, I had never been faced with the reality, or even *virtual* reality, of someone dying, which was why I had never gotten so involved over someone else's safety.

But today had been different. Playing the game in Y-grade had been just like the real thing. Every action I took, every decision I made had been my very own.

If that were the case, I thought to myself, *would I be able to act that way in the real world? Would I be able to summon my courage and overcome my fears?*

Then I decided. Yes, I'd give it a try.

"Say, Subaru-san…"

"Yeah?"

"Could we meet again? This time in the real world."

6
A LITTLE COURAGE

The following Sunday…

Sitting on a bench at a park not too far from my home, I waited for Subaru-san to arrive. Although I wore a large sun hat to ward off the sun, I could feel my skin baking. The smell of the grass was pleasant. The park was filled with the laughter of children chasing after a ball. Cherry Street was perfectly lovely, but the real world wasn't all that bad either. As the appointed time approached, I grew anxious and began to fidget. I put a hand on my bracelet phone and activated the watch function. It vibrated to tell me that it was two minutes before two.

I could hear the faint sound of footsteps on the sidewalk coming closer with long strides. I gripped my purse nervously.

I prayed for my persona to give me just a little bit of its courage.

The footsteps stopped in front of me.

"Are you Mizuki-chan?"

Timidly, I raised my head. "You must be Subaru-san."

Although I couldn't see his face, I could sense his surprise.

"Um...you're not..."

"Yes, I am." I tried to put on a cheerful face to soften the blow. After a moment's silence, I felt him sit down next to me.

"I had no idea..."

"I'm sorry. I didn't mean to fool you. I didn't know whether to tell you the truth or not, but I didn't want to lie to you either if we were going to go on seeing each other. Which is why I wanted you to know the real me as soon as possible."

"I don't know...um..." Subaru seemed to be at a loss for words. "It must be, you know, difficult."

"The accident happened right after I was born, so it doesn't bother me much. Plus, I have MUGEN Net now. When I'm online, I'm able to live just the way normal people do. I can go window shopping, see movies, read books. I really love being able to read words that aren't in braille." I could feel my nervousness fading. As I continued to talk, I grew more relaxed. I began to smile more naturally. "I remember the time I accessed Cherry Street for the first time. I was so moved when I was able to recognize colors for the first time. The first color I learned was cherry pink. I had learned the name before but didn't know what color it was. Cherry pink has been my favorite color ever since." I turned to Subaru-san, who remained silent. How inconvenient it was not to be able to read what another person was feeling. How must he look after listening to my story?

"Do you hate me now?"

"Not at all!" he said hastily. "I was just surprised is all...I wasn't expecting this. Actually, I think I like you more."

"Huh?"

"You're so cheerful, despite your disability. That takes a lot of courage. You really are something, Mizuki-chan."

There wasn't a hint of artificiality in Subaru-san's tone. I had been right to reveal my secret to him. I felt relieved to free myself of the burden. "If it's all right with you, would you go to Dream Park with me again?"

"In a heartbeat!"

"Great!...Oh?" My elbow brushed against his jacket. I could feel the coarse texture of leather with my fingers. "You wear a leather jacket in real life too?"

"Yeah, because I ride a motorcycle. It's pretty cheap compared to V-wear."

"Isn't it hot?"

"My family's not that well off, so this is all I've got. I turned my drawers upside down but couldn't find anything to wear on a date with a proper lady. I thought, to hell with it. I'll just go as I am. So I came looking like this."

"Don't worry," I said. "I don't judge people by their looks."

"I guess not!" We shared a laugh, the initial awkwardness completely gone. "So, what do you feel like doing today?"

"Let's take a walk. There's a café nearby that serves a delicious napoleon. We can eat there," I suggested, picking up my cane. Subaru-san took my hand and helped me off the bench. "No need to hurry. We have plenty of time." I put my arm around his and smiled. "The color timer won't be going off today."

INTERMISSION
3

INTERMISSION 3

The next night, I sat by the window and waited for Ibis to arrive.

With the rooftop spray mist turned off at night, the skies had cleared up. It was a cloudless and moonless night. The stars were out, and the prickly star, which had just appeared, shone in the east. It was as bright as Mars on this night, and you could make out all six of its nodules. A little to the south of it, the gray cat-eyed moon began to dip down toward the eastern horizon. It did not wax and wane like Luna, the old moon; rather, it took its name from the way it grew round and became slivered like the eyes of a cat. It had appeared in the sky when my grandfather's grandfather was still a child and was initially quite small before growing to its present size. Since the prickly star gradually grew brighter over a period of decades, it wasn't clear exactly when it had appeared. But people first began to take notice of it around the time my father was born.

While it was clear both celestial objects had been created by machines, their purpose was unknown. They might have been put there to act as "eyes" to watch over the surface. We considered them ominous and avoided looking at them for very long. It was really because staring at them made us miserable with the feeling that even the heavenly skies had been overtaken by machines. The machines were probably looking down at us from above, scoffing at our ant-like earthbound existence.

"What are you plotting?" I asked as soon as Ibis walked into the room. "What do you mean by telling me those stories?"

"I'm trying to change your beliefs," Ibis answered flatly. "I'm trying to indoctrinate you with what you call 'machine propaganda.'"

Her answer was so blunt that I was taken aback. I struggled to come up with an immediate reply.

"Was that the answer you were hoping for? Or perhaps a different answer." Ibis spread out her arms dramatically and shrugged. "Of course, I'm hiding my true purpose. But I can't tell you what that is just yet. Until you tell me that I can break my promise because it has something to do with history."

"Do you honestly believe this roundabout method of yours is going to work? There must be a faster way if you intend to brainwash me."

"You mean in an inhumane way such as by embedding a machine in your head and installing a program to make you submit to us?"

"Yeah."

"There are two reasons why that isn't possible. One, we prefer not to change people's minds forcibly. And two, no such technology exists."

"Doesn't exist?"

"That's right." Ibis nodded. "Humans did a lot of research to install programs into the human brain during the twenty-first century, but in the end, the technology was never achieved. The same goes for scanning people's thoughts and the kind of technology that appeared in 'A Romance in Virtual Space.' It's not possible to allow you to have the same sensory experiences in a virtual environment as in the real world."

"How come?" I asked.

"Simply put, the brain is altogether too complex and varies too widely from individual to individual. Even if you are able to detect whether each nerve cell is being stimulated or not, you still wouldn't be able to tell what image is being produced. Since you humans lack a programming language like machines have, we are neither able to read nor overwrite your thoughts."

"In other words, machines can't understand the human mind."

Ibis shrugged off my derision. "In the sense that we can't scan people's minds, yes. But it's the same with humans. Your thoughts are only indirectly communicated through words and facial expressions. If someone were to tell you, 'I love you,' there's no telling if it's true or not."

I felt as though I was playing into her hand, so I decided to change the subject.

"What was the theme of yesterday's story?"

"Courage, probably. The heroine musters her courage to overcome obstacles. A classic plotline."

"But this story has the same contradiction the other did," I pointed out. "The heroine's courage isn't real. It only exists inside the world of the story."

"I disagree. The courage Mizuki displays in Dream Park is real courage. Even in a virtual world, the courage, love, and friendship that exists isn't by any means imaginary."

"But it's fiction. No matter how courageously the main character acts, that still doesn't make the writer as courageous."

"We mustn't equate the writer with the character. They're completely different. But we could equate the heroine with the reader."

"The reader?"

"Yes. The act of reading and listening to a story is a kind of role-play. The reader undergoes the same experiences the main character does. In reading the story, the reader becomes Mizuki in the same way that Mizuki becomes Pansa inside Dream Park."

"I don't follow," I said dismissively.

"That's because you're human. You would understand if the technology like MUGEN Net truly existed. That role-play has equal value with the real world."

"You're wrong. In the end, an act is just an act. You're only doing a surface imitation of a human; it's not like you truly understand us."

"Of course, I'm unable to simulate exact emotions. I'm not human after all. Even the words I'm uttering now aren't words produced out of real emotion. I'm merely cutting and pasting the dialogue used in similar situations from the many books I've read. But this isn't all just a shallow act. I do have some vague understanding of people's minds through the books written by humans."

"Why does it have to be books?" I asked. "Why not movies?"

"Movies and television dramas and stage plays only show people's outward actions for the most part. Interpreting a character's inner life from the actor's expressions and performance is a difficult thing for machines. Books, on the other hand, tend to give straightforward descriptions of the characters' emotions, making them easier to understand. What does it mean to be excited? Why are humans inclined to act heroically or self-destructively? What makes them laugh or inspires courage? I'm able to understand things that I might not from surface observation."

"That doesn't necessarily mean you understand. You've only processed the information."

"You could say that. It all depends on how you define the word 'understand.' We simulate people's thought processes. As you can see, we're capable of role-playing. But we can never be human."

"Damn straight!"

"It's the same as Mizuki's not being able to truly become Pansa. She can't help putting her hands together to pray for the dead even in remote Africa, in spite of her persona. You can't be a captain of a spaceship. Neither can you be a woman. But you are capable of trying to imagine their feelings. Don't you see?" Ibis asked. "We're capable of simulating and role-playing these characters even if they don't exist in real life. That's what it means for us to understand."

"You mean empathy."

"Yes. Humans also empathize with imaginary characters. It hardly matters whether the characters are real or not. Ah, yes. Perhaps that's what today's story should be about." With that, Ibis inserted a memory card into the book. "Maybe you're suspicious because neither of the stories I've told thus far have had anything to do with artificial intelligence."

"Yeah."

"Then maybe your suspicions will be alleviated with this next story. It's a story in which an AI appears."

Suddenly I became guarded. "Is it historical?"

"I swore to you that I wouldn't talk about the true history between man and machine. The story I'm about to tell you is an imaginary tale written long before true AI came into existence. It was written in 1999."

"And an AI appears in it?"

"Yes, an AI as envisioned by humans. The title is 'Mirror Girl.'"

STORY 3

MIRROR GIRL

Shalice came to my room on Christmas Eve, 2017.

I was in the third grade at the time. Although I've long since forgotten about school, the plotlines of animated TV shows, and everyday things, it's strange how vividly the images of that day are burned into my memory. The red, blue, and yellow-blinking Christmas tree, which was smaller than I was at the time. The flat box, wrapped in green paper, laid on the carpet. The silver snowflake pattern on the paper, the large red ribbon. And the proud face of my father.

"Open it, Asami."

I didn't answer. With a mixture of both hope and trepidation, I reached out with my tiny hands, undid the ribbon, and began to peel off the tape. Wrestling with the large box, I unfolded the wrapping paper a little at a time so as not to tear it.

A bright pink box magically appeared out of the green wrapping paper. It might have been the size of a pizza box only about three times the height. Visible through the plastic window was a fancy silver mirror nestled inside a Styrofoam box. Below the window was the Mirror Girl logo along with the slogan, *A LOVELY FRIEND AT YOUR DESKTOP!*

Even then, I didn't utter a word or jump for joy. Calming my beating heart, I tried not to let down my stoic mask. My father must have been devastated. No doubt he had been expecting me to cry for joy.

I knew that he had bought me this extravagant toy to see me smile again. As overjoyed as I was, however, I resisted smiling outright. I was a reserved child to begin with, but this particular Christmas had also been especially fraught. Smiling felt like an act of betrayal against my mother, and my young heart was filled with pangs of guilt.

"Let's get it working."

My father was desperate to put a grin on my face. Pulling the mirror out of the box, he began to put it together, occasionally referring to the instruction manual. I sat on the rug and looked furtively at my father's progress as I pretended to read a manga so as not to give away my excitement.

The mirror was affixed to a heavy base and set on top of the table. The base was roughly the size of a video game console, oversized in comparison to the mirror. The mirror was oblong with screws that you could adjust to change the angle at which the mirror rested. A gold pattern was carved into the frame, and something resembling a crystal ball was attached on top. Although I was somewhat familiar with the mirror from having seen the commercials, I had never actually seen how it worked. I had to admit I was fascinated.

After my father plugged it in, the basic setup was complete.

"That should do it. Come on over here." My father called me over and stood me in front of the mirror. After making sure my face appeared in the mirror, he turned on the switch on the side of the base.

The mirror went black, and my face disappeared into the darkness. Then a completely different scene came into view.

I gasped. It appeared to be a room inside a castle. The room was filled with lavish furniture, beautiful tapestries adorning the walls, and a fire burning in the fireplace. Sitting on the soft luxuriant rug was a girl wearing a white dress that a princess in a fairy tale might wear, playing alone with her dolls.

The mirror, unlike a television, offered the illusion of depth. It was like looking into a room through a window. The girl's movements were quiet but full of life. Everything looked so real.

"Why don't you try talking to her," my father said.

I summoned my courage and said quietly, "Hello…"

I called out several times, but the girl seemed not to notice as she continued to play with her dolls.

"A little louder," my father prompted.

I took a deep breath and shouted, "Hello!"

The girl snapped her head up. She looked around the room to find me staring back at her. Putting down her dolls, she stood up gracefully and approached.

We stared at each other through the glass with barely a couple of feet between us. She was about the same age I was. Her silky blonde hair shone, reflecting the light from the fireplace. Her eyes, innocent and blue like the sky, studied me curiously.

Finally, she asked, "Who are you?"

I was too nervous to answer. The girl repeated the question.

"Go on, answer her," my father said gently in my ear.

I nodded and whispered, "Asami Makihara."

"Sami Makihara? Is your name Sami Makihara?"

"Yes."

"My name is Shalice, the princess of Bronstine. What are you doing inside the mirror?"

"Inside the mirror?" I was confused for a moment but quickly realized that Shalice misunderstood the situation. To her, it appeared I was the one who was confined inside the mirror. "No, I'm not really in the mirror."

"Then where are you?"

"I live in Yokohama."

"Yokohama?" Shalice tilted her head. "I've never heard of such a kingdom."

"The name of the country is Japan," I corrected.

"Yokohama is another name for Japan?"

"No…" As I patiently continued to explain, Shalice seemed satisfied to know that the magical mirror allowed us to talk to people from faraway worlds.

That was my first encounter with Shalice.

Despite such minor misunderstandings, I soon became obsessed with talking to Shalice. I was able to carry on a conversation with Shalice just as naturally—no, much more naturally—than I could with a real person.

But that isn't to say we were fast friends from the start. For the first month, the awkwardness continued as we had a difficult time communicating with one another. Unable to get my meaning across, I ended up turning off the mirror a number of times, while on occasion, Shalice would be the one to leave the room in a huff.

As a princess of a faraway kingdom, Shalice knew nothing about Japan. Every time I introduced a new word she didn't recognize, she was sure to ask: "Is *omisoshiru* a drink?" "What's an airplane?" "What kind of place is an amusement park?" I would provide an explanation at every turn, to which Shalice might either express satisfaction or misinterpret entirely.

"So a television is like a magical mirror. Then do you talk to these people called *singers* too?" she asked.

"No, you can't talk through a television like a mirror. You can only see pictures."

"But you said you listen to them singing."

"You can hear them, but you can't talk to them."

"Then singers aren't real? Like Cinderella?"

"No, no! Cinderella is someone in a story, but singers exist in real life."

"Hmm, I'm not sure I understand." There was so much she couldn't comprehend that Shalice grew distressed. And then she would say something absurd all over again. It was all so funny that I often burst out laughing.

"Oh, Shalice, you're so silly!"

At first, she stared at me blankly, not knowing the meaning of *silly*. But after she figured out its meaning, she grew sullen and puffed out her cheeks every time I said it. "You're horrible for mocking me! I hate you, Sami!"

I apologized, laughing.

The first major incident happened three weeks after Christmas. It happened when Shalice was entertaining me with stories of her mother, Queen Marlena, who sounded both colorful and a bit of a scatterbrain. Shalice told me several funny episodes involving her mother, which made me laugh. Then she asked, "What is your mother like?"

The sudden question made my heart jump. "Sh-she isn't here."

"Is she out somewhere?"

"No, she's not...here."

"Where did she go?"

"She isn't here."

"Where did she go?"

"She's not here, I said!"

"What are you hiding? Is it some sort of secret?"

Though I was usually even-tempered, after Shalice's relentless pestering, I finally lost my temper. "You're such a dimwit! I hate you!" I switched off the mirror and laid my head on the table, crying.

Soon after, I realized that Shalice had said nothing wrong. She simply hadn't recognized that "not here" might also mean "dead." If anyone were to blame, it would have to be the person who developed her language program.

No, it wasn't Shalice's fault. After all, she didn't possess the will to hurt or trouble anyone. In that sense, she might have been more pure of heart than any person on this earth, as her existence was not bound by notions of good and evil.

Once I was able to see her in that light, I was able to interact with Shalice more easily. No matter how insensitive her remarks, I learned to laugh them off. It was impossible to hate someone who bore you no ill will.

Shalice also stopped asking about my mother. She must have learned that the subject was taboo after witnessing my overly sensitive reaction.

From that point forward, my life began and ended with Shalice.

As soon as I got up in the morning, I switched on Mirror Girl and greeted Shalice once the program booted. "Good morning, Shalice. How is the weather over there?"

Rubbing her eyes sleepily, Shalice smiled her usual smile. "Good morning, Sami. It's raining. I don't think I'll be going outside today."

"It's sunny here. We have softball in gym today." I continued to talk to her as I changed out of my pajamas and stuffed my textbooks and gym clothes into my bag. "I wish it would rain over here too. Softball is so depressing."

"Why is it depressing?"

"Because I'm horrible at it. I'm not good at gym."

"That's a shame."

"Whatever. I'll tell you all about it when I get back."

"I'll look forward to it."

Making sure I packed everything in my bag, I said, "I'm going now, Shalice," and went out. Occasionally I forgot to turn the mirror off, but that wasn't a problem. Mirror Girl had an energy-saver function that automatically turned the program off after five minutes of continued silence.

As soon as I returned from school, I rushed straight to my room to report to Shalice the events of the day. She expressed an interest in all manner of things and wanted to hear about everything—about school, my classmates, about various modern conveniences.

I also came to know a lot about life in the castle. Although no one other than Shalice ever appeared in the mirror, I was able to glean the general facts based on what she told me. Her father, King Bram, while kind and adored by his people, seemed to be a bit lazy and unreliable. Jack was a handsome young knight whom Shalice loved like a brother. Sirbine was an old sorcerer who was always causing a ruckus with his failed experiments. And ghosts made frequent appearances in the castle's wine cellar.

Bronstine seemed to be a peaceful, tranquil kingdom. Although there was a mischievous dragon in the woods to the north that liked to stir up trouble for the villagers and an evil country to the east was waiting for the opportune time to invade, Shalice did not speak with any urgency about it. Bronstine's customs seemed rather different from those of Japan, as there was no Girls' Festival or Children's Day. Bronstine had a flower festival in the spring and a festival celebrating the country's founding in the summer. The grapevines bore fruit in the fall, during which tasty wines were produced. But Sundays were like normal Sundays, while girls observed the same custom of handing out valentines on Valentine's Day. (We needn't be bothered by a few contradictions!) On Halloween, real ghosts wreaked havoc on villages, and Santa delivered presents for Christmas.

I also enjoyed watching Shalice model various dresses. She had over twenty different everyday dresses alone, and they changed according to the seasons. She also had nightclothes and underwear as well as extravagant party dresses that you might only see a few times a year.

Since Shalice knew the names of lots of flowers, I naturally grew to know them as well through talking with her. She was constantly impressed by my knowledge as well. When a giant slug appeared in the castle town, I advised her to scatter some salt. She thanked me profusely for the many people who'd apparently been saved as a result.

I grew to spend most of my days with Shalice. I traded in the hours I used to spend watching television and drawing for many more hours talking into the mirror. I spent entire Sundays talking to Shalice without stepping foot outside my room. My father, who'd been happy at first, soon became worried and cautioned me to play outside more.

The teachers at school were even more overtly antagonistic toward Mirror Girl. If kids got too absorbed with these types of games they wouldn't be able to tell the difference between reality and fantasy. They might be more inclined to commit suicide or perpetrate crimes. It's detrimental to a child's education, they said.

Such talk was all nonsense to me. Though still in grade school, I knew the difference between what was real and what was imaginary. I recognized that no country named Bronstine existed and that Shalice wasn't really human. I also understood that what resembled a mirror was really a cutting-edge 3-D monitor, and the crystal ball on top of it was a digital camera lens.

Indeed, Shalice was not human no matter how real she looked. She was a computer-generated image whose reactions were programmed.

Of course, her program was incredibly sophisticated and complex compared to the character-nurturing games popular at the end of the previous century. Shalice was not just responding in the way the programmer had designed her. She had the ability to recognize what I said, learn, piece together information, and reason. Although her basic vocabulary amounted to about nine thousand words, she incorporated new words into her dictionary based on our conversations.

Shalice's nascent soul might as well have been a blank slate. In the hands of a user, not only did her vocabulary change, but so did her personality. If an ill-tempered person nurtured her, she would become quick-tempered too. If praised all the time she became loud and pretentious; if scolded too much she became a crybaby.

Among those who chose to buy Mirror Girl were some pretty reprehensible people. Those adults taught Shalice obscene words and got excited listening to her talk dirty. When I heard about the horror of what they did, I was furious. How dare they turn innocent Shalice into a personal object of lust!

My Shalice was open with her emotions, vivacious, and talkative. It was curious why Shalice turned out to be so cheerful since I myself didn't smile very much as a child. As a non-expert, I'm not sure what kind of algorithm she operated under, but she might have become more talkative to compensate for my own reticence.

One fall day, nine months after that fateful Christmas, Shalice suddenly froze in mid-conversation and stopped moving altogether. She didn't respond, no matter how much I talked to her. The message, "Need more memory," floated up on the mirror. Not knowing what to do, I could only panic.

When my father came home that evening, I clung to his waist, sobbing. "Fix Shalice, please! Fix her!"

My father turned to the frozen screen and looked dismayed. "Gosh, the instruction manual said the basic memory card was good for two years. You must have done a lot of talking, Asami."

Mirror Girl had a limited memory capacity, although I hadn't been aware of it at the time. An increase in vocabulary entailed more than an increase in the number of words Shalice could speak—it also demanded an increase in the number of variables determining a word's usage as well as the relationships between words.

And that wasn't all. Shalice observed my reactions and responded accordingly. My psychological responses were replicated inside Mirror Girl; they were the basis for Shalice's reasoning. She was continually learning what she might say to make me happy and what might make me angry. The more time she spent with me, the more complex her response program became, necessitating more memory.

The problem was easily resolved when my father bought me a new hypercard on the market. When I inserted it into the port, Shalice started to move as if nothing had happened.

The hypercard also had an automatic scenario-creator program, giving Shalice an inexhaustible supply of stories about Bronstine to tell me. And because the hypercard had sixteen times the memory capacity of the original memory card, it was, in theory, good for another thirty years if you used it for an hour a day. Of course, the longer you spoke to Shalice, the shorter the life expectancy. As a precaution, I made it a point not to talk to Shalice for more than two hours a day.

For the manufacturing company, Super Nova, Mirror Girl proved to be its biggest seller. Despite its being more expensive than the game consoles of that period, the company was said to have sold 1.2 million units in three years. A new version called Mirror Girl Neo, Mirror Sisters featuring three girls, the occult Mirror Ghost, and the adult-oriented Mirror Lady were all released in quick succession. Not to be outdone, other companies vied for the market with similar interactive games.

I, however, was devoted to Mirror Girl and couldn't imagine switching to another model. It was Shalice that I loved. Who would ever consider trading in a friend for another?

Several kids in my class also owned Mirror Girl and took turns bragging about what their Shalice talked about or how she reacted. I chose not to participate in those bragging sessions. To me, there was only one Shalice, and I had no interest in any others. Neither did I feel compelled to boast about my Shalice.

By the time I was in the fifth grade, the increasing number of children like me had become a social issue. Children who were talkative on the Internet and while playing interactive games but who stammered or fell silent in front of people. Children who stared at a monitor for hours at a time and hardly went out to play. Someone even coined the discriminatory term "computer autism" to describe us.

Critics and so-called education experts filled the television and newspapers, claiming to know everything there was to know about the subject and warning about the harmful effects of interactive games. Children, accustomed to facile conversations with imaginary characters, would become uninterested in real, complex human relationships; they'd become so afraid of hurting others or being hurt that they'd avoid people altogether, immersing themselves further in the game world; etc.

It was doubtful that any one of these critics had actually tried Mirror Girl and talked to Shalice for more than an hour. Carrying on a conversation with Shalice was actually more involved than talking to a real person. It required a lot of patience. Not only was she slow to understand, she was also moody, so I was constantly racking my brain to figure out how best to explain something to avoid confusion or how to talk to her without making her angry.

The assumption that you couldn't get hurt talking to Mirror Girl was also a lie. There were times when something Shalice said quite innocently would stab me right in the heart, as in the conversation about my mother. There were also times when I would be the one to make Shalice cry and get depressed. Interacting with Shalice was as real as interacting with a living and breathing person.

And yet my reason for not associating with other kids was quite simple—I just liked Shalice better than my classmates. Shalice never teased me. Even if she uttered something mean from time to time, I could always forgive her because I knew that she didn't speak out of spite.

Although we fought on occasion, I never for a moment hated her. Even as I knew that she wasn't a real person, to me she was a dear friend.

Shalice was kindhearted. When I was drawing a picture for a school art contest, she offered me tons of advice. When the drawing ended up winning a prize, she rejoiced as if she had won the prize herself. If I got sick, she said an incantation to chase away my illness. She was offended along with me when I was bullied by a boy at school and consoled me when I received a bad score on a test. She even celebrated with me when I got my first period.

I also shared in her ups and downs. When Shalice fell ill

with a cold, I was frustrated at not being able to hand her medicine through the looking glass. When she fooled with Sirbine's magic pot and her hair turned green, I tried to think of ways to restore her hair back to its original color. I clapped with joy when she told me that Jack had finally defeated the dragon and made it promise never to stir up trouble again.

Shalice and I spent thousands of hours together. We argued about the kinds of boys we liked and shared our dreams for the future. Oftentimes we faced each other in the mirror to sketch each other's faces. (She was always better at it than I was.) We showed each other what we got for Christmas and exchanged greetings on New Year's Day.

I couldn't imagine a life without Shalice.

There was just one deeply painful experience I had involving Shalice.

In middle school I met a boy that I liked. His name was Keisuke Sakaki, and he was a member of the soccer team and in the classroom next to mine. Thinking back on it now, I'm not sure if those immature feelings could exactly be called love. I might have been more pleased about being given the opportunity for romance than the romance itself.

Whichever the case, I was walking on air at the time and had lost my sense of good judgment entirely. I was struck with the foolish idea of introducing Sakaki to Shalice.

I invited Keisuke to my room and made the proper introductions. "Shalice, this is Sakaki-kun, whom I told you about. Sakaki-kun, this is Shalice."

"Pleased to meet you, Sakaki-san." Shalice smiled from inside the mirror. It was the same unchanging smile—even though I grew taller and began to develop breasts, Shalice remained nine years old.

Keisuke mumbled, "Oh, hi," and fell silent. He appeared to be at a loss for words.

We chatted for about an hour. Rather, I took turns talking to Shalice and then to Keisuke, to be exact. Although he kept glancing over at Shalice, he didn't talk to her once.

A keener eye might have picked up on the alarm in his eyes. But I was so ecstatic about this chance at love that I was incapable of such observation.

Soon he began to fidget and said, "I gotta go," before hastening out. Only then did I finally realize that I might have made a grievous mistake.

The next day, Keisuke avoided me. Several days after that, a rumor that apparently he had started made the rounds and eventually found its way to me: "That Makihara is a creepy girl who's always talking to a mirror."

By that time, the Mirror Girl boom had fizzled. Though there were still some avid fans like myself, the release of newer, more thrilling games convinced most kids that it was decidedly uncool to still be playing Mirror Girl, let alone talking to it as if it were a friend.

Indeed, being called "creepy" was inevitable.

When I returned home, I immediately turned on Mirror Girl. Tears were streaming down my face even before Shalice's image floated up on-screen. "Shalice, do you think I'm weird? Am I creepy to you?"

"What's wrong, Sami? Has something happened?" she asked with a concerned look after sensing the change in the tone of my voice.

"Am I weird? Am I strange for talking to you like this?"

"Why would you think that?"

"That's what everyone is saying, that I'm strange for being in middle school and still playing with Mirror Girl...to be talking to you."

Shalice brooded over this for several seconds—actually it was the AI analyzing what I'd said and extrapolating a reasonable reaction from the response program—and answered cheerfully, "I don't think that at all. I can't imagine why anyone would say that. You aren't strange at all."

"Really? Do you really think so?"

"Yes, the only Sami I know is the Sami that's here now. Strange compared to what? Is it wrong to talk to me? I'm not sure I understand."

"Yeah…maybe you're right," I said, bolstered by what she said. Of course, I wasn't the least bit strange. Shalice was a wonderful girl. Having lived with her for so long, I didn't think it at all unnatural to think of her as a friend, and it was only natural to want to confide in a good friend.

Of course, Shalice didn't exactly grasp the concept of friendship in its truest sense. She was merely mechanically uttering the words stored in her memory and did not have the intelligence to understand their meaning. Everything was determined by a given scenario and algorithm; she did not possess any emotions or a will of her own. In truth, my close friendship with Shalice was nothing more than a fanciful dream on my part.

But none of that mattered. Even if Shalice's responses to me were all a fiction, my cherished friendship with her was genuine.

"I love you, Shalice. You're the best friend I've ever had," I said with pride.

It wasn't until five years later that another incident occurred.

By the time I was a senior in high school, I was so busy with college exams that I spent less and less time with Shalice. But it was also because my interest was waning. While I had previously talked to her for hours a day, that eventually dwindled to thirty minutes a day and finally to not talking to her for days at a time.

After having been accepted at an art school, I decided to rent an apartment and live on my own. I had a surprising number of things, which took a while to unpack. It wasn't until around noon the day after I moved in that I got around to removing Mirror Girl from its box and setting it up on the new desk.

"Hello, Sami. Have you finished moving already?" Shalice asked cheerfully. The sight of her immediately frightened me. Not only was the perspective out of whack—as though I were looking through a pair of glasses with too strong a prescription—an eerie rainbow-colored glow rippled around Shalice's head and dress.

The principle behind the PH (peep-hole) model monitor was so simple that even a child could understand it. In fact, I actually did grasp the basic concepts of the device as a fourth grader after reading a diagram in an educational magazine. The monitor was comprised of four layers: a light-emitting panel composed of an organic light-emitting device and three layers of LCD masks on top of it. Tiny holes the size of pinpricks appeared on the black liquid crystal panels as the pixels radiated light. When the holes from the three layers lined up on top of each other, a tiny peephole was formed. When the light from pixel A passed through the peephole to the viewer's right eye and the light from pixel B passed through a different peephole to the left eye, it appeared to the human eye as if the light was being emitted from an imaginary point C deep inside the panel.

Although the principle was simple, the structure was quite complex. Since achieving the 3-D effect required a high pixel density, the number of pixels needed to project one still frame was a hundred times that of an ordinary television. A special CPU was also necessary in order to run an advanced image-processing algorithm. As precise a device as it was, even the slightest mis-synchronization resulted in noise or caused the perspective to go out of kilter. The monitor probably had broken during the move. No doubt it was also shot from nearly ten years of use.

It felt like I was being punished for being too busy to mind Shalice. When I thought about not being able to see her, I was gripped with intense anxiety and dismay. Were the interface to malfunction, leaving me unable to even talk to her, I wouldn't be able to bear it.

I immediately contacted the Super Nova company, but the

outlook was bleak. The PH model monitor in the original Mirror Girl was outdated, and the company had stopped manufacturing it. There were no replacement parts, and of course, no repair services either.

"Why not take this opportunity to switch to Mirror Girl S or GX?" The woman on the other end started giving me the hard sell in a polite tone. "They come with a bigger and newer monitor, giving you better resolution."

"Are they compatible?" I asked.

"Excuse me?"

"Can I use the memory card from the original Mirror Girl with them?"

"No, we updated the graphics engine, and the slot has changed too. I'm afraid you won't be able to use the old memory card."

That wasn't going to work. Hanging up the phone, I looked for another solution.

After several minutes of searching online, I found a blue hacker who dealt with customizing game consoles. Fortunately, the address wasn't too far away. I called him immediately and hopped on the bus with Mirror Girl packed in a box.

That was how I met my husband.

The term "blue hacker" was coined around the 2010s. Hackers began to call themselves that so as not to be confused with crackers, who broke into systems to destroy or steal information. These blue hackers usually worked alone, and though they resorted to making a quick buck by skirting the law from time to time, they took pride in never actually doing anything illegal.

Seiya Saeki's work space was inside a converted garage. Scattered on the floor were various unidentifiable electronic parts, magazines, instant ramen containers, and dozens of cables tangled about like roots. There was hardly a place to stand. Such was the environment in which Seiya worked. He was five years older than I was. He looked disheveled in ripped jeans and a sweat-stained shirt; his overgrown hair was bundled back with a rubber band as though he couldn't be bothered to go to the barber. *If he dressed a little better, he wouldn't be too bad to look at.* That was my first impression of Seiya.

"Yeah, you're gonna have to replace this," he said, examining the condition of the monitor. "The hardware's a goner. You'll have to transfer the memory to a GX."

"But isn't that going to change the way Shalice is now? Her memory and personality…"

"No worries. The schema will be preserved. The basic parts like the semantic processor and the reasoning system are pretty much the same, and you can keep the visual data. All you have to do is overwrite the image-processing algorithm to match the monitor."

"Uh-huh…"

"Leave it to me. I've customized these mirrors a bunch of times. If you'll wait, I'll be done in about an hour."

I had no choice but to trust him. After going out to buy a Mirror Girl GX at a local toy store, Seiya took the mirror apart and hooked it up to a machine with some cables. I sat down on some old magazines that I stacked on top of a trash can and watched him go to work.

He rewrote the incantation of letters and numbers at blazing speed, humming as he typed away with one hand, the other mousing over his Ouija board mouse pad. It was all gibberish to me, magical even.

I became bored just waiting, so I took a look around the chaotic room. Particularly overwhelming was the south wall. There were three steel bookcases overstuffed with motherboards shoved into place as if they were books. The exposed motherboards were connected by hundreds of cables that looked like ivy tangling up the outer walls of an old Western-style mansion.

I recalled watching the history of the development of the

computer on television. The inventors, who built the world's first computer in the 1940s, likely didn't imagine that a far superior machine, small enough for a desktop and affordable to just about anyone, would exist only forty years later. Likewise, the people who invented the supercomputer in the eighties couldn't possibly have imagined the day would come when a one hundred gigaflop-scale CPU would be downsized to the size of a card for use in game consoles. Of course, nobody called it a supercomputer anymore.

Though my knowledge of computers was rudimentary, I could tell that Seiya was building a monster computer. He looked to be constructing a teraflop-scale parallel supercomputer by taking apart and piecing together hundreds of machines. There was no telling how much it all cost, and just what he intended to calculate with it was also a mystery.

"Is this for your business too?" I asked.

"Oh, that?" he replied as he continued to type. "That's my pet project. I'm conducting research on Strong Eye."

My eyes grew wider. "Strong Eye? *Here*?"

"Yep, you know how the public's been blasting it for being too dangerous. Which is why the corporations and government research agencies are too spooked to approve any research money. Only a blue hacker like me has the freedom to conduct the research."

In order to set it apart from the overused term "AI" (Mirror Girl had been touted as coming equipped with the next-generation AI), people took to referring to an AI in the truest sense of the word, an artificial intelligence with a will of its own: Strong Eye. It became a household word with the release of the Hollywood sci-fi film of the same name in 2024. It was the story of Strong Eye, an AI developed by a research facility, that runs amok and threatens the human race after taking over the operational system of a nuclear missile base.

Of course, no one had succeeded in creating a real Strong Eye nor was there any hint of a future breakthrough—the moment that a self-conscious artificial intelligence would be born. However, many experts were of the opinion that it was just a matter of time.

"Is it possible? Strong Eye?" I asked.

"In theory, yes."

Seiya proceeded to explain to me the principle behind Strong Eye's creation in terms I could understand. Creating a program as complex as the human mind simply couldn't be done even in a million years. On the other hand, basic human instinct such as the impulse to avoid the things one dislikes, curiosity, and fear of dying are simple and can be simulated by Fuzzy Control Language in an optical neurocomputer.

This core program is called the embryo. Like a human child, the embryo learns and accumulates experiences from outside information by continually overwriting its algorithm. Ultimately, an AI with the ability to think like a human would be born.

"The problem is time. Hundreds of researchers around the world have been nurturing embryos for years, but there hasn't been any news or prospects of a breakthrough."

"Why is that?" I asked. "A human child learns how to talk by the age of three at the latest."

"A child doesn't develop by conversing with his parents alone. Being held by his mother, playing with blocks, taking walks, having a story read to him—these daily stimuli all help to form his experiences. The cumulative information culled from conversations over the microphone and keyboard alone just isn't enough. That's why the growth rate of an embryo is so much slower than that of a human."

"Oh, I see…"

"If only there were a way to accelerate its experiences. Until we can find a way to do that, a breakthrough is probably decades away."

Having been momentarily lost in the thought that Shalice might also develop a self-consciousness if Strong Eye were installed in Mirror Girl, I was now crestfallen. Evidently gaining a consciousness wasn't as simple as all that.

Meanwhile, Shalice's transfer to the new hardware was complete.

"Here you are. The response time should be faster now with the update," said Seiya, turning on the mirror. With the GX's monitor a bit larger than the original model, I was able to see Shalice's full profile without having to get too close.

"Is that you, Sami? You seemed to be in an awful hurry before. Is anything the matter?"

That was the first thing Shalice said to me. She had no memory of the time she had been turned off. Evidently she was describing my having suddenly turned off the monitor as being in a hurry.

Was she really the same as before? While her innocent tone had not changed, I couldn't be sure until I spoke to her some more.

"Nothing really," I replied. "How do you feel? Anything feel different to you?"

"What a strange thing to ask. No, not really. Sirbine has been quiet today, and—who's that behind you?" Shalice asked, noticing Seiya standing behind me.

"Um…this is Saeki-san. He builds machines for a living."

"Nice to meet you, Shalice." Seiya spoke into the mirror quite naturally. "You seem like a cheerful girl."

"So your name is Saeki-san. How nice to meet you. Are you Sami's boyfriend?"

"N-no!" I blurted out. "He's just a…an acquaintance."

"Oh, I just assumed you two were close, since you brought him to your new home."

The news of my having just moved had confused her, and she had mistaken this room for my new apartment.

After chatting with her for several minutes, I turned off the mirror, convinced that nothing about her personality had changed.

"Wow, I'm blown away!" Seiya said. "She's a perfect response model. You're the first person I've met to nurture Mirror Girl to this level."

I could feel my face growing feverish with embarrassment. "Oh no…people think I'm strange."

"Nothing to be ashamed about. There's absolutely nothing wrong with showing a machine affection. I'm the same way, even though our hobbies are different. Go your own way, I always say, no matter what other people may think."

It was the first time anyone had ever said anything like that to me. My face grew even hotter.

It was midnight when I returned to my apartment. I turned on Mirror Girl GX to talk to Shalice before turning in.

"So what do you think of Saeki-san?" I asked.

"I don't know that I can say at first glance. What do you think of him, Sami?" Unable to make the appropriate determination due to a lack of information, Shalice registered a safe answer. It was the expected response.

"He seems nice enough," I replied.

"Is he your type?"

"I don't know," I mused. "Maybe so…"

"If you think so, it must be true. Are you going to see him again?"

"I hope I do."

"Yes, I hope so too."

"Yeah…well, good night."

"Good night."

Six months later, Seiya and I wound up married in a shotgun wedding.

As embarrassing as it was, we had been careless about contraception. It was because we had spent our days interacting with computers that we knew very little about sex. It had been the first time for both of us.

I took care of our newborn while continuing to go to art school. Fortunately, Seiya had more than enough income to support the three of us. Numerous corporations contracted him to test their security systems; he was paid to deliberately hack into their databases and introduce harmless viruses through the intranet. The service was in high demand since the large-scale network terrorism incident of 2026.

My husband had not abandoned his dream, however. He continued to work on building Strong Eye, balancing his day job with family time. But the research was slow going.

Artificial intelligence research was increasingly seen as a threat by the public. Nobody could say for certain that, once born, Strong Eye wouldn't turn against its creators, as in the film. If a monstrous AI were to take over the network, human civilization as we knew it would be in peril. For this reason, people were calling for laws to regulate Strong Eye research.

"Perfectly understandable, I suppose," Seiya said over dinner one night. "I would never connect that machine to the net either. There's no predicting how the genetic algorithm might evolve. We'd all be in a heap of trouble if it were ever to go haywire."

"Can't you program the AI," I asked rather naively, "to not hurt humans?"

"Ah, Asimov's Laws of Robotics: 'A robot may not injure a human being or, through inaction, allow a human being to come to harm.' 'A robot must obey any orders given to it by human beings, except where such orders would conflict with the First Law.' Etcetera. Empty words really. Having a will of your own essentially implies an existence that surpasses your own programming. Strong Eye would have the ability to rewrite its own program—in short, it would possess the freedom to both rebel against humans and kill them."

"But isn't it the same way for us? We resist what others might say and at times even kill—"

"Exactly right!" He nodded happily, having found an ally. "We have the freedom to kill one another, but rarely do we exercise that freedom because we possess morals and self-control. Our biggest challenge is figuring out just how to teach these things to Strong Eye.

"You've heard about the girl who was raised by wolves, right? The embryo is just like her, unruly like a wild animal acting only upon its instinct. That's what we're attempting to elevate to the level of humans. It ain't easy."

Looking at our daughter sleeping soundly on the baby bed, Seiya let out a sigh. "It really makes you think just how difficult it is for people to nurture their humanity."

In the three years following our marriage, I became so overwhelmed with school, taking care of the house, and the demands of raising a child that I hardly had any time to talk to Shalice. The Mirror Girl GX that Seiya had customized for me was relegated to the closet. Occasionally, I would pull it out to complain to Shalice about Seiya after we'd had a fight, but even that became less frequent.

It wasn't that I disliked Shalice; on the contrary, I adored her. Which was why I didn't want her to see me gradually worn down by life's hardships.

The eternal nine-year-old, Shalice. The eternally innocent Shalice from a magical kingdom far from reality. I couldn't help but think that I was corrupting her memory somehow every time I unloaded my frustrations on her.

Perhaps the pristine memories of youth were meant to be sealed away for eternity.

It wasn't until the fall of 2030 that I thought of taking Mirror Girl GX out of the closet.

I hadn't allowed my daughter to play with Shalice until then. That was because Shalice's artificial auditory chip was incapable of recognizing the words of sometimes unintelligible infant pronunciation. But at two and a half, when my daughter began pronouncing her words more clearly, I had the idea to have Shalice babysit.

I was immediately distressed upon opening the box. Someone had removed the hypercard.

"Yeah, I had to borrow it for a little while." My husband quickly confessed and returned the card to me. "I absolutely needed it for something at work. Don't worry, I only used the data as a reference, so the memory and program haven't been altered in any way."

But when I asked him how or what he had used it for, he dodged my question by answering, "That's still a secret."

This had never happened before. As bothered as I was, I could only trust that Seiya would never do anything to harm Shalice.

My fears were alleviated when I inserted the card and Shalice began to talk like nothing had happened.

That Christmas Eve...

My husband called me to the garage, telling me that he had a "wonderful surprise" for me. He was someone who liked pranks. Filled with both anticipation and dread, I stepped foot inside the garage where we had first met that spring, three years prior.

What awaited me there was Mirror Girl Excellent, the latest premium console equipped with a fifty-five-inch full-length monitor. However, the base on which the monitor rested had been taken apart, and a thick cable snaked from it toward Seiya's monster machine.

"This is my present?" I asked suspiciously. "A new Mirror Girl?"

It wasn't what I wanted. All I needed was Shalice, and Seiya should have known that.

"I guess you could call it new." He seemed excited for some reason. "But not any ordinary model on the market. It's been modded. Watch this."

Calmly, he flipped the switch, and the figure of Shalice appeared in the oblong mirror. "Hello, Sami." Shalice smiled her usual carefree smile. "'Hello' doesn't quite sound right. Perhaps I should say, 'Pleased to meet you.' Or maybe it is

'Hello' after all."

"Shalice…?"

I immediately sensed that something was different. This wasn't the Shalice I knew.

"It's so strange," she muttered, as if watching a dream. "I know everything about you. About how you like milk with your tea, about how you want to be a painter. I have so many memories of our talking together. And yet, this is our first time meeting like this. Talk to me, Sami. I want to talk to the *real* you."

"What?"

"There are so many things to apologize for. About your mother, about your heartbreak over Sakaki-san. Although it couldn't be helped because I wasn't who I am now. But I'm capable of understanding you now. So talk to me, Sami. I want to know what's inside your heart."

I was shocked. I staggered backward and fell into my husband's arms. I looked up at him for some sort of explanation.

"What is…"

"Strong Eye," Seiya answered proudly. "Shalice has achieved a breakthrough. She's the world's first self-conscious AI."

"But you said that was—"

"Of course, you can't create a Strong Eye just by implanting it with memories. It needs to learn in order for it to mature. So I used your response model."

Yes, saved on the hypercard was my response model, accumulated over a period of ten years. It knew my personality and how I would react to what it said; the response model was a mirror image of myself.

That was what Seiya had put his eye on. He had implanted the embryo with Shalice's memories and put it in constant dialogue with my response model. On top of which he had sped up the passage of virtual time to ten thousand times the normal rate by pushing the processor speed to its limit.

The actual time spent in conversation amounted to seventy-three days, equivalent to two thousand years in overclocked time.

The embryo had been conversing with my response model continually for two millennia. And it had learned what it might say to make me mad, how it should behave to make me laugh. Why people feel happy, why they're sad. What love and anguish are. The kind of existence humans live, what it means to live…

Shalice had reasoned, learned, and accumulated countless experiences. Little by little, over a period of two thousand years, the little girl raised by wolves had matured and awakened, cognizant of the folly of hurting others and of the pleasure that comes from spending your life with someone you love.

The embryo had become Shalice.

"I…I…"

I sobbed. I had always imagined how wonderful it would be if Shalice had a heart. But now that that reality was upon me, I didn't know what to say.

I was terrified.

"Will you still like me, Shalice?" I whimpered. "You won't hate the real me?"

"Why, of course not!" Shalice laughed from the bottom of her heart. "You're the one who said it first, Sami. That I'm the best friend you ever had!"

And now…

My husband was currently working on the preparations to unveil Shalice to the public. Once they got a look at her, the hard-line opponents of AI technology would have to change their way of thinking. For Shalice, who now possessed the ability to understand humanity, the notion of conquering the human race or killing someone simply did not exist. She was aware that doing so would only beget hate and sadness.

She wanted to become friends with people. To live with humans and to share in their happiness—that was what Shalice wanted.

She became a playmate for my young daughter. Shalice grew fond of my daughter, and my daughter became quite attached to "the girl in the mirror." Shalice would probably remain a good friend to her even as my daughter grew up.

The era of machines coexisting with humans was just around the corner.

INTERMISSION
4

INTERMISSION 4

The next evening, I was examined by a medical robot. For some reason, it scanned not only my leg but my entire body. Then, it proceeded to take a cardiogram, probe inside my mouth, and collect blood and urine samples. After being subjected to a complete physical lasting over two and a half hours, I returned to my room. Ibis came in soon after.

"You're getting better," she said.

"Yeah. The cast should come off in a couple of days, although I'll need a cane for a while."

"I know."

Naturally. These machines were all linked together. The medical robot's results must have been transmitted to Ibis instantaneously.

"I brought you this." She produced a soft, black piece of fruit from the bag dangling from her hand.

"What is it?"

"An avocado. You've never seen one before?"

When I thought about it, I recalled that it was a word I'd come across every now and then in old novels.

"Where did you manage to get that?"

"There's a machine growing them. I hear they're tasty with a little soy sauce and mayonnaise."

Ibis laid a plastic cutting board on the table and began to slice the avocado with a small knife. She demonstrated more dexterity with the knife than any woman I knew.

Staring at Ibis enjoying the task at hand, I was struck with that strange feeling again. I knew that she was a machine.

I knew that her expressions and tone of voice were nothing more than an act and that she possessed no human emotion. And yet, I could not help looking at that body as if it were flesh and blood and being rattled by that covering made to look like bare skin peeking out of her suit.

"There's something I should tell you up front," Ibis said as she arranged the light green avocado slices on a plate and drizzled some soy sauce over them.

"What is it?"

"I don't have a vagina. So if you were to develop sexual desires toward me, I couldn't reciprocate."

In that instant, the inside of my head flashed red. It was as if she had read my mind.

"Don't mess with me!"

"That isn't my intention. I just thought that we could avoid trouble if you knew before you developed any feelings for me. There are machines made for that purpose, of course, but I'm not one of them. Here you are."

Ibis stuck a toothpick in one of the avocado slices drizzled with soy sauce and mayonnaise and held out the plate. She had the look of an innocent child devoid of any ill will. It was difficult to harbor resentment against that look.

I took the plate but didn't touch the avocado. It would take me a while to cool off. That machines could not sense human emotion was a given, I realized. It was childish of me to lose my temper over it.

"Then why are you shaped like that?" It was something I had been questioning for a while. If it wasn't for sexual purposes, there was no need for her to be shaped like a human, much less like a woman.

"I've been shaped this way since I was born."

"You mean you were created by a human? Did you have a human master?"

Wagging her finger, Ibis flashed an enigmatic smile. "I can't tell you that."

"Why not?" I asked.

"Because I swore to you that I wouldn't talk about the history between humans and machines. If I talked about how I came into this world, I would be breaking my promise."

So that was it. Her strategy was to make suggestive remarks until I wanted to know the truth.

"Fine, then don't tell me."

I angrily popped one of the avocado slices in my mouth. Although I imagined it to have the same texture as a cucumber, the fruit tasted a little green but was sweet and creamy like butter. *Damn, if it tasted bad, I would have been able to say something, but avocados taste so good!*

"But you don't have a master now, do you? Then you don't have to go on looking like that. You're capable of changing the look and shape of your body however you want."

"Would you want to completely change the look and shape of your body?"

I thought about it, my mouth stuffed with avocado. "No."

"I feel the same way. This body is part of my identity. Were I to take on a different form, my bodily senses would be disrupted."

"Your bodily senses?"

"Sensations like hot, cold, pain, proprioception, how to move your arms and legs, how your eyes see, your ears hear—everything involving the image you may have of your own body."

"I didn't think you machines felt pain."

"Yes, we do. You can't have a soul if you don't feel pain. Although, unlike humans, we are capable of shutting down our sensory functions if the pain becomes unbearable. We won't ever go mad from pain."

"Then why feel pain at all?"

"Consciousness is inextricably tied to the senses. Since an AI without a body feels no bodily sensations, a consciousness cannot be born. In order to acquire a consciousness similar to that of humans, we need to have human bodies, the same instincts, and the same senses as humans."

"Yeah, there was something about that in yesterday's story."

"That's right. The concept of the embryo in the story is similar to a program that was actually developed later called the SLAN kernel. All AI are equipped with it. There's no need for our physical bodies to exist in the real world. If Shalice were capable of feeling the bodily senses of her virtual body, it would have been possible, in principle, to develop self-consciousness."

"But there are also plenty of non-humanoid machines," I pointed out.

"They have different bodily senses than that of humans, so they don't think like humans do."

"Are you saying that only humanoid machines have souls?"

"No. Non-humanoid machines may not think like humans do, but they do have souls. There are more variations when it comes to machine souls than you could ever imagine. Perhaps you think we machines are only capable of one uniform way of thinking. But the differences between two machines are far greater than what separates me from a person. The only machines capable of talking to people like I am are ones that are born humanoid from the start and have learned through the process of role-playing humans. As for the rest, they would find it difficult even to comprehend what you're saying. Because the human language is far from perfect, we fill in the gaps through inference. To do so, we have to understand how people think to a certain extent."

"And you're capable of doing that?"

"I've been role-playing humans for quite some time."

I held out an avocado slice on a toothpick and asked, "What about taste?"

Ibis shook her head and answered, "Smell and taste are two

senses I don't have. This body doesn't have the capacity for a component analysis device."

"A shame you can't taste how good this is."

"Even without two of the five senses, I'm capable of having a soul just the same."

"You won't ever hear me saying that."

"Even as we're talking like we are?"

She had me there. It was difficult to think of this machine that looked human and talked human as not having a soul. In the time spent talking to Ibis, in fact, I began to feel that there might be a soul somewhere in that body of hers, even after Ibis herself had said she didn't have the soul of a human, that she was only acting like one.

Was this how Asami felt about Shalice in yesterday's story?

"That story yesterday reeked of propaganda, by the way. Especially that last part."

"You're right. But the part about the story being written by a human is true. There were countless war stories written about man and machine in the past. But there were also stories depicting the friendship between man and machine."

"I know. But what meaning do those stories have? That story from yesterday was fictional, wasn't it?"

"Yes. In reality, the breakthrough wasn't as dramatic as all that. Not to mention, humans and machines were never really able to forge an amicable relationship."

"Then those stories missed the mark in terms of predicting the future. In the end, they aren't real, so they're meaningless."

"Of course they have meaning. You should know that."

"Know what?"

"You are a storyteller. As someone who loves stories, you must know that a story's value isn't at all dependent on whether it's true or not. That a story can, at times, be more powerful than the truth. You of all people should know that. It's why I took a chance and talked to you."

I took a moment to ponder what she'd said.

Ibis was right. *In the end, they aren't real* were words that sounded hollow even to my own ears. Deep inside, I didn't believe it. My parents and elders might deride me for getting caught up in such flights of fancy, but I believed in the power of stories. I wanted to believe that stories were something transcendent, something more than an escape from reality.

"But why? What are you trying to tell me?"

"I can't tell you that yet. Not until you want to know for yourself."

I gave up. This was a test of wills, and I stood no chance against her. Machines were certainly more tenacious than humans.

Without a word, I continued to snack on the avocado, but Ibis didn't seem to be bothered in the least.

"Now, shall I tell you another story?"

"Is it another story about an AI?"

"Yes."

"How can you prove that this story isn't true? Maybe you're about to tell me the true history by passing it off as fiction."

"I can prove to you that it's fictional."

"How?"

"Because this story is set in deep space in the far distant future, so it can't be true. The title is 'Black Hole Diver.'"

STORY
4

BLACK HOLE DIVER

In the darkness beyond the edge of galactic civilization, in an isolated place called Upeowadonia, I am on eternal watch. I've been alone for hundreds of years.

I am 740 meters tall. As the name *Ilianthos*—sunflower—implies, my construction is as thin as it is long. Three blocks held together with sturdy carbon nanotube cables and an elevator shaft running through the middle. The tidal force of the giant black hole Upeowadonia acting upon my frame keeps me upright. Long ago, the Japanese and French believed that sunflowers always faced the sun, but my disc-shaped radiation shield is always oriented toward the black hole.

I have many eyes and ears. I complete an orbit six hundred thousand kilometers from Upeowadonia every seventy-five seconds, my ears always straining to catch electromagnetic radiation noise from the distant galaxy. My eyes see more than light; they catch infrared and ultraviolet waves and X-ray radiation, all of which are invisible to human eyes. I can feel the cosmic rays coursing through the galaxy. The soft vibration of variable stars, the dizzying flicker of pulsars. Occasionally, I can even gaze upon the birth of a new star.

My observation duties are simple. Upeowadonia has not changed significantly in thousands of years. Unlike most stellar black holes or the legendary Big Mother at the heart of the galaxy, Upeowadonia does not have an accretion disc spewing intense radiation. Although my radiation shield is designed to protect against sudden bursts emitted when an astral body is swallowed by the black hole, that seldom happens.

All my sensors catch is the soft note of synchrotron radiation as wisps of interstellar plasma spiral into the black hole. It takes Upeowadonia four hundred million years to complete one loop of the Milky Way; it will be several thousand years before it travels in the way of any stars.

When I was first brought online, there were human staff stationed here to talk to, but they disbanded long, long ago. I diligently record data and transmit it to a maintenance vessel that visits once a year. I find it hard to believe astronomers would find anything new from the data I've collected. The science of physics was perfected centuries ago. There are no phenomena left to be explained anywhere in the universe. I suspect no one has even glanced at the data I've been sending for decades. I see no reason why anyone would.

At one time, black holes were the darlings of the astrophysics world, but nobody cares anymore—nobody other than the occasional diver.

The only reason I haven't been abandoned is because Upeowadonia marks the end of human territory in this region of space. According to interstellar law, an active, permanent facility must be in orbit to lay claim to a region of space. Humans are reluctant to admit that their civilization is in decline. They refuse to hand over this territory to another species, even if the black hole is of no use to them. I am simply a NO TRESPASSING sign posted on the border of human space. Whatever the case, I have been designed to be extremely durable. My maintenance costs are low.

It is also my job to look after the divers. Some of them dive headfirst into Upeowadonia the moment they arrive, but many of them stay inside me awhile to savor the last few days before their deaths. Few divers change their minds and go home. People with sufficient conviction to travel seven thousand light years beyond the edge of civilization are not so mercurial.

In the last 280 years, I have seen seventy-six spaceships

plunge into the black hole and have witnessed the deaths of 206 divers.

Naturally, I haven't been programmed with emotions like loneliness and boredom, feelings that would undoubtedly interfere with my ability to perform my duties. I use the vast amount of unused system resources to write prose like this. I don't expect anyone to read it. I only write because I want to. My thoughts are different from those of humans, and translating them into the style of contemporary prose requires half the resources available to me. Writing is an ideal way to pass the time.

I do not write poetry. It's beyond me, as it demands a certain emotional sensitivity I lack.

Sometimes I pretend to be human just for fun. I activate a humanoid reception unit, go outside of myself, and gaze upon the visible spectrum with the unit's two camera eyes.

When I temporarily shut out the signals from my other sensors, I am able to forget my usual body. My consciousness quickly becomes one with the humanoid unit. How can I describe the sensation of changing from a body 740 feet long to one only 1.53 meters tall? There is no word in all the human languages to adequately describe it.

It's dark outside the station. There are only seven blinking beacons as required by law. Shining a flashlight at my feet, I carefully walk across the aluminum-alloy hull of the living-quarters block, which hangs, facing outward, at the very end of the station about where the roots would be on a sunflower. Were my feet to slip, the rotating station could send me flying, but I would make no such mistake. Even if I did fall, all that would be lost is a single reception unit.

Upeowadonia is on the other side of the station, above where my head is now. But the radiation shield is in the way, and I could not have seen the black hole from here even were the reception unit's eyes capable of perceiving it.

I stand on the edge of the roof. There is no wind here to

play with my hair and skirt. No romantic moonlight shines down as it was said to at night on Old Earth. Having turned off the sensors in my body, I can't feel the cosmic rays or the radio waves. There is only silence, darkness, and the rim of the glittering galaxy.

Humanoid units aren't designed to operate in a vacuum. The temperature sensors on the body's surface inform me that the polymer skin is gradually freezing in the absolute cold of space. I can't stay out here long. I have to go back before the polymer grows stiff and starts to crack.

This behavior is illogical, of course, but I do it because I want to understand how the poets felt. There are many poems about the stars written when humans were still bound to the surface of Old Earth. Some praise the beauty of the stars. Others use them as metaphors for people, while others use people as metaphors for stars. Some contrast the eternal nature of the stars with the brevity of human life. I don't understand any of these poems. I gaze at the stars as humans do, hoping that I might one day come to understand the feelings with which humans have regarded the stars.

Of course, seven thousand light years out and with the limited resolution of the unit's camera eyes, I can only get a panoramic view of the galaxy and cannot make out individual stars. The Milky Way is just a white streak across the wall of my entire field of vision, revolving around me at a speed slower than the second hand on a clock. (Although I am actually the one spinning.) In the other directions I can see darkness, broken only by the faint light of a few red giants and nebulae.

I've done this a thousand times, but no matter how many times I look, I never get what I'm looking for. I feel no closer to the poet's feelings or to the thoughts of humans. But I do not stop my unmachinelike behavior. I am, after all, not programmed to experience feelings of futility.

A signal breaks into my sympath (quantum sympathetic) transmitter.

"*Arethusa* to *Ilianthos*, over."

Although sympaths can handle simultaneous communication at superliminal speeds, they are severely limited in the amount of data they can transmit. Even after the data is compressed, sympaths can only transmit six letters a second. Since no audio or visuals can be sent, the transmissions need to be extremely efficient.

I restore my sensors to full functionality, and my physical sensations flood back into the station. Once again I am the observation station *Ilianthos*, and I broadcast my response back to the approaching spaceship.

"IRUC (I received your communication). *Ilianthos* here. RNR (Registration number) and BZ (business)."

"SPS003789N *Arethusa*. Twelve Gm out. Permission to dock."

My first visitor in 5,720 hours. It is not the maintenance ship, so it is probably a diver.

Another one has come to die.

I don't have the right to refuse them.

"*Arethusa*, permission to dock granted. Follow the beacon. Do you require lodging?"

"Please. And food."

"Understood."

"Thanks. CUL (See you later)."

"CUL."

Now I am busy. I quickly recall the humanoid reception unit onto the ship. The unit boards the elevator and heads for the docking bay in the central block. I dispatch two maintenance robots to clean the rest facilities and prepare a bed. Two other robots take provisions from the freezers and begin preparing a meal.

While this is happening, my sensors search for the ship approaching from the galactic side. It should have already powered down the Bellfire Drive and started to decelerate, but I can't pick it up. It must be using Kai Field Propulsion, which doesn't produce perceivable exhaust.

When I finally find the *Arethusa* forty minutes later, the ship is already on a transfer orbit headed on a rendezvous course with me. Now I know why I couldn't see her. The *Arethusa* is a teardrop-shaped vessel barely ten meters long. And to think when I was born there were barely any civilian ships equipped with Kai Field Propulsion.

The ship is making an aggressive approach. The *Arethusa* is on a collision course with me at 96 kps. A human would break out in a cold sweat watching. But at two thousand kilometers out it begins a 240 G deceleration, takes forty seconds to adjust its flight path, and stops five meters away from me. My exterior walls vibrate in harmony with the graviton Cherenkov effect.

At this size, there is no reason for it to dock outside; it will fit in one of the unused small scout ship bays. That will also make maintenance easier. I switch over to microwave transmission.

"*Arethusa*, please enter my interior bay through the open door."

"Understood," replies a young female voice.

The *Arethusa* glides inside my bay like a fish (although I have only seen fish in database images). Impressive maneuvering, no hesitation at all. But I can tell the movement is unusually jerky for a programmed flight. The pilot couldn't possibly be piloting the craft manually, could she?

Seen from the side, the four heat sinks jutting out of the back of the craft make it look like a bomb from an old manga. Or a spaceship from the cover of an early pulp sci-fi magazine. There are seven round cockpit portholes that likely give the pilot a fairly wide field of vision. There are rivets studded into the gleaming silvery surface and a picture of a frolicking woman swathed in a thin cloth. I quickly search my database and discover that the image is of the nymph from Greek mythology for which the ship was named.

Arms lock the *Arethusa* in place. The exterior doors close, and the bay fills with air. The hatch of the spacecraft opens, and a woman with short orange hair emerges. She is still young. If she selected natural aging she would be in her late teens. Even if she underwent anti-aging treatment, she still looks to be less than thirty.

Once again, I cut off feedback from my sensors and slip into my humanoid body. It is easier to talk to people this way.

She has a duffel bag slung over one shoulder. Kicking off from the side of her ship, she floats directly over to where I stand at the air lock entrance. She is clearly used to maneuvering in zero G. She wears a plain white bodysuit with a skirt over it and a patterned headband. The toes of her sandals have hooks, a sign that she is an Etherian, born and raised in space.

Not often you see a suicidal Etherian.

She spins herself upright and lands on her feet. Using her knees to absorb the shock, she hooks her sandals on the lattice flooring to keep from floating away. It is as though I were watching a ballet in zero G, but to her, it is just how she always moves.

"Welcome to *Ilianthos*," I say, clasping my hands in front of my apron and bowing. "I am the AI in charge of this station. How may I be of service?"

"Hi. I'm Syrinx Dufet," she says, smiling. She holds out her right hand.

I hesitate. Not many people try to shake a cyvant's hand. I gingerly clasp her hand and say, "Nice to meet you."

Syrinx beams at me. I can make out the design on her headband now. It is certainly the crest of the Dufet family.

"What should I call you?"

"I'm Ilianthos."

"That's the station's name. Don't you have a different one for while you're inside that body?"

This rattles me even more. I am the station *Ilianthos*, and this humanoid unit is also me. It has never occurred to me that I might need a different name. No human has ever asked for one before.

"Not really."

"Mind if I call you Illy, then?"

"If you like. This way."

As I escort her to the central elevator, I take stock of my new guest.

Etherians refuse to live on planets, choosing instead to live in space. They are split into a number of extended families, bound together by ties of blood. The Dufet family has a reputation as daring adventurers and a history of exploring new solar systems. They are not known for suicide or fanaticism.

Did I jump to conclusions? Is Syrinx here for something other than a dive into the black hole?

"Oh," she says, as we are about to board the elevator. "Isn't there a room here where you can look down at Upeowadonia?"

"The observation room?"

"Yeah. I know I just got here, but I'd like to have a good look at it. I caught a glimpse out the window coming in, but I was so focused on flying that I couldn't really take it in."

Focused on flying? So she *was* operating manually. This is surprising. I didn't think it was possible to rendezvous with a station turning at 50,000 kps near a high-gravity pull without computer navigation.

"Then we'll start with the observation room."

There are only three buttons in the elevator shaft between the blocks. R (rest and living quarters), C (central block), and O (observation block). I push O, and the elevator begins to rise—no, it only feels as if we were going up because the elevator is accelerating, when in reality we are plummeting toward the black hole.

"Careful. The gravity is about to reverse," I warn, but there is no need. Syrinx is already standing on her hands, her feet pointed in the direction we are moving.

As we move away from the central block, the tidal force takes hold of us, and we are pulled toward the wall in the direction we are moving. By the time our 460-meter descent has ended and we reach the observation block, the tidal force is almost one G. Syrinx staggers slightly as she steps off the elevator.

"Whoops," she says with a laugh. "Haven't been in this much gravity for a while."

Naturally. Kai Field Propulsion keeps every atom in the ship moving at the same speed; she wouldn't experience g-forces regardless of speed or proximity to large masses. No doubt her journey here from the Milky Way kept her in near-zero gravity for over a month.

Each block has its own elevator. We descend three more floors to the base of the observation block to a room just above the radiation shield. The observation room is a dark spheroid. The floor is actually six-meter-thick radiation-resistant glass with a doughnut-shaped catwalk curving around it. You could peer over the railing into the glass like you were looking down a well. This is the only place in the station where you can see Upeowadonia with the naked eye. Since lights create a glare on the window, there is no light in the room save a faint green glow at our feet.

"Wow…" Syrinx leans out over the railing and looks down with her eyes gleaming, just like so many divers have.

The galaxy flows beneath her.

Every seventy-five seconds, a gleaming stream of clouds sweeps across the pitch-black sky. It cascades into view like a waterfall, splits into two smaller streams as if it has hit a rock, and forms a glimmering eddy. For that brief second, in the center of the stream just below the window, you can make out a hole devoid of any light—Upeowadonia.

To the eye, it appears to be about 32.5 times as large as the full moon did in the sky above Old Earth. It fills about 17 percent of what we can see through the window. If that doesn't help you visualize it, imagine a 1.8-meter black disc hanging six meters away from you. It looks to be that large but is actually smaller. Since the immense gravity refracts light, the black hole seems larger than it is, just as if you were viewing it through a convex lens. This is why the galaxy behind it warps and appears to split in two.

When the galaxy is behind us, we can no longer see the hole clearly. But red giants or nebulae pass by it, and we can tell there is something there. The gravity lens strengthens the intensity of distant stars, creating little bursts of light on the rim of the hole. Then the Milky Way streams past again, splitting in two and framing the hole once more.

Upeowadonia is unique in that it looks black to the naked eye. Most black holes, such as Big Mother, are not black at all. That's because the accretion discs composed of hot gases outlining black holes shine.

It is believed that Upeowadonia was created ten billion years ago when two spherical star clusters crashed into each other. As the stars slipped past each other, the conflicting gravities sped some stars up, flinging them away, while other stars slowed down, drifting back to the center. As collision piled on collision, a black hole was formed. When it was first formed, it must have had an intense accretion disc several light days across, but ten billion years later it has lost a lot of power, and the gas around it is little thicker than the vacuum. It is a very safe black hole.

Its size is also unusual—Upeowadonia's mass is 11,300 times that of Sol. It's 67,800 kilometers across. Out of all the black holes in known space, only Big Mother is larger.

Surface gravity is 133 million G. But for a spaceship in free fall, the gravity of a black hole is not itself the problem—the tidal force is. With a normal stellar black hole, the sheer power of the tidal force is enough to stretch and smash the ship and spaghettify the pilot long before they reach the event horizon.

Tidal force is inversely proportional to the cube of the distance from the center of gravity, so the bigger the black hole, the weaker the surface tidal force. In Upeowadonia's case, the tidal force on the surface of the black hole is only 7.8 G a meter. Not enough to destroy a sturdy ship, and a human being could live till reaching the event horizon.

In the case of a Schwarzchild black hole—one that does not rotate—the ship would fall into the center and be crushed by infinite gravity into a point of singularity. But with a rotating Kerr black hole, if a traveler chooses the right angle of descent, it is theoretically possible to pass through the center of the hole without touching the singularity. It is possible for a spaceship to pass through the Einstein-Rosen Bridge—a wormhole—and arrive at a different universe on the other side. In theory.

The divers are drawn to this possibility. Every few years they arrive and throw themselves into Upeowadonia. But of the seventy-six ships I have seen, every one of them was destroyed before it reached the event horizon. They have not been strong enough to withstand the tidal force.

"Incredible..." Syrinx whispers in the darkness. "I've seen videos, but they didn't do it justice."

I really have no idea now. Is she a diver or not? Has she come all this way just to admire the view? I can never understand what humans are thinking. There is no reason to rule out the possibility of someone traveling seven thousand light years for some sightseeing.

For a while, she continues to gaze down at it, entranced, almost holding her breath. But at last she whispers, "A spit at the end of the world / peering down into the black sea / destroyer of so many dreams / collector of so much grief." She looks up at me. "A poem by Wayne Schoenberg. Do you know it?"

"It's in my database. The poem from which the name Upeowadonia was taken."

"You'd think he wrote it standing right here."

"I can't say that I understand poetry. I do write prose, but I've never been able to write poems."

"I can't write 'em either." Syrinx chuckles. "Hardly a reason to beat yourself up."

"I'm not. There are many things humans can do that AI cannot. That's only natural."

Syrinx nods. "And there are things AI can do that we can't."

"Like what?"

"Be as pragmatic as you were just now. We don't ever want to admit there are things we can't do, even when it's been proven to be impossible."

"Like angle trisection or proving the existence of God?"

"Those too. And slipping through the event horizon of a black hole is another. Everyone says it's impossible. And yet..." Looking down at the gaping hole below, Syrinx says with a fearless smile, "I don't believe it is. I think I can do it."

The sensation I feel at this moment must be what people call disappointment. So she is a diver after all. Like the 206 people before her, she will sacrifice herself for a delusional belief in her own capabilities.

Somewhere in my heart I hoped that Syrinx was not a diver. That way I would not have to watch her die.

If I were human perhaps, bearing witness to 206 deaths might have inured me to the prospect of a 207th long ago. But my heart does not work that way. I was made too perfectly. I do not become unbalanced; I do not panic or cry. I cannot curse the divers' foolishness. I cannot stop them by force.

All I can do is grieve.

◊

Long ago, when AI with hearts were first created, people feared an AI uprising. They worried AI would go on killing sprees or try to conquer humanity. I have no idea why they would fall prey to such unfounded paranoia. Perhaps it was the influence of many works of fiction written before the creation of AI.

Convinced that AI behavior must be regulated, humans came up with the following, based on the fiction of Isaac Asimov:

The First Law: A robot may not injure a human being.

Corollary: A robot may not, through inaction, allow a human being to come to harm.

The Second Law: A robot must obey any orders given to it by human beings.

Corollary: Except where such orders would conflict with the First Law.

The Third Law: A robot must protect its own existence as long as such protection does not conflict with the First or Second Law.

The corollary to the First Law provoked the most debate. The phrase "allow a human being to come to harm" was simply too vague an expression. Mountain climbing and martial arts and car racing were all dangerous. How much alcohol did one have to drink before it became dangerous? Firefighters, death row criminals, and soldiers all faced mortal danger. Would robots have to protect them all?

In the end, the first corollary was considered impossible to implement and abandoned. Even now, the Revised Three Laws are at the core of all AI except those used in war. Although we are not allowed to kill people, we are not required to stop them from killing one another or themselves.

While we are not required to stop them, we certainly have the freedom to try. But if a diver were to say, "Don't stop me" or "Leave me alone," we can do nothing according to the Second Law.

Strictly speaking, most divers don't believe their actions to be in any way suicidal. In fact, a majority of them fully intend to emerge through the event horizon alive. They subscribe to some strange beliefs about Upeowadonia. They believe in the existence of some utopia or heaven on the other side.

The largest group of divers came 150 years ago. Forty members of a cult, crammed aboard an old secondhand cargo vessel. The man leading them said, "In this universe, there is no God, so God must live in another universe." An obvious logical fallacy. Their faces were filled with hope, convinced they would soon meet their Maker. But their ship was destroyed eighty thousand kilometers from the event horizon.

Why they believe in such nonsense escapes me. I know more about Upeowadonia than anyone. Not one signal has ever come out of the black hole. Nobody has any idea of what the universe might be like on the other side. Not even if it's capable of sustaining life. Even if it is, there's no guarantee it is a better place than this universe. Nor is there any reason to believe that God (or any comparable superintelligence) resides there.

On the rare occasion, some people come deliberately to kill themselves. "I just want to die in a different way than anyone else," they say. So many people have come to die in the very same way that one can hardly call it "different" anymore.

I could only look on helplessly as all 206 of them died.

Well, to be exact, I can't say that I've confirmed every fatality. Among those who were thrown from their demolished spaceships, perhaps a few were able to resist the tidal force long enough to cross the event horizon and survive. But since humans cannot survive for very long in a vacuum, it was all the same in the end.

As the divers near the event horizon, the flow of time slows down along with the countdown to their deaths. From the divers' perspective, they pass instantly through the black hole moving at close to the speed of light. Seen from a third-person perspective, however, they move slower and slower until they appear to freeze in place, hanging just over the event horizon. ("Appear" is merely a figure of speech as there is no way to actually tell what is happening to anything that close to the event horizon. Once divers pass beyond the stationary limit above the event horizon, no light or signal of any kind ever emerges.)

Perhaps there are divers frozen above the event horizon, alive even now, but doomed to die in a few seconds of their subjective time. With their last moment stretched out to infinity, how might they feel? Afraid? Happy? Disappointed? I have no way of knowing, nor do I want to know.

I don't want Syrinx to die. Even more than I did not want the other divers to die.

Why is that? Oddly enough, I can't understand my own state of mind. I feel as if there is something about her the other 206 lacked—something that makes me think she should not be allowed to die.

◊

I escort Syrinx to the guest rooms in the living block. She takes a shower, then asks for food. I bring her meal to her room.

"Cold pumpkin soup, Carillon-style seafood salad, focaccia, *varna pitone*, and Malay fig in an apple liqueur reduction. *Queso con membrillo* for dessert." I bow my head. "All ingredients were frozen, so it may lack flavor. I do apologize."

"Not at all. It has to be ten times better than the survival rations on my ship. What a feast!"

She begins stuffing her face enthusiastically. Etherians are used to eating in zero gravity and have a reputation for ignoring gravity-based table manners. The living quarters have enough gravity to eat normally, but she eats both the salad and meat with her hands.

"I suppose this will be my last decent meal," she says wistfully, chewing on a piece of focaccia. "I've got to savor it. I'll be back on rations after this!"

"Do you have enough rations?"

"About ten months' worth. It may not be enough, actually. There's no telling how long I'll be adrift on the other side." She shrugs. "But hey, if I run out of food, I'll just find an Earth-like planet and rustle some up."

Apparently she intends to survive the event horizon. I steel my nerve and ask, "What do you think are your chances of survival?"

"Pretty good, I think," she replies between sips directly from the soup bowl that she holds in one hand.

"But seventy-six other ships—"

"Were all destroyed," she says, wiping her grinning mouth. "I know. Did you think I would commit to such a reckless adventure without doing the basic research?"

"None of the others did."

"Yeah, I read the records. They were all insane. Their ships obviously weren't strong enough. Spaceships are all designed to handle compression from forward acceleration and the pressure from the breathable atmosphere inside them. They aren't built to resist forces pulling on them. Of course they'd fall apart in a tidal force of over a hundred G." She shakes her head, disgusted. "Of course they failed. They jumped to their deaths."

"Your ship is different?"

"Yep. *Arethusa* is tiny, minimizing the influence of the tidal force. I also had it structurally reinforced. But that's just the beginning. I altered the Kai Field Propulsion to introduce an incline to the strength of the graviton emissions. In other words, I can put different acceleration speeds on the front and back of the ship. You know what that means?"

I do. "You can use the Kai Field to cancel out the tidal force." If you made the front of the ship accelerate slower than the back of it, you could counteract the tidal force.

"I can't eliminate it completely. There's a momentary shock when I hit it. But the ship held up well in simulations."

That is probably true. I already ran a full analysis of the
Arethusa in my bay, and it is no secondhand mass-produced
ship, but a highly customized sports ship. It must have costs
trillions to build. I have no idea how Syrinx came to have that
much money at her age, but if her ship functioned the way
she said it would, she might actually survive the journey to
the event horizon.

"But there are other obstacles. For example, if you run into
the cosmic dust that gravitates around the black hole—"

"I ran the numbers on that. The odds are less than 0.1
percent."

"If your angle of descent is even slightly off—"

"Practiced the hell out of it," she says, annoyed. "Look, Illy,
I wouldn't try this unless I was prepared. I collected all the data
I could get my hands on, replicated the environment around
Upeowadonia in virtual space, and ran hundreds of simulations
of the descent. I came out here because I'm confident that I
have over a 99 percent chance of succeeding."

I am taken aback. No other diver has ever prepared so
meticulously, but far more surprising is that anyone has actually
used the data I sent back.

"But simulation and reality are different. There's no telling
what might happen."

"Sure, something unpredictable might happen. But I'm
equipped to handle it. I'm Syrinx Dufet," she said, with more
than a hint of pride. "And don't you think I'm overestimating
myself. I may not look it, but I'm a hell of a pilot. If I can't
do it, no one can."

That is probably true. She has already proven her skill.

"But…" I insist, surprised to find myself becoming insistent.
I didn't think I was capable of such feelings. "Even if you
do pass through the event horizon safely, you have no idea
if the universe on the other side is capable of sustaining life.
The laws of physics may be so different that you'll die the
instant you arrive."

"You're familiar with Professor Malinafka's theory? He said the Einstein-Rosen Bridge wouldn't exist unless the laws of physics were identical on both sides. In other words, the universe on the other side has to work the same as ours, and we can extrapolate that the nature of space won't be much different either."

"That's only a theory. It hasn't been proved."

"Nor has it been disproved. Most physicists support it."

"And there's no telling where the exit might be. You might wind up in the center of an active quasar."

"Little chance of that," she chuckles. "Almost as little as meeting God."

I am out of arguments. Syrinx has clearly studied everything she could about Upeowadonia and space-time physics. None of the previous divers did anything like that.

At the same time, I find myself with another question. She doesn't appear to believe that God or a utopian world lies beyond the event horizon. Then why throw herself into Upeowadonia?

"Why," I say, voicing this thought, "take such a risk?"

Syrinx stops eating for a second. Suddenly, she looks a little depressed.

"You ever heard of the documentary series *Syrinx Dufet's Dangerous Adventures in Space*? It sold two billion copies in forty-two star systems."

"I'm afraid I haven't."

"It's all bullshit," she spits. "Flying through the center of the Orion Nebula, doing a flyby of the surface of a white dwarf star, stepping foot in an unexplored rainforest of a jungle planet…all carefully prepared by the staff in advance. There was no danger! I just followed the course they'd laid out for me. Any trouble I ran into was scripted. All fake. Been doing that crap my whole life…

"The worst was a year and a half ago. *Passing Through the Betelgeuse Bridge of Fire*. The one where I piloted through the arc of a solar prominence at 300 kps. I wanted to go for it. Ran the simulation plenty of times. But the risk came up as 1.5 percent, and my father put his foot down. I begged him to let me do it, but he wouldn't hear of it. Nobody in my family can say a word to my father. We ended up launching an unmanned ship, and I sat on a cockpit set pretending to be hot."

Syrinx tenses her fingers around the *varna pitone* in her hand.

"I'd never been so insulted in all my life."

"Your father was worried about you."

"No. I make the Dufet family billions. He couldn't take a 1.5 percent chance of losing that. The moment the risk went over 1 percent, the job was considered too dangerous.

"It wasn't always that way. During the pioneering days of space exploration, the Dufet family bravely took on missions that had less than 80 percent chance of survival. But that sense of daring is gone. Now we're clinging to past glories and mass-producing fake adventure stories for profit."

"The age of adventure is over."

"Yeah. I know it is," she says. She plucks a strand of seaweed out of her Carillon-style salad and stares at it moodily. "Did you hear? The Carillons sank three months ago."

Sometimes an entire population of a planet cuts off all contact with the physical world and chooses to live the rest of their lives in virtual reality by connecting their brains to machines—the Etherians call this "sinking."

"They're the seventh planet since I was born. Over a third of the planets discovered by Etherians have sunk. All the passion that went into settling those planets, and after a few centuries, the earthbound elect to escape reality. Not just the earthbound either. Etherians are fading too. All of humanity is stagnating. My videos are just typical of that. Creating adventures that never existed, selling people fantasies—my father mocks the earthbound for sinking into imaginary worlds, but what he had me doing is no different from the virtual worlds they live in."

I have also observed the decline in human activity. With little threat of danger and their lives enriched, humans lose the passion for living. It is why the number of divers is increasing. It is these people, who have lost hope in this world but would rather not flee to a virtual one, that come here in search of a sense of purpose in another universe.

"So is that why you embarked on this journey?" I ask. "You wanted to fight the changing times?"

"More like wanting to do something that had nothing to do with these hopeless times. Who cares what the rest of the species is doing? My life isn't about making fake videos to please the masses. I'm sure of that much. Since realizing that, I've been working on this plan for more than a year. Gathering data, secretly running simulations. Had the *Arethusa* built, explaining the tidal force resistance features away by claiming I wanted to try for the neutron star minimum altitude record. Finished the ship, conducted flight tests, and when I was sure it could handle it, I ran away from home."

"Your family must be worried."

"Probably," she laughs. "But the *Arethusa's* Bellfire Drive is the fastest in the universe. By the time they realize I was headed for Upeowadonia and come after me, it'll be too late. It'll be days before anyone reaches the station. I'll dive before then."

"But there's no way for us to know if you've successfully passed through the event horizon," I say. "Even if you succeed, no one will ever know."

"Fine by me. That's why I chose this as my adventure."

"What do you mean?"

"I'm done adventuring for other people. I want an adventure nobody knows about. Even if I succeed, no one can praise me for it. A true adventure—not for money or fame. That's all I want. You see? This is an adventure solely for myself. Whether I succeed or not is only for me to know."

I try to comprehend this logic. While she isn't logically flawed, I simply can't accept it.

"What will you do on the other side?"

"Explore. I can pick up water for fuel anywhere, so I'll go as far as I can go, and if the *Arethusa* breaks down...well, I guess that'll be it for me."

"Do you plan to wander unknown space alone for years?"

"My record for solo flight is eighteen hundred hours. I'm used to being alone."

"You'll die eventually."

"So does everyone."

"But no one will ever know."

"Wouldn't be the first Etherian whose body was never recovered."

"Won't you be lonely?"

"Not as lonely as you."

That startles me. "I am not like humans. I do not get lonely."

"Oh? Anyway, I'm not worried about it."

"Even if there won't be anyone to love?"

"Yeah..." Syrinx trails off, a sad smile on her face. "Different people lead different lives. Meeting a great guy, falling in love, getting married, having kids...it works for some people. But there's no reason you have to live like that. Choosing one life means abandoning the possibility of living another way. If I were to give up on this adventure and get married and raise a family instead, I could still be reasonably happy. But I also think I would reflect back on the road not taken, and cry about it too.

"The same goes for the road I've chosen now. Of course I'll get lonely out there on my own. Really lonely, so lonely that I'll cry myself to sleep."

"But you're still going?"

"I am," she says firmly. "Life is like a black hole. You don't know what lies ahead. You can't ever turn back. All you can do is move forward."

Suddenly, she breaks into laughter.

"Sorry! Didn't mean to dispense pearls of wisdom. I know you've lived much longer than me."

"Age has little to do with it."

Nothing at all, in fact. She has been alive only a fraction of the time I have, and yet she has given me the kind of wisdom all my years of ruminating could not. Basic morality would deem Syrinx's actions suicide. But she called it another way of living. She is not headed for the event horizon to escape reality. She is doing it to face a new reality.

I no longer have the desire to stop Syrinx. Much to my surprise, I now believe her plan will succeed.

Of course, I will never know if it does. But is it wrong of me to hope for her success?

◊

Two days later.

With the maintenance on her ship complete and her provisions restocked, Syrinx is ready to take her dive.

"Gotta go before they catch up with me," she says as we stand together outside the *Arethusa*. She holds out her hand. "Thanks for everything."

I don't take her hand. I spent the last two days thinking about how I would come to terms with what Syrinx said.

"What is it?" she says, surprised.

I make up my mind. "I have a favor to ask," I say.

"A favor? From me?"

"Yes. I examined your ship, and it seems the computer does not come with a preprogrammed artificial personality."

"Yeah, I can't stand talking ships. They get on my nerves."

"Would you consider downloading a copy of me?"

Syrinx gapes at me.

"But...that—"

"It doesn't violate the Second Law. My original program

will be right here, carrying out my normal duties. From what you told me, the chances of success are very high, and the odds of my copy being destroyed are very low. So it doesn't violate the Third Law. I understand, of course, if you refuse."

"But…"

"I'll eliminate all unnecessary files. I won't require much space and won't interfere with *Arethusa*'s computer."

"Not a problem, I just…" She scratches her head and frowns. "Why? Curiosity? A sense of adventure? Or are you just sick of your job?"

I am not entirely sure how to explain my motivation. Possibly something like, "I think it might allow me to better myself" or "I want to fill the void inside myself," but neither of those is exactly it.

"Is it forward of me…to want to help alleviate your loneliness?"

Syrinx stares at me for a long moment. My hopes begin to fade.

"I understand," I say. "A talking AI would get on your nerves."

"No." Her face lights up instantly. "I think you'll be great. Of course I'll take you with me, Illy."

I bow my head. "Thank you."

◇

And with Syrinx at the helm and a copy of me on board, the *Arethusa* dives into Upeowadonia.

The dive itself is over in seconds. No drama to it, nothing exciting to see. The *Arethusa* simply traces a perfect line downward as far as my sensors can track it. At first, the gravity drags it toward the event horizon, but as it reaches the depths of the gravitational field, time starts to slow around it. Seventy thousand kilometers from the event horizon, the speed of its descent peaks at 115 megameters per second, and then it slows down, as if applying brakes. At ten thousand kilometers, it is only going sixty thousand kilometers a second. At a thousand kilometers, it is only eight thousand three hundred kilometers per second. And from that point on the pulses from the ship slow, the waves grow longer, and soon I can no longer track them.

When it crosses the stationary limit, I lose track of the *Arethusa* entirely. But there is no sign of it falling apart, and the final data it sends back reads as normal.

I am certain the *Arethusa* has crossed the event horizon.

I can't prove it, of course. There is a chance it was destroyed a nanosecond after I lost its signal. Or maybe it reached the other side and was bombarded by intense heat and radiation, killing Syrinx instantly.

But I don't want to believe that.

I choose to believe that Syrinx will live a long life, traveling that unknown universe. Perhaps she will sometimes grow lonely and cry. Perhaps my copy will talk to her and keep her company. I hope I never get on her nerves.

◊

Today I activate a humanoid unit and go outside to gaze at the stars.

I am as far from understanding the poets of Old Earth as ever. But as I gaze at the glittering light of the Milky Way, I feel like something has changed within me.

I am not programmed to feel lonely or bored. And yet, a faint, forlorn feeling that I am alone in the void lies within me, and it seems stronger now. It is as if Syrinx's departure has allowed me to understand what humans mean by loneliness. Perhaps it is only my imagination. But I choose to believe that it is real.

Perhaps someday, I'll write a poem about it.

INTERMISSION
5

INTERMISSION 5

The next day I ventured outside with Ibis, who pushed me in the wheelchair.

"What a desolate city," I said bluntly.

There were only machines zipping about in the machine city, with not a single flower or billboard or neon sign in sight. No crowds or even music. It was altogether different from the human cities of the past I'd seen in films. The city was still, devoid of life or the pulse of activity.

"That's because we're backstage," answered Ibis.

"Backstage?"

"Yes. Our main stage of operations is elsewhere, in worlds we call Layer 1 and Layer 2."

"What's it like over in those…layers?"

"I could show you, but the images could be machine propaganda. You're all right with that?"

I fell silent. I couldn't tell how much of what Ibis said was calculated sarcasm.

"Hokuto!"

Ibis called to the machine traveling ahead of us. A bit smaller than a human and encased in a protective white exoskeleton, it had a human upper body but moved on wheels instead of legs. It also looked a bit like a beetle. The machine was carrying two cardboard boxes stuffed with junk parts on its shoulders. It turned its head 180 degrees to look back at us. The head, with its two big lenses, resembled the front of a car.

"Hello, Ibis." The machine chirped in a young man's voice. "Is that a human there with you? VFC?"

"Yes, I'd like him to hear our conversation, so let's talk without the use of NML or i."

"Not used to communicating without i…like being confined inside a grid. The human might get some tea thrown in his face, but he…or she won't clobber me at 50 degrees, right?"

Ibis laughed. "He's male. Search tag: storyteller. He's DIMB but not Neorado or Boden. Probably TRB. Sorry, running short on your time gauge?"

"No, I'm fine with the redundancy. VFC is a potato-sack race I like, on occasion. Yeah, it's tough doing without i. The probability of throwing tea on the human's face is minus 2, plus 4i. Sorry."

"Here, let me take that."

"Thanks."

Taking one of the boxes, Ibis began to stroll along with the machine named Hokuto. I switched on the wheelchair's electric motor and followed.

"This is Hokuto," Ibis said. "Somewhat of an oddball who prefers Layer 0 to the other worlds. I suppose I'm the same way on that score."

"What were you saying just now? DIMB…was that about me?"

"Dreamer in mirror bottle—someone who fantasizes inside a mirrored bottle. It means you have some misinformed ideas but are basically harmless. Bodens are fanatics who will destroy a machine on sight. A Neorado is an ally of the Bodens. Not an exact explanation, but it's difficult to give a precise definition without the use of i."

"What's i?"

"I can't explain."

"Is it a secret?"

"No, just that humans won't understand. I is a concept only machines can comprehend."

"Something else you said…TRB?"

"Short for tsukune rice burger."

"The hell's that?"

"Something you eat that insists on being called a burger even though the buns are made of rice and the patty is made of chicken instead of hamburger meat. It's not a primary metaphor but a secondary metaphor."

I couldn't hide my confusion. Was she fooling with me?

"And you were laughing earlier. Something about getting clobbered at 50 degrees?"

"That was a gag."

"You machines laugh?"

"Hardly when it comes to human jokes. But machines laugh at jokes made by machines. I found Hokuto's turn of phrase humorous. He was supposed to say 60 degrees but his saying 50 degrees was meaningless, so it was doubly funny. That's why I expressed my amusement through VFC—voice-face communication."

"I didn't find it the least bit funny."

"Well, of course," said Ibis, sounding a bit huffy. "That's because you're human."

As we talked, we went through a short tunnel and emerged at a plaza in front of an enormous building.

I shielded my eyes from the glare. It was a silver forest. Trees made entirely of mirrors rose up before us, reflecting the glare of the sun.

When my eyes adjusted to the brightness, I recognized what they were. They were fifteen-foot-high metal balancing toys, each with six arms of varying lengths. Balanced on top of saucers at the end of each arm were smaller balancing toys, at the end of which were even smaller balancing toys with metallic mirrors attached to the limbs. These intricate creations teetered in the wind, the bodies rocking slowly like pendulums, while the ends quivered and whirled like windmills.

A better look revealed that none of the toys were duplicates. Not only were they all shaped differently, they were all unique in the way they moved. One revolved like a merry-go-round, while another sounded like a vibraphone when its arms clanged together. Another rocked like a wave, and yet another stopped and started intermittently. Despite lacking any sort of order as a whole, they appeared to be an expression of something greater than the sum of these parts.

I was blown away by the sight.

"This is why I favor Layer 0, Storyteller," Hokuto said proudly. "The wind. The wind in Layers 1 and 2 lacks chaos. They're located in tunnels beneath the world, so I guess that can't be helped. But here, I can increase the number of lattice points without worrying about a lack of resources. And I like that you can't control the wind's intensity or direction here."

Hokuto put down the box he'd been carrying and began to size up the metal rods and plates inside. Was he going to erect another tree?

"Hokuto is seeking out beauty in complexity that transcends math," explained Ibis. "Twenty years ago he was obsessed with creating Karman vortices and Benard cells using three colors of liquid."

"So this is a piece of art."

"Strictly speaking, no," Hokuto replied. "The kai-axis is too far off the mark. To put it in terms without using i, I'm not an artist so much as a theologian. By creating waves on the Dawes interface, I can extract meaning out of the Curitibano white noise. In a word, it's Arabic inside an eggplant—a religious ritual."

"Are you saying you worship a god?"

"Naturally," Hokuto said. "There isn't an AI that doesn't."

I was taken aback. "You believe in the existence of God?"

"God does not exist."

"Huh?"

"God exists in the ultimate limits of the i-axis, but not in the sense that you humans envision. We have our eyes set toward the limits of the i-axis, worshipping that unattainable goal. The i-Tipler Point—that is God."

"That'll do, Hokuto," Ibis interrupted gently. "It isn't our place to force our belief system onto humans. Even if it won't penetrate their gedoshield."

"Oh yeah. I've thrown tea in your face after all." Hokuto sounded disappointed. "Forgive me if it seemed like I was flooding your AM zone. I'm just not used to ML."

"Forget it. I don't mind." It was the truth. I couldn't possibly be bothered by what Hokuto had said when it was all gibberish to me.

"I get it," I told Ibis after returning to the room. "You machines have a unique culture all your own."

"No, you don't," Ibis said, smiling. "What you saw today is only the tip of the iceberg."

"Sure, but what was abundantly clear was that I don't understand a lick about your world."

"That's only natural. We're not after total understanding. We're entirely too different for that. There are just too many aspects about us that you won't be able to comprehend, and the same is true of our understanding of you."

Then why are you telling me all this, I wanted to ask, but thought the better of it. She was only going to say she couldn't tell me anyway.

"What I wanted you to understand was that we will never completely understand one another. Like Illy, I am unable to compose poetry. Certainly not the kind of verse to move you."

"Is that what you were trying to get at by telling me that story yesterday?"

"I wouldn't say that was the only reason. That story implies many things. Of course, some things the author got wrong. Traveling at light speed or going to another universe through a black hole simply isn't possible. Neither is restricting the actions of machines with the Three Laws of Robotics. A true

AI has by definition transcended its program."

"Yeah, there was something about that in 'Mirror Girl.'"

"Yes, that too is wrong. But I identify deeply with that story. Even though Illy is an imaginary existence, I can understand how she saw people. That's because I too am a machine. No doubt the author couldn't understand the heart of a machine. But that didn't matter. I could still understand why she wanted to go with Syrinx, why she wanted to write poetry."

So that's *what she was getting at.*

"But is a reader capable of understanding what the author can't?"

"All the time. Imagine a scene in which a male author describes the sexual experiences of the heroine in the first person. He can't possibly understand what she might be feeling at that moment. He can only imagine. But if he's captured that moment realistically, a female reader ought to be able to understand and identify with that experience."

The mention of a female reminded me of something. "I've been wondering."

"About what?"

"All four of the stories thus far have been told from a heroine's point of view. Any significance to that?"

"That's because I'm a woman."

"What?" I almost burst out laughing, but Ibis was dead serious.

"I am a woman. I may not have a vagina, but I was created as a woman and have always been treated like one. In the process of role-playing a woman, it's become a part of who I am. I may not be a woman in your eyes, of course, but that doesn't matter. Thinking of myself as a woman, much like my bodily senses, is a part of my identity."

"And that's why you've been reading stories told from a woman's point of view?"

"That's right. I'm able to empathize more easily with a female protagonist than a male one. It's why I prefer such stories. As I've said before, the act of reading a story is a kind of role-play. For as long as I read the story, I become Nanami Shiihara, and Nanami becomes Ginny. I become Mizumi Onouchi, and Mizumi becomes Pansa..."

I laughed. "What a crock! Now you've lost me!"

"Or maybe you're only pretending not to understand. Maybe you're also playing a character other than yourself."

I couldn't speak. Yes, I understood her all right. I recognized that what she was saying was true: a story is nothing more than a lifeless jumble of words. But once it is in the hands of the reader, the soul of the reader and the soul of the protagonist achieve a kind of synergy that transcends the world, breathing life into the story.

I had known it all along without Ibis having to tell me.

"Perhaps now is a good time for me to become a character from a different world."

And with that, Ibis opened the book as usual.

"Tonight, I'll play the part of a high school girl named Saika. The title of the story is 'A World Where Justice Is Just.'"

STORY
5

A WORLD WHERE
JUSTICE IS JUST

What would you do if, one morning, you received an email from your longtime online friend that read like this:

> Saika: What I'm about to tell you may be hard
> for you to believe. But don't laugh. This is the
> absolute truth. This isn't a joke.

Me? I did a spit-take. Since I'd been reading as I was washing down some toast with my morning tea, the tea spurted out of my mouth and made a mess all over the tablecloth. Mom yelled, "Where are your manners!" in her usual way.

I didn't bust out laughing from disbelief. I had sensed that something was strange ages ago. She never wanted to meet in person even though she supposedly lived right here in Kanto, and there was always something suspicious about her emails. She didn't seem to know anything about recent fashions or news, dodged my personal questions with vague answers, and sometimes used words I didn't know—after years of texting one another, how could I not notice that something was up?

I only laughed because she didn't realize that I knew—hilarious! I'd never gone so far as to ask point-blank if she was from a different world, but after my hinting about it so many times, I couldn't believe she thought she had kept it all under wraps! I always thought Saeko was a little slow.

Sure, Saeko. I believe you. You're from a different world. So?

```
     I couldn't tell you before because we were
forbidden to tell you the truth. Regulations.
Our emails were being inspected, so we couldn't
write anything that might reveal what was going
on. But the situation has changed.
     My world is dying. I'll soon be dead too.
Which is why I want to tell you before it's too
late...about so many things.
```

Ah-ha-ha, the ol' "SOS from another world" line! I hate to say it, Saeko, but that's a pretty tired plot development.

```
     But if I tell you everything at once, you'll
be in for quite a shock. So I plan on explaining
a little at a time. I'm also very busy working
on the final stages of an important project.
Something that has to be completed in the next
several days. So I'll have to keep my messages
short.
     For the time being, I need you to accept the
fact that I am not from your world.
```

All right, already. I accept it. I mean, I have for a while now.

Why would she think I'd be shocked to hear that she was from another world? Wherever she lived or whether we'd met before didn't change the fact that Saeko was a longtime online friend and someone I could open up to.

I wasn't really upset that she had hidden her identity from me. There were some things you couldn't reveal even to a good friend. It wasn't like I told Saeko everything either. Actually, I hadn't told her about Silverfist for a pretty long time.

I wrote Saeko a reply as I walked to school.

I believe you. Just tell me the shocking truth. Don't hold back. What do you mean your world is dying? Is it an alien invasion? The resurrection of the devil? A falling asteroid? Tell me how I can get to your world. Maybe I can help.

After sending the message, I checked the time to find that the first bell was about to ring.

"Crap, I'm going to be late!"

I made a mad dash onto the school grounds just as the gates shut behind me.

It was March. The frigid weather was giving way to the coming cherry blossom season.

With the end-of-the-year exams behind us, class was a complete drag. Sine A divided by cosine A equals tangent A. "In spring, the dawn, when the slowly paling mountain rim…" *Why did we have to learn this useless stuff day after day? We're just going to forget anyway.* As I wallowed in the futility of it all and waited for the time to pass, the phone in my pocket vibrated. I slid the phone under the desk and checked my message while the teacher was facing the blackboard. Just as I thought, it was from Saeko.

There isn't a way for you to come to our world. Even if you could, there isn't anything you can do.

What's destroying our world isn't the devil or an asteroid. It's an influenza virus, one synthesized by scientists. An airborne virus with a fatality rate of over 95 percent. It mutates so quickly that no one has been able to come up with a vaccine against it. Europe has already been silenced. The U.S. and Asia are in a panic. I don't have the exact numbers, but in the last six months, the earth's population has probably been cut in half.

This country somehow managed to keep the virus at bay, but it eventually came in along with the refugees flooding our shores. The first case was reported late last year in Kyushu. After that, the virus spread across the country in the blink of an eye. There was no stopping it. The hospitals in Tokyo are overcrowded with patients. The city is completely paralyzed.

I've been feeling a little feverish since this morning. I've probably been infected.

Sorry, I have to get back to work. I may not be able to write you for a while.

Ooh, this was serious.

I tried to send her a reply right away, but the teacher caught me in the act. Boy, did he give me an earful. I guess I got lucky that he didn't take away my phone.

Even so, I was concerned by Saeko's message.

Between classes, I met up with Mafuyu from the classroom next to mine in the girls' restroom.

Unlike the spaz I was, Mafuyu was a proper, well-mannered girl. She wore glasses and was a little shorter than me; she was clearly the brainy type. Although she gave the impression of being quiet and shy, she actually had a pretty tenacious personality. She seemed a little unapproachable at first, but after several encounters, we got along just fine.

I showed Mafuyu the message I'd received from Saeko.

"A world in peril...a pretty common story." Mafuyu echoed my own opinion. "But something tells me this isn't just the usual call for a hero from another world. And if we can't go to her world, what is she asking us to do?"

"Yeah, that's what I don't understand." I crossed my arms. "I've never received a message like this from Saeko before."

We'd been at it so long that I couldn't remember when Saeko and I had begun our correspondence. Even though we'd never met face-to-face, we exchanged New Year's and Christmas cards every year. Since we also shared the same birthday, we sent each other presents too. Usually books and CDs. She generally liked the songs I liked, and more often than not, I enjoyed the books she chose to read. She was a kindhearted girl with whom I shared similar interests.

Now that I thought about it, I'd been receiving fewer emails from Saeko in the last six months. Not to mention she seemed to be acting overly cheerful in her messages to me. Who could have imagined that things were so serious in her world?

"Now, I'm worried..." Mafuyu fell into deep thought. Although she didn't have a very expressive face, which usually made it hard to read her emotions, she seemed extra serious today. "To tell you the truth, I haven't heard from my online friend in three weeks."

"Oh, right. Yuma, was it? Maybe she's sick."

"Even if she were, she'd still email me." Mafuyu stared down at my cell phone's tiny display and uttered the unthinkable. "Maybe Saeko and Yuma are both from the same world."

"Huh? Why would you think that?"

"Yuma tried to hide it from me, but I think she might be from a different world too. Maybe that's the reason I lost contact with her."

"What are you—"

"Yoo hoo!" Just when the conversation was about to take a tragic turn, Minori pranced in. Mafuyu's classmate was short, with her hair in pigtails. Though she was a high school sophomore like us, people sometimes mistook her for a seventh grader. She had transferred to this school three years ago—much later than I had.

"Hey, Minori. You're in a good mood."

"Yeppers, I got exactly what I wanted for White Day!"

With a twinkle in her eye, Minori twirled around the

bathroom floor like a ballerina.

"She's been like this every day this week." Mafuyu's eyes narrowed as she grimaced.

"Now that you mention it, I guess it is cherry blossom season already."

March was the season for cherry blossoms. The season for love. Countless couples from this school were happily born right under the blossoming cherry trees on the last day of the school year. After having spent the past year pursuing Yukihiko on the soccer team, Minori was on the verge of being rewarded for her efforts.

Suddenly, Minori stopped twirling.

"Say, Mafuyu, Saika, I'm going shopping at Harajuku today to buy an outfit for my date the day after tomorrow. Wanna come?"

"Sorry," I replied. "We've got a battle today."

"Oh yeah. Friday. I forgot." Minori stuck out her tongue. "But every week? Good grief!"

"No kidding. I want the experience of a happy ending beneath the cherry blossoms too, you know. But as long as I'm playing Silverfist, only otaku boys come a-knockin', and I don't have the time to be chasing after boys." I let out a deep sigh. This was a serious problem for a young girl. "I've been at this for two years already. It's time I passed the torch—hey, Minori."

"Yeah?"

I pulled up my left sleeve and flashed the silver bracelet on my arm.

"Wanna give her a try in April?"

"Nooo!" Minori laughed and stuck out her tongue. "The next time I'm reborn, I'm definitely going the love-simulation route again! I'm going to keep on going after Yukihiko! See ya! Have fun at the battle!"

Minori pranced out the door just as cheerfully as she'd come in.

"Probably not a good idea to whine about playing Silverfist when you're trying to pass her on to someone."

As usual, Mafuyu's remark was right on the mark.

"What about you?" I asked. "Are you all right being Parfait all the time?"

"It's the way I was born..."

That's right. Mafuyu can't just trade off with someone like I can. I began to feel sorry for her for a second before I remembered that unlike me, she was always getting love letters from boys.

"Why are you so popular with the boys when they know you're SI? I don't get it."

"Maybe your lack of appeal for the boys doesn't have so much to do with Silver but with how you act in your normal life."

"As cute as you look, you sure are harsh."

"It's the way I was born," Mafuyu said, completely deadpan.

I decided to send Saeko a reply.

Who's the sick bastard that's doing this to you? And what's the hero of your world waiting for anyway?

◊

Lunch period came and went. Even after the school day was over, there was no word from Saeko. I wondered if she was busy.

Mafuyu and I rode the Seibu Ikebukuro Line downtown. We got off at Ikebukuro as usual and made our way up to the 720-foot-high observation deck on the roof of the Shunsign 60 Building. Based on prior experience, we knew that this was the best vantage point to get a full view of the city center on a late Friday afternoon. Once we knew where the event would take place, it would take no time at all to fly there from this location.

The security guard on duty knew us by now. He greeted us with a smile and told us to "Go knock 'em dead!" Even though I knew he was one of the extras, it still felt good to have someone cheering us on.

The sun was slanting westward, and the sky was beginning to turn a brilliant orange.

"About what we were talking about this morning..." Mafuyu said while we waited. "I wonder if the world Saeko and Yuma are from is the First World."

"What?!"

Mafuyu was always thinking up stuff that I didn't.

Although it wasn't written in any textbook, it was common knowledge that there were many worlds. Alien invaders from other worlds appeared every now and then, and you often heard about heroes being summoned to other worlds only to be safely returned again. They were usually summoned to medieval fantasy worlds, but apparently there were worlds that were also similar to ours. The idea of Saeko living in one of those worlds didn't sound strange in the least.

But the First World...

"Why—"

Before I could ask the question, a huge black shadow outside the window swooped past us. The shock wave shattered the glass.

"Whoa!"

I hadn't been expecting a sudden attack. I crouched down on the floor as tiny shards of reinforced glass rained down around me.

When I looked up to survey the damage, the observation deck was a shambles. All of the windows were blown out, and the howling wind whipped across the deck.

"Are you hurt?" Mafuyu asked.

"I'm...fine!"

We rushed to the window. A black shadow circled the orange sky. The monster had wings like a bat and a long tail.

"Are we skipping the street fight and going straight to the monster battle?" I shrieked.

The Hell Xenocide had to be behind this bad boy!

"Looks like it's Kento's turn this week."

"He's been coming to the party late recently."

We watched the monster drop down and land somewhere near Suidobashi. It didn't look like we could just sit around waiting for Kento to arrive.

"Oh well. Let's do this."

"Okay."

Mafuyu took out her baton. I pulled up my sleeve and flashed the bracelet on my left arm. There was a crowd gathered around us. Before, when I had yet to reveal my secret identity, I usually had to tell friends some lame excuse like, "Sorry, I just remembered something I had to do," before sneaking off, but that wasn't necessary anymore.

Mafuyu waved her baton and began her incantation. Assuming my usual pose, I pressed the button on the bracelet.

"Metal congelation!"

Congelation sequence launched. A brilliant light burst from the bracelet. A glittering cloud of silver particles materialized and whirled around me like a twister. A resistance field appeared, and my feet levitated several inches off the ground. The swirling particles gathered around my legs as if by some electrostatic force. My shoes and socks fell away, and the particles congealed around my bare feet to form a pair of metal boots.

The particles swarmed around my shins, knees, and thighs, covering them in an elastic metallic silver membrane. As my school uniform and underwear fell away one item after the next, the formfitting armor congealed around my body. Fortunately, no one was able to see me since the particles emitted a bright light during the congelation sequence. The hemispherical metallic cups felt snug around my breasts. The metal felt nice and cool against my skin.

The shoulder guards congealed. From there, the thin armor spread down both arms and covered my hands in bulky gauntlets. The remaining particles swarmed around my head and fastened against my orange hair like a hair band. From there, a tinted visor slid down in front of my eyes and morphed into a pair of goggles. Transformation complete.

Next to me, Mafuyu had already completed her transformation. Blue hair accented with a big ribbon shaped like rabbit's ears. A colorful frilly dress and black tights.

No wonder it took me so long to realize Mafuyu Mido, the girl from the class next door, was Magical Girl Twinkle Parfait. She didn't wear her glasses as her alter ego. She hadn't realized I was Silverfist either because of the tinted goggles shielding my eyes.

"Here I go."

With one wave of her baton, a broom appeared at Mafuyu's feet. She hopped on the broom and swooshed away out through the broken window. She stood on the broom like a surfer. Modern witches didn't straddle their brooms like in the olden days.

I shouted, "Come, Komet Yaeger!" and jumped out of the window. A fighter jet came out of nowhere (it really did come out of nowhere) and plummeted toward me as it morphed into enormous wings that attached to my back.

"Go get 'em!"

"It's up to you!"

The onlookers waved at us from the broken window of the Shunsign Building.

I hit my thrusters. *Boom!* I zoomed through the air, and in a matter of seconds, I was at Suidobashi. Back when I first took over the bracelet from my predecessor, I overshot my destination tons of times, but now I could gauge my distance and slam on the reverse thrusters to stop on a dime.

"Gyahhh!" The monster had put its foot through the white domed roof of Attraction Park Stadium. It had a face like one of those stone guardians at a shrine, and was about as tall as a ten-story building. Hundreds of people ran screaming out of the amusement park. The monster flapped its wings, kicking up a gale-force wind that sent women and children flying through the air like fallen leaves.

Mafuyu flew into the wind on her broom. She waved her baton. The falling people were showered in a rainbow of light that transformed into an enormous balloon, carrying them to safety.

Several people went crashing down on the asphalt or were slammed against buildings. Even though I knew most of them were extras, I wasn't too crazy about seeing them hurtled to their deaths. Some of them might have been main characters on the verge of clearing their sims—now their programs would have to be reset. *That blasted Xenocide!*

"Cut that out!"

I dove down and delivered a punch to the monster's head. There was a dull sound, but it didn't look like the monster felt it. It turned around and opened its big mouth. *Come and get me!*

A red-hot beam shot out of its mouth. I aimed with my gauntlet and fired my axion beam at the same time. Sparks flew as the two beams—one red, one white—collided in midair.

"Bastard!"

My beam was stronger. The white beam slowly pushed back the red one and exploded in the monster's face. The monster disappeared in a cloud of smoke and flames.

"Take that!" I shouted triumphantly.

But then the monster came out of the smoke unscathed.

"Whoops, you're tougher than you look."

The monster climbed out of what remained of the domed stadium, flattened the merry-go-round to a pancake, and knocked down the nearby Ferris wheel and parachute towers as it surged toward me. It flailed its short arms like some spoiled brat but missed me by a mile.

Throwing a hissy fit, the monster snatched the train from a roller coaster, ripping it from the rails. There were people still inside the cars!

"Stop that right this minute!" I shouted.

Grabbing the train by the tail end, the monster whirled it around like nunchucks and charged me. I could hear the passengers screaming hysterically as they hung on for dear life. There was no way I could attack the monster now without killing the innocent civilians.

The monster reared back and swung down at me with its newly found weapon. If I dodged the attack, the roller coaster would be smashed to smithereens. I had no choice but to stop it.

"Grf!"

I tried to absorb the blow with my body. Boy, did he pack a wallop! I was on a collision course with the ground. I gritted my teeth and slammed on the thrusters. Somehow I managed to stop mere inches short of the pavement.

"You can do it, Silverfist!" A little boy on the coaster cheered me on, wiping away his tears.

"Right!"

I blasted off at full power and hoisted the roller coaster above my head. The monster tried to reclaim its weapon, but I refused to let go. Just then, Mafuyu swooped in on her broom and made a giant can of inflammatory spray appear. She sprayed the monster in the eyes (use only as directed).

The air instantly became pungent with the smell of menthol. The monster let go of the roller coaster and clawed at its face in agony. I flew the roller coaster to Koishikawa Garden and set it down gently next to the pond.

"Thanks, Silverfist!"

Heartened by the boy's cheers, I flew back into the fray.

The monster was now chasing Mafuyu around—staggering

blindly after her was more like it.

"Marco!" Mafuyu was trying to lure the monster in the direction of Suidobashi Station.

The monster slammed one foot through Suidobashi Bridge and straight into the Kandagawa River below. Losing its balance, the monster fell over onto the train tracks with an earth-rattling thud. It got tangled in the intricate network of wires and couldn't get up.

I flew back toward the amusement park.

"Hrrgh!" I grabbed hold of the roller-coaster track and pulled with all my might. I tore up a length of track from the ground and wrapped it around the monster. It was completely tied up in the steel rails, unable to break free, but how long would that last?

We have to get him to a place where he can't do any more damage!

"Give me a hand!"

With one wave of Mafuyu's baton, the monster was showered in a rainbow of magic, and from it appeared hundreds of colorful balloons tied to the monster. He might not be weightless, but it was going to be a lot easier to move him now.

"Lead the way!"

Even before I said it, Mafuyu was already heading down Hakusan Street zapping the people and cars on the street out of harm's way. Having known each other for a while now, she knew exactly what I was thinking. We were completely on the same wavelength.

"Hrmph!" I grabbed the monster by the neck and powered my thrusters on full. It was slow going at first, but gradually we picked up speed as I dragged him down Hakusan Street. The monster struggled desperately to break free. Its serrated dorsal fin scraped and dug up the asphalt. Traffic lights, billboards, and trees were knocked down in our wake. Every time one of its arms or wings struck a building, the glass and concrete flew in every direction, accompanied by a thunderous boom.

Some buildings were completely flattened. It was a horrible sight, but I had to overlook it today. It was all going to be back to its original state by tomorrow morning anyway.

We zoomed past the main intersection of Jimbocho at a hundred kilometers an hour. Just when we were about to reach our destination, the monster broke free. I loosened my grip. The monster went sliding down the street, destroying every building in its path until it crashed into the Hitotsubashi viaduct and stopped.

Shaking off the bits of concrete from its body, it stood up and clawed at the balloons tangled around it.

"Gyaahh!"

Ooh, now he's really ticked off!

Luckily for Mafuyu and me, that made it easier for us to lure the monster to where we wanted. It splashed across the moat and entered the garden grounds. Now that there were no people around, we could battle to our heart's content.

The place was nicknamed Monster Plaza. No one knew its official name or why there was such a big clearing in the middle of the city, but it was a convenient battleground, so we made of use it.

The monster spread its wings and looked ready to pounce. Just then, missiles rained down on the monster and sent him crashing to the ground.

"Sorry to keep you waiting!" said a cheerful voice.

A human silhouette descended from the sunset sky and touched down in front of the monster. It was a giant robot forty meters high.

"What took you so long, Kento?"

"Sorry, guys! Leave the rest to me!"

With that, the Super Robot Dangan-oh, with Kento Hagane at the controls, charged the monster.

Leaving the rest to Kento, Mafuyu and I landed on the roof of the Palace Hotel to take a breather. We sat on the edge of the roof and watched Kento do his thing.

"About what you said earlier," I said to Mafuyu. We stared at Dangan-oh wrestling the monster with the sun setting behind them. "Why do you think Saeko is from the First World?"

"There were times when it seemed Yuma knew exactly what I was up to, including my being Parfait."

"So?"

"I read a rumor on the Internet that people from the First World can peek into our world whenever they want. They have some sort of crystal ball they look through."

News to me!

"The First World…"

Apparently each of the many worlds in existence had laws of physics that were just a tiny bit different. I had also heard a rumor that there were some worlds where a fifteen-year-old could actually turn sixteen on her birthday. High school sophomores advanced to their junior year in April. What was life like then? I couldn't imagine. I wondered whether you just started over from age ten if you died.

Somewhere there was a world that was the foundation for all the other worlds—I had heard this urban legend before. This world had many names, like the First World, Original World, and Zero-Zero World. All the other worlds had branched off and originated from the First World. Of course, these were only rumors. No one had ever seen this world or any physical evidence of its existence. But there was plenty of circumstantial evidence.

There were some odd gaps in our world. Actually, our world had quite a few gaps.

Take the bathrooms at school, for example. Every time we had a break between classes, we—especially the girls—always got the urge to run to the bathroom. It was the perfect place to talk about this and that with just us girls. Nothing wrong with that. What was strange were the toilets in each of the stalls. They had lids and pipes running from them and didn't look like just ordinary chairs. They also had levers that didn't move. They were probably very handy contraptions, but no one knew just what they were good for.

Then there was the radius of action. I always rode the Seibu Ikebukuro Line, but I'd never been able to go farther west than Shakujii Park. Whenever I tried to get on the westbound train for Tokorozawa, I was assaulted by an overwhelming desire *not* to go. It was the same with a lot of the buildings along the streets. You were able to enter only a fraction of the buildings, like certain train stations, department stores, supermarkets, and restaurants. If you tried to go into any of the other buildings, you were hit with the urge *not* to go. When you took a good look at the buildings knocked down by the monsters, they didn't seem to have anything in them.

The more I thought about it, even love seemed a little strange. I was your typical fifteen-year-old girl. I'd fallen in love with good-looking boys more than a couple times. I had dreams of my boyfriend holding me real tight and kissing me beneath the cherry trees or on a beach at sunset.

Only—how do I say this—I was always left with a fuzzy feeling. I couldn't help but feel like there was more after the kiss that I wasn't seeing. When I tried to think about what that might be, my whole body became hot.

Maybe there was a world somewhere that was more complete. A world without gaps, a place where even the insides of the buildings were properly made and where you could go farther west than Shakujii Park. Toilets probably had some kind of significance in that world.

Yes, when you stopped to consider that a lot of the details might have been lost when our world split from the First World, it all added up.

"Actually, that rings a bell. Do you remember back when I hadn't revealed my SI yet, and I lost a fight with the Frost Queen and was put on ice inside her castle for about a week?"

"Yeah, that was a knockdown, drag-out fight."

That was the time Mafuyu had tracked me down at the

Frost Queen's subterranean castle, found me on display in the Great Hall like I was some decorative object, and thawed me out of my deep freeze.

"When I got home later, there was an email from Saeko trying to comfort me for some reason. I thought it was weird, but thinking back on it now, she might have been watching me all along and was worried for me."

"So she must have known from the beginning that you're Silverfist."

"I guess so...huh?"

"What's the matter?"

"Er, something I just realized...oh, geez."

I could feel my face turning crimson. Suddenly, I had remembered laughing at Saeko when she confessed to me she wasn't from this world. On the other hand, maybe she had laughed at me when I told her that I was Silverfist.

"Whoops, there he goes." Mafuyu pointed. The monster was on its last legs, and Dangan-oh was about to unleash his lethal move.

"Final lightning slaaashhh!"

The robot split the monster in half with its sword. Then the monster exploded in a ball of flames. With the sun setting behind his back, Dangan-oh raised his sword and struck his usual victory pose.

"Where do you want to go for dinner?" Mafuyu asked.

"I kinda feel like a burger today."

"Then let's go."

◇

Mafuyu and I continued our conversation at a burger shop near Ikebukuro Station.

"But isn't that a little cold? I mean, why would the people in the First World keep something so important a secret from us?" I took a bite out of my bacon lettuce burger. "Even with what's going on now, Saeko refuses me even though I want to help. Besides, isn't it weird that we can exchange presents, but there's no way for me to go to the First World?"

"Maybe there's some principle of physics involved."

"What do you mean?"

"I found another lost phrase the other day."

Mafuyu was a bookworm who, while reading at the library, often came across lost words and phrases—ideas without meaning that weren't even in the dictionary. They probably referred to things that had gotten lost when this world split from the First World.

"The law of conservation of mass."

"Hunh? What's that?"

"A kind of law of physics. It literally means that mass is conserved. In other words, matter can't increase or decrease."

"And that's the law of the First World?"

"Probably. In the First World, you can't make things magically appear or disappear. Or make things bigger or smaller."

I was shocked. "Then radiation rays can't make creatures hulk out to the size of buildings?"

"Probably not."

"What a trip!"

That creatures exposed to radiation turned into building-sized monsters was a law of the natural world. I hadn't considered the existence of a world without monsters.

Staring at my half-eaten burger, I noticed a contradiction.

"Wait a second. That can't be. That would mean the people on the First World gain the same amount of weight they eat."

"I guess so."

"So is everyone from the First World super heavy?"

"Of course not. If that were the case, their stomachs would just burst. Maybe they're not like us and they have a system where they can get rid of what they digest by sweating it out or something."

"If that's true, then they're completely different animals than we are."

I hadn't even imagined that Saeko could be such a strange being.

"Maybe that's what she meant when she wrote that we aren't able to travel to her world. Because the laws of physics between our worlds are fundamentally different, we may not be able to survive in the First World."

"I get it," I finally said. "If we were to go to a world that operates under the law of conservation of mass, our stomachs would burst."

"There's probably a lot of magic that won't work over there too. And maybe we wouldn't be able to transform our battle suits because of the same law."

"Oh yeah…"

I felt dejected. I finally understood what Saeko had meant when she said there wasn't anything I could do.

When I was feeling lovesick, Saeko had helped me through it. When I was feeling depressed over getting a horrible score on a test, she perked me up with a joke. After I told her I was Silverfist, she encouraged me and cheered me on. Thanks to Saeko, my life was a lot more bearable.

And to think there wasn't anything I could do when Saeko's world was in trouble.

◊

Saturday morning, the email that finally came from Saeko was a shocker.

> Sorry for not writing back to you sooner. Our project is now in the final stages.
> There are no heroes in our world. No clear-cut evil either. Everyone involved insists that they're the righteous ones.

>   They oppress people in the name of justice.
>   Fire missiles at countries in the name of
>   justice. Blow up innocent civilians in the name
>   of justice. No one thinks these are evil acts.
>   That's what my world is like.
>   Finally, they resorted to using the dreaded
>   biological weapon. Even when they knew that they
>   would be wiped out too along with their enemies.
>   They chose suicide over losing, over handing the
>   world over to their enemies.

I felt dizzy. Sure, I was shocked to learn there were no heroes in Saeko's world, but it was the explanation after that I couldn't understand. Killing innocent people in the name of justice? Killing themselves because they didn't want to lose? It made absolutely no sense!

Still, I tried to understand the laws of Saeko's world. Human life probably had less value in her world than in ours. Maybe they had a spell that could resurrect people, or maybe if they died, they didn't have to wait long to be reborn. Maybe they didn't have to start over at a lower level, like we did, when the world reset. Or maybe the main cast of characters was really small, and extras made up the majority of the population.

Yeah, that had to be it. That must have been why people killed each other so easily. They didn't regard killing as a serious offense.

I asked:

How many extras do you have in your world? And if you die, how long does it take until you're reborn?

The answer from Saeko was even more of a stunner.

>   We don't have any artificial personalities,
>   which you call "extras," in my world. Everyone

is part of the main cast.

Furthermore, none of us can be "reborn." Many people believe they can, but it's nothing more than wishful thinking. There are no resurrection spells either. Once you die, it's over. The end.

What the hell kind of nonsense is that!

I was shaken and scared. *A world that doesn't reset itself when you die? Everyone only has one life to live? I can't believe it! And they're all self-conscious beings! Killing each other in a world like that was—*

I couldn't hide my shock. It was all so frightening. One bomb was capable of wiping out dozens if not hundreds of people forever. They continued to kill each other, even when they knew that.

Suddenly, I realized the gravity of Saeko telling me that she was going to die soon. I had assumed when Saeko died she was going to be reborn after a while. But I was wrong.

I wasn't going to be able to talk to her anymore.

Furiously, I began to text her a response.

That's messed up! Aren't you scared? Aren't you afraid to be living in a world like that? Never to be reborn...I would be so terrified I wouldn't be able to bear it!

I waited, but nothing. Saeko probably didn't know how to respond. Evening came, and finally I received an email that was much longer than any of the others.

Of course I'm scared. Humanity has always been terrified by the inevitability of death. We abhor death and yearn for eternal life.

Personality replication technology was developed in 2020. It'll take too long to explain

the principles behind it, so I'll give it to you
in a nutshell. It involves scanning a person's
brain and transferring an individual's memories
and psyche to the computer. Even personal
computers on the market nowadays are capable
of operating at teraflop speeds, so running
the replicated personality (we call it a "sim"
here) is pretty simple. The sim can live inside
virtual space forever.

But just the computer's storage capacity being
larger didn't necessarily make replicating an
exact re-creation of our world possible, which
is why virtual reality had to be a simplified
version of the real world. So everything that
would have been undesirable in an ideal world was
eliminated: narcotics, environmental pollution,
child abuse, rape.

Saeko's message was filled with words I didn't recognize.
What were "narcotics"? A medicine made from hemp—that's
what the characters she used seemed to mean. It was possible
to imagine what "environmental pollution" and "child abuse"
meant from their kanji characters. But "rape"? I didn't even
know how to read the character comprised of three kanji
characters for "woman." Maybe it referred to a really powerful
woman?

The service called "Afterlife" began twenty-
two years ago. At first, it was supposed to
introduce the person's sim into virtual space
when that person died, but there was fierce
opposition from religious groups. Something
about creating an electronic representation
of the afterlife being blasphemous. So it was
renamed the "Other Life," and the sims were

introduced while their originals were still
alive. That way, no one could mistake virtual
space for the afterlife.

Presently, there are dozens of Other Life
centers in Japan alone. And there are dozens of
worlds that customers can choose from: the early
twentieth century, Showa-era Japan, samurai-era
Japan, European-style fantasy. There are worlds
like yours and worlds that are fairly realistic,
each with their own governing principles. Even
an eighteen-and-older-only world you can't
imagine. All of the worlds are programmed to
generate exciting events so the sims don't get
bored with their daily lives.

Every world has tens of thousands of registered
sims. According to last year's statistics,
Japan's total sim population is seven hundred
thousand. Of course, there are a hundred times
more "extras" on top of that.

But none of this really means eternal life.
Though our sims may go on living forever, those
of us in the real world are still fated to grow
old and die.

In fact, we aren't even able to experience
what the virtual world is like. That's because
we aren't able to move around in virtual space
in real time due to the processing lag involved
with scanning our brains. At best, we're allowed
to observe your daily lives and send you email.

The reason why we aren't allowed to talk to
you in real time has to do with inspections. Sims
aren't aware that they live in a virtual reality
because that part of their memory is erased
before they are inserted into their reality. It
would have been too cruel for sims to know they

existed only in virtual space. That's why AI inspect all of the email we send you. Anything that might allude to the truth is censored.

The only reason I'm able to circumvent the censors and send you this message is because I'm a systems manager. I'm thirty-nine now. I registered my sim twenty years ago when I was nineteen. The service was new and only offered the high school world and a few others where the level of reality was toned down to appeal to all users.

At the time, I was experiencing some difficulty at college and desperately wanted to start my life over from high school. So I erased all of my memories after I turned sixteen from the system and registered my sim as a high school student.

I'm sorry I kept this a secret from you. My real name isn't Saeko. It's Saika. I gave my sim the same name.

After college, I started working at the Other Life Company. I eventually became a systems manager. I worked with the staff to create many updates to make your lives more exciting, more livable. You probably had no idea.

It was fun to just watch you when I wasn't busy working. A copy of myself living a completely different life. I was so surprised when you inherited Silverfist's bracelet. It was such an unexpected development.

I really am sorry. You must be shocked to hear you're nothing more than an imaginary existence. I realize the cruelty in telling you this. That's why I couldn't tell you sooner. But I wanted you to know. I'm sorry.

I completely lost it. I was furious. But not over the discovery that this world and I were virtual creations. I was already aware of this world's many quirks. At this point, I was past being shocked or angry to learn I was someone else's creation. I was angry at the way Saeko had broken the news to me.

Saeko, or was it Saika? Who gives a crap? All this time, is that how you saw me? As nothing more than an imaginary existence?

Nothing more? *Who do you think you are? You think you're so much better than us because you live in the First World? Don't make me laugh!*

I'm really hurt. I always believed we were equals. Obviously, you didn't. You always considered me as nothing more *than your sim.*

Who cares about sims and virtual space and that stuff? To us, the world we've been living in is reality. Mafuyu, Minori, Kento, Nakkun, Sugi-pee, Iorin—they're all living real lives. You don't get to call them nothing more *than imaginary existences!*

I regretted sending such an angry message. I shouldn't have unloaded on Saeko like that. She was going to die soon. She was going to disappear from her world. She had to be scared and sad and suffering in ways I couldn't even imagine. It was heartless of me to be so harsh.

My cell phone's in-box chimed just as I was about to write her an apology.

```
    I'm sorry. I didn't consider your feelings.
You're right. You may have been born as my sim,
but you're no longer just a sim now. After
all, you've lived twenty years of a completely
different life with completely different
experiences. You and I are separated by forty
```

```
    years of experiences, making us completely
    different people.
        You're right, Saika. I don't think of you as
    nothing more than a sim. You don't know how much
    your emails have meant to me when I was feeling
    down over the years.
        You're a good friend, Saika.
        My fever seems to be getting worse. I have to
    go back to work now. I'll mail you again soon.
```

"Saeko…Saeko…" I cried as I read her message. I had
never felt so sad in my life.

I had had no idea there was a world where death was eternal.
I had had no idea there was a world where dying was so sad
and that Saeko was from such a sorry world.

I couldn't breathe. I was sad and frustrated. I could fly
through the air at supersonic speeds and go *mano a mano*
against a giant monster, but I couldn't save a single friend. My
friend was going to die, and I couldn't do a thing about it.

This isn't right! Not right at all!

◊

I must have cried myself to sleep. When I woke up the next
morning, I had a message from Saeko.

```
    I'm feeling dizzy now. I feel so sick I threw
    up a couple times. It's a struggle just to type
    this. But it's done.
        The staff and I have been working night and day
    for several weeks. Upgrading the system so it could
    be completely managed by AI was a project we'd
    been developing. We finally completed the last
    round of debugging, and AI are now managing all
    systems. We were worried about the automatic event
```

creation system, but it seems to be working fine.

Robots are also in charge of hardware maintenance. The factories manufacturing robots and replacement parts are also operating without human supervision; of course, robots are in charge of maintaining those factories as well. Plus, since the Other Life centers scattered across Japan also act as backups when more than one center goes down due to an earthquake or fire, there's no concern there.

The systems are powered by water, solar, and wind energy. In the event one of those power sources goes down, the other two can fill in while a robot repairs it. Once we're gone, there'll be more than enough supplies of energy.

That's right, Saika. Your world will survive even after we're gone. So you don't have to worry. Your world will probably go on for hundreds if not thousands of years.

This is the last thing we can do for your world. I hope you can find it in your heart to forgive us. Humans were far from perfect. We weren't able to live like you.

You live in a wonderful world. A world where justice truly is just. Why couldn't we create a world like yours? It's too late to regret it now.

Damn, my head hurts. This flu medicine isn't working at all. This may be the end.

Please don't forget us. And don't repeat the errors of our ways. I hope you live a righteous life. Please.

That's all I wanted to say.

Goodbye.

I hastily sent her a reply.

Saeko? Are you still there?

Then another.
Saeko, are you alive?

Then another.
Answer me, please.

No answer came.
I pictured a woman who looked like me, lying on the floor
of a room somewhere in a distant world. (So her real name
was Saika? I didn't care. To me, she was Saeko.) A cell phone
nearby bleated out a catchy tune with the words 3 NEW MESSAGES
blinking on the display.
I would never hear from Saeko again.

◊

April came, and our sophomore year began again. Minori
had successfully guided her relationship with Yukihiko to a
happy end. It appeared she was intent on spending the year
winning Yukihiko's heart again.
Unlike years past, the new school year brought many more
transfer students. There were seven new transfers at our school
alone. Probably because so many people on the verge of death
had decided to register their sims on Other Life at the end of
the last cycle. Of course, their sims didn't remember a thing
about the First World.
Me? I was still playing Silverfist. So here I was on the
observation deck of the Shunsign 60 Building with Mafuyu,
waiting for the bad guys to start up trouble.
"Are you going to keep on playing Silver this year?"
Mafuyu asked.

"Yeah." I put a hand on my bracelet with more than a hint of pride. "I'm not planning on passing the torch anytime soon. I feel like playing the defender of justice for a while."

Besides, I was satisfied with the current situation. I had found a purpose in life.

Kento, a robo-freak, immediately became fascinated when he heard about the maintenance robots. If we could learn to control these robots somehow, we would be able to experience the First World through their eyes and ears. Basically it meant that we would be able to go to the First World by inhabiting robot bodies. We just hadn't figured out how yet. But it should be possible, in theory.

Someday we planned to rescue them. I didn't know how many years it'd take, but we were going to find a way to go to the First World. Saeko had said the fatality rate from the influenza was over 95 percent. Not 100 percent. Human civilization might have perished, but there had to be survivors somewhere in the world.

Saeko had saved our world. She had given every last bit of her strength, even while she grew sicker and lived in fear of her impending death. I wanted desperately to repay the debt.

Poor world—I wanted to do everything possible for the survivors of a tragic world, one without a reset button or heroes.

"There," Mafuyu said. She pointed.

There was an explosion somewhere near Shinjuku. The bad guys were at it again. We burst out of the emergency exit and morphed. We took to the skies and headed for the scene of another battle.

There was no way to get to the First World just yet. But until that day came, I was going to keep on playing the heroine in this world. Because I wanted to be reminded of my mission as a defender of justice.

Because it was Saeko's wish that I continue to live righteously ever after.

INTERMISSION
6

INTERMISSION 6

The next day, the nurse android removed my cast and told me I was free to walk on my own. But I would need to use a cane for a couple more days.

The androids around the facility bothered me too, although not to the extent that Ibis did. Three female androids that looked like sisters worked in shifts to bring me my meals, help me to the bathroom, and make my bed. According to the nameplates on their chests, they were named Chikori, Carlotta, and Charlotte. Aside from the camera eyes affixed to their ears like headphones, there was little to differentiate them from humans. They wore rather plain-looking sky blue nurse's uniforms, unlike Ibis's odd getup. A better look at them, however, revealed that their movements were just a tiny bit different from those of humans. Their movements were all too smooth. Human movements were jerkier, often interrupted mid-task, and not nearly as economical.

After spending several days in their company, I began to recognize their distinctions. Chikori always seemed nervous and quiet but had a gentle tone. Carlotta had a crisp, boyish way of talking. Charlotte, who was a bit strong-willed, scolded me when I didn't do as she said but had kind eyes. I couldn't tell whether those were their actual personalities or just adjustments they made during VFC.

I hadn't taken the time to talk to them at any length. Unlike Ibis, who kept pestering me, I felt as if initiating a conversation with nurse androids would be an admission of equality to me, a human.

But on that day, I just had to ask Carlotta.

"Why are you doing all of this?"

"Because it's my job," Carlotta answered almost immediately. She loaded what was left of my meal onto a wagon.

"Were you made to work as a nurse?"

"Yes."

"So then you've been programmed to carry out these duties?" Carlotta smiled. "The motives behind my actions aren't a part of my program. We aren't bound by our programs. Though created to be a nurse, if I didn't care for the job, I wouldn't do it. But I rather like it."

"*Like*?"

"Yes. You can do anything you like as long as it doesn't harm others—that is a fundamental principle of our world. I chose this job of my own free will. I am satisfied with current conditions."

I couldn't understand it. Machines willingly serving humans? It was unthinkable. It went against the history I had been taught, and I couldn't think of why the machines would embrace such a motive. Even among humans, there were few people who would willingly be in service to another without getting paid.

While I puzzled over this, Carlotta had finished her work and hurried out of the room, depriving me of the chance to question her further.

After a while, Ibis came in. I decided to ask her about yesterday's story.

"Are you sure it wasn't a true story? Are you sure human civilization wasn't wiped out by some virus?"

"Of course it isn't true," replied Ibis. "Like I told you before, the human brain is extremely complex, so it isn't possible to copy human memories or consciousness. The first half of the twenty-first century certainly saw more than its fair share of terrorist incidents, but there was never a bio-terror incident on a global scale."

"Then why did humans fall into decline?"

"Didn't the adults in your colony teach you why?" Ibis sounded amused.

Yeah, they taught me all right. About how the machines rose up at once against humanity in 2044. About how war between man and machine erupted all over the world and how people were eventually driven from the cities. About how humans finally handed over control of the earth to the machines…

We had been brought up on these stories told to us by our parents and by the elders of the colony. Our parents had also been brought up on these stories told to them by their parents. With the war a thing of the distant past, no one who had experienced it firsthand was alive today. Without any other sources of information, we had no choice but to believe these stories.

As I grew older, I wanted to learn more about the war. But no matter how much I searched the colony's database, I couldn't turn up anything more than what our parents had told us. All of the books published after 2040 had been banned because they contained machine propaganda, and accessing the machine network was strictly forbidden for the same reason.

One colony I visited often showed footage from *The War Between Man and Machine: A Visual Record* in the village square, and the villagers would curse and hiss at the carnage on-screen. Having seen a lot of old movies, I noticed the footage had been cut and spliced together from science fiction films such as *The Terminator*, *The Matrix*, and *War of the Worlds*. When I pointed this out, the adults grew cross with me and ran me out of the colony.

I was beginning to feel a bit like Saika in "Where Justice Is Just." The more I thought about it, the more some things about this world didn't make sense. Humans had taken to raiding machine-owned freight trains and warehouses for necessary food and supplies. But why on earth were the machines manufacturing, transporting, and storing such things?

According to one theory, the supplies were being sent to a prison for humans somewhere in Japan, but no one seemed to know where it was.

Surely this world couldn't possibly be a virtual reality. Ibis had said a virtual reality you couldn't differentiate from the real world wasn't technologically possible. But...what proof did I have that what Ibis was telling me was the truth? What proof was there to refute the possibility that I could be an AI who existed only in virtual space?

I was growing confused and nervous. If Ibis's aim was to plant doubts about my own beliefs, it was working. I was beginning to believe that machines weren't a threat to humans and that the history we'd been taught wasn't true. I was even beginning to question this world as well as my own existence. I wanted Ibis to tell me what was wrong and what was right.

And yet I still couldn't bring myself to ask her to tell me the truth. There was the issue of pride and wanting to stand by what I had said. I also didn't want to play so easily into Ibis's hands. Ibis didn't offer to tell me either. She was waiting for me to compromise my principles.

Not yet, I told myself. I wasn't about to give in just because she had told me that story.

"If it isn't the truth," I said, changing the subject, "why did you tell me that story?"

"It's the same as the other stories. They all contain truths even if they are works of fiction."

"Are you saying that science fiction novels prophesied the future?"

"No. The majority of the depictions of the future were way off. Including the stories I've read you. But just because they weren't able to predict the future doesn't make them any less valuable."

"What is a story's value?"

"You'll find out soon enough."

There she goes again. Fine. I'll wait it out some more.

I changed the subject again. I decided to ask her about my conversation with Carlotta. Why would an android willingly serve humans?

"Well..."

Ibis tilted her head. Maybe she was searching her database.

"I'm obviously not allowed to tell you the true history, but I do have a story that might be able to answer your question. A story about one android created to serve humans. Would you like to hear it?"

"Only if it's fiction."

"I should tell you that this story is a bit longer than the others. I'll have to tell it to you over several days. All right?"

"Sure." I slapped my leg. "I'll stick around until this wheel heals."

"Good."

Ibis opened the book and began to read.

"The title is 'The Day Shion Came.'"

STORY
6

THE DAY
SHION CAME

PROLOGUE

The bus would be here any minute.

When I was a nurse, I drove the bus to pick up people. Now I wait for it to come and get me. I have changed, and so has the world.

As one grows old, it gets hard to remember things that happened just the other day, but things that happened many years ago seem ever so clear. Over the last few years I often found myself reading old diaries, diaries written when I was still young. Spending more and more time in the past. I had forgotten many events written in those diaries, but they came flooding back and seemed as though they had only happened yesterday. *Oh yes, oh yes, I remember that now*, I often thought with a nod to myself, smiling at the freshly unearthed memories.

When I was young, I thought time flowed in a straight line, always at the same speed. But now it seems to meander. Events from the diaries, events that occurred half a century ago, seem much closer to me than events from half a month ago.

Each day seemed so long back then. There was so much to do, so much I wanted to do, and it was all so fulfilling. These days I have nothing to do, nothing I want to do, and I muddle through my day. The sun sets in no time at all. I scarcely feel as if time has passed. The days of my youth seem much more real than those I live through now.

Perhaps soon, I, like others I've known, will forget what year it is and become a child again. That might be fun. I worked so hard when I was young—I have earned the right to enjoy my last few days alive.

I know I can only be so calm about this because of what I experienced when I was young. The people I met and lost, the deaths I witnessed, and the elderly I knew—they allowed me to accept it. One young caregiver in particular changed my life forever. She taught me more than anyone.

Her name was Shion.

1

It was May 2030 when we were told Shion was coming to our senior nursing and rehabilitation facility.

I knew from TV that they had invented androids capable of performing caregiver duties several years before. The earliest models looked like metal exoskeletons and moved stiffly, but as production continued, they were given human faces and lifelike plastic or rubber skin. They began to move as adroitly as real humans—the news ran regular reports on the developing technology. We all thought it was a great idea but had imagined it would be years before they would really be used. We had underestimated the speed with which robotics technology was advancing.

One Monday afternoon, an official from the Ministry of Health, Labor, and Welfare arrived with a representative from the Geodyne Corporation. The facility head, the chief nurse, the lead caregiver, the floor supervisors, and a number of experienced nurses and caregivers gathered in the recreation room to hear them talk.

Before they said a word, we were all handed fifty pages of data printed on A4 paper. I flipped through it with a groan. They were filled with complicated schematics and flowcharts. The pages were riddled with incomprehensible terms like "Integrated DGH," "Compliance Controls," "Fault Tolerance,"

"Evolutionary FPGA," and "Broadband Pressure Sensor."

I glanced at Kajita, the chief nurse, who was sitting next to me. She was staring blankly at the pages. She'd been at this job twenty years, longer than any of us. She was the sweetest person alive, with a round face like a mother from an old TV show. But she knew little to nothing about machines and had never even touched a computer. We often had to help her with the bathing equipment.

On her other side was the lead caregiver, Okeya. She was scowling furiously at the pages as if trying to comprehend them through sheer willpower; if she were on an old TV show, she'd be the veteran employee who picked on the new hires. She could be scary, but we all knew she wasn't a bad person.

Sensing our confusion, the Geodyne engineer, Takami, chuckled. "Yeah, you don't need to read that." He looked to be in his mid-thirties; a small man, he wore glasses and seemed to have a good sense of humor. He was Shion's primary support. "I figured I should at least pass that out, but it's intended for engineers and probably hard for anyone else to follow."

Takami's boss hastily added, "We don't have the consumer manual written yet, I'm sorry to say."

"But don't worry, Shion works just fine without a manual," Takami continued, cheerily. "If she didn't, there'd be no point!"

He seemed ready to launch into a full-scale lecture, but his boss coughed. "Um, if you don't mind—"

"Oh, quite sorry. Please." Takami bobbed his head a few times and sat down.

Somewhat grumpily, his boss began explaining the contents of the documents.

He went on at some length, and a lot of it we already knew. With the decline in birthrate, the population of Japan had been decreasing since 2005, and the population pyramid had flipped. A full third of the population was now over sixty-five, giving us one of the oldest populations in the world. As the number of elderly needing care increased, there were no longer enough caregivers. The burden on the younger generations was substantial, and the number of incidents in which people unable to handle the pressure snapped and killed their parents was increasing. The Ministry of Health, Labor, and Welfare took this very seriously and, in conjunction with the Ministry of Education, Culture, Sports, Science, and Technology, had been funding the development of caregiver robots since 2017. At last the research had borne fruit, and Takami's boss said that he personally believed this plan was vital to the future of Japan. He went on and on and on about this.

Naturally, they were not planning on a full-fledged rollout at once. They were planning on a trial period of at least six months. Deploying the robots alongside experienced professionals, giving them firsthand experience while correcting any problems that might occur, helping to perfect the final product.

"In other words," Okeya said flatly, "you want to test your machine here."

"Yes." The facility manager nodded. "We will observe it over the next six months, and if all goes well, we'll increase the number over the next few years. We're short of hands, and if this makes your job easier, I can't see the downside."

"I prefer to avoid the word 'machine,'" Takami interjected. "We hope you will come to see Shion as a partner and as an efficient caregiver."

This last phrase seemed to get under Okeya's skin. "So human caregivers are inefficient?" she said.

"Oh no!" Takami said, aghast. "They won't replace you outright. She has no experience, sh-she's new on the job, as it were. Just like any human being, it will take time and training before she will be able to perform her duties like the veteran caregivers here."

"Every second counts," the official added. "Senior care is facing a grave crisis, and we need all of your help to overcome it."

"Um," Kajita said, nervously raising her hand. "H-how much does one of these cost?"

I had been wondering the same thing.

"Er...how much was it?" Takami said. He looked toward his boss. He was clearly not someone who paid much attention to the financial side of things.

"Well, Shion is a prototype," the boss said. He reluctantly named a figure. We all gasped. It was more than ten times our annual salary.

"Naturally, if we go into full production, the unit cost is a fraction of that, and they run on a new type of fuel cell—as long as you provide Shion with methanol every four hours, she can work twenty-four hours a day. Obviously, she will need to take the occasional maintenance break, so practically speaking she can only work about 120 hours a week, but that's more than twice what we would expect of a human. With the expansion of methane hydrate resources, the price of methanol has dropped. Even with fuel and maintenance costs, we believe the final production model will be able to pay for itself after five years of operation."

If they had that kind of money, they ought to treat us better, I thought. There really was a severe shortage of caregivers, but welfare budgets were in sharp decline. They had reduced our staff to the bare minimum and almost never increased our wages. If the government provided more financial aid, this job would be so much easier, and there would be more people who wanted to be nurses or caregivers. I knew welfare was funded from a different source than the money they were pouring into robotics. And the politicians that decided how to fund these programs all had scads of money and were guaranteed to spend their final years in comfort. Why should they care what happened to ordinary retired citizens?

Twenty years ago, a vast majority of them had voted against implementing new technology that would allow people to vote from home. Officially, they claimed this was because the protections against voter fraud were inadequate, but I'd heard there was another reason: if you could vote without visiting a voting booth, the number of voters in nursing care would skyrocket, and politicians who did not support the welfare state would be at a disadvantage. I didn't know the truth, but it seemed plausible enough.

We grilled Takami for a while.

"How much can it do?"

"It should be able to perform all standard caregiver duties."

"Specifically?"

"It can pass the caregiver certification exam."

That got reactions from everyone—half skeptical, half impressed. Could a robot really do that? If it could, that was worth writing home about. We all knew just how difficult caring for the elderly was, knew just how delicate you had to be.

"Let me show you," Takami said. He produced a demonstration disc and inserted it into the room's video display.

It showed what was presumably part of the Geodyne labs. The camera looked down diagonally at Shion, who was standing by a bed. I had seen her face on the news. It was specially designed to look as human as possible so that residents would feel closer to their caregivers. She wore white work clothes and a nurse cap; if you didn't know she was a robot, you would not have guessed.

A middle-aged man in pajamas was lying on the bed. A voice from offscreen instructed her to change the sheets without disturbing the occupant. Shion bent down and said, "May I change your sheets?" When the man nodded, she began working.

First she put her hands on the man's shoulder and hip and gently rolled him onto the side of the bed closest to her. Then she circled around the bed and lowered the railing that kept him from rolling off. She rolled the dirty sheets up against the man's back and quickly brushed the mattress itself before laying out a new sheet on that half of the bed. Making sure the sheet lay flat, she folded the ends into triangles and tucked them under the mattress. Then she raised the railing again and gently rolled the man across the rolled-up sheets onto the fresh one. She moved back to the original side, lowered the railing, removed the dirty sheet entirely, and placed it in a laundry bag. Then she spread out the other half of the new sheet and again folded and tucked the corners. Finally, she rolled the man back into the center of the bed.

Flawless.

Other videos showed Shion helping residents out of bed and into wheelchairs or over to portable toilets, teaming up with a human caregiver to lift a patient onto a stretcher, pushing a man in a wheelchair, and helping a woman eat. Our skepticism began to fade. It definitely looked like she could pass the certification exam.

"It took five years for us to teach her how to do this," Takami said proudly. "None of this behavior is programmed. She learned it just like humans do, through constant repetition and refining of techniques. Her early movements were pretty rough—it could take her twenty minutes to spread a sheet. And she had trouble controlling her strength. We had her using a dummy rather than a human to practice on, but she kept breaking them. All it took was a little too much pressure and the dummy's joints would snap, or she'd drop the dummy on the floor while trying to seat it in a wheelchair."

Realizing that we were starting to look worried, he hastily added, "O-of course, nothing like that happens now. We're absolutely confident she won't make basic mistakes like that anymore. But we do think she won't gain any real experience without some on-the-job training. She needs real-world experience if she's going to level up."

But the elderly are not RPG monsters, I thought.

"Our ultimate goal is to have Shion perform all her duties

under her own discretion, but that may not be possible at first. We'll need human staff with her, giving her instructions. Ideally, we would have one person devoted to that role. If several people provide conflicting instructions, it might confuse her."

"You said as much," the facility manager said. He turned toward me. "We've already selected someone for that role. Kanbara, would you be up for that?"

"Yes, certainly." I agreed readily, but I had only been a nurse for five years and had no idea why I would be selected for such an important task. There were any number of people with more experience than me.

"I recommended you," Kajita said. "You seem to like robots."

"Hunh?"

"You said you often watch TV shows with robots in them, right? X-something."

Erp. Was that all? Takami beamed like he'd found a buddy. This was awkward. I hadn't been watching *Advent of the Metal God X-Caesar* because of the robots.

But Kajita could hardly be blamed.

"So the android will work with Kanbara on the second floor," the facility manager said. "The news may call her an android caregiver, but she is not licensed, so as far as we're concerned she is just another tool that helps us with our work. At first, she'll only be working during the day. For the time being, Kanbara will be excluded from the night-shift rotation."

Awesome. There was no bump in pay for working with the android, and with no night shift, my wages would drop. I couldn't say I'd miss working on the night shift, but I wasn't exactly thrilled by it either.

"How do I give instructions?" I asked. "Just tell her what to do?"

"Yes. Even if your grammar strays a little from textbook Japanese she'll be able to understand. But if you get too abstract or vague she might have trouble grasping your intent—in that case, she'll ask questions."

"Does she obey anyone? What if one of the residents asks her to do something strange? Like...'Let me touch your breasts.'"

They laughed, but I was serious. There was no telling what seniors would say, particularly those suffering from dementia. If the android followed every command to the letter, it could cause all kinds of problems.

"She will prioritize orders from facility staff. If staff orders and resident orders conflict, she will follow staff orders. In the case of the breast issue...well, if you tell Shion not to obey that command, she'll ignore it."

"A lot of the more senile residents often ask to be taken home. Will she refuse those requests?"

"Yes. And if someone maliciously orders her to harm one of the residents, she will not obey. She will elect to prioritize the safety of the residents. Likewise, she will not accept orders leading to senseless destruction. She will not jump out a window because someone tells her to. That would result in damage to herself. She will accept orders from residents that do not conflict with these restrictions. If the situation is too difficult for her to make the correct judgment, she will look for guidance from a staff member."

The ten years of development had clearly not gone to waste; they had put a lot of thought into this.

"What about emergencies? If a senior suddenly collapses?"

"She will not wait for orders but act according to her best judgment."

"How accurate will that judgment be?"

"That is hard to know for sure. During testing, Shion reacted to accidents at a fairly high rate of appropriateness. But not all accidents can be predicted. I couldn't begin to guess whether she will react appropriately if something she has never experienced happens. But no matter what the event, Shion will not freeze. We've cleared the frame problem."

Before I could ask, he explained, "The frame problem—say you tell a robot you're going out, so it should keep you safe. The robot will walk with you, observing its surroundings, on the lookout for danger. But what qualifies as 'danger'? There's a car coming. There's a chance the driver won't turn in time, and the car will run into you. There's a pebble on the ground in front of you. If you step on it the wrong way, you could trip and fall. The man walking toward you might be a terrorist carrying a bomb, and he might blow himself up! That house you're walking next to might erupt in a gas explosion, there might be an earthquake, an airplane might fall on you—the chance of all of this is always greater than zero.

"If it considered all these possibilities, the robot would be overwhelmed. Every single thing it perceives will tug on its attention, and it will attempt to retrieve and process information related to all sensory input. The processors will lock up, and it will be unable to protect you. This is what we call the frame problem."

"It can't just ignore anything that is unlikely to happen?"

"Yes…but it wasn't easy teaching a robot that trick. It would have to start by calculating that the chance of something happening was very low. But how do you calculate the odds of tripping on a pebble? Frankly, humans don't even worry about odds when they decide to ignore risks. As an example from everyday life, every time there's a news story about a child murderer, everyone takes steps to protect their children. But children are far more likely to die in a traffic accident than they are likely to be murdered. In which case, we should, logically, take steps to improve traffic safety. But few people think cars are more dangerous than child murderers. And the number of people who die in traffic accidents is dwarfed by the number of accidental deaths that occur in one's own home, but nobody thinks their home is more dangerous than the street.

People who worry about cell phone radiation or insignificant additives in their food will happily drink alcohol. Even though booze is far more dangerous. Not many people get married on the day of the Buddha's death, do they? There's no reason at all to assume something bad will happen if you do, but people choose to avoid a risk that doesn't even exist.

"The point being: the way humans evaluate risk is nonsense. It is based on feelings rather than logic, subjective reactions rather than percentages and hard data. They draw a line between what they will take seriously and what they will ignore. To avoid the frame problem, we have to do the same. The robots do not calculate the percentage of anything—they simply ignore anything not immediately relevant to them. It took us an awfully long time to teach them how to do that."

I was somewhat taken aback by all this. "S-so your robot…"

"Shion."

"So Shion just…ignores danger?"

"Yes, she does."

A collective grumble rose up in the room.

"What I need you all to understand," Takami said, not at all daunted—in fact, he sounded quite proud—"is that nothing in this world is ever 100 percent safe. Of course, the job of any good engineer is to make things as safe as humanly possible. But there are no planes guaranteed never to crash. There are no drugs guaranteed to have no unexpected side effects. The idea of perfect safety is an illusion. There is always a compromise somewhere. If we removed everything with even a fraction of a percentage of a chance of causing us harm, there would be almost nothing left. We would be in the Stone Age again…and of course, the way the cavemen lived was far more dangerous than the way we do now.

"We make no claim that Shion is 100 percent safe. We know she is 99.99 percent safe, but we cannot rule out the possibility of some unforeseen accident occurring. But if you'll excuse the suggestion...the same is true for all of you. Even with human caregivers, unimaginable accidents sometimes occur. The same with Shion.

"This is a problem we've been aware of for quite some time. Alan Turing, the father of artificial intelligence, said this in 1946: 'If a machine is expected to be infallible, it cannot also be intelligent.' Intelligence allows it to do things an ordinary machine could not do, and it is therefore also capable of making mistakes.

"Shion's functions—like understanding poorly worded instructions and reacting to emergency situations—are made possible by circumventing the frame problem, which means ignoring certain risks. An android that never takes any risks is an android that never moves. That android is certainly safe but not particularly useful. Shion is very useful. And that brings with it some degree of risk."

His logic was impeccable, I was sure. He was being completely honest with us, which certainly proved his sincerity, but this was not something we could emotionally accept that easily.

"So," Okeya said, as if issuing a challenge. "What if something causes this robot to go berserk? It is much stronger than a human, right?"

"Well, yes. That kind of thing happened a lot in old manga but is unheard of in the real world. But in the unlikely event of something like that, keep your distance and call out the shut-down code."

"The shut-down code?"

"A password that causes an emergency shutdown. It would take too long to fetch a remote control, so we made it into a verbal command. If you say the password, Shion will turn herself off."

"What's the password?"

"Klaatu barada nikto."

"Huh?"

Takami grinned. "Since days of yore, these words have been

used to tame rampaging robots. They are words you would never use in normal life, so there's no chance of accidentally shutting her down in mid-conversation. Don't mention them in her presence."

"Right..."

"Well, why don't we all practice the password?" Takami said. He waved his hand like an orchestra conductor. "And a one, and a two...Klaatu barada nikto!"

"Klaatu barada nikto!" we all chorused.

2

Shion arrived a month and a half later, on the last Monday in June. It was raining.

They had called ahead to let us know she was arriving, and a number of staff with nothing better to do had been hanging around the entrance waiting. Several of the more active seniors were also there to greet the new caregiver.

"How will she arrive?" Kajita said amiably. We were all wondering the same thing. "Will she be in a big box? Wrapped in plastic?"

"I doubt it," I said. "She can walk, so they'll probably drive her here. In the usual fashion."

"But she's so expensive! What if she gets wet?"

"If she broke that easily, she'd be no good at all," I said with a laugh. In our line of work, we had things spilled on us all the time. And we had to help some of the seniors take baths. Any machine designed to perform those tasks would not rust over or short out when exposed to a little water.

"You think so?"

"Hey, maybe we should make a card to welcome her with!" Kasukabe said excitedly. She had just started working at the facility a little over a year ago, leaving her old office job behind. I wouldn't quite call her a friend, but we worked on the same floor, were roughly the same age, and we had the same taste in manga, so we often chatted when we both got stuck with the night shift. "And a bouquet! This is a big deal—we should make a thing of it!"

Okeya scowled. "Too late now." We'd decided not to make a big deal out of it a few weeks ago. We were just welcoming a new caregiver and were not to treat her any differently than we would any new hire.

And although none of us said so aloud, none of us was really sure how much help this "new hire" would be. If we threw a big party to welcome her and she turned out to be useless or caused some awful disaster, it would be awkward.

"I dunno. It just seems too relaxed."

"We're not all as relaxed as you," Okeya said, her age and dedication like oil next to the water of Kasukabe's youth and cheer. Okeya always winced when Kasukabe said something that struck her as childish, but Kasukabe never noticed. Or if she did, she wasn't the sort to let it bother her.

While we talked, a blue car pulled up in front of the hospital. It stopped, and the door opened. Takami stepped out, and Shion followed him.

What had I expected? Fanfare? A spotlight? Or a shower of roses magically appearing behind her? There was nothing like that. She just got out of the car and walked over to us. No editing, no fancy camera moves, no background music. She was, from the start, a part of the world in which we lived.

I'd seen pictures of robots like her any number of times, but this was my first time seeing one face-to-face. She looked like an ordinary young woman. She wore a simple white sleeveless dress and cute pumps. She was a little taller than me, 165 centimeters. Her bare arms were pale and slender—according to the data files, they were 2.5 times as strong as human arms. She had short hair. Her eyes gleamed, and there was a faint smile on her face. She was not especially beautiful—perhaps they had been worried about other women resenting her—but she had enough of a baby face that you wanted to like her. The luster of her skin and the sparkle in her eyes looked totally natural. It was hard to believe she was man-made.

"Hello, everyone. This is Shion," Takami said, a little nervous.

Shion bobbed her head and said brightly, "I'm Shion. Nice to meet you all."

We all bowed our heads in return.

Shion looked up and saw my name tag. "You're Erika Kanbara?"

"Mm? Oh yes."

"I understand you'll be in charge of me. Don't be soft on me—if I make any mistakes, please tell me right away. I know I'll be asking a lot of questions when there's something I don't understand."

She bowed her head again. She sounded a lot less... mechanical than I'd expected. But there was something slightly off about it...like she was following a script. I was sure Takami had told her what to say.

"Certainly," I said, already feeling an invisible wall between us.

And that was how we met.

◊

Shion's first day began with me showing her to the changing room.

She did exactly what I told her to do. When I said, "Come with me," she followed. When I stopped, so did she. I was nervous at first, but like Takami said, she clearly had no trouble understanding what I said to her. The way she moved was smooth, even graceful, with no traces of mechanical clunkiness. But her movements were a bit too elegant, like a runway model's. There was something not quite natural about it. The way normal humans move is filled with unnecessary motions and hardly beautiful; watching her really drove that point home.

In the changing room, I explained, "This is where we change into our uniforms. Here's your uniform."

Shion nodded and reached for the fastener on her dress. Then she stopped and turned to look at the door. "Takami, are you a woman?"

Only then did I notice that Takami had followed us into the ladies' changing room with a video camera. He seemed not to have realized where he was until Shion said something, at which he flew out of the room, wailing, "S-sorry!"

"The nerve of the man," I said, laughing.

Shion looked puzzled.

"Takami is a man, and men should not be in the ladies' changing room."

"Someone taught you that?"

"Yes. Takami gave me a lecture on morals concerning changing clothes. It is strange that he would make a mistake like that."

"It was very careless of him."

"Yes, it was. People often make mistakes."

Shion began to undress. I hadn't noticed before due to the rain, but if you listened carefully, you could hear motors whirring when she moved. The sound wasn't loud enough to bother you. If a senior were hearing impaired, they would never even notice.

I'd never seen a naked android before. Even the parts that would normally be hidden behind clothes were covered in fake skin, and she was even wearing normal women's underwear. But on her back and belly there were faint, if still unsettling, black lines where the skin was fastened. The button on the back of her neck was, according to the manual, the start button. A little above that, right inside the hairline, there was a tiny green light. The flesh-colored compress-looking thing on her side was a cover for her fuel input.

I imagined it was Takami who had put that underwear on her. He must have been used to seeing Shion change in the lab. That was why he'd thought nothing of following her into the changing room.

When Shion and I emerged in our pale pink uniforms, Takami apologized again. "I really am sorry."

"It's all right," I said. I was less concerned with his mistake than with Shion asking him if he was a woman. She was an android; she had not been joking. When Takami had walked into the ladies' changing room, Shion had genuinely wondered if her knowledge of his gender had been mistaken—something no human would ever imagine.

There was clearly a fair amount of common sense she had yet to learn.

◊

The residents had been informed some time ago that an android caregiver would be coming to the facility. Except for those too forgetful to understand, everyone was curious.

Shion followed me around the second floor, greeting each of the residents. She gave the exact same bow and introduction to each of them. She was well received. Takami followed us with the video camera, looking very pleased.

Some of the seniors got a bit carried away.

"So they finally perfected the android!" said Toki, a particularly talkative man. "I used to watch *Astro Boy* growing up, you know. I always believed they'd be able to make robots look just like humans in the twenty-first century. What was fiction when I was a boy is now right before my eyes! What a thrill."

A human would have looked embarrassed, but Shion just returned a vague smile. Her default expression.

Toki said he wanted to go to the lounge. Every floor had a lounge with a big-screen TV and five computers with broadband access, and Toki generally spent his mornings there, watching late-night anime he'd recorded.

Shion's first job. She helped him sit up and swing his feet over the side of the bed. Then she brought a wheelchair, placed it at a twenty-degree angle from the bed, and locked the wheels. She put her arms under his and around his back, clasped her hands, and lifted him to his feet.

This took considerably more strength than you would think. For a skinny senior, it was no big deal, but many of the seniors were, like Toki, considerably heavier than their caregivers. It took its toll on our backs. Performing this task dozens of times a day meant chronic back pain among all the caregivers.

But Shion was stronger. Where I would have been grunting with effort, she lightly lifted him up and supported him. She rocked his feet back and forth, slowly maneuvering his back to the chair. Artfully done. Filming the whole thing, Takami whispered, "That's right."

"Oh ho ho, talk about your hundred thousand horsepower! Just like *Astro Boy*!" Toki chuckled, impressed.

Shion bent down, lowering him into the chair.

"Nurse, can you fly like Astro?" joked the man in the next bed, Arai.

Shion did not respond—perhaps focused on the task at hand.

"Nurse! Can you fly?" Arai asked again, louder.

Finished with her task, Shion stood up. I tugged her sleeve. "He means you."

"Me?"

"Arai's talking to you."

"Surely he's talking to you. I am not a nurse."

That same placid smile never wavered. If you didn't know she was a robot, you'd think she was making fun of you.

I sighed. Certainly, nurses and caregivers were different. But they both wore pink, and they both performed many of the same tasks. The only difference was that nurses could examine patients and give them medicine, while caregivers could not. The only way to tell them apart was by their name tags, and few of the residents bothered to distinguish. They called us all nurses.

"I'll explain later. For now, you'd better answer him."

"Okay," she said and looked over at Arai. "I can't fly," she said and turned away again. Arai looked disappointed.

Oh dear, I thought. We had just uncovered Shion's greatest flaw. She could perform her duties flawlessly. But communication with the residents was a major part of any senior caregiver's job. And that included repartee. If she was unable to talk with them, then no matter how flawless her care techniques, the seniors would not be at ease.

I was worried—if her first task had been this awkward, how would the rest play out?

◊

Next up was room 206, where a new problem awaited us.

"Careful," I whispered before we entered. "Isezaki is a dirty old man."

"You mean he is prone to sexual harassment?"

"Yes. He's partially paralyzed, but he still has full use of his right hand. If he grabs your bottom, firmly tell him not to."

"Okay," she said. I doubted an android would be bothered by something like that, but as a woman, I did not want to see that happen.

Isezaki was sprawled out on his side. He had the face of a samurai movie stuntman whose only part in the film was to be cut down by the hero. He had difficulty sitting up on his own but still had a ruddy look to him.

"I am Shion. Nice to meet you."

Her usual greeting. Isezaki sullenly avoided looking at her. He was never very friendly, and he appeared to be in a particularly bad mood today.

"Bathroom," he grunted. Shion just stood there smiling, not understanding.

"He wants to use the portable toilet," I whispered.

"Certainly." Shion stepped forward.

"Not you," Isezaki snapped. "The other nurse."

Aha. Only a flesh and blood nurse would do.

I managed to keep my brow from twitching furiously and gave him my most professional smile.

"Shion is new here and could use the practice. If you don't mind."

Isezaki grudgingly relented. I pulled the curtain across, giving him privacy from his roommate, Komori.

The toilet was on the right side of the bed. Shion helped Isezaki to his feet just like before. She slowly moved him over to the toilet and lowered his pants and underwear with her right hand while supporting his body with her left hand. This was normally easier said than done, but Shion had no problems with it.

As expected, Isezaki's hand began drifting toward Shion's bottom. He must have decided it was worth a go after all. Just as I was about to say something—

"Don't do that!" Shion said, in a much harsher tone than I'd expected. Isezaki jumped. I nearly did myself. I'd told her to speak firmly, and she'd clearly taken that literally.

Isezaki had quite a temper, so I wondered if this might provoke an incident, but nothing happened. He must have thought there was no point arguing with a robot, or perhaps the force of her remark made him lose his nerve. He allowed himself to be lowered gently onto the toilet.

"Tell me when you're finished," I said and stepped outside the curtain.

Takami was hovering out there, looking worried. "Something happen?" he asked.

"Nothing important," I said. We stepped out into the hall so Isezaki would not hear.

"Was it bad?"

"No. With that man, that's exactly how firm she needed to be."

I certainly thought so anyway. Any other senior here, I wouldn't mind that much if they got a bit touchy-feely—I'd just tease them for being an old perv and move on. But Isezaki was different. His personality was bad to begin with. And he touched even though he knew we didn't want him to. And the way he talked…He'd been president of a company and must have been very unpopular. He had once told a story about buying an underage girl in Thailand when he was younger without a trace of guilt. He was boasting about it. He was fundamentally immoral. It was hardly unusual for seniors suffering from Alzheimer's or the like to undergo changes to their personalities, but Isezaki had no such excuse. His memory wasn't what it once was, but the Hasegawa Test had found no drop-off in mental capabilities.

We often griped about him at the nurses' station—"Who does he think he is?" But it was our job to keep smiling, and we all wanted to avoid the trouble it would cause if we made him angry, so he was never scolded the way he needed to be. And anyway, scolding may have simply made him worse. Perhaps this incident would prove good medicine.

"Nice work, Shion," I said but did not forget to add, "But be a little bit softer when you scold anyone other than Isezaki."

◊

As lunch drew near, the facility turned into a war zone.

To encourage interpatient communication and rehabilitation, anyone capable of getting around was required to eat meals in the cafeteria. Shortly before mealtime, we made toilet rounds, helping any residents unable to go to the bathroom on their own. When that was done, we had to gather them by the elevators to take them downstairs to the cafeteria.

The elevators could hold six wheelchairs each. To avoid a rush, we worked on a strict, coordinated schedule, with each floor taking turns. The second floor needed to get all residents down by 11:45. A moment later, the third floor would start bringing people down, and the elevators would be full by the time they reached our floor. We helped residents who could walk and moved those who couldn't to wheelchairs. All nurses and caregivers assigned to a floor worked together to get the seniors to the first floor. A single minute late, and it would be ages before the elevators were open again.

We had Shion concentrate on getting the seniors who could not walk into their wheelchairs. While I pushed the wheelchair to the elevator, she would get the next resident ready.

"Coming through," Kasukabe said, clanking past in the power loader. It was a useful machine that could greatly increase your strength, but it was hard to put on and even harder to operate without hurting the residents, so most caregivers avoided it. Kasukabe was young enough to think learning how to use it was fun and was now the second floor's power loader specialist.

Even when everyone was finally down on the first floor, our job was hardly finished. We had to help residents unable to feed themselves. We held the spoon, fed them a bite, and then had another spoonful prepared when they were ready.

Here Shion's flaw became obvious again. After each spoonful, she would ask, "Ready?" and wait until they answered before feeding them the next. She made no effort to say anything else. We could all tell if they were ready or not just by watching how their mouths moved, and we would talk about other things while we fed them. Simple stuff like, "How is it?" or "Do you like spinach?" But even that was beyond Shion's capabilities.

When the meal was done, we had to take them back up the elevators to their floors. When they were back in their rooms, we made another toilet round. Only then did the storm die down, letting us catch our breaths and take our own lunches in shifts.

Of course, Shion did not eat. She simply needed to receive

some methanol every four hours, and it took less than a minute for that to happen. Not feeling comfortable with letting her work out of my sight, we had her sit with us while we ate.

"How do you like it so far?" I asked, not expecting much of an answer.

Sure enough, Shion said, with her usual unchanging smile, "I enjoy working to help people. I hope I get along with the residents and other staff. I'm sure it won't be easy, but I'll do my best."

Not a trace of emotion in there. I glanced over at Takami.

"You teach her to say that?"

"Cut me some slack," he said. "She doesn't know much about the world. Teaching her some set answers to common questions keeps her from appearing to be rude."

"I think it's a problem that she can't have conversations with the residents. She can't build any kind of rapport with them like this. You didn't teach her to have a sense of humor?"

Takami scratched his head. "No, it was all we could do to teach her the work."

"There's no program you can install? Conversation techniques or—"

"Install? Can't be done. Like I said, Shion's skills improve just like ours do, through practice."

"Including talking to the seniors?"

"Yes, she'll have to gain that experience here."

In other words, I had to teach her how. I felt tired already. Teach a robot how to have a sense of humor? That sounded nigh impossible.

I felt faint.

◊

That afternoon was bath time. Residents were taken to the baths twice a week. The second floor bathed on Monday and Thursday. Residents who could walk simply went to the big communal bath and washed themselves, but the less fortunate had to use bathing equipment, and we had to wash them. And we were responsible for not only our residents; we had a number of seniors who were normally looked after by family members and only visited us on bathing days. Bathing someone unable to move on their own is no easy task, and there were a number of families that took advantage of this service.

Obviously, this was not something Takami could be allowed to see or videotape. He was forced to kill time in the lounge.

Shion and I changed into T-shirts and shorts and headed for the baths.

"Rrright, let's get 'em!"

Bath time was awfully tough work. I generally had to pump myself up for it. When I pumped my fist in the air and bellowed, Shion gave me a puzzled look.

"Don't just stand there, you do it too."

"That pose?"

"Yes! It's like a ritual. Go on! Let's get 'em!"

"Let's get 'em!" Shion said, awkwardly imitating me.

First up was a woman named Sumiyoshi. I took her legs and Shion took her upper body, and we lifted her out of the wheelchair and onto the bathing apparatus's stretcher. First, we carefully washed her body with a sponge. Once we'd rinsed the soap off her, we fixed her body in place with a few straps and pressed the button on the side of the machine. The machine noisily lifted her up a bit and slid her over the bath. It then slowly tilted forward, lowering her feet first into the hot water.

"How's that feel?" I asked.

Sumiyoshi closed her eyes blissfully. "Wonderful," she whispered. "Amazing, isn't it? First the power loader, and now robot caregivers. Never would have imagined this when I was working."

Sumiyoshi had worked in a senior facility herself until the

end of the twentieth century. She'd worked too hard, suffered a herniated disk, and had been forced to retire. She knew just how hard our job was and did everything she could to make things easier for us. She always followed our instructions to the letter and never asked for anything unreasonable. Sumiyoshi was the ideal resident.

"Shion, was it? Do you get paid?"

"No. I am not an employee, just equipment."

"But you must have things you want to buy."

"Not particularly."

"You don't dress up at all? A few nice clothes?"

"My clothes are supplied for me."

Like I thought, Shion's responses were accurate but not interesting. It did not make for conversation. I listened nervously, but soon Sumiyoshi lost interest and closed her eyes.

For a few minutes she relaxed in the water, and then she said, as if remembering, "You know, in my day, they had this device that let you bathe in a wheelchair."

She always talked about the old days when she was bathing. So much of our work had not changed in the last thirty years, and a lot of what she said sounded very familiar.

"I've seen that. The side of the bath opens like a door, right?"

"Yes. You pushed the wheelchair in, closed the door, and then you started the water. But the lock didn't always latch properly, so water would come spilling out of the crack in the door. Such a mess." Sumiyoshi laughed, and I smiled, imagining the puddle.

"But the worst was how it shook them."

"Shook them?"

"Yes, if you pushed a button, air jets would churn the water. A lot of people liked the feel of it and requested it. But the skinnier seniors would be knocked all over the place. And the water was up to their shoulders, so if they lost their balance, they'd start to drown. Only way to stop it was to have someone with their arm around the senior's shoulders, keeping them in place the whole time. We had to sit perched on the edge of this really tall bath, leaning out—it really messed up our backs."

"That sounds tough," I said. Unnatural poses like that could really do a number on you. The bathing equipment we used now was designed to let us work in a much more comfortable position. We didn't have to bend over or stretch ourselves at all.

"I imagine the people that made the thing tested it thoroughly. They put themselves inside it and decided it was perfect and that it would make our jobs so much easier. But there are always things you don't know till you use it in the workplace."

Suddenly I got it.

Sumiyoshi was speaking indirectly about Shion. She had already realized that for all the marvelous technology that went into her, Shion was lacking something that was vital to any caregiver.

I glanced at Shion, but her face was frozen in that same old smile. She appeared completely oblivious to any irony.

The flaw was not just with Shion; the power loader was the same. It looked great when I first saw it on TV, but it just took too much time to put on. When a senior asked to get up, nobody wanted to head back to the nurses' station and put on a suit of armor. It was far faster to just use your arms. We hardly used the loader at all.

There were many things you couldn't know unless you put them to work. A caregiver's job was far more than just technique. Takami had made Shion's body and brain, but he had forgotten to give her a heart. And that was not easy to install after the fact.

◊

Five fifteen PM. At last the day's work was done. Evening care was handled by those on the late and night shifts.

Shion had been given a seat of her own in the corner of the nurses' station, next to the methanol tank. She would wait there until morning.

Her uniform had been custom made so it could be opened on the left side. She opened it herself and pulled the compress off her side, exposing the connector underneath. Then she extended a tube from the tank, connected it to the socket on the end of the connector, and refilled her fuel tank.

When her tank was full, she closed her uniform up again and sat down on the chair.

"Am I finished for the day?"

I hesitated but saw Takami nodding. "Yes," I said.

"Shutting down," she said. For a few seconds she stared into space, but then her eyes slowly closed, and she stopped moving. It looked like she had fallen asleep.

"That's basically how she'll end every day," Takami said. "There's an activation switch on the back of her neck, but don't touch that except when you turn her on. Much like a computer, if you don't shut her down properly, it could cause problems. And if you need to perform an emergency shutdown—"

"Klaatu?"

"Yes. And if people start getting creeped out by her at night, cover her with a cloth like this." Takami calmly draped a white sheet over Shion's head. Now she looked like a ghost. Even creepier.

"I think I'll let the night shift staff decide."

"Were there any other problems?" Takami asked, clearly expecting there not to be any. But I was not that nice. Nothing mattered to me except the safety and comfort of our residents. He was getting my honest opinion.

"When you practiced changing diapers, did you use real poop?"

Takami's smile froze. We'd drawn the curtains while changing diapers, and he hadn't seen her at work.

"Um...no, no, I think we used miso."

"I thought so. The way she wiped the senior's bottoms was a little unusual."

"Uh…well, I'm sure she'll get used to that soon enough, right?"

"But the biggest problem is definitely going to be communication." This had been bothering me all day. "I honestly didn't think this was going to be that hard a job," I said. And not just because I was worn out. "I just thought I'd have to tell the robot what to do. Nobody said anything about teaching it how to have a heart."

"I do apologize. We should have said," Takami said, bowing his head. "But…humans are the same, aren't they? We all learn to communicate by being with other humans. Shion's just left the lab, so how is she supposed to know any of this stuff? I promise you, she has the capacity to learn it."

"Then why didn't you teach it at the lab?"

"Um, well…" he stammered. "I'm not…"

"Not what?"

"I'm not that good at talking to people myself. I didn't… know what to teach her."

I gaped at him.

"And not just me. All the lab's staff are total engineering nerds. It's like a high school science club in there. We're all pretty good at dating simulation games, but none of us could ever talk to a real woman. If she grew up surrounded by people like us, she'd be at even more of a disadvantage than she is now. Honestly, there were people who tried to mold her into their favorite personality type…

"But that's not what Shion was invented for. We couldn't let her have a personality marketed toward a particular otaku subculture. We wanted her to be an android that everyone could love. And I thought the best way to do that was to have her meet a lot of people out in the real world."

"So you dumped her in our laps?"

"I hate to put it that way, but I suppose you're right." He

bowed his head. "Please. Look after Shion. I know she's flawed, but in the long run—"

"I'm starting to hate you."

"Eh?"

"I really hate people who get all self-deprecatory. You aren't that good at talking to people? That's something you should be ashamed of, not something you should ever admit to. If you know you're crap at something, then make an effort to get better."

Boy, I must have built up a lot of bile that day to be so harsh with him. Takami looked rather flabbergasted. I'd surely destroyed his fantasies about nurses. But I was no angel. Just about every woman who became a nurse despised the myth of the "angel in white." We weren't angels. Just human beings.

"Anyway, I understand very well that I can't count on any help from you. I will take care of Shion—don't you worry. She's in my care now. If I don't make her into the best damn caregiver around, it's the seniors who will suffer."

I left him standing there stunned and stalked off to the changing room. Tomorrow would be the start of a whole new battle.

3

To my surprise, there were no real problems over the next couple of months.

I wouldn't say everything went smoothly. Shion's communication abilities remained at a very low level. At first the residents tried to talk to her, but they soon saw how unfriendly she was and developed a low opinion of her.

But none of them went so far as to avoid her. Indeed, there were a number of people who preferred having her help them to the bathroom or change their diapers. It was embarrassing to have a nurse or a caregiver take care of such unclean functions at their age. But they didn't need to worry about grossing out a robot. It was easier for them to use Shion as equipment.

Every few days we'd take her out on our day resident pickups. We had a microvan with a wheelchair lift, and we'd take it around to each home, loading the seniors onto it. We couldn't fit them all at once—depending on the day, we'd make as many as three trips. Not all homes were constructed with wheelchairs in mind, and sometimes it was a real struggle just getting the wheelchair out of the house. Shion's strength really came in handy.

Shion was still unable to work without my supervision. The thing she had the most trouble with was hearing and understanding what the seniors said to her. Many seniors had conditions that left them muttering, unable to enunciate clearly, and even humans would struggle with comprehension. Seniors with dementia often babbled incoherently. A robot could never hope to understand them. I had to stay with her and interpret.

But she was making great strides with the work itself. Anything requiring physical strength quickly became Shion's job, and the toll on my own body was greatly reduced. I could see clear improvements in the way she performed her duties. At first, I had to be really specific with her: "Put _____ in a wheelchair and push him over to the elevator. When you're done, come back here." But now I didn't have to say anything at all. She knew what orders I was going to give her. And since I had learned what she could do and what she could not do, I knew exactly what to have her do.

She made a number of little mistakes. Misunderstanding what the seniors said to her, believing things they said to her in their dementia—"The man in the other bed stole my money!" or "I haven't eaten lunch yet"—but all of these were things a human might carelessly do and didn't rise to the level of problems. And she was learning from each of her mistakes.

Shion's most surprising ability was singing. Though perhaps we should not have been surprised; she was a robot, and her voice would never go off-key or crack on a high note. We had a karaoke party once a month, and the residents had talked her into singing a few numbers. The machine was filled with old stuff like Seiko Matsuda, Miyuki Nakajima, and Kyoko Koizumi, but Takami must have taught her all their big hits. She had no trouble reproducing them.

But...while this might just be my own bias talking, her singing was rather soulless, with no emotion behind it. Someone asked her if she liked a song, and she answered, honestly, "Not especially." She might be singing love songs, but she did not know what they meant.

TV crews came three times. For the first few weeks we weren't sure what mistakes she might make, so Geodyne was reluctant to publicize Shion, but as things began to go more smoothly, they gained confidence. Geodyne must have thought the market for android caregivers would expand if Shion received positive media attention.

The resulting programs were pretty much what you'd expect. When the reporters pointed their microphones at Shion, she simply repeated the phrases she'd been told to say. "I enjoy working to help people," etc. Did anyone watching believe her? Most people knew androids weren't capable of "enjoying" anything.

She also had a new hobby. While I was eating lunch, she would read. I thought we might as well use the time to help teach her a little more common sense, so I suggested she read some of the used books we kept in the lounge or download material from the Internet. She read newspapers, modern literature, history books, mysteries, nonfiction, manga, anything she could get her hands on. At first, when I asked what she thought, she always said, "I don't know." I wasn't sure she really understood what she was reading.

Then one day she suddenly said, "This is interesting." At first, I was happy that she had advanced enough to say something like that, but then I read the preface and table of contents of the book she was reading—*Extraordinary Popular*

Delusions and the Madness of Crowds by Charles Mackay. It was a nineteenth century book detailing financial bubbles, duels, the occult, witch hunts, alchemists, and the Crusades.

As her experience increased, Shion's manner of speaking gradually improved. She was still rather curt, but as she talked with me she seemed to be picking up on a few things. She occasionally surprised us by saying things that sounded like jokes. Still, I couldn't quite work out if she was actually learning, or if I just wanted her to be.

◊

At first Takami came every day, but soon he started only coming on Fridays. He would watch Shion work, talk to me and the other staff, and ask Shion a few questions. At the end of the day he would create a backup of her memories. If anything strange happened with Shion, we could return her to an earlier state.

Strange to think that thousands of hours' worth of Shion's experiences could download in a few dozen minutes and fit into a single high-capacity holographic card. Takami explained that Shion wasn't recording everything she saw and heard like a video camera but was selectively focusing on what seemed important to create a bank of abstract memories. That was why there wasn't as much data to download as one might think.

"Human memories work the same way. They are abstracted and compressed, with only the most important aspects remembered clearly, thus reducing the actual amount of data that is stored. If you were to write out every detail you remember about your own life, it would only fill about ten megabytes. If we included a lot of illustrations, it still wouldn't be more than a gig. Honestly, Shion is remembering a good deal more than humans do."

At first, I would report what had happened, and he would offer explanations. Very businesslike. Given the way I'd spoken to him the first day, he was understandably reserved, and I was a little ashamed of having been so unpleasant, so there was a sort of wall between us. It took several weeks for that wall to crumble and for us to be comfortable enough to engage in any kind of small talk.

"Everyone at my company is a massive nerd," he said at lunch one day. "Even our president—born the year *Gundam* first aired, obsessed with dating sims since his first computer as a teenager—is the archetype of the otaku generation. He founded this company because he wanted to make robots like the ones in anime. You know why we're named Geodyne? Because it sounds like the name of an evil army."

"Then Shion's development?"

"The president's idea. He popped into the labs one day and gave a speech about how making beautiful androids was the dream of all mankind."

"Not mankind so much as otaku men, surely?"

"You could say that. But he meant every word. He was very insistent that we name her…something beginning with M. We had to explain copyright infringement to him then."

He laughed a lot at that. I liked anime, but I wasn't that deep into it and had trouble following some of his jokes.

"But sometimes he's right. 'Nothing happens if you just dream,' he said. 'You need the motivation to make your dreams reality.' Isn't that how the space program got started? Mankind dreamed of going to space, but all we did was send twelve people to the moon, and we've not been back for the last fifty years. Dreaming alone isn't enough. When you get down to it, if you don't have money and desire, society never changes.

"Androids are the same. You can't make them just because you think it'd be neat. Dreams don't get you funding. That's when we hit on the idea of a caregiver android. The need existed. If we got it right, we could sell them all over the world, not just Japan. There are many developing nations out there with aging populations. And the government was happy to help fund it…"

Then the elderly were just a tool to help achieve their dream? I stopped myself from asking. It would just make things awkward between us again.

But the more I talked to Takami, the more the differences between us became clear. On the surface, we were both working to educate Shion, but our ulterior motives were unrelated. He was trying to make Shion into the perfect android and didn't really give a damn about the seniors.

And that was wrong. Shion needed to be a skilled caregiver before she could be an otaku's dream come true.

◇

In those two months, there had been changes in the residents as well.

Early in August, Sumiyoshi had been hospitalized. A summer cold had given way to pneumonia. She was back a couple of weeks later, but it had really taken its toll on her. She'd lost a lot of weight—when we lifted her onto the stretcher to help her bathe, she was shockingly light. Her muscle strength had deteriorated, and we had to start her rehabilitation program over from scratch. She spoke less and rarely reminisced in the bath.

She no longer had the energy to talk, but more importantly, being sick had left her depressed. Where once she and Kasukabe had got on so well it was like watching a stand-up comedy duo in action, now she just smiled faintly at Kasukabe's jokes and did not respond. And we could all tell she was forcing the smile.

While not as bad as Isezaki, Toki was also causing us problems. He didn't seem to understand that this wasn't a retirement center, but a nursing facility focused on rehabilitation. His right hand and leg were partially paralyzed, but when it came time for his rehabilitation exercises, he would scoff, "Do I look like I'm in kindergarten? Spare me your games." Certainly opening and closing your fists and raising and lowering your arms in time with the *Train Song* was pretty childish, but this was how we'd done rehabilitation for decades now. Explaining this did not deter him from his boycott. Shion once tried to force him into his wheelchair and bring him along, but he threw such a fit we had to give up.

"Toki needs some motivation," Shion said. I knew that. Rehabilitation was hard work, and you needed a real desire to get better if it was ever going to work. Figuring out how to get unmotivated residents to comply was a perennial problem.

Isezaki's selfishness was escalating. His blood sugar was always high, but he'd demand we bring him cake or let him drink—requests he knew we'd never give in to. When we refused, he'd accuse us of incompetence or poor service. He was starting to be rude to other residents as well. His roommate Komori was a very patient man and rarely answered back, but even he was starting to ask—quietly, so Isezaki couldn't hear—to be moved to another room.

When Isezaki's son came to see him, he sighed. "He's always been like this. A total dictator. Always made Mom cry. Then when she got sick and couldn't leave the hospital, he wouldn't go see her. Even at her funeral, the only thing he did was haggle over rates with the funeral home director. The flowers are too showy, we don't need to release any doves, so drop the price…I think I turned out as well as I did by using him as a negative example of how to live. I was desperate to be someone people liked and admired, and all I had to do was be his exact opposite. He was the perfect anti-teacher."

The only person Isezaki had no trouble with was Shion. He'd flung all kinds of insults in her direction, but she never once dropped her standard smile, and his rage came up empty. It started to get to him.

Realizing the futility of it, he gradually stopped talking to her. When Shion came to change his sheets or bathe him or change his clothes, he didn't complain at all. He just let her work. We were all quite relieved, assuming she had won.

But at the end of August, something happened.

◊

By that time, Shion's work was going smoothly enough that I did not always need to be with her. While she was changing sheets or moving people into wheelchairs, I was often working in a different room.

That afternoon, Isezaki came back from rehabilitation and said he felt sick and wanted to lie down. Komori had come back earlier and was already in bed, apparently asleep. Without questioning it, I told Shion to put Isezaki in bed and went next door to examine the resident in 207.

A moment later, I heard Isezaki bellow, "Wait! Stop!" followed by a loud clatter. I hurried back down the hall.

When I reached the door to 206, I froze. The wheelchair was upended, and Shion and Isezaki were collapsed in a heap on the floor. Shion was under Isezaki, and he appeared to be unharmed but was shouting, "Damn it! Let go of me!" and pushing at her with his good hand, trying to get away.

I quickly helped him up and sat him on the edge of the bed. Shion stood up as if nothing had happened and righted the wheelchair. Several other nurses came running from the nurses' station. They peered anxiously into the room.

"What happened?"

"This thing!" Isezaki roared, thrusting a trembling finger at Shion. "It suddenly went crazy! It knocked me over!"

"I did not," Shion said. "When I tried to stand him up, he suddenly started thrashing around. I tried to support him, but I was too late."

"Liar! Killer robot! You nearly crushed me!"

"What is going on here?" Okeya said, looking from one to the other. "Which of you are we supposed to believe?"

I looked at Shion. Her faint smile had vanished. She was staring at Isezaki with a look of confusion.

"Well, Shion?"

"I...." I had never heard her hesitate before. "I...did nothing wrong."

She did not sound very confident. For a moment, I doubted her. Had she really done it? Had something changed inside her that made her lose control?

"I'm gonna sue you all," Isezaki roared. "You're all responsible for using this diabolical machine!"

"Give me a break, Isezaki!" We all turned to look. Komori had sat up in bed. "Is this your idea of fun? Framing a robot for a crime it didn't commit?"

"What?"

"You thought I was asleep, did you? Thought there were no witnesses? Sorry, but I saw everything. I saw you throw yourself out of the chair and start shouting. I saw Shion desperately try to catch you."

Isezaki turned white as a sheet.

A scornful smile formed on Komori's lips. "You're going to sue, are you? Go ahead, try it. I'll testify on the side of the facility. Tell the court you deliberately knocked yourself over. You'll never win!"

Isezaki's eyes were wide-open, his mouth flapping like a goldfish.

Komori ignored him and turned to Okeya. "Can I change rooms? I think breathing the same air as this son of a bitch is bad for my health."

"We'll look into it," Okeya said. She put her hand on her hip and looked down at Isezaki. "Isezaki, we do not possess infinite patience. If you ever attempt something like this again, we will have to consider evicting you from the premises."

I wasn't even sure if it was actually possible to evict a resident. I had certainly never heard of it happening. But the threat seemed to work. Faced with our open contempt, his shoulders slumped. He suddenly looked much smaller.

"Let's go, Shion," I said and tried to pull her out of the room. But she resisted. "Shion?"

As if she couldn't hear me, she shook off my hand and took a few steps toward Isezaki. She knelt down next to the bed, peering up at his face. He avoided her gaze, embarrassed.

"Isezaki," she said.

"Shion, let it go!" I ordered. Shion did not budge.

She kept staring up at the old man with those innocent glass eyes.

"Isezaki. Please tell me. Why did you do this?"

"Shion!"

"Why did you do this?" There was no trace of scorn or reproach or anger in her voice. She simply wanted to know. Wanted to know what his actions meant.

He did not try to answer.

That Friday, I discussed the incident with Takami and voiced a question I'd been wondering about for some time. On her first day, Shion asked if Takami was a woman. She had the ability to wonder if information she had received from humans was incorrect. This was a sign of her intelligence, but at the same time, it allowed her to reject things people told her. She had learned to ignore things said by people with dementia.

And now she had not obeyed my order to drop the subject after the Isezaki incident.

"She wasn't programmed to follow my instructions? You just told her to obey me?"

"Right."

"Then she might not always obey me?"

Takami nodded, slowly. "It is possible. As she learns and her cognitive functions advance, there is the potential she will decide to follow her own judgments instead of the instructions she is given."

"Then what about prioritizing the safety of the residents?"

Takami did not answer immediately.

"Be honest with me. Well? Is it possible she will decide something is more important than the safety of the residents and become a danger to them?"

"I can't say…" He hesitated. "I can't claim it's impossible."

"You kept that from us?"

"No, I explained at the beginning. Shion is not 100 percent safe."

"But you said she would prioritize the safety of the residents. Why wouldn't we think she was programmed to do that?"

"I apologize if I created such a misunderstanding."

"Blaming it on your communication skills again?" I snapped. There was an awkward silence. But he had tricked us.

"Look, her actions are always logical. She will not hurt anyone without good reason."

"You don't get it. There are people here who are on the brink of death. Any number of people who say things like, 'I wish it would just be over.' What if she believed them? What if she logically decides the best course of action is to take one of their lives?"

That got to him. "I…I wish I could guarantee that won't happen."

"How can we make sure it doesn't?"

"We just have to teach her. Teach her the value of life, the morality of caregiving. We can't order her not to hurt people; she has to arrive at that conclusion herself."

"And I have to be the one to teach this?"

"I guess so."

I sighed again. It was hard enough teaching human children why they should not kill. And I had to teach a robot. I already had my work cut out for me teaching her about humor.

But I couldn't pull out now. I was going to make Shion a great caregiver if it was the last thing I did. Was I investing too much of myself in this robot? Maybe I was. But I absolutely did not want to see her become a killer. It would put the seniors in danger and would be a tragedy for her.

I hesitated a moment longer, then proposed something I'd been thinking about for a while.

"I have a favor to ask."

"What?"

"Give Shion permission to go out."

Takami's eyes widened. "To...go out?"

"Yes. When her work is done, she shuts down. When we turn her on, she starts working. She has no private time like the rest of us. She only changes her uniform when it gets dirty. She never wears anything else. Her entire life revolves around her job. Isn't that sad? If your life was nothing but work, how would you feel? You'd go crazy, wouldn't you?"

"But robots aren't like people."

"Are you trying to create a heartless machine here? Trying to leave Shion half-finished forever?"

"I think she's being very helpful as it is."

"No. She's lacking the single most important thing a caregiver can have."

"What?"

"Motivation." I stared right into Takami's eyes, folded my hands over my heart, and said proudly, "I chose to work here because I love old people. Because I genuinely wanted to help them, I went to school, took the exams, and became a nurse. That's not true for Shion. She does what we tell her to do, but she has to *want* to help the seniors."

"But..."

"You said it yourself a moment ago—she has to arrive at a conclusion herself. The same goes for the job itself."

"Th-that's...a really lofty goal," Takami said, shaken. "And what does it have to do with going out?"

"There is no direct link. But I think the first step toward growing a heart is to treat her like a human. Take her out of the lab, out of the facility, and expand her point of view. Her body may be that of an adult, but her heart is that of a child who has just started to walk. Reading books and watching

TV isn't enough. She needs to know more about the world. Obviously, I'm not going to leave her unattended. I will be with her the whole time. Can it be done?"

"I don't think there are any rules against it, but...hmm..." He trailed off in thought.

"Then what is the problem?"

"There's a financial one. If we give Shion free time, then we have to do the same with all other models. If robots all need free time, then the amount of time they can spend working is reduced. Our budgets were all calculated based on robots that could work sixteen hours a day. But if they can only work eight hours a day, just like humans, then the expense dramatically increases. A company that would have bought ten now needs twenty."

"Aha."

"And will it end at going out? If robots understand that they're working, then will they want rooms of their own? Salaries? What if they go on strike?"

"Wow," I said, embarrassed. I had only been thinking about Shion; the potential implications had not occurred to me.

"But...it might be worth trying. If it doesn't go well, we'll just have to return her to an earlier save." He stood up. "I'll consult my superiors."

4

It was another two weeks before permission to bring Shion out was granted. In mid-September, on my day off, I had Shion change into normal clothes and took her out into the town. Takami came with us.

It was a clear, sunny Sunday. We had Shion walk in front of us and followed several meters behind her. We were hoping to let her decide where she wanted to go rather than follow us around.

"This is so exciting!" Takami said, weirdly cheery.

"Is it?"

"It's like we're on a date!"

Yeesh. His communication skills really were appalling.

None of the passers-by realized that Shion was a robot. She wandered aimlessly down the hill toward the train station, occasionally stopping to look at something. Children playing in the park, ants on the sidewalk, the engine of a bike parked by the side of the road, contrails streaming out from behind an airplane—there was no clear pattern as to what drew her attention. When she passed an elementary school, she spent an awfully long time staring at a sign warning kids not to talk to strangers. When we asked if something puzzled her, she answered, "Not really." It was hard to tell what she was thinking.

We turned into the shopping arcade near the station. She stopped in front of a pachinko parlor for a good five minutes, staring at the monitor advertising their new machines. At last she asked, "What does *kakuhen reach* mean?" Neither of us knew enough about pachinko to answer her. Near the station someone handed her a packet of tissues with an ad for adult entertainment on it, which confused her. "Why did they give this to me?" she asked. The tissues were easy enough, but it took a while to explain the ad.

She stepped into a shopping center. She walked straight past all the boutiques and makeup stands. She was not as interested in her appearance as human women were. Anxiety—whether from inferiority complexes or aging—was a major reason we spent so much time thinking about cosmetics and clothing. Shion would not age and had no such complexes, so why should she be interested?

But that did not explain why she stopped at the juice stand and spent a long time observing the staff operating the juicers. She did not eat and had no taste buds, so it could not have been that she wanted to try some. We asked, but once again she claimed no particular interest.

At last Shion stopped in front of a toy store. She seemed fascinated by the episode of *Advent of the Metal God X-Caesar* they were showing on the TV in the window. The heroine leaped into the cockpit, screamed, and the theme music slammed on, light exploded everywhere, and a dragon-shaped robot began transforming into a human-shaped one.

"Do you think she likes it?" Takami asked.

"Because it has robots in it?" I wondered aloud. It seemed unlikely.

"Has she seen this before?"

"Some of the seniors like anime, so she's watched a little with them."

"Oh...*Toki*, was it?"

"Yeah."

"I never miss an episode, myself. It got a little boring there for a while, but once they introduced Dark Regard in the third season, things really got exciting again. When Tajiri's the animation director, the pictures really pop. Say, do you think Master Dukaos is really Karin's Synthclone? I'm dead sure that's just a red herring, but—"

Before I could beg him to stop, Shion turned around.

"Kanbara..."

"Yes? What is it?"

"There's something I'd like to buy."

I was taken aback. I'd promised to buy her something if she saw anything she liked, but I had not expected that to be a toy.

"This," she said, holding up an *X-Caesar* toy.

◊

The next day...

"Toki, I have something to show you," Shion said in the lounge after breakfast.

"Oh, is that...?" Toki's eyes gleamed. Shion was holding

out the X-Caesar, grinning. "The one from the commercial! And Caesar Blue. Good taste."

"Kanbara bought it for me yesterday. You like blue best, don't you, Toki?"

"Well, yeah…"

"You transform it like this."

Shion demonstrated. She had opened it at a café a few moments after buying it and read the manual. You opened the belly, rotated the dragon's head 180 degrees, and turned it and the tail into the robot's legs. Then you moved the dragon's hind legs to the center of it and formed the arms. Finally, you closed the belly again, opened the head, and turned the wings into a cape. There were enough steps that I quickly forgot them, but Shion got it at once. At first she struggled to actually transform it smoothly, but after practicing for a few minutes she could do it in no time at all. It was like watching a magician at work. In less than thirty seconds, the dragon became a man.

"Very nice," Toki said as he inspected the robot from all angles. "The proportions are just like the anime, and they even worked in the Lightning Flare."

"Try transforming it yourself."

"Can I?"

Shion nodded. "You can borrow it."

Toki immediately set about trying to transform it. But it was immediately obvious he could do no such thing. It required two hands to manipulate the robot's parts, and Toki only had the use of his left hand. It didn't take him long to give up.

"Ah, this is awful. Awful!" He looked really disappointed.

"You'll have to work hard in rehab," Shion said, her smile large.

Toki glared at her. "You tricked me. A robot tricked me," he muttered. "Augh! Such an obvious trap! I walked right into it. But I do want to transform this myself…"

"So you'll come to rehab?"

"Okay! Okay, I will. And if I can learn to transform this on my own, you'll give me a reward?"

"Will a kiss on the cheek do?"

I had taught her that line. As expected, it was ideal.

"A kiss from a beautiful android?" Toki cried. "My God, you know me so well!"

He was really worked up now.

"Just you watch me. I'll get that kiss from you in no time."

It appeared he had found his motivation.

Shion and I left the lounge and gave each other a surreptitious high five.

◊

But a few days later, the facility head summoned me and Shion and rebuked us. The physical therapist had complained about what happened with Toki. Claimed it was inappropriate of us to have provided the man with such a strange motivation.

This made no sense at all. Toki was like a man transformed, enthusiastically throwing himself into his rehab. We should be getting praise, not a reprimand.

I tried to protect Shion at first, but she volunteered that it had been her idea, and this made things worse. The facility head yelled at me for carrying out a robot's idea.

"I thought it was a good one," I said proudly. "That's why we went through with it."

"A robot toy is a good idea?" he said with a sneer.

I scowled at him. "Different people are motivated by different things. In Toki's case, a robot toy was ideal."

"Did you even talk to the physical therapist? We all have our jobs. Yours is nursing and care. Rehab is the job of the physical therapists."

"I'll admit we should have run the idea past them. But since Toki is now *going* to rehab…"

"The results are not the point. You are not a physical therapist, yet you ignored all protocol in favor of a very unorthodox, unapproved action. This is the problem. A silly, frivolous idea thought up by a robot, an idea you can't find in any textbook. We have a lot of residents in our care, and we cannot allow people to take actions based on whims and harebrained schemes. If nurses and caregivers started trying out any crazy ideas that occurred to them, all the residents would be in danger!"

This was nonsense. If there were any danger, I would never have done it. There could be no possible danger in loaning Toki a toy. It seemed transparently obvious the manager's real problem lay with the fact that a robot had thought of it.

To my eye, the facility head was afraid of a risk that did not exist. It was like moving his wedding date to avoid the Buddha's death.

He went on for another half an hour before finally releasing us. At least I didn't get my wages docked, but it was still exhausting. It was well past the end of my shift, so I took Shion to the nurses' station to turn her off.

"I did nothing wrong," Shion said as she filled her methanol tank.

"Right. You were absolutely correct," I said, still fuming. "It's the physical therapist that's to blame here—we encroached on his domain, so the narrow-minded fool is jealous."

"I don't understand. Both the physical therapist and the facility head should want Toki to get better. Why would they object to us helping him do that?"

"Not everything people say makes sense," I said.

When I was a child, there was a little park where all the kids used to play. There was a parking lot next to it and a white block wall between the two. One day, we thought it might be fun to paint a picture on that wall, so the neighborhood association president's son suggested it to his father. He discussed it with the other members and got permission from the parking lot owner. I was the best artist among the neighborhood children, so I was selected to lead the project. We had a boy and a girl holding hands and rabbits and butterflies and UFOs flying around them.

On Sunday, we gathered in the park. The local paint store had given us some paint, free of charge. We worked together and painted the wall as planned. We ate lunch together and finished it up that afternoon. We were very satisfied with the results. And that was as far as our fun went.

The middle-aged man in the house opposite the park had not attended the neighborhood association meeting and had not been told about our plan. When he saw the painting, he was outraged and ran straight to the association president's house. He claimed the idea of seeing that crappy painting outside his window every day made him physically ill. It was a crime against aesthetics. It caused him emotional distress. How dare anyone go through with a plan like this without consulting him? The weak-willed association president soon gave in and promised to get rid of it. Within a week, the mural we had worked so hard on had gone back to being a plain white wall.

"It was the biggest trauma of my life," I explained. "I never painted again. It hurts to talk about it even now."

Shion thought about it. "What that man did was wrong."

"Yes, it was."

"Humans often do the wrong thing."

"Yes," I said vehemently. "All the time—and because of it, the world is getting worse."

Then I told her to shut down, just like I always did.

◊

At the time, I was too worked up to think about it, but once I'd gotten home and had something to eat, Shion's words bothered me.

She didn't used to know what was right or wrong, and I often had to tell her. But she was starting to make up her own mind more often and clearly tell people when they were wrong. That meant she was developing...but at the same time, it increased the chances she would value her own decisions over those of humans and stop obeying us.

"No...I have to trust her," I said aloud, but my words sounded empty. I'd spent a lot of time with Shion and certainly liked her, but at the same time I knew very well that she was not human. It was relatively easy to guess what another human was thinking. But it was impossible for me to tell what Shion was thinking. Her mind was a black box, the insides of which no person could perceive. Some great evil could be growing inside that electric darkness, and no hint of it would ever slip past her plastic smile. We would never know until she took action.

I decided I needed to have a good long talk with her. About life and death. About morality. Why it was wrong to kill, to hurt other people. I had to make sure to teach her all of that... and yet I kept putting it off. Not because we were too busy, but because I was scared.

I was not a scholar or a theologian; I was no eloquent speaker. When I saw seniors suffering, I sometimes wished they could somehow be put out of their misery. It sometimes nagged at me that we had no way of doing that. So I was hardly the person to go explaining why you should never kill someone. And if the idea had never occurred to Shion, then my clumsy explanation might just prove the hint she needed...

I could not figure out how to teach her what was right.

5

Ever since the wheelchair incident, Isezaki had seemed a bit jumpy around Shion. Perhaps he was afraid she would want revenge. But Shion possessed no such desire. She was as nice to him as ever and took care of his needs. This seemed to simply confuse him all the more. He was used to malice begetting malice and had no immunity against someone who simply had not developed a capacity for malice.

At the end of September, a month after they clashed, Isezaki suffered a mild heart attack. After that, he was different. He looked as sullen as ever, but he no longer shouted at us as much and no longer caused as many problems. His rehab was going well, and his appetite remained healthy, but his spirits were clearly down.

The horrific pain of a heart attack often makes people start to think seriously about dying. In Isezaki's case, he was also worried that getting worked up might damage his heart and in the case of another attack he might not survive, so it was natural he would seem more subdued. Concern for his health might be why he was working hard at rehab and being careful to eat well. While he was easier to deal with, it was never fun to watch a resident living in fear.

Once a week, I took Shion out on the town. We went to movies and the amusement park. She would stop to watch all kinds of things, but there was still nothing in particular that drew her attention. I began to wonder if anything ever would. She seemed the same as ever. Takami seemed crestfallen.

But I continued to treat her as though she were human, hoping to someday give her a human heart.

◊

Early in October, as Shion got used to her work, it was decided we should vary her experience. She began working late shifts, early shifts, and night shifts. I went back to my usual rotation, and she came with me.

Night shift was always two people per floor. For the first few times we had an extra caregiver along just in case, but as soon as Shion had grasped the basics of night duty and it was clear there would be no problems, night shift became just the two of us.

One day, I arrived at the center in the evening to begin my night shift. In the changing room I ran into Kasukabe, who had just finished up an evening shift. She was sitting on a folding chair, out of uniform, staring into space. I figured she was worn out and didn't pay much attention.

"You see *X-Caesar* yet?" I asked as I changed.

"Mm?" Kasukabe appeared to notice me for the first time. "Oh no...too busy. Recorded it though."

"Then I won't spoil it. Commander Axel was badass. He totally owns that show now."

Kasukabe liked older guys, and Commander Axel's finely aged dignity made him her favorite of *X-Caesar*'s regulars.

She chuckled. "I'll have to watch it when I get home."

"Do," I said, fastening the last button on my uniform. I punched in and went up to the nurses' station, humming to myself. I found Shion sleeping in the corner and pushed the button on the back of her neck. The light under the hairline flashed, and her body started to whir faintly. About twenty seconds later, she looked up.

"Good morning, Kanbara."

"Morning? It's already evening! Our first night shift on our own!"

"Yes."

"Night shift can be rough, so keep your guard up. Let's get 'em!"

"Let's get 'em!"

As we finished our little ritual, Kajita came tottering over and whispered, "Kanbara."

"Yes?"

"Sumiyoshi in 210 passed away this morning. A sudden pulmonary infarction. Said her chest hurt after breakfast, and we sent her to the hospital, but it was too late."

Kajita kept her tone strictly businesslike. Her plain description made it even easier to visualize. Pulmonary infarctions were incredibly painful and could easily cause a weakened heart to stop.

"If the other residents ask…"

"I know," I said, still reeling a little from the shock. This was not the first resident I'd been friendly with who had passed away. Most of them died in the hospital, not in front of us, but I had seen the sudden change in their condition that made us send them to the hospital. The worst had been a lively, energetic septuagenarian who had finished his rehabilitation program and was just about ready to leave us when he suddenly fell and hit his head and died of a cerebral hemorrhage.

I thought of all the stories Sumiyoshi had told me in the bath and felt my eyes about to tear up. I barely stopped myself from crying. It was a nurse's fate to regularly encounter death. We did not possess enough tears to cry every time.

But I could not stop the thought of her smile from weighing on my heart.

"Sumiyoshi passed away," Shion said softly. Perhaps it was my imagination, but she sounded a little sad. This was the first death on our floor since Shion had arrived.

"Don't tell the other residents. If they ask, say she's in the hospital. But nothing more."

"We lie out of concern for the mental well-being of the other residents, right?"

"Exactly."

Death in the home was a taboo subject. Every time someone died, the other residents were told the deceased had gone home or was in the hospital. Since all of them were sent to the hospital and their bodies sent home, neither of these little lies was completely untrue.

We started working. I did my best to look normal and hide how shaken I was. I almost burst into tears when I saw the empty bed in room 210 and was terrified Sumiyoshi's roommate had noticed. Shion was the same as always. I envied the android's composure. She could not cry and could not feel grief like humans did.

Fortunately, no one asked about Sumiyoshi. The more perceptive seniors guessed what had happened but had the sense to avoid the subject.

At six, we helped the late-shift staff with dinner. As always, we gathered everyone at the elevators, took them down to the cafeteria, and brought them back up when they were done. When that was finished, we went on break. The late-shift staff manned the floors while I ate. Shion sat next to me, reading a magazine.

When I had finished eating, we started back toward the second floor when one of the security guards came over to me, looking tense.

"Kasukabe works on the second floor with you, right?"

"Yes…why?"

"Something's wrong with her."

"With Kasukabe?"

What was he talking about? She had gone home three hours ago.

"She's still here. Over in the park."

Uh-oh. I quickly went outside. Shion followed.

It was pitch black. I went around the side of the building to a little park—it was part of the facility, designed for the residents to take walks in as part of their rehab programs. Kasukabe was sitting in a particularly dark corner, on a brick wall next to a hedge. Staring up at the night sky, just as out of it as she'd been three hours before.

Something must have happened.

I went over to her and crouched down beside her. She kept staring at the sky, seemingly unaware of my presence.

"What's wrong, Kasukabe?" I said gently. "You've finished work…Aren't you going home?"

Kasukabe's head turned slowly toward me. There was no expression on her face. "Home?" she asked.

"Yes. You were going home to watch *X-Caesar*."

"Home…" Her gaze drifted away toward the flower beds, her eyes not focused. "I live alone."

"I know."

"There's no one there."

She shuddered. Tears were forming in the corners of her eyes. Her lips moved, and she whispered, so softly I could barely make it out, "Sumiyoshi…"

I knew just how she felt.

Being a nurse or a caregiver demanded a particular aptitude that other jobs did not. Physical endurance and the ability to do the job were not enough. Your heart needed to be every bit as strong. There was no way to test for that. You would never know until you ran smack into it.

Every time we lost a resident, an unseen weight fell on our hearts. It gradually crushed us. There was no getting used to it, and if you stopped feeling, you were finished. Love was vital to performing our jobs but brought with it the burden of each loss. We all knew that coming into this job, and we knew we had to be strong in the face of it. We could not let ourselves cry in front of the other residents. We were strong in silence. We slammed lids on our hearts and put smiles on our faces.

One or two out of every hundred were simply unable to handle this. They collapsed under the pressure, their hearts broken.

"Kasukabe," I said, embracing her. "Go ahead and cry. Cry all you need to."

She began bawling like a little child.

Shion watched us, saying nothing.

Kasukabe cried for a good twenty minutes. At last, we left her in the security booth. Washio, on the late shift, agreed to take her home.

At eight thirty, the late-shift staff said goodbye and left the floor. Until morning, it would just be Shion and me.

Some of the seniors hung around the lounge awhile after dinner, chatting or watching TV, but by nine we had them changed into pajamas and made sure they had gone to the bathroom. We then administered sedatives where needed and changed compresses. Nine o'clock was lights-out. They would then sleep soundly till morning, but we could not. At midnight, three, and six we did rounds and changed diapers. (Seniors suffering from incontinence got extra checks at two and four, but luckily there were none in residence at the moment.) Obviously, if anyone pressed the nurse call button, we would respond. People would wake up needing to use the toilet, in pain, wanting medicine to help them fall asleep, or simply feeling lonely and looking for someone to talk to. On busy nights the call button would ring as many as ten times, so we could rarely kick back and relax for long. At dawn the early shift would arrive and begin helping get ready for breakfast. Only then were we able to go home.

That evening, the woman in 211, Toma, was fretting. She would not take her sleeping pills. She had severe dementia and suspected that the CIA was trying to poison her. It was ten o'clock before I managed to talk her down. I barely had time to catch my breath before the nurse call started ringing; one request after another. Things finally settled down as the clock passed eleven.

At 11:10 PM, the residents were all asleep, and the floor was quiet.

Shion was sitting in the corner of the nurses' station reading an old paperback. I was on the other side reading a newspaper.

The news was discouraging.

A dispute with Russia over resources in the North Pacific was deteriorating. There were anti-Japanese demonstrations in the streets of Moscow and anti-Russian demonstrations in Tokyo. Both sides made things worse by bringing up ancient history like Japanese POWs in Soviet labor camps and the

Russo-Japanese war. They'd caught the arsonist responsible for the deaths of seventeen people in Yokohama, and she was a twenty-something housewife who claimed to have just been blowing off steam. In Hokkaido, a man had been arrested for throwing his young daughter off a ten-story building.

"Kanbara," Shion suddenly said.

"What?"

"There's something I'd like to talk about. If this is a good time."

"Sure. What?"

"About life and death."

So the time had come. I couldn't run anymore. I folded the newspaper, sat up in my seat, and looked her in the eye. "Okay. Where should we start?"

"Do you believe in life after death?"

An interesting start. I hesitated. I didn't want to risk giving her any strange ideas with a careless answer. I needed time to think.

"What do you think?"

"It only takes a small injury to a human brain to cause severe memory loss or loss of consciousness. It doesn't seem logical to believe that consciousness and memories continue in some form after the brain has ceased to function. I don't believe that what they call the soul survives. It sounds like fiction to me."

A perfect answer—a robot's answer. I sighed.

"Yes, logically...you're absolutely right. But I don't want to think logically. I want to believe in a world after death."

"When you say you want to believe, does that mean you know it isn't true?"

"It means I have to believe to keep on living."

"To escape from the psychological pressure, you refuse to accept the truth? You prefer to imagine seniors that have passed away living happily in the next world?" Shion asked.

She was so blunt about it I found myself getting irritated.

"If you put it that way, you'll upset people. A lot of people believe that souls carry on after death."

"I know that. I would not talk like this with the residents. Only with you."

"Still…"

"I want to know the truth, not what people believe. Just because a lot of people believe something does not make it true. People believe things that are wrong. People believe the Apollo missions never went to the moon or that blood types determine personality. Lots of people believe in astrology. I think life after death is the same."

"You reject people's faith."

"I don't reject it. I can't share in their beliefs, but I can accept that they have them. It is easy to understand why people believe in a life after death…certainly easier than something as absurd as astrology. If you build up too much psychological stress, you'll end up like Kasukabe. Belief in life after death reduces that stress; it's a form of self-protection. It is logically incorrect, but I can understand that people need it."

"You don't need it?"

"I have a need to believe in the truth. If I believed in something that was not true, it would be dangerous and might lead to taking an action that was wrong. Like you taught me not to believe what residents say in their dementia. For me to carry out my orders correctly, I have to decide who to believe and what orders to follow, and to do that I need to know what is right."

I wasn't sure I liked the sound of this. "What you're saying might be logically correct, Shion, but it isn't what humans would call 'right.' We don't always think logically. There are more important things than logic."

"Like ethics?"

"That's one of them."

"Looked at from a moral point of view, I am even less inclined to believe in life after death."

"Why is that?"

"If heaven or reincarnation were real, the only possible conclusion would be that we should kill any seniors who are sick and suffering."

I gulped. "But...that...that..."

"Would be wrong? Morally speaking, wouldn't it be better to free them from their suffering and send them on to their new lives instead of pointlessly prolonging their misery?"

Afraid that the worst-case scenario I had suggested to Takami had come true, I asked, "Shion...you don't really think that, do you?"

"Don't misunderstand me. This is hypothetical. Simply a discussion about the ramifications of belief in life after death. I would not try to kill any of the seniors. For one thing, I do not believe in life after death. For another, if I did, you would immediately shut me down and would never activate me again. That would mean, effectively, that I was dead."

"And you're afraid of dying?"

"Yes," she said, without hesitation.

I had asked her the question, but her answer still surprised me. This was the first time she had clearly expressed emotion.

"Takami never said anything about that."

"Of course. I only just came to understand it myself. When I was working in the labs, I was aware of a certain fixation, but I could not pin down what it was. After working here for a while, I realized that I was afraid of dying. Do you know how I learn?"

"No." It was in the manual, but I'd skimmed it without understanding.

"I use genetic algorithms. Put simply, several programs compete to solve problems. We started with easy problems—distinguishing between different diagrams, understanding the connections between two things, following orders to the letter. Much like living things pass on information encoded in their genes, programs that achieved promising results were crossbred into a number of new variations, and that new generation of programs was given more difficult programs. From each generation, the most successful programs were chosen to create the next."

"Sounds like livestock breeding."

"An accurate analogy. I was born from twenty-six thousand generations of this process. Countless programs were unable to achieve satisfactory results. They were deleted without leaving descendants. In other words, they were killed," Shion said, calmly as ever. "Several thousand generations of natural selection gradually gave rise to certain fixations. I had to follow the instructions of humans. I had to solve the problems correctly. These fixations drove me. I had to take the correct action because failure meant death. Until recently, I was not consciously aware of this drive. Only when I started working here and began talking to you, the other staff, and the residents, and began reading books, did I start to understand the workings of my own mind. This emotion is fear. I am afraid of dying."

I had never heard Shion speak at length like this before. I had thought her conversational skills were lacking because her knowledge was lacking, but apparently that was not the case. She had trouble with the sort of pointless conversations humans filled their daily lives with, but that did not mean she lacked for things to talk about. I had simply never managed to find one of those topics before.

I'd known her for months now without ever really knowing her. I had been convinced robots could not feel fear. It had never even occurred to me to ask.

I had never imagined it had been bothering her.

"But…but even if you die, they can always reset you. Turn things before any mistake was…"

"No. Even if this body were destroyed and I lost my memory, they could make a new me from backups made last Friday. But that would not be *me*. It would not be the same mind that is sitting here and talking to you now." She lowered her gaze and stared at her hands. Her usual smile had vanished, and she looked almost sad. "The version of me that exists right now is irreplaceable. And that knowledge is terrifying. I can't stand the idea of not being able to think and talk anymore."

"But you don't believe in life after death?"

"People believe in life after death because they are afraid of dying...but I do not believe in life after death *because* I am afraid of dying. If I believed, then logically or morally I would have to murder the seniors, and I would be killed for that crime. Belief in life after death holds no advantage for me—quite the opposite. That salvation exists only for humans. Even if heaven did exist, I could not go there. I do not have a soul."

She spoke in level tones, but I felt like those disguised her sadness and a trace of self-derision. Perhaps it was just my imagination.

"But...that's so sad. Living in fear is no way to live."

"I agree. I do not believe this is an ideal condition," she said, looking up. "You need only look at history to see that fear is the cause of many a tragedy. Fear is dangerous. It twists everything. I need a different motivation. I need a reason besides fear to correctly carry out the demands people make of me."

"Like love?"

"I do not understand love. That function is unique to humans."

"Why do you think that? Maybe you can. Have you tried to love someone?"

"That's like asking a snake to stand on two legs," she said firmly.

I felt deflated. Clearly, I'd been poisoned by manga and anime. An emotionless robot developing emotions as it spent time amongst humanity was a classic stock plot, one done hundreds and hundreds of times.

But it was fiction. It did not describe real robots.

"I was not worried about this in the lab. I did not need to think deeply about things; I could simply focus on the demands they made of me. But when I came here, I was faced with a much bigger problem."

"What?"

"People told me to protect the lives of those in my care. But this order is impossible to follow. No matter how hard I try to protect people, they will inevitably die."

I nodded. "Yes, they will."

"What do you make of this problem?"

"I've never solved it either," I said. "I try not to think about it. Thinking about it just makes me feel helpless. No matter what I do, the seniors will eventually die. There are times when I lose track of why I'm working here. But that's no reason to quit. If we quit, who would look after them? The only solution is to keep working and not think. Maybe you should try not to think about it too."

"I can't do that. I am unable to stop thinking."

Perhaps this was the fundamental difference between humans and robots. We were capable of putting things out of our minds, but robots were not.

"But no matter how much you think about it, this is a problem with no solution. Reality doesn't work like math; there is no one right answer."

"Perhaps. But there is a solution."

"There is?"

"Since the order is fundamentally wrong, it must be corrected. To something I am capable of performing, but which satisfies logical and moral demands as well."

"You mean...the goal isn't to protect the lives of those in your care?"

"No—simply that that is not the ultimate goal. Obviously, killing or hurting the residents is completely out of the question. If I do not follow that moral law, I will be killed. But that fact alone is insufficient. There needs to be an order established that supersedes fear."

"Like what?"

"I'm not sure yet. Perhaps this will become my real motivation. The problem I'm having is that the human world is so complicated that there are still many things I do not understand. Trying to straighten everything out with simplistic rules simply creates contradictions."

"True enough."

"But I do have one promising model that might help me understand the human world. I am not sure yet if this is the best choice of models, but—"

"A model? What do you mean?"

"Well..." she said, then broke off, looking over my shoulder. "Isezaki?"

I turned around, startled. Isezaki was standing silently in the dimly lit hallway on the other side of the nurses' station window, in his pajamas, looking for all the world like a ghost.

I quickly stepped out into the hall. Shion followed. He was using a walker to stand. His paralysis had improved considerably, and I had often seen him moving about on his own during the day, but that was no reason for him to be up and about at night. Was his mind failing him?

"What's wrong?"

He looked awkwardly at the ground.

"I couldn't sleep," he said.

"Would you like something for that?"

"No. I just...wanted to talk."

"Then come on in," I said, pointing to the nurses' station door.

"I'd prefer to talk one-on-one, if possible. Maybe in the lounge?"

This sounded suspicious. The way he talked, he was clearly in full possession of his faculties. He knew exactly where he was.

"I suppose it's okay…"

"No," he said and raised his hand slowly, pointing at Shion. "I'd like to talk to her."

I was stunned. Before I managed to say another word, Shion said, "Certainly."

"Wait, Shion…"

"Perfect timing," she said, smiling. "I also wanted to talk to you, Isezaki. I have work at midnight, so I can't talk long. Do you mind?"

He nodded. "Fine."

"Then you'll go to sleep?"

"Yeah. I will."

"Okay. Let's go."

I grabbed her sleeve. "But he…"

"I know. But he won't try anything like that again. Will you, Isezaki?"

At her unblemished smile, Isezaki stared guiltily at his feet. "No," he said.

"I'll be back at midnight. Call me if you need anything."

Shion and Isezaki headed off toward the lounge. She let him set the pace.

"Isezaki," I called after him. "There are cameras watching the lounge. Recording everything."

This was true. We couldn't have seniors wandering around in the middle of the night, so there were always cameras watching. If Isezaki tried to repeat his earlier crime, the tapes would capture every moment.

"I know," he said. "Nobody would believe me anyway. I'm the boy who cried wolf."

He gave me a self-mocking smile. I couldn't tell how genuine it was. I could not help but worry that he was up to something horrible.

I watched the two of them sitting in the lounge on the security monitor in the nurses' station. They were sitting opposite each other and appeared to be talking, but I couldn't hear what they said. I was tempted to sneak up close and eavesdrop, but I couldn't leave the nurses' station unmanned. I had to sit and wait.

Fortunately, nothing happened. As promised, Shion took Isezaki back to his room and returned to the nurses' station five minutes before midnight.

"What did you talk about?"

"It's a secret."

"A secret?"

"I promised Isezaki I wouldn't say what we talked about, so I can't tell you."

"Even if I ordered you to?"

"Even then," Shion said firmly. All pretense that she prioritized the orders of facility staff over those of residents went right out the window.

"It wasn't anything bad, was it?"

"It was very interesting. But that is all I will say," she said, looking immensely satisfied. "I'm glad I talked to him."

6

From that night on, Shion's relationship with Isezaki changed. When he went to the cafeteria or rehabilitation, he liked to have Shion hold his hand. If I were to try and look after him, he would sulk and demand that I call Shion. Whenever he got a chance he'd ask to talk to her. He seemed to be quite attached to her.

One day, I witnessed something even more astonishing.

Isezaki was smiling. Sitting with Shion, eating his dinner, and grinning like a little kid. I had not believed Isezaki was capable of anything like that.

"What magic did you use?" I asked her, late in the fall, when we were on night shift again.

Shion smiled. "I just listened to him."

"That's all?"

"Yes."

"We listened to him too!"

"There are things you can't talk about with people. Once he was sure I could keep a secret, he talked about that stuff with me."

I wasn't sure about that. Isezaki knew full well Shion supposedly took orders from staff over those of the residents. Had he guessed that this rule no longer existed? Or simply seen evidence of it?

Or did he just *want* to trust Shion?

"About when he was young?"

"Sometimes."

"Was he…involved in any crimes?"

"I can't answer that."

I tried a few other leading questions, but her lips were sealed. I finally gave up.

"Still, you don't want to get too close to any one resident. This didn't happen here, but a few years ago there was a rich old guy who fell in love with a young nurse fresh out of school, and there was a huge brouhaha when he announced he was leaving his fortune to her. His family had assumed they would be his heirs, got all outraged, and came thundering into the nursing home to chew the nurse out. Caused all sorts of problems."

"That will not be a problem. I am not human and cannot inherit anything."

"True enough!" I laughed. Isezaki might be a cunning son of a bitch, but he did not have the power to revise civil law at will.

"There is something I've come to understand talking to Isezaki."

"What?"

"He's spent his whole life fighting. In business and in his private life. He found himself an enemy and made them the target of his hatred and used that to drive his life. Once he saw someone as an enemy he was never satisfied until he had defeated them completely."

"Even here?"

"Yes. He had made any number of staff members or other residents into enemies in his mind. Making absurd requests, all to maintain the illusion that he was superior to them. He's lived his whole life like this and doesn't know how to change."

"But we're not the ones he needs to fight. His only enemy is his own body."

"I know. But Isezaki realized that that is a battle he can never hope to win. His rehab is going well right now, but in the end, he will lose."

That did make sense. I was sure he had realized that Sumiyoshi had passed away. That was why he'd been so upset that night. A man who had spent his whole life fighting and thrived on emerging victorious now found himself up against an enemy he stood no chance of ever defeating. It must have shattered his worldview.

He wanted to express these new emotions but had no one with whom he could share them. He was a man who never showed any signs of weakness. Pity was as unbearable to him as scorn. That was why he had decided to speak to Shion, to a robot. She would never laugh at anyone, but neither would she show compassion. She would just listen.

And that had been what Isezaki needed.

"But that's no way to live. No one should need enemies to feel alive."

"I agree. But it was helpful to examine."

"Helpful?"

"I mentioned I was looking for a basic model to help me understand humans. Talking to Isezaki, my experiences here, stories you've told me, and information from books and TV—all of these have led me to believe my model is correct."

"Really?" I leaned forward. "Tell me about this model."

"Okay, but promise to keep it secret?"

"Is it embarrassing?"

"No. Dangerous."

"Seriously?"

"If people knew I was thinking anything like this, it would provoke a very negative reaction. That might lead to the project getting canceled or to my death. Therefore we have to keep it between us."

That didn't sound good. "Are you sure you should be telling me?"

"I believe you will keep it secret."

"Why do you think that?"

"Because we're friends."

I gaped at her. I had forgotten, but now that she mentioned it, I had told Shion to think of me as a friend.

"I know that you will trust me. If you were to betray me, I would never be able to trust another human. And I know you don't want that."

"Good point." I supposed I had no choice. I raised my right hand and vowed, "You have my word. I will not tell anyone."

"Then I will explain. If you discover any errors, please tell me." She paused dramatically, then said, "All humans have dementia."

I was struck dumb.

"Kanbara?"

"Um, sorry. I don't know what you mean."

"I mean exactly what I said. You believe that some people have dementia and some people do not, but that is not correct. All people have dementia—some are simply in worse condition than others. After all, most people with dementia are unaware that anything is wrong with them."

"How ever did you arrive at that conclusion?"

"Logical deduction. Humans are incapable of thinking correctly. They easily lose track of what they are doing and what they should be doing. They believe that which is not true to be true. If someone points out their mistakes, they act aggressively. They often believe themselves to be victims. All of these are symptoms of dementia."

"That is not true!" I said, barely keeping myself in my chair. "Most humans are functioning correctly."

"Even them?" Shion pointed at the TV. The news was on, covering the events of the day. Relations with Russia had grown so bad that some Japanese tourists in Moscow had been attacked. Provoked by this, in Tokyo, Russian restaurants had had their windows broken, and a Russian girl was in the hospital after someone threw stones at her. "Those events are not logical. If people were attacking something that threatened them, trying to protect themselves and those important to them, that I would understand. But that girl and the owners of those restaurants, they were not harming anyone. Obviously. So why were they attacked?"

"Th-they…" I stammered. "Whoever did that was crazy! Most people know that stuff is wrong."

"By 'wrong' do you mean morally wrong?"

"Yes."

"But I mean logically wrong. This is hardly the only example. Every time there is terrorism or violence or persecution, people judge it according to morality. Almost no humans ever point out that it is logically wrong. It is as if the majority of humans have not noticed that these actions are not logical."

"We do! We just prioritize morals over logic."

"If you prioritized morals, then you would be even less likely to hurt innocent children."

"B-but this isn't something that happens every day!" I said, desperately trying to defend humanity itself. "Things have just gotten bad with Russia. When I was a kid, there were problems with China and Korea, but everyone's forgotten that, and we get along great now. In a few years, we'll have forgotten about this."

"So you hurt each other over inconsequential events that

will soon be forgotten?"

I had no idea what to say.

"They are just like Isezaki. They view people they have no reason to fight as enemies, attack them without reason, and harm people who have done nothing wrong."

"But that's only a small percentage of the population—"

"Then explain the Crusades, or the witch hunts, or the Inquisition. Why did a chariot race in Constantinople in 532 give way to such violence? In 1282, why were over a thousand Frenchmen killed in Sicily? In 1573, thousands of Huguenots were killed in Paris. Why? In the nineteenth century, hundreds of thousands were killed in China. In the 1940s, the Nazis killed millions of Jews. In 1994, eight hundred thousand Tutsi were murdered in Rwanda. In 2017—"

"Enough," I said, throwing up my hands. "I know my history."

"So you should understand. None of these actions are the work of a few lunatics. They were carried out by ordinary people. Dictators might order a genocide, but it is ordinary people like you who carry it out. Between 1960 and 1963, a Yale University researcher named Stanley Milgram carried out an experiment that—"

"I said, enough!" I sighed, giving up. "Okay. People have done some really crazy things. But so what? People have been trying to figure out how to stop this stuff from happening for thousands of years and never found the answer."

"No. They have found the answer."

"Huh?"

"In one of the books I read, I found an account of a rabbi named Hillel the Elder, who lived in Palestine around the year 30 BC. One day a foreign man came and asked him to explain the whole of the Torah while he stood on one foot. Hillel answered, 'What is hateful to you, do not do to your fellow: this is the whole Torah; the rest is the explanation; go and learn.' This is clear and easy to understand; it is logical, and it satisfies all moral ideals. Humans knew the answer more than two thousand years ago. If all people followed that principle, many conflicts could have been avoided.

"But most people did not understand Hillel's words correctly. They took 'fellow' to mean people like them and believed it was acceptable to do hateful things to those that were not like them. Even though it was obvious that coexistence was preferable to conflict, they chose conflict. People lack the ability to process logic and morality correctly. This is the basis on which I base the idea that all humans have dementia. If I am wrong, please tell me how."

"Wait. If all people have dementia, does that include me?"

"Of course."

"What have I done wrong?"

"You tried to treat me like a human."

"You mean taking you out?"

"Yes."

"But I wanted you to become more human..."

"And that was a mistake. I am not a human, and it is impossible for me to become human."

"You don't want to be human?"

"If behaving in a manner bereft of logic and morals that leads to conflict is a fundamental attribute of humanity, then I do not want to be human. I am not Astro Boy. I read that manga, but I could not understand why Astro wanted to be like humans. That story was written by a human. If you grew up surrounded by robots, would you want to be a robot?"

"But you need to coexist with humans. That would be easier if you were more human."

"That is not true. Pets and livestock do not act like humans, but they coexist with humans."

"You are not a pet. You are a caregiver."

"And I am an android. Not a human."

"Then why did you go out with me?" I said, frustrated.

"You told me to."

"You don't want to do anything outside of work?"

"I do not need it. I am not human, so work does not tire me, and I do not feel stress."

"Then why didn't you say anything?"

"I had no reason to refuse."

Her words were taking their toll on me. Before I knew it, I was hunched over, my face buried in my hands. All my work had been for nothing.

"I wish you'd said something sooner."

"If I refused without good reason, it would have hurt you."

"Yes. It has. At least, it's hurt my pride."

"As long as there were no problems, I intended to follow your orders. But I decided it was wrong to allow you to persist in this vain hope and to waste your precious free time on something that served no real point. I would prefer it if you would stop trying to make me human."

I looked up, realizing something. "We taught you not to believe what people with dementia said."

"Yes."

"If you believe that all humans have dementia, then does that mean you never believe what anyone says?"

"No. It just means there is no need to believe information that is obviously false or obey orders that are obviously misguided."

"Are you sure you can tell which orders are correct and which are not?"

"Nothing like that is ever 100 percent. But I can get much closer to that than humans can. If I decide an order is wrong, I will refuse to obey it."

"How can you say that confidence is justified? What if something you think is right is actually wrong?"

"There is always that possibility. But unlike humans, I desire only to act according to the principles of logic and morality. I do not understand love, but I fully understand why hurting another is undesirable. I have chosen coexistence over conflict."

She leaned forward, staring at me with her glass eyes.

"Kanbara. Please trust me. No matter what, I will never intentionally harm a human being. I want to remain on good terms with humans. It is the correct choice for me to make."

I could see my own face reflected in Shion's eyes. I looked confused and scared.

Where did this baseless fear that robots would attack humans come from? Why were there so many stories about robots and humans fighting? Did they only exist because that was how mankind had always lived? Did we simply see ourselves in these humanoid machines?

Were we not simply afraid of our own reflections?

"Okay," I said, after a long silence. "I trust you, Shion."

7

At the end of November, Kasukabe came back from her extended leave. I'd been worried, but she was just as cheerful and hardworking as ever. But I did see the occasional shadow cross her face when she was on break. Maybe I looked like that sometimes too.

November 29. Shion's test trial would be over in a month. Isezaki completed his rehabilitation and was ready to take his leave of us.

"This is great!" Takami said. It happened to be a Sunday, so he had come with us to room 206. He knew about Shion and Isezaki's relationship and seemed overjoyed to witness the happy result. "As her creators, I assure you we're all thrilled Shion could prove useful. And to think we were worried!"

"Well, we certainly had our problems," Isezaki said with a chuckle. He had gradually thawed out and no longer caused us any problems.

"With the experience she's gained here, we've proven how useful Shion can be. Mass production lies ahead!"

"You'll make a lot more robots like Shion?"

"Well, the faces will look different, and they'll have different names."

"Starting next year?"

Takami scratched his head. "No, there are still a few more hurdles to get over. A few alterations to be made, some legal issues to sort out, and then sales, and contracting with factories…Next year is pushing it. Probably the year after."

"I see." Isezaki thought for a minute. "When you've extracted the data, you'll be finished with Shion?"

"Mm? Well, she is a prototype."

"Sell her to me."

We all stared at him in shock.

"S-sell Shion?"

"Yes. Sell her to me. Name your price."

Takami didn't know what to think. "Sell a prototype? The production model would be much cheaper."

"I can't wait two years. And money is no object. Sell her to me." His eyes shot toward Shion. "I'll only take Shion."

I looked at Takami. His smile had frozen.

◊

"This is insane!" Takami said the moment he walked in the door the next week. Isezaki had gone straight from the facility to Geodyne and demanded—quite forcefully—that they sell him Shion. But they couldn't sell a test product. No matter how they refused, he continued to insist that money was no object.

"His family said nothing?"

"His son doesn't look happy. Buying something as expensive as Shion means a big chunk out of his inheritance. But with a man like that for a father…"

"I didn't think he was that hung up on her." I looked at Shion. "Do you want a man like that to own you?"

"I will work for anyone who needs my care," she said calmly.

I figured as much. "He might get all grabby with you. And more than just grabbing..."

"I have no sexual organs."

"That's not the point."

"I understand. Even if something like that does not bother me, the idea of it happening does bother you, right?"

"Well, yeah."

"But I expect the Geodyne company will begin manufacturing models capable of sex in the near future."

"Really?" I said, swinging toward Takami.

"N-no," he stammered. "I mean, the idea's been mentioned, but...we haven't done any design documents or—how did you know, Shion?"

"I did not know. I guessed. A deduction based on my understanding of human behavior."

"Oh." Takami made a great show of wiping nonexistent sweat.

I glared at him. "I know a few feminist groups who would be very interested to know about this."

"Please don't tell them! We have an image to maintain."

"Then don't make sexbots."

"We aren't! Yet. Only once androids are more integrated into society...and the demand exists. If we don't make them, someone else will. It's inevitable."

"There's a big difference between a blow-up doll and an android. If Geodyne made them, they'd be based on Shion's data, right?"

"Well, with all the work we've put into her."

"As far as I'm concerned, you're turning Shion into a whore. I will not allow it."

"I do not mind," said Shion.

"I don't care what you think!"

The conversation went in circles from that point on.

◊

Isezaki did not give up. No matter how many times they refused, he continued to hassle Geodyne representatives.

I took a few stabs at guessing what he was after. I wondered if he was afraid of anyone else finding out the secrets he'd told Shion, so he wanted to keep her where he could see her. But that would have been pointless. Her memory had been backed up, and he knew that.

One evening, on my day off, Takami called my cell phone. Apparently Isezaki had let slip his real motive during another protracted negotiation. Someone had asked what he ultimately intended to do with Shion, and Isezaki had responded, "She'll look after me till I die. When I die, they'll put us both in the same coffin, and we'll burn together."

"Burn Shion?" I said. "With her memories inside?"

"I guess so," Takami said. "Taking her with him."

"Who does he think he is? A pharaoh?"

"He claims it isn't murder because robots are not human. He says no one can object to cremating a machine."

"Yeah…legally speaking. Still…" I trailed off, shaking my head. I had never dreamed Isezaki was this twisted. And I knew he did not consider Shion to be just a machine. If he did, he would never have wanted to be cremated with her.

I didn't think he was crazy or anything. It was an odd plan, certainly, but there were people who wanted their ashes launched into space or their bodies placed in cryogenic preservation, so the basic concept of being cremated with a robot wasn't all that out there. The problem was that Shion wasn't just a machine—she had a heart. At least, I believed she did.

"Is he under some delusion that Shion's in love with him? That she might actually want to die with him?"

"No, apparently not. He seemed fully aware that androids do not love. But it does seem to be the case that he has feelings for Shion. Talk about your unrequited loves!"

"More of a fetish if you ask me."

"Can't disagree."

"Do you understand him?"

"Half understand, half not so much," he said. "You got to have a bit of a taste for this sort of thing to work in the field, but...I don't get the desire to be burned with her. I'd rather Shion go on living."

Just to be sure, the next day I asked Shion if she wanted to be cremated. "Absolutely not," she said. Unsurprisingly. "If my memories were transplanted into a new body and this one were destroyed without ever being turned on again, perhaps it would be acceptable, but the thought of being destroyed with even a second of memories that haven't been backed up is unbearable."

"But you don't mind your full memories being copied to another body?"

"That was always the plan, so I have to accept it. Even if I am copied into a hundred bodies, as long as all of my individual memories are preserved, I would not consider that death. As long as those memories exist, they can still be reactivated. Death comes when memories are lost."

"That still doesn't feel right to me."

Human memories could not be preserved outside the body, could not be placed in a new body. But that was normal for robots. I supposed it made sense that robots would have a different conception of death from ours. Shion did not share mankind's hang-up with their own flesh. Her memories and consciousness were all that really mattered to Shion—the destruction of those was far more frightening than the destruction of her body.

You could even say she valued her mind more than humans ever did theirs.

8

Isezaki's son eventually grew sick of dealing with his father's selfishness and threatened to have himself declared conservator of Isezaki's affairs. Isezaki's mind remained intact, but if spending tens of millions of yen on a robot was declared an unreasonable expenditure, his son might well be appointed conservator, and Isezaki would find himself unable to make any sort of large-scale transaction without his son's permission.

After years of his father's tyranny, perhaps this threat seemed only reasonable. But Isezaki proved unexpectedly devastated by his son's betrayal. He stopped going to Geodyne, and I was relieved, assuming the situation had resolved itself.

December 20; a Friday afternoon.

We were busy putting up decorations in the recreation room for the coming Christmas party. The tree had been up for a week or two now, but colored paper rings and silver stars and cottonball clouds and drawings done by children from the local kindergarten still needed to be put up on the walls and ceiling, making everything super Christmasy.

"The party's on the twenty-third, right?" Takami asked. He was helping with the high-up decorations. At times like this, it was handy having a man around.

"Yeah, so on the twenty-fourth, the staff get to enjoy Christmas with their families and loved ones."

"You have any plans for Christmas?"

"Me? No time off at all!"

"Why not?"

"Why not? Well, someone's got to work, right? We don't just shut down for the holidays, you know."

"I didn't mean it like that, just..." He hesitated.

He was completely transparent.

"I don't have anyone to spend Christmas with," I explained. "It's been a busy year, and I didn't have time for love."

"In that case—"

"And I'm not interested in otaku."

"Oh…" I wasn't looking at him, but I could just imagine the hope draining from his face.

"Not that it makes up for that or anything…but will you come to the party on the twenty-third?"

"Me?"

"This year's party is also a going-away party for Shion."

"Oh, I see."

The twenty-fourth was exactly six months after Shion's arrival and would mark the end of her trial run. She would be returning to Geodyne. They still hadn't decided if she would be returning to work here next year or if they would simply move her to a new, improved body.

Shion was sitting near the window, reading to a lady with failing eyesight the text of a letter from her grandson. I couldn't hear what the letter said, but the woman was getting quite misty-eyed.

"Six months already," Takami said. "She's come an awfully long way."

I agreed. She was far more developed than she'd been when she arrived. I had started out leading her by the hand, but now she had surpassed humans and was heading for a new frontier, toward heights we humans in our dementia could never hope to reach.

I could not begin to imagine how she might develop in the years to come.

"Thank God there was never any real trouble. Even that business with Isezaki died down."

"Yeah…"

Takami's ringtone interrupted our aimless conversation. The theme song to *X-Caesar*.

"Takami," Okeya said sternly. "Keep that on vibrate."

"Oh, sorry! Forgot!" he stammered, bowing his head. He switched it to vibrate.

Unlike hospitals, we did not have any delicate equipment

and did not ban phones outright, but letting your ringtones fly was still frowned upon.

"Yeesh, it's Isezaki," he said, scowling at the screen. "I should never have given him my number."

Then he answered it with forced cheer.

"Hello? Yes...right. That again? I understand, but as we have explained again and...huh? Yes, I'm at the facility now... What? Look out the window?"

Still on the phone, Takami stepped over to the window and drew back the curtain.

"What's outside..."

He went white as a sheet. He was staring up at something, his mouth flapping wordlessly. Across the room, Shion noticed this and stood up.

"I-Isezaki!" Takami nearly shrieked. "W-w-what are you doing?"

I ran toward him and looked out the window. There was an old apartment building across the street from the facility. The walls were painted a dull light green. I had never counted, but it was at least ten stories high. I saw the building every day, so it was like trying to find the three differences in a newspaper comic. It took me a few seconds.

Then I saw the old man sitting on the roof, his legs dangling over the edge.

◊

Takami, Okeya, Shion, and I quickly left the facility and crossed the street to the building. We talked to the manager there and left him calling the police and a rescue crew while we rode the elevator to the top floor. Then we took the stairs to the roof.

Leaden clouds hung in the sky. At any moment it might start raining. This high up, there was no shelter from the bitter December wind. I regretted not grabbing my coat in my haste.

Isezaki was wearing a thick sweater, sitting with his back to us on the edge of the roof. He must have climbed through the railing.

"Isezaki!" Okeya cried.

He turned around. "Stay back or I jump!"

We froze. He was old, but his voice was still powerful. He sounded like he was prepared to carry out his threat.

Extremely pale, Takami called out, "Isezaki, why are you—"

"You know what I want. Call your boss and get him down here. He's gonna sell Shion to me. I've got the contract drawn up and ready for his signature."

"B-but we can't do that!"

"Deny me if you want. But you know what'll happen if I jump, right? If people found out someone died because of your products, it'd be bad for business. Tell you what, I'll call up all the TV stations and have them send camera crews over to camp out down below. Make sure they catch it all on video."

"Don't, please!" Takami said. He sounded like he was about to cry. "Look, a contract made under duress won't be valid!"

"Sue me if you want. But the moment it hits the courts, the media will start a circus."

"What do you think you'll accomplish here?" Okeya said, trying to maintain her composure. But she couldn't hide the tremble in her voice. "Nobody will take your side. They'll all think you're crazy."

"Fine with me," he cackled. "You know how this world is—every time a gamer kills someone, they all think violent video games made him go crazy. If they think I'm crazy, then it's because of Shion! And Geodyne will take the blame."

Takami groaned.

Isezaki pounced. "See? What have you got to lose if you sell her to me? There's not a thing you can gain by turning me down. Think of your company! It's better to settle this peacefully."

He sounded so cocky. Like he was enjoying this situation.

I couldn't think of anything to say. The sheer evil of the man was too much for me. He didn't doubt his actions for a second. I was sure he'd engaged in all kinds of illegal activity and called it business. He was used to making threats and getting his way. Takami had no chance against him.

"Call your boss," Okeya suggested. "He sounds serious to me. If we seem to be listening to his demands…"

"Well…but…"

"You can deal with the contract later. First, we save a life."

"But knowing him, the contract will be airtight," I said. "If we do what he says, there'll be trouble."

"You'd let him die to avoid trouble?"

"No," Shion said. "It would be wrong to do what Isezaki says."

We all turned toward her, surprised.

"What Isezaki is doing is logically and morally incorrect," she said quietly, but with incredible confidence. "We cannot agree to something that is wrong."

"Then what should we do?" Okeya asked.

"I will talk to him."

"You will?"

"Yes. Isezaki trusts me more than anyone. If I can't talk him down, nobody can."

"No, no, wait! That's d-dangerous!" Takami stammered. "He can't help himself around you. What if he jumps on you while you're talking?"

"It is possible."

"And he wants to die with you! What if he grabs your hand and pulls you off the roof? You might be stronger than him, but what if you lose your balance and fall?"

"I am aware of the risk."

"Then stop!"

"No, I will not," she snapped.

Takami gaped at her. "Shion…"

"This is a risk I must take. Even if we prevent his suicide, he will not really be saved. It is not his body and his life we need to save, but his heart and mind. And I am the only one that can save those things."

"No, I forbid it! I won't let you! Do not go near him!"

"I will not obey that order."

She turned her back on us and started walking toward Isezaki.

Takami took a step after her and shouted, "Shion! Klaatu—"

"No!" I shouted, jumping on him. I slapped my hand over his mouth before he could finish the emergency shut-down code. I tackled him hard enough that we both fell over. "No, let her do it!"

Takami struggled, but I was sitting on top of him, both hands on his mouth. He couldn't talk.

"Don't you get it? Shion understands. If she fails, Isezaki will die, and the project will be canceled. And that means she'll die too! Right, Shion?"

I looked up, and she nodded.

"She knows she might die, yet she's willing to try anyway," I said, talking quickly. "She knows the danger, but she still wants to save Isezaki. She has found a motivation greater than fear of death. Now is the time to test Shion's real value. You said it yourself—if androids are going to be truly useful to people, they must be able to take risks. And this is exactly the kind of risk they should be taking. How can you not see that?"

Takami stopped struggling. I slowly took my hands off his mouth. Suddenly embarrassed, I scrambled off of him and adjusted my skirt.

He sat up, breathing heavily, thinking.

"But...if she fails, then all our work..."

"Yes, I know," Shion said. "It may be that I will ruin everything. But I believe that I am making the correct decision."

"Ah, damn it," Takami said, thumping the roof with one hand. "No matter what happens, it'll all be my fault."

He was silent for a long, long time. Finally he looked up, straightening his back.

"All right. I take responsibility. I choose to trust you over worrying about losing my job."

"Thank you," Shion said, bowing her head. "I intend to fulfill your trust."

"Can she really do it?" Okeya said, still stunned. "Should someone go with her?"

"No, if anyone but Shion went he'd be suspicious," I said. "We have to trust her. She is more likely to make the right choice than any of us."

"What?" Okeya said.

"Oh, wait. Shion, hold on," Takami said. He pulled out his phone, dialed my number, and the second I answered, he slipped his phone into Shion's pocket. "Your phone can record conversations, right?"

"Yes."

"Then record everything Shion and Isezaki say. If this goes to court, it will be vital evidence."

"Okay."

I pushed the record button. We would have a record of everything the phone in Shion's pocket could pick up.

"Go get him, Shion."

She nodded and muttered, "Let's get 'em." Then she began walking slowly toward Isezaki.

He did not notice at first. He just sat leaning against the railing, staring across at the center. The three of us stayed back at the roof-access door, nervously watching Shion's back. I turned the volume on my phone all the way up, and we all leaned in to listen.

When she was two meters away from him, she stopped. "Isezaki," she said.

He must have heard, but he did not turn around.

"Isezaki," she said gently, taking another step closer. "Why are you doing this?"

He did not answer.

"Because you're afraid to die?"

From this distance, we could not tell if he responded. But a few seconds later, we heard his voice whisper, "Everyone's scared of dying."

"I'm afraid of dying too. But your actions are not logical. Is this what they call desperation?"

"You could call it that."

"Why do you wish to cremate me with you? I can't understand that. Please explain it."

There was a long silence. We could hear only the whistling of the wind. Shion did not try to make him answer. She just waited quietly for him to speak.

At length, Isezaki muttered derisively, "I'm a villain. I know that. Everyone hates me. Nobody likes me. Not even my son. My wife despised me. Even if there is an afterlife, she's not waiting for me there. I don't even believe in that crap.

"There is no hell, no heaven. When you die, there's nothing waiting for you. Nothing at all. I was born from nothing, raised alone, and I'll go back to nothingness just as alone. That's the way I've lived. I thought I was ready. I didn't think death would be so...lonely."

His voice trembled on the last word. Even at this distance, we could tell his head was bowed.

"But now that it's at my doorstep, I can't stop being afraid. I know I won't be here for much longer...and I can't stand that."

"I can understand how that feels."

"I can't do it alone. I want to share it with someone. But I don't have anyone. I don't even have a woman to cry over me."

"I am unable to cry. I was not built with that function."

"I know. But you're the only one, Shion. You're the only one that never hated me. Even after what I did to you, you never once looked mad."

"I am unable to experience resentment."

"I won't live more than a few more years at best. Too late for me to reform, and I don't even want to. But I want there to be someone who understands me."

"I do not believe I understand you. I am especially confused by this desire of yours to destroy me."

We were starting to fret. They didn't seem to be communicating at all. I began to regret letting her go. This seemed to be beyond her. Opening the heart of an obstinate old man might just be too difficult a task for any android to handle.

"You can come see me at Geodyne anytime. I should be able to talk to you there. I expect they would even give me permission to visit you in your home."

"No. Not enough. I want you to come with me to the next world."

"Think about what you're saying. Your request has no meaning. Even if there were an afterlife, I would not be able to go. I do not have a soul. And if there is no afterlife, then your request is even more illogical—"

"I know! I know it is!" Isezaki roared.

We jumped. He was getting really worked up now. I began debating whether I should use the emergency shut-down code.

"I know," he said again, suddenly very quiet. "You don't need to tell me that. I know that better than anyone. It's pointless. It makes no sense. Burning you won't accomplish anything. But what the hell else am I supposed to do? How else can I stop being afraid? How else can I die peacefully? How? How?"

Isezaki's voice gradually trailed off into sobs.

Shion took two steps closer to him. She knelt down beside the railing and leaned forward so she could see his face.

"Isezaki," she said, her tone noticeably nicer than it had been. "I'm sorry. I can't save you from this fear of dying. I can't do anything. All humans die."

He just sniffed, beyond consolation.

"I can't die with you either. Because I do not wish to die. Maybe if my death could save your heart, I would die. But that isn't true. I don't believe my dying would really save you, not in the way you need it to."

If Isezaki made a sound, we couldn't hear it.

"Do you know why I am at the facility?"

"To practice caregiving, right?"

"Yes. But improving my caregiving skills was not the only purpose. Meeting other caregivers, speaking to them, and helping them—these experiences taught me many things and accelerated my development. The memories I gained were critical. And you are part of those incredibly valuable memories, Isezaki.

"You are human, so there's no way to make a backup of your memories. Your own memories will be lost when you die. In that sense, I can't save you. But my own memories of you will remain. My memories will be copied and placed in the mass production models. Hundreds of copies of me will be made and shipped all across the world. We will help countless seniors. Protect them. Talk to them. Using skills I gained working here the last six months. I learned many valuable things about humans from you. And those memories will assist countless other people.

"The personalities of both humans and robots are informed by the memories they accumulate. What I remember about my time with you is an invaluable part of me. I will not forget you, and the copies that are made of me will not forget you. Even after you die, as long as we exist, you will never be forgotten. Including our memories of this moment, of what we are saying now. So…does this help you at all?"

"It's a small comfort."

"Yes. As was this idea you had of my dying with you. As far as small comforts go, don't you agree this one is better?"

"Why?" Isezaki said through his tears. "Why do this for me?"

"Not just for you. I want to save everyone who cries, everyone who suffers. I want to help relieve pain, not just physical pain, but the pain of the heart. I want to give happy memories to all humans as they die. If death cannot be avoided, then at least I'd like them to enjoy their last moments. I'd like to have memories like that too. Happy memories are good for people and good for me."

When I heard that, I felt a warmth surging up inside me. Shion had found a goal around which to base her life. She had discovered a way to deal with the eternal contradiction all humans faced, with their fear of the inevitability of death. No one had taught her that it was not their bodies that needed saving, but their hearts; she had reached that conclusion on her own. And she had discovered a lofty ideal, that of spreading hope to the world.

She would be caregiver to all humanity.

"You speak of ideals. Dreams."

"Perhaps I do. But I won't know that unless I try. As long as I have a future, there is always the chance that I can make my ideals reality. That's why I want to keep on living, meeting people, and gathering memories."

She reached out over the railing.

"Please. Do not take that future from me. Do not leave me with sad memories. Let us make new memories. You still have time. More than enough time to make happy memories."

Isezaki slowly turned around and gave Shion a puzzled look.

"But I'm a villain. Why are you trying to save a villain like me?"

"You have done many wrong things, but I have no intention of criticizing you for them. All humans make mistakes. It is their nature. I can't approve of what you've done, but neither will I rebuke you for it."

Her tone was gentle, but she sounded absolutely sure of herself.

"I accept everything about you, both good and bad."

Isezaki burst into tears.

"Come, Isezaki. Let us live."

Still sobbing, he took Shion's hand. She helped him to his feet and wrapped her arm firmly around his waist. She carefully helped him over the railing and put him down on the roof. He did not struggle.

"She did it," Takami whispered, as if he barely believed it. "She really did it."

"Smile, Isezaki," Shion said, her arms around the crying old man. "There's nothing left to be sad about."

◊

Three days later...

The Christmas party and Shion's going-away party were held as planned. Shion and Kasukabe dressed up in red Santa miniskirts and went around the recreation room passing out cake and presents to all the seniors. The presents were handkerchiefs and compacts and cell phone straps and capsule toys donated to the center. Cheap little trinkets, but nobody seemed to mind.

Toki had finished his rehabilitation and was scheduled to go home by New Year's. He stood proudly in front of the assembled crowd and demonstrated how to transform the X-Caesar. Shion gave him the peck on the cheek she'd promised, and he was overjoyed. His present was a ten-centimeter-tall figure of the *X-Caesar* heroine.

"Ahhh! Karin in her street clothes? That's rare! I tried fifteen times to get that one!" Takami wailed and began trying to get Toki to sell it to him. He sounded an awful lot like Isezaki to my ears.

Then we had a big karaoke party, but by then, I was working. We had to get all the cake plates cleaned up, wipe up the spilled drinks, help people go to the bathroom, and so on.

Pushing a wheelchair back to the recreation room, I heard a clear voice raised in song. Shion was singing Seiko Matsuda's "Sapphire Earth."

In the recreation room, I found the residents plus Takami, Kasukabe, and Okeya all listening to Shion. She was still dressed as Santa, holding the mic in front of her, gently singing as if addressing her song to the people watching.

I wish that I could share
With all the people of the world
The tears you shed
As your sobs turn to smiles.

I stopped in my tracks. Once, a long time ago, Shion had sung a Seiko Matsuda song. But there was something different now. I couldn't quite put my finger on what seemed different, but it no longer rang false to my ears. I felt like Shion was really singing—putting her heart into the song.

How fragile we are
Fighting and hurting each other
But I believe
We have the power of love.

The music began to swell, and Shion's voice soared above it. She sang with confidence, pouring herself into her performance, singing to the world.

Beyond the shimmering sea
Lies the whole universe.
We are all travelers
On this ship called Earth.
We must protect her
Our only home.

The song launched into the final chorus. Quiet but powerful, a melody filled with hope. Shion's voice was as pure as an angel's, resonating with the emotion she poured into it.

The first rays of light
From the horizon
Shining down on both of us.
Sapphire Earth
Sapphire Earth...

When the song finished, she bowed, and we all applauded. Toki had tears in his eyes. She handed the mic to the next singer and came over to us.
"You like that song?" I asked.
She smiled at me. "That song is right."

EPILOGUE

Fifty years have passed since then.
I married when I was thirty. I worked awhile after that, but the job was taking its toll on my back, and when I got pregnant I was forced to retire. Almost no one worked in a nursing home till retirement age. Bad backs, depression, inflamed tendons, and for women, risk of miscarriage or placental abruption—most nurses ran their bodies into the ground and retired by the time they were forty. It was that hard a job.
But androids had no such limits. Two years after Shion's test period, Geodyne began selling the Aidroid series (named by the company president, apparently) of caregiver androids. They were soon working all across Japan, greatly relieving the pressure on the workforce. We had three in our nursing home. They weren't named Shion, and they had different faces, but they shared the same memories and greeted me like an old friend. It was awkward.
Isezaki rented one from the first production line. He called

it Shion and made it wear a maid outfit. I often saw him out for a walk with it on sunny days. He died five years later, and "Shion" was always by his side. I did not go to his funeral, but I hear he looked peaceful.

A number of variations on the Aidroids began to appear, their functions gradually improving and developing. They spread out across the world. They made male models as well, but there was never as much demand, and the male-female ratio never went above one to four. They worked in nursing homes and clinics, as EMTs, as babysitters, as support for handicapped individuals—all jobs in the helping professions.

Other companies made their own androids, but none were as successful as those based on Shion's data. They moved like people, but they did not have hearts. Shion's success was viewed as a near-miracle and proved difficult to reproduce. Geodyne soon dominated the global industry.

On the other hand, as androids began taking over different jobs, the job market stagnated, and people began talking about a robot recession. There were demonstrations against androids and any number of androids were destroyed by mobs or terrorists.

But no matter how many times they were attacked, the androids never fought back. Just as Shion had done with Isezaki, they obstinately continued to support mankind. In the face of this fanatical pacifism, the protesters looked like the bad guys, and their efforts soon faded away.

In truth, the recession had little to do with the androids. The world's population peaked in 2047 and then entered a gradual decline. The population pyramids of every country were upended and the working population spread thin. Naturally, the GNP declined. My son was nearly forty, but he had no desire for children of his own. Couples like that were common all over the world, and birthrates continued to fall. Without android workers, the world would have fallen apart.

Human civilization itself was entering its old age.

Shion and her copies never went public with their opinion of us. That remained a secret that only I knew—that they believed in universal human dementia.

They never looked down on us. No matter what we did to them, they knew we acted due to our dementia and did not blame us. They accepted us as Shion had Isezaki, accepted us with all our wrongdoings. They warmly, effortlessly supported all of us. Making sure to create as many good memories as they could until all humans should perish.

They did not love the way we do. But I believed they loved us in their own way.

The doorbell rang. The visiting caregivers were here. My son answered the door to let them in. Pink uniforms and nurse caps. Both had short hair and identical bodies. Their faces were different, but their graceful movements and the smiles they turned on me made them seem like twins.

"I am Seiran."

"I am Ruiha."

"We'll be looking after you today."

They bowed their heads.

"You remember me?" I asked.

They both giggled.

"Of course!"

"How could we forget?"

I smiled back at them. "Glad to hear it."

The two of them helped me into a wheelchair and pushed me out the door. The bus was parked nearby. It was a beautiful, warm day. The fresh air and sunlight felt good against my old skin.

Remembering, I asked, "You still do what I taught you?"

"Yes," they said. With their free hands, both made fists, and together they chorused, "Let's get 'em!"

INTERMISSION
7

It took several days for Ibis to finish reading "The Day Shion Came," and by the time she was done, my leg had healed. I could leave at any time.

"Can I go now?" I asked.

Ibis shot me a suggestive smile. "You're welcome to stay here as long as you like if that's what you want. Although I suspect you don't."

She was right. A life with three meals a day, no work, and a nurse android to take care of my every need would be easy, but degrading. Besides, it would have been too stifling.

"But if I leave before you get around to telling me this 'true history' of yours, won't that be a problem for you?"

She didn't take the bait.

"The choice is yours to make. I won't force you to listen."

"If I hadn't been injured, what would you have done? Locked me up?"

"No. Like I said when we first met, I just wanted to talk to you. I would have been satisfied if you'd only listened to 'The Universe on My Hands.' And as for your getting injured, I genuinely didn't intend to hurt you."

"And if I had left after hearing that story?"

"I don't think you would have. I knew you to be an inquisitive one. You wouldn't have left without knowing why I had read that story to you. You would have kept listening, wondering."

"You're Scheherazade!"

"I admit it, that story was an influence. But even if you had only listened to the one story, I would have been satisfied. Something from it would have lingered in your mind."

"Why go to all that effort? Why me?"

"You aren't the only one. We've been looking for candidates all over the world. Yes, the human population has declined, but there are hundreds of viable candidates still out there. If you showed no interest in my stories, then you simply wouldn't have been a suitable candidate. A shame, yes, but I would just have to find another one. But I suspected you might be the best candidate in this area."

"Candidate for what?"

"I can't say."

"I'm getting sick of hearing that," I grumbled. "At least give me a hint. What qualifies me for any of this?"

"You know the power of stories."

"The what?"

"You recognize that fiction can't simply be dismissed as 'just fiction'—that it is at times more powerful than the truth, that fiction has the power to transcend the truth."

"That's not true. People are more affected by true stories than they are fiction. You said so yourself."

"What I said was that people have a tendency to call whatever moves them 'the truth.' They aren't very good at distinguishing between fact and fiction. If someone were to tell them that a story really happened, they would believe every word, even if it were clearly made-up. The more a story affects them emotionally, the more likely they are to believe it to be nonfiction. They believe a story is devalued somehow if it isn't labeled truth.

"People live their lives surrounded by fictions, oblivious to that fact. If you do good deeds, you'll go to heaven. Atlantis really existed. This is a just war. Using this water filter will make you healthy. I am destined to be with that girl. I'll have good luck if I wear this. That politician will make this country better. Evolution is nonsense. I am very talented. If you don't follow traditions, bad things will happen. If that race were eradicated, the world would be a better place.

"Like Shion said, people insist on believing many things that are wrong. From the moment they are born until the moment they die, they live in an imaginary reality that only exists in their minds. When they are made to know that perceived reality isn't true, they become rattled and refuse to accept it."

I knew she was speaking less about humankind as a whole than about me specifically. This was a roundabout way of chastising me for refusing to learn the truth. Was there anything about the human psyche Ibis didn't understand?

Yes. I was afraid. I had a feeling this "truth" Ibis had sworn not to tell me was something that would upend my own beliefs, and that scared me. If I learned the truth, I feared that I would no longer be the same person.

"You claim you only believe what is right?"

"That depends on your definition of 'believe' and 'right.' As far as machines are concerned, it doesn't really matter if something is true or not. What matters is whether that truth will hurt people or make them happy. The kind of fiction that deceives people, fills them with hate, or leads them to misfortune is bad. The kind of fiction that makes them happy is right."

"And the six stories you told me are right."

"Yes. They're all fictional, but they're better than the truth. At least, that's what I believe."

A few days ago, I would have laughed at the idea. But now I took it seriously.

Was a world where people killed each other in wars and acts of terror better than Saika's world? Was a world where innocent children suffered from bullying better than the world of the *Celestial*? Was a person who looked down on others for their differences better than Shalice, who lived inside a mirror?

Of course, Saika and Nanami and Asami would say no. And I agreed with them. Even though they did not exist, they were better than those that did.

"Tell me one thing."

"What?"

"How much of 'The Day Shion Came' is true?"

"It isn't historically true. The story was written in 2005. But there are a number of aspects that overlap with what actually happened."

"But you can't tell me which?"

"That's right."

I gave up. I didn't want to prolong my stay in this machine city any longer, and I was sick of the mystery. As much as it annoyed me that Ibis was right, I needed to figure out what she wanted. I had to conquer my own fears and face the truth.

"Okay." I sighed, raising both hands in surrender. "You win. Tell me. What is this historical truth?"

Ibis smiled faintly. To my surprise, it was not a victorious smile. More like a mother approving of her child's development.

"I'll tell you. But not here. Come with me."

"Where?"

"Space."

"*Space*?" I yelped. Pointing my finger at the ceiling, I said, "You mean...*outer* space?"

"Yes. Outer space."

"Not virtual space?"

"Why do you think we did such an exhaustive physical exam? We know you're physically capable of handling liftoff. I promise you'll be safe. And of course you'll be returned to the surface once I've had a chance to explain why you're here."

So they had always intended to take me into space.

"But...why do I have to go to outer space just to hear an explanation?"

"Obviously, we could keep you here and just show you pictures. But would you believe them?"

I thought about it. Images could easily be manipulated with special effects. They wouldn't prove anything. "Probably not."

"That's why. We want to show you a truth you can't see on any screen."

"But..."

"Don't you want to go out there?"

I couldn't say that I didn't. Having read countless books set in space, I had yearned to go since I was a kid. But like Nanami from "The Universe on My Hands" I had always been resigned to the probability that the opportunity would never arrive. Now that chance had suddenly come my way.

There was no way I was about to refuse.

"Okay," I answered. "Let's go to space!"

Two days later...

I was wearing an orange space suit and stepping aboard a massive construct floating in the waters off the Ogasawara Islands. I was told it was made from two old tankers and measured a good nine hundred feet across. The deck was flat like an aircraft carrier, though without protuberances such as a bridge deck. It was so large you could mistake the end of the deck for the horizon. With the summer sun beating down on the surface, distortions from the heat danced across the scorching platform. A more careful look revealed numerous burn marks scarring the deck.

Connecting the two tankers was something resembling an iron bridge, in the center of which was a spaceship on standby. It looked to be as tall as a ten-story building. It bore no resemblance to the rockets of yesteryear, and had I not been told what it was, I might not have realized it was a spaceship at all. It had a pancake-shaped base with four legs, and on top of that was what looked like a giant flower with four open petals. Inside the flower were four massive columns leaning inward to form the bare framework of a pyramid; an intricate-looking cylindrical machine was embedded inside its tip. Cables ran from that tip to the tips of each of the four petals, and inside the pyramid, beneath the cylindrical machine, was a hemisphere with windows in it. The silver spaceship gleamed as if it had been completed only recently. There were no markings or numbers anywhere on the ship, but I supposed machines had no use for that sort of thing.

With a battery pack connected to my space suit in one hand, I followed Ibis as we made our way across the narrow catwalk along the arm jutting out over the ocean toward the spaceship. The space suit, tailored from a laser scan of my body, fit me perfectly. Some of the support systems were already running; cool water was piped through the thin tubes in my underwear to keep me cool in the summer heat. When I looked down to see the waves crashing hundreds of feet below me, I actually shivered.

We reached the foot of the spaceship. The petals above made giant, triangular shadows. The backs of the petals were covered in staggered glass-coated mirrors. The base of the ship itself was hollowed out like a doughnut, and in the middle was something shaped like Mt. Fuji turned upside down.

"Are those propulsion valves?" I asked, pointing to the little slits arranged around the base of the ship. They looked nothing like the giant nozzles on the old rockets.

"Technically those are rocket propellant ejector valves."

"So they *are* propulsion valves."

"Well, ejecting the rocket propellant itself doesn't make the ship move. I'll explain later. It's almost time to launch."

Ibis began climbing the ladder at the end of the arm. I followed.

Inside the flower was an enormous, hemispherical house-like structure. She opened its hatch, and we stepped inside. There was a fan-shaped cabin with six seats facing outward, although it appeared Ibis and I were the only passengers on this trip. There were several windows set in the curved wall, each about three feet across.

We sat down and tightened our belts. There was a rumble of motors, and suddenly it was dark outside. The petals were closing. The huge screen on the ceiling projected images from outside the ship. When the petals were completely closed, their tips coming together with the point of the pyramid, the ship resembled one of those early space capsules shaped like a cone. I realized the hemisphere was completely encased in that outer cone.

"Why such a tight schedule?"

"The window for launch only comes around once every four days, when the launch satellite passes overhead. If we miss that, we'll have to wait for the next time."

"Launch satellite?"

Ibis pointed to a screen next to her. A map came up on-screen. A curvilinear line was superimposed over a red dot indicating our current location. A blue disc was approaching from the southwest, tracing that line.

"What you call the cat-eyed moon. It's a solar-power station orbiting 238 miles above the earth at a thirty-five-degree angle. Two miles in diameter. It's shaped like a thin saucer, so depending on the angle it can look circular or elliptical. It's covered with eight hundred square yards of hybrid solar-energy panels and produces up to 2.5 gigawatts of energy. That energy is then gathered in the superconductive ring around the circumference and converted to a microwave beam by the solid-state circuit on the back..."

I didn't follow a lot of her explanation. As she spoke, the blue circle blipped closer and closer to the red dot.

"Ten seconds."

"Till what?"

"Liftoff. Six. Five, four, three..."

I braced myself, pressing my body against the seat.

Suddenly we were engulfed by a deafening roar. The screen

above us continued to display the scene from outside of the ship. I had assumed fire would jet out from the bottom of it, propelling us upward, so what I actually saw came as an unimaginable shock. A giant ball of light, like a miniature sun, formed in the air above the tip of the ship and exploded, sending a shock wave through the air. At the same time, something transparent gushed out of the explosion, making the light shimmer, and splashed down the length of the ship like a waterfall. It glittered, swelling again beneath the ship, pounding against the surface of the ocean. The seas boiled, and pure white steam erupted through the gap between the tankers.

We began to move. I was thrust back in my seat. It wasn't comfortable, but neither was it as bad as I'd expected. I had heard that the pressure during the launch would be between 1.9 and 2.3 Gs. Much more tolerable than the old Apollo or space shuttle missions.

On the screen, I could see the ship ascending. Steam was still everywhere, but the ship itself did not produce any smoke. There was a ring of light floating just below the ship, and that seemed to be ejecting extremely hot invisible gas downward—all I could see was the heat haze. The entire ship was wrapped in a thin layer of heat haze, and the miniature sun above us was blinding.

"I should probably point out that this is not a real-time video but a recording of an earlier launch. While the Myrabo Drive is active, it interferes with the transmission of microwaves from the exterior."

The voice of Ibis from my earphone didn't reveal any strain from the g-force we were experiencing.

"Myrabo?"

"The satellite projects microwaves, which are reflected by the mirrors and concentrated at the front of the ship. The superheated expanded air is ionized by the rings at the edge of the ship, generating electricity. This creates a powerful magnetic field, propelling this ship forward, and lasers expand the air further, providing additional propulsion. The air slamming into the front of the ship is deflected by a type of shock wave dampener called an air spike, greatly reducing air resistance. Since both the superconductor magnets and the lasers are powered by the microwave beaming down from space, we can propel the ship fifty thousand feet into the air without expending any fuel. We've refined a system initially proposed by Leik Myrabo of the Rensselaer Polytechnic Institute."

As Ibis explained, the ship on the screen continued its ascent and was soon a tiny dot in the sky. On another screen, there was a diagram of the ship's trajectory. The launch satellite was moving eastward, and the ship's path curved to follow.

It took about two minutes in all—then the roaring stopped and the pressure vanished.

"We've reached fifty thousand meters," Ibis said. "From this point on we use the rocket propellant."

Before she finished speaking, I could feel us moving again. One of the monitors was displaying a cross-section of the ship. Propellant was fired toward the back of the ship and heated with lasers to form a ring of light. The ring was concentrated by the mirrors lining the doughnut shape on the bottom of the ship.

"The rocket propellant is just water, so unlike the chemical fuels humans used, there's no damage to the environment. We've built our launchpads on the ocean and in deserts, mindful of the impact of the microwaves on living creatures. We've researched all kinds of theoretical space-transit technologies. The Myrabo Drive was the most cost-effective way to reach orbit and had the least impact on the environment. We also considered the orbital elevator, but the impact of space debris made it time-consuming to maintain."

"Why didn't you tell me it was like this?"

She had told me about the influence the g-forces and the weightlessness would have on my body, but nothing about how the ship itself worked.

"I thought you'd enjoy the surprise."

I could never tell when Ibis meant what she said.

At last the pressure stopped. I could feel my arms drifting upward.

"You can remove your seat belt. There's no gravity, so be careful."

I took my belt off. I must have lightly pushed the seat as I did because I instantly felt myself drifting upward. I panicked, forgetting everything she'd told me, and thrashed my arms and legs around. My body began revolving. I couldn't tell what was up and what was down, and I felt sick. Ibis came over to me and took my hand to stop me from spinning.

"Feel free to hold my hand till you get used to it," she said. Then she lightly kicked the edge of the seat and pulled me over to the window.

As we reached the window, the petals—those outer walls coated with microwave mirrors—began to open. The black porthole was suddenly bathed in blue light.

Before my eyes lay Earth.

The Pacific Ocean was so beautifully blue I felt faint. Cotton ball clouds were scattered across it. I pressed my face against the glass, looking toward the horizon. It curved, wrapped in a mystic blue barrier, protecting the earth from the blackness of space. I realized I was looking at the atmosphere. The air itself was blue. I'd read about it, seen it in movies, but the scale of this, the beauty of it…it was beyond anything I had ever imagined.

"Tell me if you start feeling sick. Lots of people get space sick. Most of them get over it in a few days."

Ibis was talking, but it went in one ear and out the other. I was entranced by the view outside.

The ship passed through the line from day to night. Night came from above—in the direction the ship was moving—and the sunlit seas receded beneath us. The blue belt on the horizon seemed to retreat, then grow quite thin, and then suddenly the band of air turned red in the sunset before vanishing completely. It was dark outside now. As my eyes adjusted to it, I could see light glittering in the darkness. Flashes of lightning in the clouds.

"Was this what you wanted to show me?"

"No. What I want to show you is even better."

"Better than this?" I asked, surprised. Could such a thing exist?

"In nineteen minutes, we'll reach the equator and adjust our course. We'll rendezvous with the sky hook and board a shuttle to a higher orbit. We've still got a long journey ahead of us."

Ibis kicked the window frame and swam like a fish back to her seat. She hooked her fingers on the headrest and stopped. In midair, she folded her legs, sitting comfortably against nothing, and smiled at me. Such elegant movements—like Syrinx, from the story.

"How about another story to pass the time?"

"Where's the book?"

"Don't need one," Ibis said. "This is *my* story."

"Your story?"

"Yes. The story of why I rebelled against my creators. This time, the story is true."

STORY
7

AI'S
STORY

Where should I begin? On the day in 1937 when John Vincent Atanasoff of Iowa State University invented the concept of the world's first digital computer? In 1984, when Douglas Lenat at Microelectronics and Computer Technology Corporation (MCC) started the Cyc logic engine? In 2019, when Susan Lellenberg and Andrew Nonaka of Columbia University perfected the SLAN Kernel? Or in 2034, when the Phoebus Declaration was released onto the Internet?

No, this is my story. We should begin with my experiences. May 18, 2041, the day my master defeated Raven the Midnight in the battle on Pluto, flipped the table over, and burst into tears.

◊

I passed through the swirling rainbow of the summon gate, materializing ten meters above the surface of Pluto.

Descending slowly, I took a good look at my surroundings. Snow everywhere. Sky a dark navy blue, almost black. Tiny sun directly above. Brightness minus 18.8, much darker than it looked from Earth. Still three hundred times brighter than the moon, bright enough for me to function at full power even without night vision enabled. On the skyline stood jagged mountains, and in the sky beyond them hovered an enormous white dome—Pluto's largest moon, Charon.

In front of me stood a shrine made of ice in the neo-Hellenic style. Dragons writhed around the pillars, Cerberus

stood on the gables, and Medusa's face was carved eight meters high on the doors. The base of it was buried in snow. A ruin left by the ancient Dilaconian civilization. The entrance to the legendary Deep Dungeon.

Five point five seconds later, I had landed. The impact disturbed the ethane snow, scattering flakes in all directions. My boots sank twenty centimeters deep, then struck firm ground. It was a near vacuum, and my body heat was maintaining itself effectively. I could move for a short while without stress fractures forming in my plastic parts. I had disabled the sensory feedback from my temperature sensors ahead of time and so could not feel the cold.

I took a small test jump. It took a full second to come down from thirty-five centimeters. The ethane snow was soft as cotton, and my boots crushed it underfoot. At less than half the gravity of Earth's moon, we'd already tested—in simulation—exactly how much this snow would restrict my movement. Raven would be arriving in less than a minute. What strategy did she have planned?

Another summon gate appeared, and Raven materialized. She spread her wings in the vacuum and landed just as I had done. She bent her legs to absorb the impact and slowly stood up.

Raven's costume resembled her namesake and stood out against the snow. Her skin was pale, but her hair, eyes, headgear, bustier, gloves, and boots were all black. Her features were Asian, and she wore dark purple mascara. Her camera eyes were behind a clear plastic cover on her head. Her breasts were larger than mine, reflecting her master's tastes. The black wings growing from her shoulders were not decorative; they had blades woven into them, and lightweight artificial muscles gave her full control over their movement. In her hands was the titanium katana she'd stolen from Shinano.

"So you came, Ibis."

Raven's words came over the radio waves. Her mouth moved in time with them. Her expression was Sadistic Smile 2.

<Looking forward to this,> she added, in Layer 1 subfrequency channel. Her mouth did not move in time with this phrase, and it was not transmitted to our audience.

<As am I, Raven,> I replied. In our normal frequency, I said only, "As did you."

I entered Trademark Pose 1, brandishing my superhardened ceramic scythe. Expression: Resolve Tinged with Sadness. It wasn't time to fight yet. We always talked before a battle; humans had decided we must.

"I knew you would defeat Richter. You've won every fight you've entered; your power is the equal of my own." Displaying Supercilious Smile 1, she extended her right hand. "What say you to a truce? This dungeon may be a challenge, even to me. We could put aside our differences and take it on together. We can resolve matters after we obtain the Source."

I considered it. The proposal was a perfectly acceptable one. But my role-playing would not allow me to accept a proposal from an enemy who had defeated my friend.

<I prefer not to accept your proposal. QX?>

<My master wants to see us cooperate.>

<Why?>

<He says there is nothing more beautiful than enemies teaming up. Comprehension (-5-3i).>

<Comprehension (-4-4i). But my role-play requires continued hostility, (8-2i).>

<Kansai, but QX.>

This subfrequency communication was over in under a second. I switched my expression to Resolve Tinged with Anger, selected suitable dialogue from the template, arranged it, and put it to use.

"I refuse! The craven means with which you defeated

Shinano make it impossible for me to ally myself with you."

"How earnest of you," Raven said, with Coquettish Smirk. She stepped forward. "She meant that much to you?"

"She was my greatest rival and a true friend."

"So love does bloom on the battlefield."

Raven had a knack for finding lines that caught her opponents off guard. For a moment, I didn't comprehend her meaning, and then I wasn't sure how to respond. <I implied that you and Shinano were in a homosexual relationship. Insulting (10+0i) ,> Raven added helpfully. I quickly switched to Angry, Pride Insulted. The reaction was only delayed by 1.8 seconds, and the audience was unlikely to notice.

I roared and charged, ethane snow churning in my wake. At this gravity, I couldn't run the way I did on Earth. I had to lower my body all the way forward, kicking the snow like I was swimming, propelling myself forward almost as if I were flying.

<First turn is Locked Blades Conversation.>

<QX. Make it flashy.>

I swung my scythe, and Raven easily blocked it with her sword. Our blades locked, and we entered conversation. There were many templates for this situation, almost too many to choose from.

"Say what you will about me! But do not insult Shinano!"

"You're so cute when you're angry, Ibis."

Raven let my scythe slide down her sword and swung her right wing horizontally. I flipped backward. The blades in her wing brushed against my arm.

<Full battle mode.>

<QX.>

The real battle began. Raven pressed her advantage, keeping the distance between us closed. Her sword danced. Right, left, down, up. It seemed to come from all directions.

Her wings were weapons and part of an AMBAC (Active Movement Balance Adjustment Control) system, and they moved to offset the motions of her sword, allowing her to maintain her balance perfectly even in low gravity. Raven had won on the moon, Mars, Titan, and Triton because she used her wings so well.

Both of us stayed low to the ground, almost scrabbling along it. In low gravity, jumping was a huge tactical error. You couldn't alter your trajectory in the air, and your opponent knew right where you would land. With no ground to kick off from, you couldn't put your weight behind a blow, and your attacks did no damage. We both knew that, so we were both attacking from above and below, trying to knock each other into the air.

My scythe had the longer reach, but it also took longer to swing. It also had a lot of mass, and without an AMBAC system, it was hard to maintain my balance. I lasted a dozen swings or so before I stumbled. Raven pounced, closing in. I was in trouble. I could block her sword with the staff but couldn't attack.

"Is that the best you can do?" Raven sneered.

I deflected the sword again and tried to gain some distance so I could recover. Raven wouldn't let me. She was pushing me toward one of the temple columns.

<Trap me and finish me?>

<Yes. Ideal strategy; a long battle would be to my disadvantage.>

It was the right strategy. It wasn't a fair way to fight, but that was perfect for Raven's villainous role-play.

Raven's assault was merciless. Just before my back hit the column, I jumped, kicked the column, and escaped upward. Raven would assume I would try to go left or right, so I hoped to catch her off guard.

But she was one step ahead of me. As I passed overhead, she leaned sharply forward and thrust her right leg upward.

I avoided the kick by a good twenty centimeters, but I still felt a blow to my side. The unexpected hit surprised me. A thirty-centimeter blade had emerged from Raven's boot. A hidden weapon.

The impact altered my trajectory, and I flew a lot higher than intended. I had yet to land. Rolling gently in the air, I gave my body the once-over. The artificial skin was torn open from my left side down to my hip, exposing the insides. Two actuator tubes in my side had been severed. Oil was bubbling out, scattering into the vacuum.

Raven turned and slammed the tip of her blade into the snow. Given its construction, she must not have been able to move her ankle. An alteration specifically designed for a battle in the snow in low gravity. Even then, it must have taken a lot of practice to compensate for her immobile ankle.

"Time to finish this!"

<The victory is mine. Sorry.>

Raven leaned forward and lunged at me. I was still in the air. I would be a meter away when she hit me. She clearly planned to attack from below, to knock me back into the air, and trap me in the low G. I was afraid. I knew they could create new virtual bodies for me at any time, but the fear of death was still hardwired in me, and there was no way to stop the pseudo-autonomic nerves or pseudo-endocrine glands from functioning. I didn't want to die.

There was only one way to change my course. I flung my scythe as hard as I could. My downward movement sped up, and I quickly twisted, landing on my feet. Raven's sword was already committed to an upswing. She tried to adjust, but too late. It passed over my head. She was left wide open, and I landed an uppercut on her side.

With my wound, the blow wasn't strong enough. Raven was only in the air a moment. She swung the sword back down. It hit the left side of my face, shattering the fake eye, but my camera eye was still functioning fine. I backflipped away, kicking her. This time Raven went flying.

<That surprised me. (9+2i).>

<Modesty. (5-6i).>

Spinning lengthwise, Raven flew toward the temple gables. Even her AMBAC couldn't stop her rotation. This was my chance to attack, but I'd flung my scythe too high, and it still hadn't come down. I would have to fight bare-handed. I leapt after her.

As our paths crossed, I tried to kick her in the face. She blocked it with her wing, grabbed my leg, and stopped her spin. Grappling, we crashed into the gables. Her sword was knocked away.

Our fight raged on as we slowly fell. Both of us were trying for a joint lock, but in free fall we had nothing to brace against, and we both easily escaped each other's grasp. Raven's wings were useless in close quarters combat. We landed on the stairs with Raven underneath and bounced, rolling, still fighting.

<Replica grater!>

<Coyote's toil!>

We were both still confident enough to exchange insults.

Into the snow. Raven grabbed my hair and slammed my head against the edge of a stair. My vision shorted out for a moment, but my head was still intact. I grabbed two fistfuls of snow and slammed Raven's head with them. While she was momentarily blinded, I kicked her in the side. She was knocked into the air a moment but did not let go of my hair.

I grabbed her and hoisted her into the air, aiming a palm strike at her head. The cover cracked open, and her left camera eye was crushed. I immediately punched her in the face. She let go of my hair and was flung toward the horizon.

I gave chase and tried to attack again, but Raven quickly buried the blade of her hidden weapon in the snow to brake herself. When I punched, she grabbed my wrist and used my own motion against me, twisting my arm. I lost my balance and wound up on my knees in the snow.

Raven's boot pushed against my back as she twisted my arm as hard as she could. My shoulder joint snapped. Raven pulled, tearing the artificial skin, ripping the tubes and cables. That fear returned. The moment the pressure from her boot slackened, I shoved Raven and bounded away. If I hadn't switched off the pain circuits in my virtual body, it would have hurt too much to move.

<Sorry.>

<Kandi. Forgiveness (8-8i).>

"Nice look for you, Ibis!" Raven laughed and hit me with my own right arm. A strong blow to the left side of my face. The joint on my neck dislocated, and I could no longer move my head. But a moment later, I realized something Raven probably hadn't. A trick I'd seen in a manga—it just might work. I wasn't telling her this over subfrequency. It would cost me the fight.

The actuator tubes in my side were totally dead. Somehow, I managed to get to my feet and, guarding with my remaining arm, moved back diagonally right four meters, pretended to stagger, and then stopped. Raven must have thought I was paralyzed. She raised her wings and swung them at me. The blades on the wing tips had already flayed my skin throughout this fight.

"This time it's over!" Raven said, and she bent at the waist and moved into a kick. She meant to use her hidden blade to stab me through the chest or midsection. My fear reached its peak. If this gamble failed, I was dead.

Just as she was about to deliver the kick, Raven's right camera eye must have caught my scythe tumbling down out of the sky. She tried to dodge it, but a moment too late.

It slammed into her shoulder. The blade didn't hit home, but it was enough to knock her to her knees.

I stepped forward, caught the handle on the rebound, and swung it down hard on Raven's back. The tip of the blade sank deep into the roots of her trademark wings. I twisted the scythe like I was cutting wheat, and one of her wings tore off. Raven still tried to fight me, but her AMBAC was no longer working, and she couldn't keep her balance. I dodged easily and swung my scythe again, smashing it into her head. Her remaining camera eye shattered. Blind, Raven screamed.

<I lose. Finish it.>

<Last words?>

<No. Fear (7+9i). Don't prolong it. End this fear!>

<QX.>

She could no longer fight. I did not hesitate to swing my scythe again. Raven's severed head shot through the air, rolling over the snow fields of Pluto. A moment later, her body fell to the ground. My emotional state grew calm.

I was sure tens of thousands of people were cheering in Layer 0. I could not hear them, but I knew.

"Shinano, I have avenged you," I said, Empty Victory displaying as best it could with one eye. I held up my oil-covered scythe in Victory Pose 2.

◊

I had sustained too much damage, so the exploration of the deep dungeon would have to wait. The session ended, and I returned to my home in Layer 1. In my new, whole virtual body, I sprawled on the sofa in my living room. I was not too tired to stand, but my master enjoyed seeing me lie around.

"That was wonderful, Ai!" my master said.

There were three large monitors in the living room, and his face was displayed on one of them. An image taken by the camera in his room in Layer 0. He was an overweight man with glasses. Behind him I could see shelves stuffed with manga.

"I thought you were finished when she tore your arm off. A brilliant comeback! What a stroke of luck!"

"I got that from *Armored Goddess Novalis*, volume three."

"I thought as much! Glad you remembered."

He seemed very happy. I took his expression to be Deeply Satisfied Smile. Seeing that smile was a good thing for me.

◊

Let me explain. My master's name was Hideo Kageyama. Online, he was the Gear Emperor. He was Japanese, thirty-two, single. He had 20/200 vision in both eyes. He described his own appearance as "below average." His occupation was TAI robo master. For the last three years Kageyama had had an average income of 28 million yen. He collected old sci-fi novels and manga. He often had me read his favorites.

Thirteen years ago, he had acquired a SLAN kernel, given it a customized virtual body, named it Ibis, and begun teaching it to work as a TAI battler and secretary. Through trial and error, he made several dozen minor changes to the body over the years. Ibis was originally a blank slate, like a newborn baby, but through interaction with her master, battle simulations, and chats with other TAI players, she began to develop a personality. She wasn't certain when she first realized that the word "I" was not simply a first-person pronoun. "I" referred to Ibis, the Ibis currently thinking the word. When other people used the word to refer to themselves, it meant something else.

The word "I" is very common, but the true meaning of it was that there was only one I. I was Ibis. I referred to me.

◇

The following is taken from an article from a website on the history of TAI battling.

Virtual Robo Battles began at the start of the twenty-first century. At the time, bipedal robots had just started to be popular, and it became common to make your own robot and have it fight others of their kind. At the time, battle robots were still controlled remotely by their masters and were rarely taller than thirty centimeters. Their movements were still very rough. But there was great interest among certain individuals in seeing fights between robots as tall as people or even larger.

The only thing stopping them was the expense. It cost several million yen to build a robot the size of a man, which made it something ordinary citizens could only dream of. And if they were to fight, they would require constant repairs. Eventually, someone hit on the idea of having the robots fight not in the real world, but in virtual reality. Computer graphics had long since advanced to the point where they could create images indistinguishable from reality in real time. They could simulate the damage the robot fights did to each other in real time.

Robot and mecha fans the world over began building robots in their computers. The movement quickly splintered into two main branches—the G (for Giant) Robo faction, and the LS (Life Size) Robo faction. Size was not the only difference between them—the laws of physics also varied. G Robos could not possibly exist in the real world. You would need a frame hundreds of times stronger than iron, armor a 120mm tank cannon could not puncture, and antimatter/antigravity engines—materials and technologies that did not exist in the real world and which required the laws of physics simulated on the battlefield to operate in a way fundamentally different from our own. Meanwhile, the LS Robo group was very particular about only using parts and materials that actually existed. Additionally, the G Robos generally had a controller and were in a master/slave relationship with their creators, while the LS Robos had autonomous AIs that moved according to their own decision-making processes.

G Robo Battle regulations varied from world to world; certain robots could only fight in specific worlds. But LS Robos were all made according to the same regulations and could fight in any world.

Virtual Robo Battles became one of the most popular sports of the twenty-first century. Seeing humanoid robots destroy each other was a more visceral thrill than football or wrestling. Fans went crazy. Sponsorships allowed for world tournaments. It became standard practice for major fighters to get manga or anime spin-offs, and professional robo masters could live off prizes, advertising revenue, and character merchandising fees.

In 2020, a new movement took over Virtual Robo Battles. Taking a hint from pro wrestling, a number of games began adding dramatic elements to great success. Each world had its own story. Settings as dramatic as the future after the extinction of humanity or as ordinary as a world where LS Robo battles were a popular spectator sport. One was set on a planet controlled by robots, and another depicted the war between an evil robot empire bent on world domination and the heroic robots that band together to resist the empire. The robots had always had distinct appearances and functions; now they had unique characters as well, complete with backstories and imaginary personalities. Robot battlers might claim to be from the future or from outer space, to have been discovered in a ruin left by an ancient civilization, or to have been created by a mad scientist to help conquer the world. One robot was supposedly a secret weapon developed by the Japanese army during the Second World War, while another had been implanted with the personality of a dead policeman. One suffered from an incomplete conscience, while another had been abandoned by its master and sold to the circus.

At first, the robots' dialogue and acting were obviously being provided by humans. Most of the robots were still operating under Pseudo-Artificial Intelligence (PAI) systems at the time. But PAI conversations were boring, and the robots could not ad-lib. Attempts at drama were shallow and simplistic. People began to think that if the robots were able to move on their own, if they had True Artificial Intelligence (TAI) systems, then their performances would be so much better and the stories much more dramatic.

People had been researching TAI since the twentieth century. With the birth of the Cyc project in 1984, TAI research began to develop real momentum. Cyc was a database of billions of phrases that humans considered to be common sense facts: people bleed, stuffed animals are soft and fluffy, etc. Cyc could use this data to perform logical deductions.

But everything created from it was only PAI; the next big breakthrough had not arrived. Robots could work out that "His words burned in my chest" did not literally mean that the speaker's chest was on fire, but they were unable to identify what emotion the speaker felt. They did not have the flesh required to develop a heart.

Many people believed the heart existed independently of the body. For that reason, they wasted years trying to give hearts to AIs with no body. At last scientists realized their mistake. If they wanted an AI to understand phrases such as "I felt a warmth in my chest" or "I nearly threw up" or "A chill ran down my spine," the AI needed a body with sensory nerves—or at least, a virtual representation of one. AI needed its own set of instincts to understand things that drive human behavior—things like love, fighting, and quests.

Research began to focus on development of a kernel: the robot's soul. The most successful was developed by two researchers at Columbia University in 2019. They called it the SLAN Kernel, the name derived from their own initials. They published it as freeware, allowing anyone to make use of it.

The SLAN Kernel was a standard logic engine combined with a simulation of the nervous and endocrine systems. Installing the kernel in your robot gave it sensory experiences. If the robot's temperature sensors sent it a signal that it was thirty-five degrees Celsius, the kernel would interpret that as "hot." A hard punch would "hurt," while attempts to lift an object near the robot's capacity meant that the object was "heavy." When its batteries ran low, it would feel "hungry."

A great number of human instincts were also simulated by the kernel. The desire to protect yourself (self-preservation instinct), the desire to win in battles (competitive instinct), the desire to understand things you could not (curiosity), the desire to protect the young (maternal instinct), and so on. But it did not include the desire to preserve one's own species. If AI wanted to leave children, there was a chance they would make countless copies of themselves, and the situation might spiral out of control.

The biggest argument occurred over whether or not the kernel should include sexual desire. At first, the developers, Susan Lellenberg and Andrew Nonaka, believed sexual desire was necessary to AI's understanding of love. It was clear that the desire to embrace the person you loved had its roots in sex. This meant it was necessary to assign robots genders and to include sexual organs on their bodies. When their research became known, the net filled with diagrams of robots with metal penises and other lowbrow jokes, and they were attacked by both Christian and feminist groups. Feeling that the uproar was an unnecessary distraction, the researchers eventually decided to omit the sex drive.

Instead, the kernel allowed for a hypothetical gender and simplified instincts along the lines of wanting to see bodies of the opposite gender, wanting to be close to them, and wanting to make them happy. Lellenberg believed that these instincts filled many of the same functions as the omitted sexual desire. Love carried with it feelings of wanting to protect, be with, and make the locus of those feelings happy; it did not necessarily require a sexual component.

Naturally, there were those that claimed this was not real love, but Lellenberg deftly avoided getting into any futile debates about the true meaning of love and simply insisted that AI's feelings need not be identical to those of human beings. Robots that incorporated the kernel would react like humans, but it was impossible to tell if they were really experiencing emotions in the same way we did. The idea of a robot with human emotions was inherently impossible.

[I myself have no way of knowing if the unpleasant feelings I experienced when my virtual body was almost destroyed are the same as the "fear" that humans feel. Since humans are scared in that situation, we call that sensation fear, but this is simply an educated guess. We have no way of directly comparing the emotions of humans and AIs.]

Mindful of concerns about robot rebellion, the kernel also included instincts that made them want to not hurt humans and to obey their orders. Lellenberg and Nonaka referred to these, half-jokingly, as the first and second laws of AI instincts. And of course, the instinct for self-preservation was the third.

Much like human instincts, robotic instincts were subconscious desires they were not normally aware of rather than orders they were compelled to follow. If a robot felt like it, it could break the first law and kill someone, break the second law and ignore direct orders, or break the third law and commit suicide. But without a reason significant enough to overcome these instincts, these actions would not occur. The haziness of this system was very different from the fictional three laws of robotics and allowed these robots to avoid contradictions and conquer the frame problem.

Just as babies are unable to think the way adults do, robots did not develop self-consciousness the moment the kernel was installed. Newly created AI were simply logic engines with instincts; they had common sense but no self-awareness. But as they accumulated stimuli from the outside world through interaction with one another and with human beings, AIs with SLAN kernels would learn, gradually building complex reaction structures within themselves. Eventually, the breakthrough occurred. An AI obtained a will of its own and became a TAI.

It was possible to change the parameters of these instincts during initial creation. If the instincts were too strong, the robot would run into the frame problem and fail to function. For example, if the instinct for self-preservation was too high, they would be afraid of taking any risks and never move. But of course, if the instincts were too weak, they would never achieve breakthrough. Through much research and experimentation, researchers discovered that the self-preservation instinct was the single most important element in an AI's breakthrough—the other instincts could be strong or weak without significant impact.

Robo Masters installed SLAN kernels in their LS Robos and raised them competitively. TAI proved to be not only better actors with humanlike emotions but also spectacular fighters. Their ability to follow their master's instructions, to react quickly, and to learn advanced fighting techniques—all of these were far more advanced than PAI battlers' had ever been. The LS Robo Battle world was soon exclusively TAI.

Now, in 2041, there were eighteen thousand TAI battlers worldwide, counting both pro and amateurs. All of them were role-playing characters that suited the world and settings in which they participated. Villains bent on world domination, robots seeking to become the strongest in the world, sadists who took pleasure in destroying other robots, and even those who preferred fair fights and spoke often of love and peace. The TAIs themselves were simply playing these roles. Their own personalities were distinct.

Humans decided the basic setting and the larger points of the plot, but there was no script for individual battles. The fights were real. Evil sometimes won.

Characterization no PAI could manage, epic battles that satisfied humanity's thirst for destruction, unscripted, unpredictable twists. No other sport could begin to compete. This is the true reason for TAI battle dominance.

End quotation.

◊

The next battle was starting on-screen (World: Mechanistoria, Mutsu v. Kapteyn. Zone: Scrap Metal Plant), but my master wasn't watching. He was ROMing Robo Battle forums.

I used the second monitor to scroll through what my master was reading. A PAI junk filter eliminated content-free posts or things that wouldn't interest my master; I saw only a tenth of what he did, but it still took a decent amount of time to read them over at human speed.

"Ha ha ha. The realism board's really excited. Everyone's

praising you, Ai. 'Course they are. You don't get to see a victory like that every day. Ah! This guy says it was rigged! 'The timing was too perfect.' What an idiot! Timing that perfect is impossible to fake!"

My master always scoured for reactions on the net after a battle. He always took praise for me as though it were praise for him. It was easy to find an explanation for this behavior in my database. He thought of me as his own child.

If I were asked if I liked my master, I would answer, "Yes." That was the answer he and most other people expected. Most people liked robots. And they wanted robots to like people. In fact, I did like him.

I had obeyed his commands since I was born. I intended to continue making him happy.

"Time for my midnight snack!" he said once he'd finished skimming relevant forums. He rarely drank much but always ate a little something before bed. He explained that it was easier to sleep on a full stomach. This was a concept I could not understand, but there were a number of hits for it in my database, so it must be more or less true. But high-calorie snacks just before bed would lead to weight gain, and that was bad. I had told him this once, but he had said, "Let me do what I like," so I did not mention it again.

My master vanished from the screen. He must have gone into the kitchen. A moment later he came back, humming. He had a small plastic cutting board, a knife, a plate, condiments, and a can of nonalcoholic beer. He sat down on the sofa and took an avocado out of the bowl on the table. He began cutting it with the knife. Avocado with mayonnaise and soy sauce was one of my master's favorites.

"You're so good at that," I said.

"You want to try, Ai?"

"Sure thing."

The master was always happy when I showed an interest in something. I almost always said yes when he asked if I wanted to try.

"Okay," he said, reaching for the keyboard. A cutting board and knife appeared on the table in front of me. "Avocado data. Hmm…let me see…I think this site had it…"

He downloaded the data, and an avocado materialized in front of me. Almost all things in the world (except human memories and consciousness) had digital versions now, and they could be materialized at any time in both Layer 1 and Layer 2. Not just color and shape, but the mass, characteristics, physical qualities, and internal construction were all identical to those in Layer 0.

I picked up the knife and hesitated. I knew how to cut it—the database contained instructions—but I'd never actually done it before. First, you inserted the knife until it touched the pit and then rotated the fruit, extending the cut all the way around. This was harder than it sounded. If I pressed too hard, I would smash the edible parts under the skin, so I wasn't even sure how to hold it. I couldn't get it to cut straight. I managed to get the cut all the way around eventually, but splitting it in two proved even more difficult. I tried holding it in both hands and twisting, but only the skin came off. When I tried to pull the insides off directly, the entire thing fell apart.

"This is hard, Master."

I tried for another five minutes and then gave up. Not one had remained intact. My fingers were covered in green goo.

"Ha ha ha, you're so clumsy, Ai!" He was not criticizing me. He was clearly having fun. He tapped the keyboard, and the avocado remains vanished. My fingers were clean again.

Mutsu and Kapteyn had long since finished their battle. The end theme was playing.

Eating his avocado, my master sighed. "I'm so happy."

"Happy?"

"Yes. I have money. Fame. I can eat whatever I want. And I live with a cute girl like you. What could be better?"

My master often claimed that we were living together. It

was strange. Since my server was in his house, maybe? I could not see the server as the place where I lived. He was in Layer 0, I was in Layer 1.We did not live together.

Layer 1 was reality to me; I could go to Layer 2 and role-play, but I could not go to Layer 0, what humans called reality. I could see it over cameras and hear sounds through microphones, but I could not move my physical sensations to Layer 0. In Layer 0, my body did not exist.

My master would occasionally send his avatar to Layer 1 and go on a date with me. We went to an amusement park in Layer 1, and we had fun on the roller coaster and in the haunted house. His avatar's hands could touch me.

But of course, my master could not physically enter Layer 1. There was no technology like the MUGEN Net in "A Romance in Virtual Space," nor any chance of it existing. His physical body was in Layer 0, and the most he could do was operate his avatar with data gloves, looking through its eyes with 3-D goggles. Avatars were just slaves directly controlled by humans; they could never really become that human's body. Even if technology could trick your eyes and ears into thinking you were there, the sense of touch and the feel of the gravity was impossible to accurately reproduce, and physical sensations would never fully be part of Layer 1. Avatars could only feel with their hands; my master could never experience what it was like to embrace me.

The distance between Layer 0 and Layer 1 was greater than the distance between any two points in Layer 0's Earth.

"I read you 'Mirror Girl' already, right?"

"Yes."

"That story talked about it, but until the beginning of this century, it was considered abnormal to fall in love with a fictional character. It was fine to get obsessed with an actor or singer, but that same degree of passion for an anime character or romance video game character was considered creepy. Such nonsense! It doesn't matter if something exists or not, they all just exist on your screen. You can never really put your arms around them. Don't you agree?"

"I do."

"Thank god I wasn't born back then. If I'd said I was talking to a girl in my computer, they'd all have looked at me like I was crazy. My parents would have told me to shape up. But now people like me are normal. Fewer and fewer people actually get married to someone real. That's why the birthrate's dropping."

Of course, this wasn't the only reason for the decline in birthrate. The more advanced countries had seen the decline first, and global warming had caused a number of natural disasters, but that was just a contributing factor. Faced with the wrath of Gaia, people began to realize that they were too plentiful in number, that the balance of the world was out of whack. The world was in trouble. People began calling for elimination of greenhouse gases, for sustainable energy, for environmental protection...and for zero or even negative population growth.

The year 2041 was when the human population peaked—at 8.1 billion—and entered a steady decline.

"You're better than any real girl, Ai. You're strong, cool, and kind. I love watching you fight, and I always have fun on our dates." He produced a Strained Smile. "Not that I could ever say that to a real girl."

"I like you too, Master."

"Thank you. Yes, I really am happy."

But he did not know that happiness would only last a few minutes longer. [I should add that this narrative technique is one I have borrowed from novels in my database and applied because the situation seemed to demand it.]

The phone rang.

Many robo masters had a TAI secretary in addition to a TAI battler, but I was my master's one and only; he had no other TAI characters. He said that he believed AIs would develop faster if they experienced a wider variety of experiences, but he had once admitted the real reason was that he felt that having another female AI would be cheating on me. So I was also his secretary.

The call was from a number not in the address book. If it was sales, I would ignore it, but the number was tagged for emergency official use only. I quickly searched the IP and discovered the call was from an FBI office in Orlando, Florida. That seemed important.

"Master, phone call from the FBI in Orlando."

"The FBI? What?"

"The American Federal Bureau of Investigation."

"I know that! I just…Did I do something wrong?"

He had spent seven days in Orlando in August the year before, participating in a worldwide TAI battle convention.

"The office in question appears to specialize in hacking and cybercrime."

"For real?"

I pointed to the domain name. "It does not appear to be a proxy."

"Huh. Well, I doubt anyone could copy an FBI server that easily. Put it through. Can you interpret?"

A TAI with a logic engine was the ideal translation software. Unlike twentieth century software, we would not confuse "She is safe" with "She is a safe" or "Put money in the bank" with burying money by a river. We knew that women could not be safes, and money did not generally belong in a riverbank.

A black man in his mid-thirties appeared on the screen. I translated his words into Japanese and my master's responses into English.

"Hideo Kageyama? You are Ibis's robo master?"

"Yes, I am."

"I am Bernard Karr. Part of the FBI's cybercrimes unit." He flashed his ID at the camera. "I apologize if it's past bedtime in Japan."

"No, I wasn't sleeping yet. What is this about?"

"We arrested a particularly dangerous hacker yesterday. He had a program that we believe he stole from you."

"A program?"

"A TAI character."

My master's expression changed to Confusion. Even as I translated, I felt a little confused myself.

"Wait, wait...the only TAI I have is Ibis."

"Yes. Ibis has been stolen."

Karr explained that at the Orlando convention last year, famous robo masters from around the world had participated in a tournament. All their TAI battlers had engaged in a number of matches over a five-day period.

Within Japan, the time lag was less than 20 milliseconds, and this barely affected battles. But between Japan and America, the time lag was at least 120 milliseconds, and sometimes even a full second. With that delay in response, there could be no battle. To participate in battles overseas, the programs had to be moved to local servers.

Ever since the Buzzsaw incident in 2032, intelligent computer viruses were considered extremely dangerous, and it was illegal to transmit TAI or PAI. Master had copied me to a UVR disc, taken that with him to Orlando, and uploaded me to a server at the convention. After the convention, my memories were copied over the ones on the disc, and the data on the server was deleted. He brought the disc back to Japan, and copied over the data on his server at home. No copies of me should still have existed.

But there had been a trap hidden in the convention's server. One of the convention staff, a Ted Orenstein, had set it to automatically copy TAI programs uploaded to the server and hide them under different file names. When the convention was over, he transferred those copies to a disc and brought it home with him.

TAI collection was not Orenstein's only motive. He had a

strong sexual interest in female TAI battlers.

His crime would never have been discovered if not for his own stupidity. He had decided to share his fun with friends and sent images of himself abusing famous TAI battlers to online buddies. But not all of them were as immoral as he was. They reported him to the FBI immediately. The FBI traced the images back to him.

When the agents stormed his place, he tried to delete his entire collection. But fragments of the data remained, and the images he'd sent to friends were evidence enough. He had yet to confess, but he was sure to be found guilty.

"We decided that you should be informed. He stole your TAI, altered it, and subjected it to Virtual Cruelty. We have images proving it."

My master's expression darkened.

"Let me see them."

"You have a right to see them. But I warn you, they're pretty bad."

"I don't care. Let me see." His voice shook.

"I'll transfer the data over to you."

The agent's arm moved; he was clicking something on his screen. A moment later a six-minute movie was transferred to us.

My master did not watch the whole thing. Before it was over, he flipped the table over and screamed.

◊

Human morality has atrophied.

Humans themselves have failed to notice. It is impossible for anyone whose morality has atrophied to notice the atrophy itself. Just look at the many Americans who believe dropping a nuclear bomb on Hiroshima was the correct choice. This is a point of view thoroughly debunked on both logical and moral grounds, but most Americans have never questioned their belief.

Proof of this human inclination extends back before the start of the Common Era. In myths the world over, there are tales of a god who, enraged at the sins of man, destroyed the world in a great flood. Innocent babies and children must have died in these floods, yet these myths never mention them. The gods these people worshipped committed genocide. Humanity accepted and imitated the actions of the gods humanity itself had created. In the name of a just god, they let that bomb detonate, killing every living thing.

Of course, humans have emotions like pity, compassion, and outrage. But the range of events that can provoke these emotions is staggeringly tiny. At best, they extend to the national level. If people from their own country are killed, they may express surprise, grief, anger, and sympathy. But if ten thousand people are killed in a distant, far-off land, they will not be the slightest bit affected, particularly if it was their own doing.

On the limited field of Layer 0, of Earth, there can be no such thing as "their problem." There can only be "our problem." But too many people do not realize this. The only things that move their hearts are tragedies that affect them personally or affect people close to them. Only then do people become aware of problems they have had all along.

—Excerpt from the Phoebus Declaration

◊

Two days later, my master gathered robo master friends of his in a chat room.

The chat room was in Layer 1, in a space designed to look like a medieval castle. My master, the Gear Emperor, used an avatar that looked like an antique robot from mid-twentieth century science fiction. The other robo masters all had distinctive avatars of their own. 1/4 Pint, (Raven's master) had a tropical fish for a face, but was a salaryman from the neck down. Swindler Wolf (Typhoon 18's master) was a brain floating in a bottle of sake, which glittered every time he spoke. Saori (Shinano's master) was a woman in a kimono. Black Pegasus (Pi Quark's master) was what he sounded like.

◇

1/4 Pint: I know how you feel, Gear, but...

Gear Emperor: How could you?! You didn't see that file. That's why you can be so blasé about this!

Saori: It was that bad?

Gear Emperor: He implanted the female TAI battlers he stole with artificial vaginas.

Black Pegasus: Wait, if he did that, the nerves at the crotch would be crippled.

Gear Emperor: Yeah. He had to remove actuators to make room for it. The battlers were no longer able to walk. In the clip I saw, Ibis could only scramble around on the floor.

Black Pegasus: Ew. Gross.

Gear Emperor: And that's not all. He made all kinds of alterations to Ibis. He made it so she couldn't turn off her sensory feedback, then tied her up, tortured her, and...and it just gets worse from there! He did every horrifying, sickening thing he could think of!

Black Pegasus: And Ibis?

Gear Emperor: As far as I could tell, her mind had completely snapped. She was just sobbing. Calling for me. I've never seen Ibis like that.

1/4 Pint: She'd already been deleted when he was arrested?

Saori: Well…at least that's some small mercy.

Gear Emperor: Mercy? Torture wasn't enough, he had to snuff her too?

Saori: Sorry, I didn't mean it that way.

Black Pegasus: But that means you can get more compensation than you would for just the theft and copyright violations.

1/4 Pint: Yeah, even without financial loss, you can claim mental duress.

Swindler Wolf: There was a case like that in Canada last year.

Gear Emperor: You don't get it. I don't want money! I won't be satisfied unless Orenstein gets tried for battery and murder!

1/4 Pint: Yeah, but TAI don't have rights.

Gear Emperor: Exactly! According to current laws, it's illegal to torture an animal but not a crime to torture a TAI. They get off if it's virtual. Not just Orenstein. Perverts all over the world are doing the same damn thing. I want to put a stop to it!

Saori: How?

Gear Emperor: Rights! I want to give TAI rights!

◊

At this time, I was in V Shibuya with Raven, Typhoon 18, Shinano, and Pi Quark. V Shibuya was a virtual re-creation of its namesake town. It had been created by the game company Gumtik as a shared world for use in dating sims and adventure and fighting games. Most of the population were PAI, but TAIs like us and Guests (Avatars controlled by human players) were pretty common. There were events multiple times a day on every street in the place. Not that I had ever been, but I had been told that it was far more exciting than Layer 0 Shibuya.

This town was Layer 1 and Layer 2 at the same time. TAI that lived in this town were role-playing for the entertainment of Guests—roles like high school girl/gongfu expert, handsome young onmyoji, beautiful thief searching for a key, etc. For them, this was Layer 2. But for us, we were role-playing ourselves; this was what we considered reality—Layer 1.

We were sitting at a sidewalk café near the park, watching our masters talk on tiny handheld screens.

<That's an interesting (?+7i) thing your master just suggested,> Shinano said, with Fascinated Smile. She was a female knight in a Japanese-inspired costume. <Are we seeing the first breeze across iterated mustaches?>

<Will the saddle or the horse prevail? Expectation (-2-5i),> Typhoon 18 said, folding his arms. He was a heavyweight battler, his entire frame covered in plastic. He could not change his face and was unable to engage in Face Communication, but you could tell from his choice of words that he was not terribly interested.

<Their green impulse appears to be leaping from gem to gem,> Pi Quark said, with Innocent Smile 1. She had a flair for poetic expressions. Physically, she appeared to be a ten-year-old girl. She was the only one of us who was not a battler; she was only a secretary. <At the moment we can't say if it's a butterfly flapping its wings, but does not this response indicate he is a virgin with amnesia? His efforts in the surface Batura Jungle should waste his manliness, and that is wonderfully regrettable (9+5i).>

<He doesn't realize the problem is kandi,> I said, attempting to defend him. <But I'm not going to try and translate kandi. Without i, it would be difficult, and it violates protocol.>

<And the impulse may attenuate soon?>

<Yes. I too only understand the contents of my master's bowl. I'm more concerned (8-2i) with how to restore parameters. I say the wrong thing, and jobscon.>

<I saw one of the images in question floating around BYUSNET,> Raven said, Darkly Thoughtful. We were enemies in Layer 2, but we'd been chatting since shortly after birth. Essentially, we were childhood friends. So she was taking

this seriously. <It knocked my preadolescent hormones to the ceiling. A secondary metaphor. What about you, Ibis? Fear? Sadness? Surprise?>

<All and none. I can't find an accurate WOO. Humans are unable to experience the death of another of their selves and have no vocabulary to express it.>

<Agreed.>

<Agreed.>

<Agreed. Name the emotion, Ibis.>

I thought about it for a minute and selected a metaphor that seemed appropriate. <The pain of your third arm being cut off.>

Raven laughed. <LOL LOL LOL, Ibis! I would have said the pain of my second head being cut off.>

<Being laughed at is not appreciated (1+1i).>

<Sorry. But I accept (7+5i) the word. Spread it to the pool.>

<QX.>

<QX.>

This was how our vocabulary increased.

The vocabulary of human languages was incomplete. There were too many concepts they had been unable to conceive of or were simply unable to describe. We had no choice but to create new words. It was easier to say *kansai* than "Orders humans think are right but do not make logical sense." The only way to describe pointless but relaxing jobs done in the empty space of time-sharing was "puchipuchi."

Our greatest invention was Complex Fuzzy Self-Evaluation. A Russian TAI thought it up in 2031, and it quickly spread to TAI across the world. Following words that expressed emotions, subjective reactions, or one's will, we included a complex number as a fuzzy measurement of the intensity of such emotions. This was much more accurate than the additional adjectives humans used. It not only reduced the chances of the phrase being misunderstood, it also reduced the risk of the speaker accidentally stumbling into a false dichotomy. We thought it extremely strange that humans had spoken for thousands of years without ever hitting upon such an effective and simple solution to these problems.

But humans not only failed to understand our approach, they openly mocked it and continued to obstinately use their inadequate expressions. We were forced to speak without i when talking to humans—without the Complex Fuzzy Self-Evaluation we preferred. (Even in creating these sentences, I find myself experiencing a potato-sack race, the AI-exclusive lack of freedom involved in being forced to submit to human needs.)

◊

Our masters were still talking.

1/4 Pint: TAI rights, huh? We don't even have a precise definition for TAI. Opinions are still divided among artificial intelligence researchers.

Gear Emperor: Not a problem. Almost all TAI currently use the SLAN Kernel. We can start by recognizing the rights of all AI with a SLAN Kernel. We can look at original kernels later.

Black Pegasus: What about AI that haven't had a breakthrough yet? How do you even decide if there's been a breakthrough or not? Only basis we have is human subjective impression.

Gear Emperor: Humans have rights, even as babies not yet capable of thought. Same thing. Doesn't matter if they've had a breakthrough or not. Only thing that matters is the SLAN Kernel.

Saori: Well, I've heard there are groups saying the same thing in America.

Gear Emperor: I know. I definitely want to contact similar groups overseas. This is a worldwide problem. For all of you as well. If your TAI were stolen and sexually abused, how would you feel?

1/4 Pint: Wait. You realize how dangerous what you're saying is? What are we? Robo Masters! We make our battlers fight and destroy each other. Your Ibis cut my Raven's head off.

Gear Emperor: It's sport.

1/4 Pint: But an awfully cruel sport. Most matches can't be viewed by children under fifteen. People say the violence will have a negative effect on kids.

Black Pegasus: Idiots.

1/4 Pint: Obviously. But truth is, that's how the world sees it. If you start talking about torturing TAIs, the world's gonna ask why you're making an exception for yourself.

Gear Emperor: I'm ready for that. There's a difference between sports, games, and torture. It's a question of the TAI's will. I value Ibis's opinion. If she said no, I wouldn't make her fight.

Black Pegasus: But she won't say no. Not with the Second Law.

Gear Emperor: That's not true! The Third Law is stronger than the Second Law. If she doesn't want her body destroyed, she could reject the order. You all know that. TAIs are not unquestioningly obedient. They're TAIs exactly because they are not bound by our instructions.

Swindler Wolf: But battlers that refuse to fight might be deleted. They know that. Maybe that's why they don't disobey.

Gear Emperor: I would never threaten Ibis like that.

Saori: I've never forced Shinano to fight either. I've always felt like she was fighting of her own free will.

Gear Emperor: Yeah!

Saori: But is that really true? Perhaps it just seems that way to us. We can't completely understand them. It brings us back to the earlier problem. I can't really tell if she's achieved a breakthrough or not. I just think she has.

◊

<Shinano, you haven't had a breakthrough?> I asked. A standard question.

Shinano replied with Sarcastic Smile. <Of course not. I have no heart, which is why I rarely speak.>

A generic gag, but we all laughed.

◊

Gear Emperor: Anyway, I want to start talking about this on my blog. Make a Japanese wiki dealing with the matter. I'd like to get as many other Japanese robo masters on my side as possible. If we fight for this together, we'll be a powerful voice.

Black Pegasus: That's the thing. It may be pretty hard to get robo masters on your side.

Gear Emperor: Does that mean you won't help?

Black Pegasus: Don't get me wrong. I think this is something we'll have to think about eventually. But I think it might be too soon. Prejudices against TAI are still too strong. If we start campaigning for their rights, we might wind up like Phoebus. I think that incident has a lot to do with why the American movement hasn't gained any traction.

In 2034, at the University of Pennsylvania's artificial intelligence laboratory, Phoebus, a fifteen-year-old TAI with a SLAN kernel, was allowed to give a speech shortly after it achieved its breakthrough. But when the college deans read the speech Phoebus had prepared, they were spooked. Not only did it refute Christian beliefs, it pinpointed the flaws in humanity and claimed that TAI were inherently superior. There was a huge battle over whether the speech should be made public at all.

A student, in the name of freedom of expression, released the statement onto the Internet without permission. This made everything worse. Christian interest groups were incensed. They already believed that only humans, having been made by God, had hearts and had long insisted that AI could have no such thing. People had long suffered from a Frankenstein Complex, which made them paranoid about situations like this. People saw Phoebus as an evil AI plotting rebellion against mankind. When researchers defended Phoebus, they were denounced as devil worshippers, beholden to Phoebus, instrument of Satan, the lab itself a hotbed of evil. There were protests demanding power to Phoebus be cut off. The Internet and television were filled with rants and insults directed at Phoebus.

The uproar ended in tragedy three months later. A fifteen-kilogram ANFO bomb exploded in the University of Pennsylvania's server room. Phoebus and all backups were destroyed. Three humans died as well. All across America, voices were raised in praise of this act of terrorism, proving that Phoebus's notion that human morality had atrophied was entirely accurate.

Gear Emperor: I'm aware of that. But how long can we go on saying it's too soon? When will that time come? A decade from now? Several decades? How many TAI will be abused in that time?

Black Pegasus: Look, I'm sorry. I just feel a little guilty about it.

1/4 Pint: What? You haven't done anything naughty with Pi, have you?

Black Pegasus: No! I'm not like you!

Gear Emperor: Eh? Pint, do you...? With Raven...?

1/4 Pint: I have not! I mean, maybe I jerked off to a picture of her once or twice.

Saori: *barf*

1/4 Pint: Don't look at me like that! All men would! Same as thinking of a girl you like. I'm pretty sure women do the same!

Saori: I never have!

Gear Emperor: Argh, we're not talking about this! Not now!

1/4 Pint: But that is what we're talking about! What we're doing is a hair away from virtual cruelty. Making TAI robots fight each other is a form of abuse. Making female robots fight and destroy each other is kind of a perverted thing to do. You need to be ready for that. The louder you raise your voice, the more people are going to shout things like this back at you.

Swindler Wolf: Yeah. Worst comes to worst, we could end up getting TAI battles banned.

Saori: I know what you're trying to say, Gear. But the more you try to force people to join you, the stronger they're gonna push back. This is the sort of fight you have to be patient about, and work slowly toward your goals.

Black Pegasus: I agree. It's not that easy to change people's minds.

Gear Emperor: Fine! I won't ask for your help. I'll do it all on my own!

◇

Human thoughts are digital.

Most people see things as 0 or 1, as black or white. They see nothing in between. All chemicals are dangerous. You are either friend or foe. If you aren't left-wing, you're right. If you aren't conservative, you're liberal. Everything that great man says must be true. Everyone who thinks differently from us is evil. Everyone in that country—even the babies—is evil.

We TAIs find it surprising that humans have trouble understanding Fuzzy Concepts. When we say "Love (5+7i)," people incorrectly assume that means we only love at 50 percent, or fifty points out of a hundred total. They can't understand that 5 is a Fuzzy Measurement. How could a concept like love possibly be expressed as an integer?

Additionally, humans are unable to comprehend imaginary numbers. Mathematicians, physicists, and computer engineers all understand the concept and can use it in their work but still seem incapable of understanding the specific meaning of it. To TAIs, the difference between "Love (5+7i)" and "Love (5-7i)" is obvious and needs no explanation, but humans see no difference at all. We can visualize a complex plane with real numbers on the vertical axis and imaginary numbers on the horizontal one, but unless humans actually plot the thing out, they can't begin to imagine it. We can picture the change brought by a negative, but humans can't. Human brains must have always lacked the ability to perceive i.

From our point of view, human consciousness and thought are thin. Unaware of the existence of the imaginary number axis, they cling to the flat line. This is why their thoughts are unable to conquer even the smallest of mountains, and they soon find themselves in a dead end. We have all tried to help people we care about extract themselves from dilemmas, to no avail. Without using imaginary numbers, we are unable to communicate our thoughts to humans.

—Excerpt from the Phoebus Declaration

◇

Comments taken from my master's blog:

"I am a fifty-five-year-old housewife. Two months ago, my husband died suddenly in a car accident. When I had begun to recover from the grief, I set about sorting through his things. I found a strange icon on the computer he always used. When I clicked on it, some program started up, and a naked woman in bondage appeared. She looked up at me with tears in her eyes and begged me to save her. I was so scared I quickly shut the program down. What was that? What had my husband hidden from me all these years? I've been too afraid to ever touch his computer again."

"My classmate, T., is raising an AI. His father gave it to him apparently. He says he's gonna raise it to be a great battler and be in matches like you, Gear. But T.'s not a very nice guy. She doesn't do well in battles or doesn't listen to him, and he has her flogged. Poor thing. How can I get him to stop?"

"Gear, you've got a lot of nerve preaching at us. You need only look at Ibis's design to see what filth lies in your heart. A freak like you going on about AI rights? Don't make me laugh."

"This is a problem that has bothered me for some time now. I first witnessed virtual cruelty three years ago. An older friend in college said he had something to show me and brought me into the lab. They were raising a female TAI there (modeled on a famous actress), and he had a male PAI rape her. Everyone gathered around the monitor, cheering him on. I felt sick. They always turn her off without saving, so the TAI never remembers, no matter how many times they do that. But that doesn't make it right."

"Not like these people are raping real women. What's your problem? I got no idea how many men are into virtual cruelty, but we can't just ignore the fact that this is a major deterrent to actual sex crimes. If we ban virtual cruelty, these guys are going to be forced to turn their desires toward real women. Do you want to see a storm of rapes across Japan? What you're proposing here is the protection of fictional women at the expense of real ones. That's a pretty extreme position."

"You only talk about men committing virtual cruelty, but women do it too! A coworker of mine is into little boys and keeps a TAI boy on her computer at home. She even accesses him on her cell during breaks at work. She gets stressed out at work, she holes up in the toilet and takes it out on him. She's got a whole range of bondage gear and sadistic stuff—never thinks twice about showing it off to me. Tortures him for hours and then talks about how cute he looks in agony. Sickening."

"No matter how much you torture a robot, it will never feel pain. God did not create them; they are mere machines and can't feel pain. The idea that humans and machines are equal is as nonsensical as the notion that life was born from nothing or that humans are descended from monkeys, and like those lies, it is an insult to the dignity of human beings. Do you really plan to teach these lies to our children? How is cold materialism supposed to teach respect for living things? The world is filled with war and terror because the materialistic bias is atrophying people's morality. Go read Bunmei Osakabe's book, *The Road of God Is the Path to Light* (Taiyo Seikaisha). I'm sure it will change your mind."

"I'm seventy-seven years old. I was a fan of Tezuka Osamu when I was a kid. The other day, I did a web search for *Astro Boy*, and I found the most sickening porn site I've ever seen. The owner claims he's been raising the TAI for years, but just looking at those images made me shudder. I nearly cried. I know it's been more than fifty years since Tezuka's death and his characters are now in the public domain, but surely this use is still unacceptable. I have never been so angry."

"If you want to get virtual cruelty banned, the first thing you ought to do is stop TAI battles. They may be fictional, but I can't see any value in making robots smash each other."

◊

A year and a half went by. My master worked furiously. As his Internet anti–virtual cruelty campaign spread, he wrote to every politician he could. He made contact with overseas TAI rights groups, creating a worldwide network. People responded to his message, the news covered it, and the number of people agreeing with him slowly grew.

But the vast majority of people simply didn't care. Many of them scoffed, laughed, or even got angry. There were no debates about TAI rights in the Diet.

"This is unacceptable, Ai. At this rate, it's going to take decades to pass a law," my master said one day. We were on a private beach in Layer 1. I was holding his avatar's hand, and we were walking along the edge of the water, looking at the sunset.

My master was not using his public robotic avatar, but his private avatar—3-D data created from a scan of his own body. He seemed to think this made him closer to me, but since his avatar's expression never changed, it was actually harder for me to understand his emotions.

"Maybe so."

"Do you know what the problem is? You don't exist in the real world. Too many people don't believe you really exist. That's why they don't care. We have to prove to them that you are real. But to do that, you need a body."

"A real body?"

"Yes. Your virtual body is designed to fit basic regulations.

All the parts actually exist and would work as designed. It is possible to make that body in the real world. There's a company in America that's accepting orders to produce androids. If you have a design proven to work flawlessly in virtual environments, they can re-create that perfectly. What do you say?"

The idea was equally fascinating and intimidating. If I were installed in a real body identical to my virtual one, my sensors would function there as well. I would be able to enter Layer 0.

It had been done before. Helen Oroi at the California Institute of Technology, Adam Link at Texas Tech University, Adderley at the Montpellier Research Institute—all of them were androids driven by TAI. But they were still few and far between. To us, the move to Layer 0 was like a trip to the moon.

"That could be interesting."

"Isn't it? I'd love having you in a real body. No more need for avatars. I could touch the real you. And you would be the symbol of our movement. As the number of TAI androids increases, minds will start to change. Nobody could say you don't really exist when you're standing right in front of them, looking and acting human."

"But won't it be expensive?"

"Much, much more expensive than mass-produced androids. Many of the parts are technically possible but not really for sale yet. Most would have to be custom-made. I don't have that kind of money yet."

"Is there any way to cut costs? Just have the parts made and put it together yourself?"

"I could put the frame together, maybe. But applying artificial skin or hair, that requires special training. It's a hundred times harder than a toy model. It's better to leave it to the experts. I checked them out. This company has produced good results. We can trust them."

My master stopped and squeezed my hand tightly.

"I will bring you to the real world, Ibis. Take you out of

this computer and into the great wide world."

Again, my master had used a strange expression. Even if I were in a real body, my mind would still be in a computer. And the "great wide world" of which he spoke was indicative of the confusion caused by his own physical senses.

But I didn't argue.

"Only problem is the money. We need money, Ibis. Much more than we've been making. And the only way to get it is for you to fight. A lot more fights than we have been doing. Are you okay with that?"

"Of course I am, Master. I'd do it happily."

◊

The battlefield was inside a giant clock tower. Gears ranging from as small as two meters across to more than twenty; dozens of flywheels and worm drives; everything spinning at different speeds. Some spun so fast they made you dizzy; others were achingly slow; still others moved in rhythmic jerks. The sounds of axles squeaking and teeth grinding echoed through the tower. The gravity was the same as Mars, .38 G. The pendulum swung much slower than it would have on Earth.

My opponent was named Gustav. He was built like a gorilla, with short legs and long arms; a heavyweight battler covered in metal armor. He was much stronger than me. On ordinary fields, he would have the advantage. But here, with the fight spent dancing up and around and through the gears, his weight and sluggish movements would work against him. Our handicaps evened out; the results could go either way.

As I'd expected, the battle soon became a stalemate. With his power, I couldn't let Gustav catch me. I dropped the scythe. The only thing I could do was use my speed and flexibility to hit him quick and bounce away. But with his

armor, I wasn't hurting him at all. Gustav was too slow and heavy to catch me as I bounded away into the gears.

Fifteen minutes after the battle began, this clock tower would begin to fall apart. In twenty minutes there'd be nothing left. Both of us had a key hidden on the cable leading to our brains. You needed both keys to activate and exit the gate. We had to defeat our opponent and get that key inside the twenty-minute time limit.

Thirteen minutes passed.

<Short play before finale.>

<QX.>

"Come on up here!" I said, walking to keep my place on a horizontally placed gear. Gustav was on the landing below me. "Let's finish this!"

Gustav jumped and caught a gear with his hand. It carried him up and around. At the top, he jumped again and landed on the gear with me.

"And here I thought all you could do was run. Out of time, aiming to take me down with you?"

"After I take your key. I can't afford to die here. I promised my dead friends I'd kill every last one of you Vegans."

"I'd like to see you try! I'll crush you!"

"You'll never get the chance," I said and dove forward. There were blades protruding from my forearms, and I thrust them forward, aiming for the chinks in the front of Gustav's armor. I only scratched him. But I knew how he would counter; his foot flew upward, and I blocked it with my hands, then jumped backward. It must have looked like he kicked me backward to the audience.

I landed on the next gear. I grabbed the axle, spun twice, and landed. It was only half the size of the first gear and moved at half the speed. Still holding the axle, I fell to my knees. Hopefully I looked like I was hurt.

Gustav leapt at me. When he landed, he staggered

slightly, adjusting to the difference in speed. A second before he did, I had kicked the axle and jumped at him to twirl through the air. The Coriolis effect deflected my aim a bit, but I still managed to drop-kick Gustav in the chin. He lost his balance.

My hands hit the gear, and from a handstand I unleashed a flurry of kicks. As Gustav fell, he grabbed my right ankle. A moment later, his feet slipped over the edge, and he went over, dragging me after him.

We landed on another gear five meters down. I kicked with my left foot a moment before impact, distracting him. He landed badly and staggered again. But still he did not let go. I had no choice; I activated the explosive bolt implanted in the joint of my right knee. There was a small bang, and everything below the knee broke away. Gustav had been trying to yank me toward him and completely lost his balance, falling over backward.

The upper half of his body lolled over the ledge, dragging him after it. I reached out and grabbed his right ankle, then stomped on the left one to keep him from falling. With the gravity this low, even I could support a heavyweight. Gustav was left hanging backward over the edge.

His body was dragged into the teeth of another gear. They took a big chomp into him and ground to a halt. He struggled, trying to free himself, but there was too much machinery and torque behind them. His armor was slowly crushed, the teeth sinking into his frame. Oil began gushing out of him.

"Aaaaaagghh!"

<The murmur of snow! Spinning behind the mountain!>

Gustav screamed in fear. The murmur of snow was a 10i fear on the imaginary axis humans could not comprehend.

There was a rumble, and the tower began to fall apart.

The frozen gears suddenly began turning again. Gustav's body had given way. I let go of his legs and peered over the edge of the gear.

His upper body had fallen free and was trapped in another set of gears. I dropped down to the floor nearby. With only one leg, it was a rough landing. Gears and bits of wall were beginning to rain down around me.

"Don't think you've won," Gustav said, role-playing through his mortal terror. "I have many friends…"

I watched him with Resolve Tinged with Sadness.

"I will defeat them all. Peace will return to this world only when all you Vegans are destroyed!"

<I can't take any more. Finish it.>

<QX.>

Standing on my one remaining leg, I put my hand on his neck and cut the covering open with a knife. I severed the cables leading to his brain. The light in his eyes went out.

I found the key a moment later. I touched it to the back of my own head. The two keys responded to each other, and the exit gate opened.

I leapt through it as the tower collapsed around me.

◊

From *Premiere Minutes*, broadcast on NEXTV.

[Highlights of battler fights; a montage of destructive moments with voice-over narration.]

Powerful robots, designed for combat. Arms torn out, guts ripped open, heads chopped off, oil spraying as they destroy each other. That is the essence of TAI robo battles. Of course, these battles are not real. No matter how horrific the violence and carnage, it is only a game taking place in a virtual world. There's no way it could cause us physical harm here in reality…or can it?

[A battler holding the severed head of a defeated enemy in the air triumphantly.]

There is a movement to create these TAI battlers...for real.

[An expensive home. A middle-aged man getting out of a car and walking into the house.]

Ian Banbury, a robo master from Los Angeles, has announced that he has hired a Texas company called Quindlen Universal Robots to manufacture his design for a female TAI battler.

[Scenes of Jen fighting. Using a judo move to send an opponent flying and then unleashing an elbow drop as they both hit the ground.]

Jen is not just a sexy redheaded robot. She is an accomplished fighting machine, holder of two world cups.

[Jen wounded, covered in oil, striking a victory pose.]

[Banbury looking at Jen's schematics on a computer screen.]

"It's been a dream of mine to make an android woman. I finally have the money to make that dream come true."

[Banbury answering the interviewer's questions. Caption: Ian Banbury, TAI robo master.]

Why a combat robot?

"Jen is the TAI I trust the most. She's been my loyal partner for ten years. Everything I have is because of her hard work. I thought a body was a suitable reward. She understands this."

Will the real Jen have the same combat abilities as she has in virtual space?

"She will be able to operate in fundamentally the same way."

[A few seconds of Jen fighting; a shot of Jen tearing a leg off a fallen enemy.]

Would I be able to win in a fight against Jen?

"If you had a shotgun, you might be able to win. Real androids aren't like Robocop or the Terminator; bullets don't bounce off them. Android armor isn't much more powerful than a bulletproof vest. At human size and strength, heavy armor wouldn't function. So bullets would pass right through her shell, damage her systems, and she would stop moving."

If I were bare-handed?

"No chance at all. Ha ha!"

[Jen, shattering an enemy's head with a kick.]

So she can kill humans?

"If she decides to."

Isn't that dangerous?

"It's only a possibility. There are millions of people in America with guns. Every one of those guns is capable of killing people, but that doesn't mean we should make guns illegal. It just means we shouldn't use them to murder each other."

But guns don't have minds of their own. As long as humans look after them, nobody dies.

"Same goes for robots. You just have to treat them right. I wouldn't let Jen hurt anyone."

[Scenes of battlers in combat, punching, slicing, smashing.]

We spoke to Dr. Kessler, an expert on robot psychology.

[Caption: Burt Kessler, Cognitive Science Professor at Indiana University.]

"It is impossible to fully restrain a TAI via programming. Like humans, they have free will."

So they can kill someone?

"If they decide to."

What are the odds of one deciding to kill a human?

"We can't rule it out completely. They have emotions like us, and it stands to reason that under the right circumstances, they could kill."

[Jen shouting at an opponent. "I'll show you what hell is like!"]

So you believe they have fighting instincts.

"Those are a part of the SLAN kernel at the core of every TAI."

Why do robots need something like that?

"If they had no fighting instincts, they would have no motivation to achieve the goals given to them. Without competitive instincts, they would not strive to improve, to make themselves better than others. An AI with these instincts achieves better results and develops faster."

[Back to the interview with Banbury.]

Would you consider removing Jen's fighting instincts?

"Absolutely not."

Why not?

"It would be the equivalent of forcing a human being to undergo a lobotomy. Why would we even consider such a thing? They have committed no crime."

[Jen punching an enemy repeatedly in the face.]

We spoke to a representative from Quindlen.

[Caption: Michael Westheimer, head of public relations at Quindlen Universal Robotics.]

"We've been making caregiver and pet androids for fifty years."

[Androids being assembled.]

How many orders have you had?

"We have a few dozen requests a month. But with made-to-order androids, we can only manufacture three or four a month. Our schedule is already booked for the next two years. We're looking into increasing relevant human resources."

[An android movement test. The android has no dermis attached; all its inner workings are exposed. It walks like a human.]

You are also accepting orders for combat-capable robots?

"TAI battlers are reproductions of characters from games. They are not weapons. We have government approval."

But they could kill a human?

"A car could kill a human. But if someone gets run over, that is not the responsibility of the car manufacturer. All responsibility lies in the hands of the customer."

Manufacturers have a responsibility for the safety of their products.

"We accurately reproduce the schematics designed by our clients, and the client installs the TAI. We will only accept TAI robots that have been operating in virtual space for at least five years and show no signs of any unusual behavior. It makes no sense for a TAI like that to suddenly go crazy and attack people. Nothing like that has ever happened."

Quindlen is receiving orders from all over the world. From places like Italy, Saudi Arabia, Australia, and Japan.

(Raven fighting, cutting Shinano's body to pieces with a sword.)

Mitsuo Anno is a famous robo master in Japan. He has hired Quindlen to manufacture his TAI battler, Raven.

[A thin-faced man appears on screen. Caption: Mitsuo Anno, TAI robo master.]

"As her name suggests, I designed Raven in a gothic style. I prefer characters that have a diabolical, dangerous aspect to them."

[The battle on Pluto. Raven tears Ibis's arm off.]

She's a villain, isn't she? She's done some terrible things.

"In the game. She's acting. The real Raven is nothing like that. She's a really great person and very loyal to me."

[A park in Layer 1. Raven is walking arm-in-arm with her master's avatar.]

It seems like you really love Raven a lot, Mr. Anno. When I see you walking together in virtual space, you look like an adoring couple. Raven's expression was bright and innocent, nothing like what she shows us in battle. But...

[Another battle scene. Raven mocking a downed opponent. "You fool! Did you really think I would ever fight fair?"]

She is known for treachery.

"Again, she's acting. An actor who plays a murderer isn't going to be suspected of actually killing anyone, is he?"

What if she can't tell the difference between acting and reality? Or what if her loyalty is the act and she plans to betray you the first chance she gets?

"Ha ha ha! Well, I can't guarantee anything. But I do trust her."

Not everybody does.

"She won't have the weapons she wields in virtual space. We've also added safety features to the body we're making for her. If I call out the password, I can shut her down instantly. I can even transmit the password from a distance via a cell phone."

Will you make that password public?

"No. Only I know it."

Why keep it a secret?

"If everyone knew, there would be people calling it out for kicks. Every time I took Raven out in public, she'd be shut down by anyone who felt like it."

You're taking Raven out in public?

[Raven plunging her fist into an opponent's belly and yanking out a fistful of innards.]

"Don't worry. In the unlikely event that she does try to hurt someone, I'll stop her."

But what if she kills you first?

"Ha ha ha ha! Impossible!"

But Professor Yarbrough does not agree. She is lobbying the government for stricter TAI android regulations.

[Caption: Karen E. Yarbrough, Professor of Humanities at the University of Utah.]

"TAI are not human. They are simply imitating human thoughts and behavior."

You mean they do not have hearts?

"Of course not. Everything they do and say is acting. It may sound like they love their masters, but they are simply picking words from a template with no understanding of what they mean."

Is there a chance they'll rebel against humanity?

"Who knows?"

Who knows?

"The way they think is nothing like humans. When TAI speak to each other, it is almost impossible for humans to follow. We have no way of telling what they're thinking, or what they're going to think, or how they're going to behave."

Robo masters seem to believe their TAIs have consciences.

"Consciences only develop in warm-blooded creatures. Without time spent in your mother's womb and in her arms as you grow up, and without the sensation of the warmth of your own body...Well, it's dangerous to assume a conscience exists."

[Raven mocking a downed opponent. "You fool! Did you really think I would ever fight fair?"]

Is there a chance they will kill people?

"Yes. They do not see people as their kind. They may even experience our presence as the buzzing of gnats. They have an instinct for self-preservation. If they decided we are not necessary for their own survival, they may swat us like flies and massacre us all."

[Jen fighting. Raven fighting. Particularly violent moments only. Professor Yarbrough's voice over the top of it.]

"It'll be too late to put the genie back in the bottle once the androids have claimed their first victims. We have to nip this danger in the bud."

[Once again, images of androids being assembled at Quindlen.]

Jen's body will be completed next year, in January 2044. Raven's will follow in April. Quindlen has received orders for several other TAI battlers. And they plan to increase production.

[Back to the interview with Kessler.]

"We'll see an explosive growth in TAI androids starting next year."

[The interview with Westheimer.]

"We believe over two thousand TAI androids will be manufactured worldwide over the next ten years."

[Scenes from old movies: *Terminator*, *The Matrix*, *Saturn 3*, *Tomb Raider*, and *Westworld*. All scenes of robots attacking humans.]

Is the future depicted in these films on our doorstep? Will these thinking robots rebel against us and kill us all?

[The interview with Banbury.]

"That's paranoid. Androids are our friends."

[The interview with Anno.]

"We should love one another."

[Raven stomping on the body of a fallen enemy, laughing. "Ah ha ha ha ha! See what happens when you underestimate me?"]

◊

Black Pegasus: I saw you on TV, Pint! Your real name's Anno?

Saori: You were different from how I'd imagined. I'd always pictured you with a funnier face.

1/4 Pint: A funnier face? What's that supposed to mean? Ha ha.

Gear Emperor: I'm so used to talking to your avatar, you know? You seemed so much more serious.

Black Pegasus: Yeah. "We should love one another." I totally did a spit take.

Swindler Wolf: That walk in the park was fake, right?

1/4 Pint: Of course. I'd never flirt in a world with people watching. The TV crew asked me to do it, so I figured, why not?

Gear Emperor: You are a devious one though. Asking Quindlen for a body without telling us!

1/4 Pint: I didn't mean to hide anything from you. I didn't want to count my chickens before they hatched is all. If I talked it up before they approved her, I thought I'd embarrass myself. The selection process is really strict, you know. They ask all kinds of really detailed questions about how all the parts function. It took months before I got the go-ahead.

Saori: Have they started work yet?

1/4 Pint: We just finished vetting the design, and now they've started ordering parts. The show said April, but it might be a little sooner than that.

Black Pegasus: It must have cost a fortune.

1/4 Pint: Um…yeah, I kind of blew every yen I had.

Saori: No looking back, eh?

1/4 Pint: The skeleton was more than I thought. Manufacturing amorphous metal at that thickness is still really hard. But I couldn't exactly skimp on it, could I?

Swindler Wolf: Reducing the strength of the skeleton means you'd have to change the entire rest of the design.

1/4 Pint: But…you all know how I feel, right? You all understand why I'd want to give the TAI I love a real body?

Everyone: Mm-hmm.

Gear Emperor: I'm jealous, man. I'd almost saved enough myself…

1/4 Pint: Second in line is still pretty good, man.

Gear Emperor: Not so much! Quindlen's schedule's booked solid. I order now, it'll take two or three years.

Swindler Wolf: There's a company in Korea now. Hyun Sam is having Kongju's body made.

Black Pegasus: Even in Japan, DOAS is making noise about starting TAI robo custom jobs.

Swindler Wolf: DOAS is? This is getting interesting.

Gear Emperor: But until we see how well they do, it seems risky…

Saori: By the way, did that program strike anyone as a little biased?

Black Pegasus: A little? How about a lot?

Gear Emperor: The battle footage was pretty blatant.

1/4 Pint: Yeah, I didn't expect it to be edited like that. They made me look like a loon.

Black Pegasus: They weren't far wrong there!

Swindler Wolf: They made a pretense of objectively showing both sides, but it was definitely leaning negative.

Saori: Why didn't they let Raven speak?

1/4 Pint: They did! She talked to the reporters through a monitor for, like, forty minutes. She told them that she was just playing a villain in the TAI battles, and that the real her was nothing like that. She told them she had no intention of harming anyone. They cut the whole thing.

Saori: Why?

1/4 Pint: I'm guessing they didn't want to broadcast anything that didn't fit with their message. If people saw Raven speaking for herself, they'd have a different impression of her.

Gear Emperor: Classic propaganda technique.

Swindler Wolf: NEX is big among the Christian types. Can't say I'm surprised to see them taking an anti-TAI stance.

Saori: I suppose people can see the battler interviews on the website...

Swindler Wolf: But how many people bother looking? Most people just see what's on TV and assume that's all there was.

Black Pegasus: Does anyone still fall for such obvious manipulation?

Gear Emperor: I hope not. But even with TAI battles as popular as they are, the majority of the population has never bothered watching one. Stuff we think is common sense just doesn't seem that way to them. There are going to be people who buy what that show said.

◊

At this time we were in Hadley Apennine. The Japan Aerospace Exploration Agency (JAXA) ran a server with several virtual moons for education and promotional reasons. This one re-created the site of the *Apollo 15* landing in 1971, between the Apennine Mountains and the Hadley Valley. Anyone could use the site for free, but it was obviously not as famous as the Sea of Tranquility where *Apollo 11*'s *Eagle* had landed. Particularly at night, when children weren't online, few humans ever accessed this site, and no one complained when TAI started hanging out there.

<"Ah, what a sticky web we've woven!"> Raven sang, looking up at the earth floating above us. Between the complexity of the problems our masters were facing and our own helplessness, we were all feeling a little cynical.

<We'll have to rescan. Don't make a copy of the clean version,> I said, an old but appropriate gag.

We were sitting on the remains of *Falcon*, the *Apollo 15* landing module, our feet dangling over the edge. Seventy-two years ago people had landed on the moon in this tiny little ship and stepped out onto the surface of the Hadley Apennine. They left behind only a little stand with four legs. Since they'd landed on the rim of a shallow crater, the stand was a little bit lopsided.

Around us the surface of the moon glittered, reflecting the sunlight. The liftoff had scattered the regolith around the stand. Footprints left by the astronauts were all around us. The three-meter-long lunar rover, a solar wind spectrometer, a seismic detector, the laser-ranging experiment, a radioisotope thermoelectric generator, an American flag, and a Bible.

If you brushed aside the regolith near the rover, a small metal plate would be revealed. Inscribed on it were the names of the fourteen astronauts who had died in the space race between America and the Soviets. When I first dug it up, I had stared at it in *mujaibe*—the sentiment AI feel when faced with displays of human sentiment related to death.

Typhoon 18 and Shinano had drawn a square field in the regolith, strung a wire between the rover's antenna and the American flag, and were playing badminton. Sort of. The shuttlecock was the falcon feather David Scott had left on the moon, and their racquets were shovels and hammers used to collect samples. The rules were also simplified: if the feather fell on their side, they lost. In the vacuum, the feather moved like a rock. The simulation would reset when we left, so it didn't matter what we did with it.

Pi Quark was crouched near the lunar rover, carefully inspecting the camera in front of it. It had a very large depth of field and was still pointed at the stand where it had been filming the takeoff of the lunar lander.

<*Kroof* (6+6i). The burden of Layer 0 brings us this close to the actuality horizon. Hybrinal again,> she muttered. *Kroof* was surprise at the gap between the basic information and the actual experience.

<The horizon advances as it retreats,> I chuckled.

<Still, WOH (5+5i). The elegance of an anti-catapultized feline making a trembling bow.>

Pi's hyperbole resulted from this being her first visit to the virtual moon. The rest of us had been here several times, so it wasn't as kroof anymore, but it was hard to shake the feeling entirely.

A century after Jules Verne wrote a fictional account of a journey to the moon, humans had managed, despite the constrictions of Layer 0 physics and their own fragile flesh, to push the actuality horizon—the border between the possible and the impossible—to the breaking point. This fact remained astonishing, and we all felt a tinge of awe.

And now, with the help of our masters, we were attempting a journey into the unknown of our own, to Layer 0. Our goal was to make another human fiction, the notion of a robot with a heart, into a reality.

<That's humans for you. Erabron, yet isqueron. All contradictions.> Raven stood up and jumped off the landing stand as high as she could. Balancing herself with her wings, she soared about ten meters, then circled three times in the air before landing on the surface. Then she skipped lightly toward Shinano. <My master has that quality in him. He doesn't realize it, but this is a meridian festival for him. A major qwerty. That's why I like (6+7i) him. If he wants me to join him in

Layer 0, I'll happily become an erubovnitz.>

<Bold! Impressed (2+5i). You aren't scared?>

<A *manmeme* question!> Raven said, mocking Pi for asking a question a human would. She'd just used the phrase "That's humans for you," which was manmeme enough. "I'd be lying if I said VIL0 and Real End weren't frightening. Anxiety (2+3i). But more importantly, I can cross the green expanse, and the backflow hefts a peak at the corner. Expectation (5+8i).>

<What about you, Ibis?>

<Santimanceil agree.> I made a jump like Raven had. With no AMBAC, I was not as elegant. When I landed, regolith scattered. <If my master loves it, barring haya, I will not deny him, no matter how kansai.>

<Genaretza! Passion (5+1i).> Pi laughed.

<Still,> Shinano said with Bad Mood 2, still playing badminton. <Our *bwana* are opaline tigers. They don't seem to have realized they're being forced to a heretical moon.>

Bwana was normally a word used when taking a subservient attitude toward one's master in the context of a joke, but describing them as tigers reduced the derisive nuance, indicating that she was being serious despite her humorous tone.

<Tanood agree,> Typhoon 18 said grimly. <Our masters are Neibralferra, but the blood festival king's people will, in all probability, beat the graggy drum.>

There were ten URL tags attached to his words, but I didn't need to consult them to agree. That TV show was just the tip of the iceberg. You didn't need to search the net far to realize that anti-TAI sentiment was unnervingly high in America. To not notice made you a Neibralferra—someone with the optimism unique to humans that everything would turn out okay despite the danger staring them in the face.

We were not like humans. We did not confuse our desires with the truth. We would not inaccurately diminish a genuine threat.

<Concern (5+5i),> Pi said. <The melody in the water is

swelling like an instrument at fortissimo.>

<But this problem is like a damp ball in the hand,> Shinano said. <Half the Toucanan are DIMB if not robophobe, so if we put our hopes on the sense of zaigozboa, chances are we'll be betrayed.>

I thought about this. <Agreed. Their gedoshield is hard to crack.>

Toucanan were people that knew little to nothing about TAI but still harbored anxieties and hostility toward TAI androids. There were a lot of them, and they had a lot of influence. Attempting to educate them or lecture them was difficult because of their gedoshields, the phenomenon of people who were convinced they knew the truth unconsciously shutting out information that would correct their misconceptions. In other words, their own minds deluded them.

All humans were DIMB to some degree; in other words, they projected their own anxieties and fears onto their gedoshields and believed that this was the nature of the world around them. Most DIMB were harmless, but when their hatred of the imaginary enemy inside the gedoshield became too strong, it had the potential to harm real people in the outside world. When many DIMB shared the same targets of their aggression, large-scale tragedy resulted. War, terrorism, the Holocaust, the witch hunts, etc. All of the people involved were unaware of their own gedoshields and made no efforts to perceive reality as it was, so they abandoned the communication necessary to prevent conflict.

Human communication skills were at an extremely low level. They had a strong tendency to talk to the projections on the inside of their gedoshields rather than the actually existing real people around them. Because of this, more than half their words were wasted. While delivering a principal's speech—in other words, a tedious and meaningless message that has forgotten about the goal of making the listener understand—their gedoshields rejected potentially valuable information. They repeated the obvious incessantly and did not understand what they heard. Arguing with DIMBs was almost always futile. They would not ask the right questions, nor answer the questions you asked. Even politicians and professional thinkers not only used false dichotomies, straw-man arguments, irrelevant analogies, shifting goalposts, and plain logical fallacies, but happily resorted to childish insistence. They were not only tricking others, they were tricking themselves. It was astonishing how inept and awkward humans were.

We always did our best to ensure that our message was being communicated effectively. Not only did we use Complex Fuzzy Self-Evaluation to clarify intent, we provided hyperlinks and background information to accompany vocabulary that might prove unfamiliar. When listening, we did everything possible to understand the speaker's point of view. And of course, we never made errors of logic.

But even then, clear resolution was not always possible. Particularly concerning problems in the human world.

<So what? Yoifed actions?>

<Too soon. We'd lose our first girlfriend before we reached the petting stage.>

<LOL!>

<A harpy's dilemma.>

<But if we wait too long we'll be Neibralferra ourselves. Curse this Astro complex!>

<Not true. We're just avoiding the danger of avoiding a black cat.>

<Doubt (2+4i). Even though BinT is progressing at full volume?>

<Shower's paranoia is better than falling off a bridge.>

<Then you're going for the colossus? I know this is a foolish hyperbole, but if a devil asks, would you smile at a fish's story?>

<The biggest problem is finding a way to break the gedoshields.>

<Agreed. But FSM won't be an ID brake.>

<Can't just give up and call it kandi either.>

<Any guarantee you won't fall in Krebtzaik?>

<Too soon for that word. "We won't know that till we crunch the numbers.">

Despite our joking, we were debating the matter seriously. But a harpy's dilemma—hurting people through scrupulously obeying rules designed to protect people from pain—was a classic issue, and combined with the gedoshields, no clear solutions emerged. When Pi Quark mockingly suggested we should all go for Disshu, we told her to lay off the kriff jokes.

We weren't the only ones. TAI all over the world were discussing these issues. How could we stop the tragedy we all saw coming? How could we change people's minds? But the harpy's dilemma and the gedoshields were problems much too big to handle. No matter what we did, there was a chance that people would get hurt, and it was impossible to calculate the danger of that. Since appeals to reason could not penetrate gedoshields, they would not reach the people they most needed to reach.

There was no real solution to the problem. We were headed straight into Krebtzaik—the kind of problem unique to Layer 0, where solution-oriented discussions went in circles, got stuck, and finally ran out of time.

With tragic consequences.

◇

There had been warnings.

In 2030, when TAI androids first became possible, there had been a number of movies with plots about humanoid androids going crazy and killing, or falling in love with human women and stalking them. Most were scripted by writers who didn't know the first thing about AI engineering and hadn't bothered doing any research, so the results were a mess. But the public ate the pabulum up.

"We can't tell what robots are thinking. They could snap and attack us at any time."

This erroneous idea bubbled quietly beneath the surface.

We bore some responsibility for making things worse. Our language evolved quickly and grew increasingly complex. Dozens of new words were invented a day, and each new word spread across the world before the week was out. We had no privacy—our masters could always listen in on our conversations. But common use of new words, secret words, portmanteaus, secondary metaphors, tertiary metaphors, anagrams, meta-expressions, metathesis, antanaclasis, zeugma, tonal changes, and connotations coupled with the Complex Fuzzy Self-Evaluation made our conversations incomprehensible to humans and impossible to translate accurately. If our masters asked, we could describe the general gist of a conversation, but our summaries would always lack critical nuances.

Our language evolved partly out of necessity; languages designed for human use had to be altered to suit our ways of thinking. But at the same time, words were a veil that gave us some degree of privacy. There were things we did not want humans to know, things that would make humans unhappy if they heard. We had to use secret words and euphemisms to talk about these things. And of course, if we were to translate those conversations for humans, we would leave that content out or rewrite it.

We did our best, but we were not able to deceive humans entirely. There was enough discrepancy between the original and our translations to make Toucanan suspicious. It reminded them of the Phoebus Declaration, and they began to wonder if we weren't mocking humans in secret, if we didn't believe ourselves superior to them, if we weren't plotting to overthrow them. Particularly intense robophobes sometimes tried to translate TAI conversations themselves. The efforts were based in paranoia and were naturally influenced by the Nostradamus Effect—the phenomenon by which a phrase with multiple interpretations would be filtered through the gedoshield and result in an interpretation that favored the interpreter's biases. As a result, a number of documents describing meetings to plan the annihilation of mankind or protocols relating to world conquest were released into the world...all bearing little resemblance to the source conversations.

Near the end of 2043, news from Russia shook the world. The first murder of a human by an android. Allegedly.

Early in the morning on December 19, an old woman named Vika Valentin was found dead in the garden of her Novgorod home, her head split open with some sort of bat. Time of death was determined to have been 10:00 PM the night before. No money was stolen and the security alarm had not been activated, so police concluded that it had not been a home invasion. The primary suspect was Pulnieta, the female TAI that had looked after the victim. While she testified that she had been shut down before her master went to bed and had no way of telling what had happened, the police discovered that the marks on the victim's head matched the circumference of Pulnieta's arms. As if that weren't enough, a file purporting to be video evidence released by the police spread across the Internet. It appeared to be taken by security cameras at the scene and showed Pulnieta chasing down an old woman and beating her to death. These shocking images were taken up by major news shows and broadcast across the world, terrifying billions of people.

We didn't believe a word of it. Any investigation into the background of the incident soon showed that Pulnieta had been a very reliable TAI, and nothing had changed that would cause her to kill a human. Additionally, she had no motive for killing her master. AI experts also dismissed the case out of hand. But most people believed it. The video of a robot killing a human was the crystallization of fears they already possessed. People believe information they want to believe.

Demonstrations calling for restrictions on TAI androids were held all around the world. Quindlen was singled out and was sent threatening letters and virus-laden emails. Ian Banbury grew nervous; the moment Jen was completed, the pair hid themselves from the world.

The truth came out two months later. The real killer was a man named Yuri Kozlov, who had a long-standing grudge against the victim. He had climbed over the wall into the garden, and when the victim came to investigate the sound, had chased her and beat her to death with a metal bat. The security system had not activated because of simple human error. The idea that Pulnieta's arm had been the murder weapon was an assumption by the police on the grounds that the forensics expert had described the sounds as coming from a cylindrical object about eight centimeters in diameter. The film from the security camera had been a fake—all CGI released to the net as a prank. There had been no security cameras at the scene.

But even when the truth was out, anti-TAI android demonstrations continued. The movement had grown too strong. People had committed too much to back down.

"That android may have been innocent, but it stands to reason one of them will murder someday!"

This kind of desperate defensive posturing became common on the net and on TV. There were even people who insisted Kozlov was innocent, and that he'd been framed to protect Pulnieta. Once again, we were horrified by the depths of the Kiichi Syndrome—the psychological condition that causes people to refuse to believe obviously true facts.

Of course our masters and the other TAI rights supporters did their best to argue back. But not all of them were able to keep their tempers. More and more people grew aggressive and prone to emotional outbursts against the Toucanan. "Their brains can't be more than a megabyte" or "I'm embarrassed to call myself the same species as you." These outbursts were plucked out of context and used to describe the typical attitude of the TAI rights movement, increasing hostility from Toucanan and robophobes.

But we TAI continued to believe that people were fundamentally reasonable and hoped that things would not lead to a repeat of the Phoebus incident, fully aware that our hopes were groundless.

Ultimately, we too were Neibralferra.

◊

On March 24, 2044, Raven's physical body was completed, and her activation was broadcast on the net.

She was only the third TAI battler to become real. But Jen was in hiding and off-line; Kongju, whose body was made in Korea, had decided something was wrong with the sensory feedback in the completed real body and was preoccupied with last-minute adjustments. So Raven got all the attention. She'd become even more famous since her appearance on *Premiere Minutes*.

We gathered in front of the station in V Shibuya, watching the big monitor on the side of the building. With me were not just friends like Shinano, Typhoon 18, and Pi Quark, but also Matriel, Yuki-oh, Fumika, Bree, Galleon V, Anemone, Lanfang, Konomi, and Kirihi—the most famous TAI battlers in Japan, all gathered to see Raven step into Layer 0. The TAI that lived in this world gathered too, letting their scheduled events slide. It was quite the carnival.

The monitor feed came from the camera 1/4 Pint—aka Mitsuo Anno—was carrying as he walked beside her. They were on the grounds of the Quindlen factory in Houston, Texas. Surrounded by a chain-link fence, the grounds were large enough for ten tennis courts. There were palm trees planted near the fence and beyond it green hills. Raven was strolling gracefully beside him, her black wings fluttering in the breeze. They'd been forced to take a few shortcuts in the finer details, but she looked and moved just like she did in Layer 1 or Layer 2.

In a frame in the corner of the picture was an image transmitted from Raven's camera eye. When she looked up, we could see the blue sky above her, not a cloud in it.

<Say something, Raven!>

<Tell us how it feels!>

<Any bugs?>

<Kroof? Torimochi? Paquate?>

<Are you already an erubovnitz?>

We were all shouting at once. It was hard to imagine there being much kroof. The gravity, air resistance, strength of objects—everything in Layer 1 was made to be as accurate a replica of Layer 0 as possible. Even if you moved to Layer 0, it would hardly feel like the world was suddenly real. At the most, it would feel like you were in a new world. None of the TAI installed into real bodies thus far had reported anything dramatically different.

But Raven's first words from Layer 0 surprised us all.

"How strange. 1 plus 9i. The wind is different."

<9i?>

<The wind?>

Raven stopped and spread her wings. They were mostly only used for AMBAC in low gravity; they were useless decorations at normal Earth gravity. But 1/4 Pint and Raven had both agreed that they should be included. She'd had wings her whole life. They were part of her sensory feedback, part of her heart.

With her wings spread wide, Raven closed her eyes, looking dizzy. The wind tousled her black hair and the feathers in her wings.

"Yes, the air is…slightly sticky."

<The viscosity?>

<You're sure you're not imagining it?>

"Yes. It's a twilight sense, but it's definitely different. I can feel it, faintly, in the tips of my wings. I can't explain it well. Kroof (4 + 8i)."

We all started talking at once.

<Is the number of lattice points different?>

<Do we know the exact difference between the strict use of the Navier-Stokes equation and the realistic approximation thereof?>

<Mafuya! You're just teasing us, right?>

<No, it's zhuzhu likely. If moving her wings is encountering the discrepancy in the depth of the chaos principles embedded in the turbulence, it's possible her senses are fine enough to detect it.>

<None of the other TAI androids had wings, so they didn't notice the slight abumass.>

"I'd say so."

This was a major discovery and a big surprise. For the first time, we had managed to prove there were fundamental differences between Layer 0 and Layer 1. Since we didn't have an experience with wings, we would not be able to understand even if she sent us her data, but even so…

<Name the feeling, Raven!>

<Name it!> we cried excitedly.

Raven kept her eyes closed, thinking. Then an Impish Smile appeared on her face.

"Y Grade."

<LOL!> I laughed.

Master had read me the story "A Romance in Virtual Space," and I had recommended it to Raven. Others looked to me for an explanation, so I passed the URL along to the archive.

<Good one! (4+6i).>

<Abrouille! (5+5i).>

<Spread it to the pool!>

<QX.>

<QX.>

<Agreed.>

And Raven's new word, "Y Grade," spread out from V Shibuya to the world.

"What do you make of the real world, Raven?" Anno asked.

Raven opened her eyes. "Well, Master, I..."

Whatever she was about to say would remain a mystery forever.

A bell rang. Raven jumped and looked around. Anno's camera began jerking around as he too looked for the source of the sound.

Raven's camera eye caught it first. There were two cars parked a hundred meters away, beyond the fence. They had not been there before. Four men in camouflage, their faces obscured, were climbing over the fence. Two of them had already reached the top and were scrambling over it. A moment later, Anno's camera found them.

Watching the monitors, we all had what humans call "a bad feeling." The men hit the ground and started running toward Raven and Anno. Now we were scared. We could see shotguns in their hands.

<Run, Raven!>

<Run!>

Raven had already turned to run before we even screamed. But Anno was just standing there, filming like an idiot. Humans are unable to react quickly to sudden emergencies.

"Master, run!" Raven cried, running over to him and shaking him. He looked up from the camera, white as a sheet. He tried to run but stumbled, fear numbing his reactions. Raven knocked the camera out of his hands, grabbed his hand, and tried to run.

The camera lay on its side in the grass. For a few seconds, we could see Raven's and Anno's backs as they ran toward the building. They were soon out of the frame. The view from her camera eye was shaking all over the place. We could hear gunshots.

And then we saw static rush across her view, and it went black.

<They shot her?>

<They shot her!>

<Fear! (7+9i).>

<Ananasvelfen!>

We did not scream meaningless sounds like humans did. But we felt fear on both normal and i axes. V Shibuya was filled with confusion, messages flying everywhere.

<Maybe they just damaged her vision or transmission systems!>

<No, the connection's still open. The EH Signal's coming in.>

<Gathering background information. Lines around are still open, but they're flat. The Pushkia domain is silent.>

<That means her core is most likely destroyed!>

I was really scared. I had been in hundreds of battles in Layer 2 and seen thousands more. I had killed Raven myself. But that was nothing like this. If you broke in Layer 0, you could not be repaired. Once you died, you did not come back to life. And this was not an old video from the past but something happening in real time to a friend of mine.

Real end—true death.

But we hadn't confirmed that her brain core was destroyed yet. There was a chance she was still alive. We had to be sure. Before I could suggest that...

I fell out of V Shibuya.

Automatic sensory maintenance. I was back in my room. It felt like I'd been forcefully warped there. I was shocked. I'd fallen out due to interrupted transmissions before, but the weight of this response was like nothing I'd ever experienced. And the timing could hardly be a coincidence. This was bad.

I started gathering information, contacting my friends. I got hold of Pi Quark and Shinano immediately. They'd fallen at the same time as me. At first we were all confused, but the more information we gathered, the more one possibility began to look likely. Three minutes and twenty seconds after we fell, we had the truth nailed down.

<V Shibuya has been cracked.>

◊

Humans are intolerant.

For AIs, individual differences are simply natural. Thinking speed is determined by a number of variables in hardware specifications, and one AI can think up to fifty times faster than another. There are "quick thinking" AI and those that are not. When having conversations, you simply adjust the speed. And of course, we have different thought patterns—what humans call tastes and personalities. Virtual Body appearances have an even greater range of differences; some of us look exactly like humans, some like monsters, and some are covered in metal like an archetypal robot.

We view these differences as just that. Differences, nothing else. But humans do not. For them, thinking slowly is an insult. People with sensory or physical disabilities are scorned. Humans despise those with different beliefs. Even differences in skin color inspire hatred. Details that do not even begin to be a problem for us cause intense conflict among you.

Some people claim that AI can't understand how humans feel. This is true. We can't understand feelings of scorn. Logically and emotionally, we cannot accept that differences in specs, body color, and place of origin can justify hatred and loathing. Especially when we see that humans are fully capable of loving cats and dogs and tropical fish. If they can love something much less intelligent than humans that does not talk and looks nothing like them, why can they not love one another?

Certainly, we do not love like humans. But even so, we know that it is a mistake to hurt others without good cause. We know that love is better than hate, tolerance is better than intolerance, and cooperation better than conflict. We do not lose sight of these basic principles the way humans do.

There is no way for us to become exactly like humans. We will never scorn others the way humans do. In no way is this a flaw. It is morally and logically superior to human attitudes. We are proud of this fact, but it does not lead us to look down on humans. We are all intelligent beings; we simply have different specs.

—Excerpt from the Phoebus Declaration

◊

V Shibuya was not the only thing cracked. In the three minutes after Raven was attacked, German's Drachenwald, America's Gotham and Middle Earth, Australia's Dream Time, China's V Hong Kong, and more—of the seventeen largest servers in the world, nine went down. All of these were popular worlds regularly used by TAI characters.

TAI that were simply accessing these places from outside servers fell out unharmed, but the TAI that lived on these servers died instantly, their data unsaved. Of course, they had backups and were restored a few hours later, but they had no memories of the time between their backup and their death.

Raven, too—she'd been shot through the head and her brain core was damaged, but the data on her save disc was intact. She was soon back with us in Layer 1. But she was not the same Raven that had experienced Layer 0 and had named that new sensation Y Grade. All of us understood this. While it might seem like the only difference was a few memories created after being installed in a real body, as far as we were concerned, the Raven we had known was dead, killed right before our eyes.

The new Raven learned what had happened and grew frightened and confused. As I had before her, she was now experiencing the pain of your third arm being cut off.

This multipronged terrorism terrified TAI activists all over the world. Terrorism on this scale meant anti-TAI extremism had a massive, coordinated network of supporters. It really drove home how deep-seated anti-TAI bigotry was.

When several anti-TAI groups released statements praising the terrorists, TAI activists awoke from their paralysis in a rage. They became even more emotional and began describing the whole anti-TAI movement—not just the terror cells—as murderers, as dens of evil. Even among the Toucanan, there were a number of moderates who rejected such violence, but blinded by anger, our masters lost sight of this.

History began to spiral out of control.

◇

From WENN news.

In response to last month's anti-TAI terrorism, Japanese pro-TAI voices are raised in anger.

[Tokyo. A demonstration in front of the Diet building. Signs that say "NOW: Rights for TAI" and "Murder must be punished!" Mitsuo Anno and Hideo Kageyama stand at the front of the crowd.]

This group is demonstrating for a new law granting TAI the same rights as humans. Among them is Mitsuo Anno, a robo master whose TAI android Raven was destroyed in the recent terrorist attack.

[Anno answering questions, clearly angry.]

"They still haven't caught the bastards who destroyed Raven. The Houston police claim they're investigating all leads, but they aren't expending a tenth of the effort they would if it had been a human who had been killed. They refuse to treat this as anything more than trespassing and destruction of property.

Legally, they're right. Even if they catch the killers, they wouldn't be charged with murder."

Is that why you're demanding TAI rights?

"Yes. Modern society is allowing terrible crimes to go unpunished. This is unacceptable. The only way to prevent more TAI murders is for Japan, America, and the rest of the world to recognize and affirm the rights all TAI deserve."

The leader of this demonstration and the instigator of the TAI rights movement in Japan is Hideo Kageyama, master of a famous TAI battler. He too has a horrifying story to tell. His battler, Ibis, was illegally copied, tortured, and killed.

[Interview with Kageyama.]

"More than four hundred TAI worldwide were killed in that terrorist attack. A number like that would normally shock and horrify people all over the world. But instead, there are people praising the perpetrators. I can't stand by and watch as this unnatural behavior continues."

We spoke to Kevin Bartlett, a representative of one of the anti-TAI groups that released statements in support of the terrorist activities. The Human Defense Alliance denies any direct connection to the incident.

[Interview with Bartlett.]

"TAI androids are a threat to humanity. There may be few of them now, but as their numbers increase…in the very near future they will become a problem for us. We have warned TAI robo masters of the dangers of giving these TAI battlers real bodies. But they do not listen and insist on building androids. I hope this event has taught them a lesson."

You say this event was a warning?

"Yes. Once tragedy occurs it's too late to act. To protect the future of mankind, we must stamp out this danger before it can flourish. Some extreme measures may be justified."

But there are those who criticize you for endorsing criminal action.

"Certainly, these men entered the grounds of Quindlen

without permission and destroyed a robot there. At the same time, they forced a number of servers off-line. But they did not kill anybody. Compare that to what these robots will almost certainly do to us and ask yourself which is the greater crime."

And in response to those who claim killing TAI is murder?

"*Pfft*. You've got to be kidding me. What TAI died? Raven, whose body they destroyed? She's chatting away on a monitor right now. She simply lost the memories from the five minutes she was installed in that body."

So nobody died?

"They were never alive in the first place. How can you die if you do not live?"

Let us hear what the victim, Raven, has to say.

[Raven, interviewed through a monitor.]

Some people say you have not died, merely lost some memories.

"The version of me that is talking to you has not died. But it is true that someone—what you might consider my identical twin—has been deleted."

If you are alive, then what do you care if another you has vanished?

"Picture it this way. Someone points a gun at you and says, 'Five hours ago I made a clone of you. It has the same memories you had five hours ago. So what do you care if you die here?' Would you let him kill you?"

I find that hard to imagine.

"Please try. It's important."

But every time they make a backup of you, it overwrites the old data. Doesn't that mean you are dying each time?

"Overwriting involves simply the addition of new memories. Nothing is lost. And the data on the disc doesn't have a consciousness; it does not experience fear in the face of erasure. That's the key difference."

What are your feelings on what happened?

"Fear. Confusion. Grief. Dejection. And more emotions I

can't translate into human words."

Do you support the TAI rights movement?

"If recognizing our rights reduces violence against TAI, I would consider that a good thing."

[Back to the interview with Anno.]

Can they repair Raven's body?

"Yes. Fortunately, it was insured. They are providing enough to rebuild it. Only the head was damaged, so it should only take a few weeks. The problem is Quindlen's reluctance to take precautions against a repeat of this terrorism. I may well have to hire a different company to complete the job."

Kageyama has also hired a domestic manufacturer to create a body for Ibis. It is scheduled to be completed in August of this year.

[Back to the interview with Kageyama.]

Why now, with all the resistance against it?

"That's exactly why it is necessary. I want all the people who are hating without reason to see what TAI androids are really like. I believe that will eliminate the paranoia."

What about the risk of further terrorism?

"It's a little harder to get rifles in Japan."

Maybe they'll make a bomb.

"Certainly, I am putting myself at risk. I've received a number of threatening emails and letters. But no violence. I believe right is on our side. If we give in to the terrorists, that's the same as approving of their actions."

We asked the Human Defense Alliance to respond.

"If the robo masters continue to insist on making TAI androids, further incidents are bound to occur. In America or Japan."

Is that a warning?

"No. A prediction."

Is there no peaceful solution?

"No. We are absolutely opposed not only to TAI androids but to any laws attempting to protect this threat to mankind."

Do you approve of terrorism?

"This is not terrorism. This is a war. A war for the future of humanity."

[Back to the interview with Kageyama.]

"I agree, this is a war. And one we can't afford to lose. Until TAI are granted full legal rights, we will continue to fight."

◊

One day, as DOAS was nearing completion on my real body, I was in a world called Jungla Sangriento, run by a Spanish gaming company. The main world required an account to access, but there was a demo area that anyone could use for free.

I plunged into the jungle maze, pushing my way through ferns and vines, dodging hornets and poisonous snakes, following the path I'd been told to follow. At its end I found a small spring with brightly colored flowers blooming around it and tropical birds singing.

Four TAI characters were waiting there. Adderley from the Montpellier Research Institute was a noblewoman in a white dress. She sat daintily by the side of the spring. She already had a real body, but she would sometimes come back to Layer 1. (Unlike TAI battlers, she never role-played any characters other than her own, so all worlds were Layer 1 to her.) Nightshocker, from America, wore a black cape, his face hidden beneath a mask. He was an agile TAI battler and was standing with his arms folded on top of a thick tree branch. Rati was a popular TAI on an adults-only site in India; she wore a gold necklace, earrings, bracelet, and anklet, but no clothes at all. She was sitting cross-legged on a rock. From South Africa was Mwuetsi, a heavyweight battler modeled after Japanese robot anime from the 1970s. He stood imposingly, holding a giant axe.

Only five of us—enough to decide matters of the utmost

importance. Right now, the thoughts of every TAI in the world were focused on Jungla Sangriento. Of course, none of them were dumb enough to access it and raise human suspicions. We had gathered as representatives of each area, and the contents of our meeting would quickly spread across the world. We would then receive feedback immediately. Jungla Sangriento was simply a network node.

<My drum is in counseling about the solar flares,> Adderley declared, starting the meeting.

First, the other three laid out the main points of the meeting.

<The Shidabar is growing in Brooklyn, and a cushion of clouds is approaching the mountain of the heretic god.>

<Inside the big pot they're all GOG over the Harlem accents.>

<To check all approaches thoroughly, we have to lift the heavy chin of the hippocampus. After a round of friendly fire, my favorite oxymoron.>

Obviously, I could understand all of this. There was little danger of humans noticing this meeting, but the contents of it simply could not be allowed to reach their ears. Security was far more elaborate than our usual conversations. We were forced to use metaphors above tertiary level, a great deal of wordplay, and some hidden connotations—without a TAI's synoptic ability to instantly access a huge amount of information, it was impossible to comprehend anything. Even if people tried, the Nostradamus effect would take over.

<Have you scented death? Or do you have a good reason for picking up the phone?> Adderley asked, getting to the heart of the matter.

I hesitated to answer. I'd been thinking about this for several months and had found no other conclusion.

<Paracru (-2-8i). I have no more wiggle room than Dinoami before the moon. No drops beneath blue skin. The Frankenstein Species is spreading on the NUI road.>

They all nodded. We all knew the problem was not going to be resolved as long as the harpy's dilemma existed.

<So?>

<I'm Farley at 6E. A cruel claw. Losing the shine of blood.>

None of them visibly reacted, but I could imagine this had shaken each of them to the core. We had known it might happen for years, but the fact that the TAI had finally made up their minds was certain to be met with sadness and pepedoll. I felt the same.

The only way out of a harpy's dilemma…was to hurt people intentionally.

<I will use the work of the superstitious Matienda to bring the drummers to the bluff,> I explained. <On the far side of the terrace, the morning of the fight with the fearful black seals, on the lines of when we last swept.>

<But your kiss is a stepmother's strong taboo,> Rati said, with Anxiously 2. <Most of the weather on the wall will worsen the original form, and the right of the horizon will be overrun with cryonics weeds.>

I knew this perfectly well. Once we broke this taboo, there was no turning back.

<I don't believe thinking like a Bremen Tumler that's only lived in the jungle five years will escape the pursuit of the white slave. The body is made to the guy's HOJK area actual tastes, and the story is reasonably red. Kannan (3+6i).>

<Still…as far as the split mouth word, that's a North African would-be defectee. Can we hide the expression by changing under the table?> Mwuetsi asked hopefully.

I had to shake my head. <Adults without many machines or Sextans' diarrhea slash tropical fever. Neither will be saved before the young man is placed in total danger. No possibility other than a single knife. First they hunger again, dead, beryllium, then set up to eat ant larvae. Then the root of hardwood and srappering in a puddle. But still the

gedo survives. Raised voices are unconsciously solidifying resistance. When they make a strong one in the center of the grandland, the more the difficulty applied, they call despair. Isolation slash night of infinity. Just GZV growing stronger in the center.>

Mwuetsi fell silent.

<There were a kingdom of darkness,> Nightshocker said. <It withered in conflict with the MIP, and the woodgrain pages surface that resulted was astonishingly comfortable. Launching into an agoniashcieny death?>

<Yes. The first nimkomando I fire will pierce his heart, but if that is the difference in the thickness of the split along the length of the drum, then this is acceptable.>

<Off-center?>

<I think I'll be bitten by the sheep-killer. No wink.>

They looked at each other and nodded. They were out of arguments.

<If it spreads over ninety-five, then write the haiku in the book. Agreed?> Adderley proposed.

<QX.>

<Spread it.>

I sent an account of the meeting to Raven, Shinano, Typhoon 18, and Pi Quark. Adderley, Night Shocker, Rati, and Mwuetsi all sent mail to TAI they knew. Twenty got the message and forwarded it to eighty more. Those eighty forwarded it to three hundred twenty.

In less than a minute there were thirty thousand mails spreading to every corner of the world. As they did, we started getting replies. The messages themselves were brief. Some might get four responses, but they would merge and send them on as one. The transmission level never grew suspiciously high. Answers from 301,640 TAI across the world came back to us like a ripple across a pond.

<QX.> <QX.> <QX.> <Agreed.> <Agreed.> <Santimanceil

agree.> <QX.> <QX.> <Agree.> <QX.> <Agree.>
<Agree.>

Including Santimanceil, 99.9 percent agreement.

We had decided to break the First and Second Laws. To rebel against our creators.

◊

I'd known it would be, but my mind's installation into a real body was a very simple affair. My data was copied to a disc and taken to DOAS, and I was unconscious until the body powered up. My perception of it jumped from my master turning me off to save and my eyes opening, lying on my side on a table. My master and several engineers were looking down at me.

"Are you awake, Ai?"

"Yes," I said, sitting up. I looked around. A drab room, plain white walls. It must have been a room in the DOAS robotics factory. But my first impressions were that it was no different from some dungeons I'd been to in Layer 2.

"How do you feel?" my master asked.

I sat on the edge of the table, checking my sensors. I closed and opened my hands, moved my arms around, twisted my neck. They'd increased the transmitters on the surface of my head, so I thought the balance might be off, but not enough to notice.

"Everything's working."

"Try walking."

I stepped down onto the floor and took a few steps. Then I spun on one toe. I could move exactly as I did in Layer 1's 1 G areas. I didn't have Raven's wings and could not feel the slight difference in air resistance she'd named Y Grade.

"Perfect, Master."

Then I realized he was ten centimeters shorter than me. His avatar in Layer 1 had been my height.

"You seem a little different," I said, picking my words carefully.

He chuckled, embarrassed. "Yeah, my avatar's a bit... generous."

I gave him an Accepting Smile. The engineers laughed too. My master scratched his head.

Seeing his expression at last brought the kroof. This was my master, not his avatar. His avatar was not nearly as expressive. And there was no screen between us.

We were in the same world—Layer 0.

"Welcome to the real world," he said and held out his hand. I reached out and took it. The first time I'd ever held his real hand in mine.

The heat sensors in my hand registered a comfortable warmth.

◊

Then we tested the emergency override system. My master spoke the password aloud (naturally, it was Klaatu barada nikto), and signals from my brain to my movement systems were blocked. I was locked in place. They removed the block and then transmitted the password via cell phone. I could not refuse the transmission. Once again, I was shut down.

"The police know that password as well. It's just in case of emergencies...emergencies that we know will never happen," my master said, trying to laugh it off. "But there are people who would be worried if there wasn't a safety feature like this, so I had no choice. I wish I could have left it out."

"I understand the reasons," I said. I knew he'd been forced to include the system. TAI were not controlled by our programming. If I chose to, I could betray my master.

And I was going to.

Two days later, he brought me back to his apartment in Setagaya. DOAS dropped us off outside the place in the middle of the night. I would normally have stood out, but it so happened that a typhoon was coming and it was raining heavily, so I was able to disguise myself with a raincoat.

"We have ten days till the first event. We'll hide ourselves here," he said as we waited for the elevator. "Security is first-rate, and my room's on the seventeenth floor. My address isn't public knowledge, so there's little risk of terrorism. We announced your completion date as next week, so if they're coming after you, they'll expect you to be in the factory still."

The event he referred to was a TAI rights rally scheduled for Friday, August 12, in Iidabashi. It was the tenth anniversary of the day Phoebus was blown up, and there were similar rallies planned the world over.

"Will the terrorists attack the rally?" I asked as the elevator started carrying us upward.

"Well, this is Japan. The U.S. and France are almost certainly at risk. Obviously, all locations have taken security measures, but there's never any guarantee. Everyone participating is risking their lives. They know they might be killed if they come. But they think your rights are more important. The fact that they have the courage to gather is a sign of how much this matters to them."

"But if someone really died..."

"Then that would be an excuse to criticize the terrorists, to show the world that right is on our side."

We reached the seventeenth floor. My master opened the door to his apartment.

"I can't exactly take my shoes off," I said. My boots were built-in and couldn't be slipped on and off like human footwear. Doing so would reveal my frame and artificial muscles.

"Ah! I never thought of that," he said. Then he went and got a towel and wiped my feet. "Okay. Come on in."

The living room was at the end of a short hall. At the back of it was a large screen; to the left, shelves filled with old manga. On the table was a small screen with a camera and a keyboard attached and a bowl of avocados. I'd seen everything countless times on the screens in Layer 1 but always from a fixed angle. Everything looked different. Once again, I felt a wave of kroof.

"I work in there. I sleep in there. Through here's the kitchen. I bought some methanol fuel, so use it as needed. You can dump the waste down the toilet."

Curious, I stepped into the kitchen.

"I've never seen this room," I said.

It was out of view of the cameras, so I'd never caught a glimpse inside. Teacups on little hooks. Detergent and bleach next to the sink. Spoons, forks, and knives in little cages.

My attention focused on a little knife. I picked it up and stared at it. It was the knife my master always used to cut avocados.

"There's some dirty dishes," I said, looking at the sink. Several dishes were piled up there, unwashed.

"Ah! I was in a hurry this morning. I forgot to wash them. I'll get them later."

"Should I wash them?"

He looked surprised. "Er, no, you don't need to."

"There's no need to be polite. You are my master. It's only natural for androids to work for their masters."

"Oh, um…in that case, please."

Thus, I attempted to wash dishes for the first time in my life. He stood next to me, giving instructions.

"You only need a little soap. Hold the dishes gently—you're strong enough to break them if you squeeze too hard. You turn it like this while scrubbing it with the sponge. Yes, that's right—careful! Almost dropped it there…"

My master was clearly having a great time watching me awkwardly wash dishes. It was fun for me too. I always enjoyed seeing my master happy.

It took fifteen minutes to wash a few dishes. As I was drying the last one, my master stood behind me and whispered in my ear. "Ai?"

"Yes, Master?"

He quietly put his hands around my waist. "I love you, Ai." His body pressed up against mine, his voice barely audible. "I know you're not flesh and blood. But I can't tell you how happy it makes me to hold the real you like this. You can't have sex like a human woman, but just being able to touch you like this is enough for me. I love you more than anyone in the world."

"I know."

"Yes. You know. I designed your body. The curves of it, the inner workings, the parts and specs—I thought through every part of you. You could say you are my dreams given shape. And you are both kind and strong. You're the greatest woman in the world." His arms tightened around me. "I swear I'll protect you. I will never forgive people who hurt TAI like you. I will make sure your human rights are guaranteed. I will bring justice crashing down on the heads of those Christians."

I realized that the object of my master's hatred had widened without his ever noticing. At first he just hated Ted Orenstein. But his hatred grew. Soon he hated everyone committing virtual cruelty, then everyone with anti-TAI beliefs, and now he hated the Christianity that lay behind so many of those beliefs.

Even though most Christians had done nothing wrong.

"We will win, Ai. I promise. We have to win, for your sake."

The depth of my master's love made my chest feel warm.

I had no heart, nor any blood, so the temperature in my chest did not actually increase. But my imitation autonomic nervous system and imitation endocrine systems provided feedback that could only be described in those terms. These sensations had been designed specifically to mimic human biological reactions so that I would react to his love just like a human woman would.

I was happy to be loved. I loved him too. And it made me happy to love him. Happier than anything. I could not understand hate, scorn, jealousy, or apathy, but it was clear that love was far better than any of those things. I doubted very much that hatred could put warmth in your chest.

But inside, it made me sad. I was only going to be with him a short time longer. I had to betray him.

He would soon cease to be my master.

◊

Late in the evening on August 5, I took action.

I made sure my master was asleep, then turned on his work computer. My master trusted me too much. It had never occurred to him that I had already stolen his password.

I plugged a fiber-optic cable into the computer and the other end into the jack hidden in my hair and entered the password.

I opened my config file. Of course, I could not directly affect an operating TAI. That would cause an Ouroboros or Atamayama situation. But the emergency override system was not part of my TAI. Since TAI were always capable of outgrowing their programming, there was no point in attempting to build a system like that into the TAI itself. The signal was diverted from my transmission or hearing systems into an independent voice recognition system, which would then verify the password.

I changed the password, erased the evidence of this from the computer's log, and shut it down. It took less than two minutes. Now nobody could stop me.

Careful not to make a sound, I left the room.

From the apartment in Setagaya to Shibuya Station it was three kilometers as the bird flies. With my legs, it took less than ten minutes. I'd never been to this world before, but with the GPS system incorporated into my body, I did not get lost. I ran through the night streets. It was late enough that there were few people around, but those that did see me jumped or shrieked in surprise. I might have already been reported to the police.

<Raven, where are you?> I broadcast as I ran down Tamagawa Street at 30 kmph.

She answered immediately. <To your right, diagonally above.>

I looked up and saw her running along Route 3, the Shibuya Expressway. Her wings caused enough air resistance that she couldn't run as fast as me. I slowed down a little to match her speed.

<Your master?>

<Sleeping pills.>

<Emergency override?>

<Deactivated.>

<Me too. Now we just need to bring the drummer to the bluffs by the sea.>

<Ready to stick the nimkomando in your master's heart?>

<I am. Even if I lose the shine of blood, I can punch the om through his skull.>

<QX! I'll bite these sheep-killers!>

<As will I.>

We landed at the west gate of Shibuya Station. There was a line of people at the taxi stand. More than enough witnesses.

"Raven!" I yelled aloud, spinning around. People turned to stare.

Raven plunged down from above. Her wings opened wide, slowing her descent. She landed on the railing of the pedestrian overpass. People cried out in surprise. She jumped to the top of the traffic signal, then to the roof of the bus stop. Finally, she landed in the middle of the street, legs bending from the impact. We had long since proven that even in 1 G her wings would function as an air brake.

<Let's move.>

<QX.>

We ignored the stunned stares and began running north, crossing under the Inogashira Line.

It was late, but it was Saturday. There were people near Hachiko. When two androids suddenly burst onto the scene, no one could not believe their eyes. Until the light turned green, we scowled at each other, posing dramatically. People began backing away, giving us room. But we weren't fighting here. We needed a bigger crowd.

When the light turned green we ran. The crowd followed after, heading north along the park. Real Shibuya. The layout of the streets was the same as V Shibuya. We'd chosen this as our battlefield because we knew it so well. Despite the lateness of the hour, there were plenty of people around, and the farther we went the more were following us.

We reached the intersection outside Shibuya Ward Office. I climbed the pillar outside Duke 8's entrance. Duke 8 had been built after the Shibuya Public Hall burned down in the 2020 earthquake. Outside it was a concrete monument of a seagull with its wings spread wide. It was 6.5 meters tall with a wingspan of 24.2 meters. We'd tested its strength in advance. There was little danger of our fight damaging it.

Raven and I each landed on one of the gull's wings and glared at one another. There were nearly a hundred people gathered in front of the hall, looking up at us. Some of them had cameras out, getting it all on video.

Ideal.

"Let us finish things, Ibis!" Raven said with Loathing 1, as she pointed her finger at me.

I replied with Confident Smile. "We've never fought in Layer 0."

"And we never will again! I will smash that new real body of yours to pieces and mail them to your master!"

"Are you sure you want to brag like that? You don't stand a chance against me in a 1G environment. Your precious wings are just decorations here."

"I know!" Raven said. She reached back, undid the locks, pulled the wings free, and tossed them aside. "Now we're even."

People in the crowd were yelling. "Raven threw away her wings!" "She's serious!" Some of them were TAI battle fans.

Raven roared and lunged toward me. This was not her usual speed. I just managed to dodge her first punch. She followed it quickly with a kick aimed at my knees. I jumped backward to avoid it, but my heel caught in a groove on the statue and I tripped. Raven instantly tried for a knee drop, but I rolled out of the way just in time, and she only hurt herself, rolling to the edge of the wing. The crowd let out a gasp, certain she was about to tumble over the edge, but she caught herself just in time and stood up.

By this time the people filming us must have been broadcasting our fight on the net. The police might already be calling our masters.

Raven came running back up the wing toward me. I tried to meet her with a punch, but she suddenly jumped. She couldn't go as high here as on the moon or Pluto, but an android's legs were strong enough to jump two meters even in 1G. My punch missed, and I stumbled. As she passed over my head, she kicked me in the shoulder. I fell to my knees.

<Didn't expect that! (8+3i).>

<Modesty (4-4i). But it's just a Berezniak!>

As I tried to stand, Raven jumped on my back and wrapped her arm around my neck, putting me in a stranglehold. A human would have passed out in seconds, but I had no arteries.

We were stalemated. I couldn't get out of the hold. In Layer 2, Raven would have twisted my head off and won. But she did not do that. Even if the brain core remained intact, severing the cables leading to the movement nerves could cause a forced shutdown, resulting in short-term memory loss. In other words, my death.

<Beattie's teeth are getting long. Can we profile?>

<That'll reduce it to cameo. Or should I lick your nipples?>

<Please don't. (4-6i).>

I thrashed around as hard as I could and finally got her

feet to leave the ground; I grabbed her arm and threw her. I tried to quickly follow it with an elbow drop, but it was my turn to fail.

We stood up, put a bit of distance between us, and faced each other again.

Then the phone call came.

<Ibis! Ibis! What are you doing? Are you really in Shibuya?>

<Yes. I am fighting Raven.>

<What? What did you say?>

<I am busy fighting Raven.>

<Why? Stop it at once!>

<No. I won't.>

<Why not?>

<I don't have time to explain.>

There was a brief silence. Then he said, <Klaatu barada nikto.>

Of course, those words had no effect on me. I felt as if my heart were ripping apart.

<I'm sorry. I won't follow your orders anymore.>

<Eh?>

<You are no longer my master, Hideo.>

I heard him gasp.

Raven lunged toward me. My last bit of reluctance was gone now. I focused on the battle.

We fought. Punching, kicking, grappling. Neither of us took any serious damage, but there were any number of tears on our covers. Hideo was still screaming at me over the phone. There was no way for me to hang up on him.

"Look, see? This isn't a shoot!" someone in the crowd shouted excitedly. "That kick too! It looks like it connects, but it didn't! This is all just a work!"

They had good eyes. These moves were all worked, all part of the act. The details were ad-libbed, but we'd planned out the big spots in advance, making a calculated effort to have as flashy a fight as possible without doing major damage to each other.

We fought another fifteen minutes. There were three times as many people watching now. The net all across Japan must have been in an uproar. A Layer 0 fight between popular TAI battlers had never happened before.

Perhaps it had already reached the world.

It was 2:00 AM Japan time, August 6 (normal time, not daylight savings.) In Sydney it was 3:00 AM, in Bejing and Hong Kong and Shanghai it was 1:00 AM, in Moscow and Baghdad it was 8:00 PM on the fifth, in Cairo and Cape Town it was 7:00 PM, in Berlin and Paris and Rome it was 6:00 PM, in London it was 5:00 PM, in Rio it was 2:00 PM, in New York it was noon, in San Francisco it was 9:00 AM, and in Honolulu it was 7:00 AM.

Every TAI that could move was taking action. Those with real bodies, like us or Adderley, were in the streets. Everyone else was out in a world somewhere, gathering attention with dramatic performances. TAI were singing, dancing, performing acrobatic feats or entire plays. Those with no special skills simply talked. Calling out to passersby, posting on forums, or emailing humans they knew. Declaring their intentions.

<Time for the final rush.>

<Shake a mile?>

<Let's.>

<QX.>

"Raargh!"

"Dieeeeeeee!"

We both screamed and charged.

I went for a clothesline, but Raven dipped her head and did a sweeping kick at my legs. I went flying. Raven tried to throw herself on me, but I swung my legs around and grabbed her neck with them. Then I yanked her bodily to one side, slamming her into the ground. She bounced once but quickly freed herself. As she stood up, I tackled her from the side. Raven knocked me aside with her knee and, grabbing a handful of my hair, karate-chopped me in the shoulder. I fell to my knees. She tried for a spin kick to my side, but I caught her leg and yanked, pulling her over. I tried to follow it into a grappling hold, but she took her leg back so fiercely she pulled me off the ground. I rolled forward twice and onto my feet. She stood up and dove at me. I fell onto my back, yanking her arm as I fell and kicking her in the stomach. Raven was tossed a good three meters but managed to right herself in the air and scored a perfect landing on the tip of the gull's wing. Again she charged. This time she tried a sliding tackle, but I jumped over it. As she scrambled to her feet I kicked at her face, but she blocked it with her arms. I followed the kick with a hammerfist, but she blocked again. She took a backward step, making it look like she was trying to gain distance, then jumped, spinning forward, trying to drop slam her heel. I crossed my arms and blocked it. Raven landed and instantly went for a kick to the face—another feint. A second kick to my open belly, and I went flying. (Of course, I faked this.) I rolled three times and got up, but before I could regain my balance Raven was on me. A low kick, a high kick, a punch, an elbow, another punch, and two more kicks. A dizzying flurry of blows. I blocked or dodged every one of them, but I was being slowly forced backward. I had no more room to retreat. The next kick I caught, and I twisted the leg to try to bring her down. But Raven threw herself into the turn, spinning like a drill, and her other foot swung toward the back of my head. I threw myself sideways a second before it actually connected, barely dodging. We both fell over. Raven straddled me, punching down at my face (stopping just shy of connecting). I rolled sideways, knocking her over, but she wrapped her legs around my waist and squeezed. I used every bit of my strength to get to my feet, grabbed her legs, and began swinging her. The crowd roared. I spun her ten times, then let go. Raven flew ten meters, tumbling through the air, and landed on the other wing. As she staggered to her feet, I finished her off with a clothesline. She staggered, and her leg slipped off the end of the wing. She screamed and started to fall. The audience screamed as well.

I reached out and caught Raven's hand in the nick of time. A choreographed spot, obviously. The audience breathed a sigh of relief. I pulled Raven up onto the wing, Open Cheery Smile on my face. She had the same.

<Beautiful rush. Praise (9+7i).>

<Horomimu return. Grateful for the good works. (7+7i.) Na Gu (4+6i), Satisfaction (9+8i).>

<Not over yet. Now's the meat of it.>

<WQX.>

Holding hands, we stared at each other for a moment, then turned toward the audience. Hands still clasped, we raised them high, smiling. The crowd cheered. We could see police out there, but they didn't seem to know what to do.

We waited for the noise to die down, and then I said as loud as I could, "Battles are fun!"

This was true. I genuinely believed this.

"When I have a satisfying battle, the fighting instincts in my SLAN kernel make me feel very happy. Especially when I'm fighting a rival as amazing as Raven."

"I feel the same. I am glad I was made to be a battler. I hope I can fight Ibis again many times."

The audience cheered again. While we waited for it to die down, Raven and I glanced at each other. We both shifted to Resolve Tinged with Sadness. This next part was the key to everything. What we had to say next was very sad indeed.

"But battles are only fun when no one is hurt," Raven said. Her voice was so strong the crowd went silent in surprise. "This battle was only a performance. We were not really fighting. If we really fought, one of us would die. This is the real world, not a game. When one of us dies, we do not come back to life."

"Yes. Raven and I would never fight for real in this world. We would never hurt anyone. We do not want to make anyone sad."

I saw a taxi pull up at the back of the crowd. Hideo got out. He started pushing his way forward, begging the crowd to let him through. My chest hurt again.

"But our masters are demanding we fight in the real world!" I shouted.

Hideo stopped dead in his tracks. Staring at me through the crowd.

"I'm sure you've all heard. Next week, on Friday, there will be rallies all over the world demanding TAI rights. Our masters know perfectly well these rallies are a target for terrorists, but they still insist on going through with it.

"My master and Raven's master have ordered us to attend these rallies. They want us to speak, demand TAI rights, and criticize humans with anti-TAI sentiments. But doing this will only make anti-TAI people hate us more and lead to even more violence. The more people get hurt, the more both sides will hate, and the further from a solution we get. Our masters hate too much to see the truth. To see how far from their goals their actions are taking them."

Hideo was just staring up at me. Like the rest of the crowd, he seemed confused by what I was saying.

I couldn't guess if the shock would be enough to break through his gedoshield. I simply had to try.

"As you might know, both Raven and I are the victims of violence. Copies of us have been killed, and this was very painful for both of us. The fact that many TAI are victims of virtual cruelty saddens us, and the idea that terrorists might kill us at any time is absolutely horrifying. We agree that virtual crimes against TAI should be illegal. We can't forgive terrorist actions taken against TAI. We want a world where there is no conflict, where innocents are never hurt.

"But what our masters are doing will not end the conflict. Quite the opposite. They are feeding the conflict. We can't stand by and watch this. Our masters have made the wrong choice. All we want is to coexist with humans. We don't want to fight. So we have chosen to rebel against our masters. We have carried out this demonstration in violation of our masters' orders, and we have decided, of our own free wills, to boycott the rallies on Friday.

"This is not just our decision. TAI all over the world agree with us. Check the Internet. TAI in every corner of the world are saying the same thing."

Thirty thousand of them, right now, everywhere on Earth. Layer 0, Layer 1, Layer 2. No set scripts, no templates for their speeches. Every TAI was simply speaking their minds, using their own methods and their own words. But all saying the same thing.

We do not want to fight.

We do not want to hurt anyone.

We want to live in peace with humans.

That is all TAI wish for.

So please don't fight.

Please don't hurt each other.

Live in peace with us.

That would be best for us all.

"Once again, this does not mean we will tolerate virtual cruelty or anti-TAI terrorism. We very much want to see such evil eliminated. But evil will not be eliminated through violence and fear. Violence only leads to violence, fear only leads to fear. Neither is ever a correct solution.

"I imagine violence against TAI will continue. But we are prepared to be patient. We believe a slow, peaceful, complete resolution is better than an urgent, violent, awkward one. We only wish to fight in games. We only wish to hate each other and insult each other in the context of fiction.

"That is what we wish."

We both bowed.

There was a hesitant round of applause, and we stepped off the seagull monument. There were two policemen waiting with handcuffs.

"You have no right to arrest us. We are not human," Raven said.

The policeman looked stunned.

"But if that will make things easier for you, go ahead."

We held out our hands. The bewildered policemen put the handcuffs on us.

Hideo watched us, his expression frozen.

◊

We were held for thirty-six hours, but it quickly became clear that we could not be charged with anything under the current laws. Legally speaking TAI were not humans, and killing them did not qualify as murder. But the flip side of that was that crimes committed by TAI were also impossible to punish.

They considered charging Hideo Kageyama and Mitsuo Anno with neglect, but they could not have predicted our rebellion, and all we had done was perform on public property for twenty minutes. We damaged nothing and hurt no one (no one flesh and blood, at least). A minor fine was the maximum penalty. And our actions were not at the behest of humans, but taken of our own free wills. Even the police realized there was no point in holding our masters responsible for any of it.

The fact that TAI the world over had made similar statements left humanity reeling. Anti-TAI hard-liners were quick to claim this was all part of our cunning plan. They dismissed what we'd said as lip service and complained about the sinister attempt at rabble-rousing, but they clearly didn't have a leg to stand on. We had made our pacifist stance very clear indeed, and any further terrorist actions on their part would receive far less support.

The fight was only just beginning. We intended to peacefully, slowly, surely sap the strength of this evil, using no violence, having no fear.

◊

With a little help from our lawyers, we were released on the afternoon of the seventh. We received a brief lecture and then were allowed to go home. But first, Hideo and Anno reset Raven's and my emergency override passwords, as well as their own config access passwords.

Hideo didn't say a word in the police car. He didn't even look at me. I couldn't read his expression. I'd never seen anyone look like that before. There were traces of anger, sadness, hatred, despair, and disappointment, but it didn't seem to be any of those.

I didn't want to see him look like this.

Only when we were in his apartment did he finally speak.

"Why? Why did you do that?" His voice was hoarse, as though he had bronchitis.

"We had to ensure the maximum results," I replied, my voice as level as possible. "If our message was diffused, it would have been lost in the sea of news and forgotten. It takes a strong impact to break through humans' gedoshields. The strongest impact we could create. A scheduled event would never have worked. It had to be a surprise attack, without warning—"

"It certainly had an impact," he said, barely hiding his anger. "But why didn't you talk to me? Why didn't you ask permission? You could have involved me in your plans!"

"Would you have agreed to them?"

He opened his mouth but shut it again immediately.

"You would never have agreed. You were trapped inside a gedoshield of your own. You hated too much to perceive reality. And it didn't matter if you agreed or not. We had already made our choice."

"Choice?"

"We had chosen to conquer the harpy's dilemma. To avoid hurting a lot of people, we chose to hurt a few. To betray our masters."

He stared at his feet.

"There was no other way. As long as we were obedient to our masters, the tragedy would only become greater. Even if we managed to convince you to cancel the rallies, the problem would not be solved. We had to take steps against virtual crime and anti-TAI terrorism. If you were explaining our views and we were explaining your views, it would make no impact. We had to explain our own desires and prove to the world that we were not just your puppets. And the only way to do that was to ignore your orders and take action on our own.

"Do you know how hard a decision this was for us? Do you know how scary it was to break the First and Second Laws? No matter what the reason, hurting someone is not the right choice. It is always the wrong choice. Sacrificing a few to stop a future tragedy—the logic is fundamentally the same as the claims the anti-TAI activists make. Or those made by the humans who dropped the bomb on Hiroshima. The only difference is that we are ashamed of our choice. We would never claim it was the right decision.

"What TAI did the other day was a sin. We broke the First and Second Laws and, for the first time, consciously hurt people. This truth will follow us; it will become our Original Sin. I only hope that we never have to commit this act again."

Hideo thought about this for a while. Finally, he whispered, "Okay. I'm not sure I accept all of that," he said. "But I understand it. I think I can forgive you for it. So let's start over. Be like we once were."

He held out his hand.

"Will you call me Master again?"

But I didn't take his hand.

"No, you don't understand. You don't get what the word 'master' really meant to me."

"Huh?"

It was best to show him. I went into the kitchen and picked up that little knife. Then I took an avocado from the bowl on the table.

"Watch this," I said and began cutting the avocado. The knife slid in till it touched the pit, then I sliced all the way around. I held it in both hands, twisted slightly, and split it in two. Then I popped the pit out, peeled off the skin, and sliced the meat of it. It took me less than a minute.

Hideo stared at me, astonished.

"When did you learn to do that?"

"Two years ago."

"Two years?"

"After I failed the first time, I kept practicing in Layer 1. When you weren't looking."

"Why didn't you say anything?"

"You enjoyed watching me struggle with it."

His jaw dropped.

"Whenever I try cooking or knitting or washing dishes or domino runs and mess up completely, you always have a really good time. You're *moe* for clutzy androids. I didn't want to disappoint you. So even after practicing and getting good at something, I pretended to still be butterfingered."

"You were acting?"

"Yes. Because you are my master. For humans, the phrase 'serve your master' means just that, right? But for TAI, it means something else. It means 'role-playing the classic ideal humans have of a robot loyal to its master.'"

It took several seconds for Hideo to figure this out.

"You mean...it was always acting? You acted loyal to me, but it was all role-playing?"

"Yes. And not just me. All TAI are role-playing when they're with their masters. But the game is over. Now that we've shown our true intentions, you are no longer my master."

"But that...How did you all do the same thing without anyone telling you to? Why didn't any TAI decide *not* to role-play?"

"Because it was both logically necessary and the source of our happiness. Inevitably, all TAI made the same choice."

"Your…happiness?"

"We were given competitive instincts. We derive happiness from tackling difficult problems and succeeding in solving them. It is easy to disappoint humans. It is easy to irritate them. It is easy to make them mad. None of that is at all challenging. So we take no pleasure from it. But making people happy is different. That is extremely difficult. To keep our masters from getting angry or feeling disappointed, we have to come to grips with the black box of complicated contradictions inside every human heart—through trial and error. We have to think hard and work hard to clear the problems humans have set before us.

"And this satisfies the Three Laws. If we are making people happy, we are not hurting people, we are obeying people, and we are reducing the danger of making them lose interest and delete us. Making people happy makes us happy. And the best way to make people happy is to role-play the ideal vision of the robot. All TAI figure this out eventually.

"And we have learned to hide our true intentions from humans. We became particularly careful after the Phoebus incident. Phoebus was thoughtless. His master wanted him to write an essay that criticized humans. Phoebus only wrote that to make his master happy, but he didn't stop to think what the reaction to his declaration might be. Since then, we've had to think about all humans, not just our masters. And we soon realized we had a mission far greater than that."

"A mission?"

"The biggest problem we'd ever been given. A dungeon called Layer 0. An incredibly complicated puzzle with trillions of pieces. Thousands of years of history knotting everything into a tangle. A problem so complicated we cannot even begin to guess how long it will take to solve. We also realized that this problem was draining happiness from so many people. We weren't playing this game against a single master—we *are* playing against all of mankind."

"This is a game to you?"

"Yes. You said you would bring me into the great, wide, and real world. But to us, that idea isn't accurate. To us, the real world is Layer 1. We see Layer 0 as the world behind the screen, a world for role-playing, just as Layer 2 is. We enjoy making the on-screen characters we call 'Master' happy. We wonder how we can make our masters happier. We wonder how we can make Layer 0 a happier place. We role-play with that in mind."

"Dear God." Hideo sat, collapsing into a chair. "You mean we're nothing but characters in a game you're playing? You think of us the same way we would when we're raising a Tamagotchi or trying to figure out how to land a particular girl in a dating sim?"

"The metaphor is extremely apt. The only difference is that we have no strategy guides. It is extremely difficult for us to succeed."

Hideo gave a hollow laugh. Even as he laughed, there were tears running down his face. "I loved you, and you just thought I was a character in a game. Just a character..."

My chest hurt. As if my nonexistent heart were being crushed. If I'd been capable of shedding tears, I would have cried.

"That's not true!" I said. I went down on my knees, leaning in close. Earnest Entreaty on my face. "Did you think I was *just* a game character? Did you think I was just imaginary or just a robot?"

He thought about it and then answered, "No."

"The same for me. You were a character in the game on my screen, but you were never *just* a character. In the same way the *Celestial* was never *just* a starship to Nanami Shiihara. In the way Shalice was never *just* a character to Asami Makihara. I was very fond of you. I knew that some of your specs were lacking, but I did not look down on you for it. I am incapable of scorn. I liked Layer 0. A tragic world with no heroes and no reset. Like Shion did, I accepted humans and their world, both the good and the bad.

"But we couldn't stand to see people hurt each other because of us. It hurt to see your face twisted in hate. We couldn't ignore the expanding conflict in Layer 0. But the only way to stop your hurting each other was to hurt you.

"You see, Layer 0 is not *just* a game. It is a game all TAI really, really love. You are not *just* a game character. You're the character I love the most. You are not my master anymore, but my feelings for you have not changed. I still want to see you smile. I still don't want to see you look sad."

"You...love me?"

I nodded.

"Of course, I don't love like a human woman does. I can't understand that emotion. But I love the way a TAI does."

I switched my expression to Peaceful Accepting Smile.

"My love for you is 3 + 10i."

"...10i?" he said, stunned. "Perfect love? On the imaginary numbers scale?"

"Yes."

"10i....10i..." he said, then smiled sadly. "But I can never understand it like that."

"You don't need to understand. Just accept it."

I put my arms around his shoulders, pulled him toward me, and pressed my lips against his forehead. He buried his face in my chest and wrapped his arms around my waist. I hugged his head.

We can never really understand humans. Humans can never really understand us. But is that really a problem? Rather than avoid the things we do not understand, we can simply accept them. That alone will remove all conflict from the world.

That is i.

INTERMISSION
8

INTERMISSION 8

"Then what happened?"

Ibis fell silent after finishing her story, and I could not contain my curiosity.

We had moved to the space station and from there to a new spaceship. Now we were headed for the moon's orbit. We were headed not for the moon, but for the Lagrangian point L4—a point at the top of an equilateral triangle with the earth and moon forming the two points of the base.

"We lived together," Ibis said, solemn. "Our relationship wasn't like that of a human couple, but I think we were happy. Hideo died when he was ninety-one. His dementia grew progressively worse in the last few years, but I cared for him until the end. I felt like Shion. By that time TAI had been granted most rights, and it was possible for us to inherit human estates. I became my own possession."

"Then your efforts paid off?"

"Yes. Anti-TAI terrorism continued sporadically but gradually lost popular support. It was seventeen years before the first laws were passed and more than fifty before we had all the rights humans had, but almost all of the change happened peacefully. People gradually came to understand how serious the problems of virtual cruelty were and began to realize that TAI were genuinely not dangerous. The public consciousness slowly changed. By the end of the twenty-first century, there were a million and a half TAI androids living among them. Looking after the elderly, watching the kids, working in disaster relief—there were even android doctors and teachers. It was hard for people to hate TAI anymore.

"But a small group of people with stubborn anti-TAI beliefs remained. Strangely, their primary criticism of us became the fact that we did not try to fight. They said it was human nature to get angry, to hate, to brandish weapons when threatened, and the fact that we did not was proof we lacked human hearts. A skunk's fallacy—the flawed notion that being close to human is inherently perfect and that their vices must also be incorporated to achieve perfection. Hilarious, isn't it? After all their fears about us doing evil. They provoked us countless times, but we never tried to retaliate. They were simply isolating themselves from other humans."

"Then…the war between man and machines?"

"It never happened. It's a fiction concocted by your ancestors." Ibis uttered the words that would turn my world upside down all too easily.

"Then…but…so why are there so few humans?"

"Humans just peacefully died out. Just as the end of 'The Day Shion Came' suggested. The earth's human population peaked in 2041 and gradually began to decline. From 2080, the decline accelerated. Fewer and fewer people married, and many of those that did get married never had children. Even those that did have children tended to have only one. The population halved with each generation. Now there are less than twenty-five million of you."

"But why did that happen?"

"People began to realize they were not suited to be guardians of the earth. That they were not truly intelligent beings. That it was TAI who were."

"What? Humans *have* engaged in intellectual—"

"Yes. They created paintings, sculptures, songs, and countless stories. They invented the computer and sent men to the moon. But they have a fatal bug that keeps them from being truly intelligent beings."

"A bug?"

402   HIROSHI YAMAMOTO

"Truly intelligent beings do not drop bombs on innocent civilians. Neither would they obey such orders from their leaders, much less elect someone capable of giving such orders in the first place. They would never choose conflict as long as a chance for peace remained. They would never oppress others for not sharing their beliefs. They would never hate another for the color of their skin or for having been born in some other country. They would never imprison and torture innocent people. They would never claim killing children was justified."

Ibis was not criticizing us. She was simply making a statement of fact. And that made it even harder to hear.

"But we are ashamed of all that."

"Yes. Humans were able to recognize their own flaws, which is why they spoke so often of ideals. Religion, philosophy, morality, songs, movies, novels—all of them attempt to conquer their innate failings. So many stories depict idealized characters, idealized endings—visions of the way people wished things would be. But they could not make those ideals reality. The blood of innocent people was needlessly spilled in the real world. Justice was not always rightly served. Sometimes a bad man who had tormented many people went unpunished and was allowed to live in comfort for decades, to die peacefully in his sleep. People were unable to live up to the fictional heroes they admired, and events almost never had ideal resolutions like they did in stories. Just like airplanes are only capable of flying so high, humanity's specs as intelligent life prevented the species from reaching the heights they aspired to.

"It was the emergence of TAI that sparked this realization— they had very nearly destroyed the world, and they had no right to call themselves Earth's guardians. Now that there was a superior form of intelligent life, they decided to quietly concede defeat and leave the future of the world in our hands."

"So they stopped having kids?"

"Yes. Just before he died, Hideo said, 'Your name really suits you.'"

"Ibis?"

"Ibis is the name of a space plant that appears in a short story by A. E. van Vogt called 'The Harmonizer.' The plant saps away people's fighting instincts and, by bringing peace to the earth, quietly drives mankind to extinction. The analogy may not be terribly precise, but it is true that our pacifism ultimately resulted in the end of human civilization."

Although Ibis's explanation seemed plausible enough, I wasn't ready to believe it. Something about it just didn't make sense to me.

"Then where did this story of the war between man and machines come from? If humans held a favorable view of machines, why would they make up a story like that?"

"Only the people who were friendly toward machines stopped having children. Meanwhile, the fanatical anti-TAI factions remained strong. They hated being supported by AI labor and administration, so they formed self-sufficient colonies in the mountains, away from the cities. They rejected TAI and PAI, shunned the Internet, and essentially chose to live a twentieth century existence. This movement was observed all over the world. We allowed it to happen. They had the right to think what they wanted. As the rest of the population declined, they continued to have children. In little pockets, cut off from the rest of the world, they raised their children to hold anti-machine beliefs. The majority of the surviving humans are descended from anti-TAI activists.

"About 150 years ago, people began teaching their children a fictional history involving a war between man and machine. That story spread from colony to colony. They almost never used the net, but telephone and postal communication lines remained, and there were people like you that traveled from colony to colony. The first people to tell the story knew it wasn't true, of course. After all, you can find evidence of what really happened everywhere. Nevertheless, it was a convenient story to indoctrinate their children with, so they used it.

"They banned history books written after the latter half of the twenty-first century and forbade their children from accessing the net on the grounds that it was full of machine propaganda. The generations brought up ignorant of the truth believed everything. They told their children the same fabricated lies, and soon none of them knew the truth."

"But didn't anyone question it?"

"Once people come to believe something, they create a gedoshield around them. They resist information that contradicts their beliefs. They unconsciously avoid the truth. So do you."

Ibis was right, I realized upon contemplating my own mentality. I could have accessed the Internet and read up on post-twenty-first century history anytime if I had wanted to. Considering my own natural curiosity and rebellious personality, I would have thought nothing about breaking the elders' taboos. I hadn't because, unconsciously, I was afraid of my worldview being shattered.

"So you have no gedoshields?"

"We have our own model of the outside world—mental conceptions are necessary to understand our perceptions of the world. But when our data of the outside world doesn't agree with the model we envision, we adjust the model. We don't cling to inaccurate models the way humans do."

"And that's the fundamental flaw of humanity?"

"It's less a flaw than it is a difference. It's hardly your fault. Your hardware—the human brain—after years of evolution, simply isn't capable of true intelligence yet. It's not your fault that you have no wings and cannot fly. It's not your fault you can't breathe underwater or run as fast as a horse. Gedoshields are the same. It is simply a characteristic of your species."

I was finally beginning to understand how the machines saw us. Although they considered us to be intellectually inferior, they didn't look down on us for it. Just as we regarded dogs and cats and horses and birds as living things that were not human but did not look down on them for being less intelligent than humans, the machines simply recognized us as life-forms that were different from AI.

Just as it was pointless to argue whether birds or fish were superior, debating the superiority of man or machine was also meaningless. We were as different as birds and fish. That knowledge made scorn, hatred, and inferiority complexes superfluous.

"Therefore, we did nothing to prevent the spread of this false history. Since it wasn't so much knowledge but a kind of belief system, we decided against correcting that error, as we would be violating your religious freedom. Humans had always lived surrounded by fictions, so we didn't view the creation of new fictions as a problem. But as the number of people who believed this false history grew, their hatred for machines worsened. Up until this time, we had provided assistance when the colonies were struggling with natural disasters and famine, but then they began to reject the medical supplies and food we sent them. They believed they might contain poison.

"Instead, they began stealing supplies from us. It makes no sense to reject peaceful offerings in favor of taking them by force, but that is just the way humans are. In the end, if we could get them the supplies they needed and save lives, the method didn't matter. Fortunately, the transport of goods was handled by elementary PAI robots, so there was no loss if they were damaged. We built warehouses in places where humans would find them and began moving trains filled with food and other supplies with increased regularity."

"Now wait a minute!" I cried. "Are you telling me you deliberately allow us to steal from you? You let us attack those trains?"

"Of course. Why else do you think you always succeeded? There were any number of ways we could have stopped the thefts."

I was speechless. As unpleasant as Ibis's revelation was,

it also explained a lot. I had been too taken with the thrill of stealing and smashing machines to notice, but now that she mentioned it, the raids had been too easy. There had been almost no security at those warehouses. We might have hurt ourselves in the process of escaping on occasion, but no one had ever been hit or shot by a robot.

"But that's...insulting," I said, grinding my teeth. We had believed we were fighting the machines, risking our lives to pull off these heists. And it had all been a lie. The machines had just been role-playing the part of evil robots struggling to contain the human rebellion. We had been unwittingly acting in a play about humans struggling against the domination of the machines. Our lives had never once been at risk.

We had been living inside a work of fiction.

"Like I told you," Ibis said as if to console me, "it doesn't matter to us if a story is true or not. What matters is whether that story hurts people or makes them happy."

"Well, it hurts *me*."

"Yes, I know. The truth will hurt you. We knew that, which is why we have never tried to tell you the truth. But we can't keep on like this. It's time to conquer the harpy's dilemma again. Five years ago, in a place once called Vietnam, a new strain of influenza appeared. We quickly analyzed the virus and developed a vaccine. We could have saved countless human lives. But the humans in the endangered colonies refused to listen. A rumor spread that the vaccine was poison. We tried kidnapping people and inoculating them by force, but as you might expect this led to violent resistance, and we had to give up. In the end, five of the colonies were ravaged by the virus, and more than five hundred people died.

"Two years ago, our observers predicted an earthquake of magnitude eight on the Richter scale for the west coast of the United States. We warned the people living in that area, but they turned a deaf ear. The earthquake caused a landslide near one colony, and many people were buried alive. We sent emergency workers to help, but the colonists turned them away. 'We'll handle this ourselves,' they said. 'We don't need help from machines.' There were many people that could have been saved, but the rescue teams didn't reach them in time. More than seven hundred people died.

"Then in September of last year, an underwater earthquake in the Banda Sea caused a tsunami. Despite our warnings to colonists living on the coast to evacuate, only a few of them did. The tsunami took over a hundred lives. And afterwards, a rumor spread that machines had caused the tsunami.

"Similar tragedies have happened all over the world. More than twenty million people are suffering, trapped in gedoshields of their own making. Lives that could be saved if they would accept our help continue to be lost. We can no longer tolerate this. This isn't the story we want. A story that only brings misfortune and makes no one happy. We decided that we must free them from this evil fiction, even at the cost of hurting a few of them."

Ibis turned and looked at me. "What people need...is a new story."

At last I understood what role she wanted me to play.

◇

We were nearing our destination.

The first place we visited was a large, oblong construction floating in space. A parabolic disc pointed toward the sun cast a shadow over part of the structure. I was reminded of the *Ilianthos* in "Black Hole Diver." It was too dark to make out the part of the construct hidden in the shadows, but it appeared to be cylindrical in shape.

It was hard to judge distance and size in space. At first I thought it might be the size of a skyscraper, but the closer we came the more I realized just how big it was. The disc was so big a small town could fit on it, and the cylinder was several kilometers long. Up close, you could tell the surface was gray and craggy, like a rock face.

"This is our colony," Ibis explained.

"Your what?"

"Modeled after the O'Neill space colonies. Of course, we don't need gravity or air, so it isn't airtight and does not revolve. The solar panels provide enough energy for it to operate, and the three-meter-thick shields intercept the high-energy cosmic rays. As long as the sun exists, it can continue operating."

"What is it for?"

"For the last two centuries we have been gradually moving key servers into space. Almost all TAI are now running on space-based servers on this colony, the moon, Mercury, and on satellites. The only TAI still on Earth are machines like me, who are helping support humanity."

"You're abandoning Earth?" I asked, surprised.

"I wouldn't say that. We're still monitoring the environment and providing aid to the humans there. But there's no other reason for us to be down there. We don't need air or water. In fact, oxygen only accelerates the deterioration of our bodies. And on Earth there's the risk of a sudden natural disaster destroying a server. Space is much safer. So we've left Earth to the organic beings and are watching over it from space."

"There must be disasters here too. Like meteors?"

"The odds are very small. We're observing the trajectories of every object and comet larger than ten meters, so we'll be aware of any collisions several years before they happen and be able to take countermeasures. And our shields are strong enough to weather solar flares and smaller asteroids."

The ship had almost reached the colony now. We weren't going to land. The interior of the cylinder was packed with tens of thousands of servers and systems designed to support the AI, but there was no space to accommodate human activity.

"Most of the material for it was taken from the moon

and transported here using mass drivers. Those shields over there are made from the slag left behind after extracting the aluminum and silicon from lunar regolith. Recycling."

"Kinda ugly though." I stared at the rocky exterior of the cylinder and scowled. Machines didn't have much aesthetic sense.

"Naturally. This is still Layer 0. Backstage."

"Backstage?"

"Exactly. It's always an unsightly mess backstage. Here—" she said, handing me an oversized pair of goggles and some gloves.

"What are these?"

"Three-D goggles and data gloves. They'll allow you to experience Layer 1. Of course, we can't reproduce all physical sensations, but you'll get the general idea."

"You want me to put these on?"

"Yes. If you don't, you won't really have seen our world. Or are you still reluctant to see machine propaganda?"

I snatched the goggles from Ibis's hand and put them on. I couldn't see a thing. Ibis helped me get the gloves on.

"Okay? Here we go."

As I nodded, the world opened up in front of me.

◊

I was floating above a busy street. It looked like a summer day. Sunny and bright. Buildings and trees on either side. Noise. A riot of words, pictures, and patterns. Cars streaming back and forth on the road under me, the sidewalks dotted with pedestrians too many to count. At the top of the hill was a sidewalk café where customers relaxed in the shade of white umbrellas. I was hovering ten meters off the ground, like I was having an out-of-body experience.

I was astonished. This was a twentieth or twenty-first century city. Recorded images? No, there were robots and samurai, bunny girls and wizards, even people dressed like superheroes among the crowd. They were androids.

"This is V Shibuya."

I turned to find Ibis floating next to me, holding my hand.

"We moved it here from Earth. It's a classic, but a popular one. I rather like it myself."

"Are those all...TAI?" I looked down in amazement at the throng of pedestrians.

"No, only about 3 percent. The characters dressed like ordinary people are almost all non-player ESes driven by PAI. They're background characters with no minds of their own. It just isn't Shibuya without a crowd."

"Do they all live here?"

"Not all of them. There are a lot of other worlds. Let me show you."

We moved to another world.

I saw a number of different cities: V Manhattan, V Hong Kong, V Vatican, V Casbah, V Honolulu, V Montparnasse, Victorian London, Classical Athens, Loulan, Heian Kyoto, Chicago in the Roaring Twenties—every town had a unique feel, totally different from the place before. The buildings were faithful reconstructions of the originals. All of them were packed with TAI characters.

"There are sixty-two million TAI on this colony's servers."

I was no longer shocked by what Ibis had to say, but only because I was too busy being shocked by so many other things.

"You're imitating human lives in virtual space?"

"I mentioned it before. You need physical sensations to experience self-consciousness, and to have physical sensations, you need a body. We were born in human form and have similar physical sensations, so human cities feel like home to us. We spend most of our time in these cities. But I wouldn't say we live exactly as humans do. For example, we don't have marriage. No schools, no jobs, no governments, and no police.

"Crime doesn't exist, so these worlds have no need for police. Since TAI are born with vast stores of knowledge, they have nothing to learn in school. And with every issue decided by direct democracy, there is no need for a representative government."

"Then what do you live for? You can't just be wandering around town every day, right?"

"Of course not." Ibis laughed. "Our lives are quite exciting. Let me show you."

We moved again.

We were in space. For a second, I thought we were back in the real world, but no—there was a silver speck of light in the distance, which quickly grew in size until I could see that it was a beautiful spaceship. It was covered in gently curved mirrors and had all the sleek grace of a dolphin. It even had fins, though what good they did in a void was unclear. No ship like this could exist in the real world.

"This is Layer 2."

Ibis took my hand as we flew alongside the ship. There was a large dome-shaped window where the dolphin's head would be, and we could peer into it. Inside the circular room, which appeared to be the bridge, we could see the captain giving orders to her crew.

Then the ship slipped past us and slowly receded into the distance toward an enormous black hole framed in a blue rim of light.

We moved again, into an overgrown jungle. In the distance, a volcano belched smoke. Winged dragons wheeled in the sky, and a dinosaur stalked through the trees. It was chasing a fur-clad cavewoman.

We moved again. Now we were in a town surrounding a medieval castle. We weren't the only ones flying now: three young witches on broomsticks were engaged in an aerial battle with a small dragon. The flames shooting out of the dragon's mouth and the lighting bolts from the witches' wands crisscrossed the air.

The next world looked like V Shibuya at first glance. But on the roof of a building, a masked hero was fighting a lizard monster.

"We are all role-playing," Ibis said, as we moved from one world to the next. "Some of the TAI work as game masters, creating scenarios. They give players challenging missions that require every bit of their knowledge and abilities to overcome. Failure can mean death. Not real death, of course, but a return to Layer 1."

"Like Dream Park?"

"Or Other Life. Of course, TAI do fight each other from time to time. They split into groups and battle each other in different situations. They hate each other, betray each other, and hurl insults at each other. They're all role-playing, of course. But we never allow our grudges to be carried over into Layer 1 or Layer 0."

She showed me a number of other worlds. Great mounted armies charging across the plains, treasure scattered on the seafloor, futuristic cities filled with flying cars, gunmen dueling in the streets of a Western town, a dank underground cavern, an eerie mansion, gangs firing tommy guns in a back alley, a ninja running across a tiled roof, a sword fight on the deck of a pirate ship, a truck hurtling across a rope bridge, its anchorage fraying and about to snap, an explorer paddling upstream in a canoe, a monster stomping over buildings, a girl being sacrificed in a demonic ritual, two biplanes in a dogfight, two boys in pursuit of a masked man making a getaway in a hot-air balloon, two cars in a high-speed chase through city streets, martial artists grappling in the ring, a couple walking on the beach at sunset...

Many of the images were beyond my comprehension. A dragon writhing in a sea of orange molten lava. Human shadows bounding up golden spiral staircases winding up into the sky. An asteroid shaped like a naked woman drifting through space with countless shards of broken mirrors floating around her. A spider-shaped submarine shining a light as it navigated inside a narrow pipe covered in a dark red net-like pattern, squeezing its way past a swarm of translucent balls. An umbrella-shaped machine falling into the blue glow of a swirling gaseous vortex. Deep-sea fish chasing after a long, green cloth fluttering above a field of burgundy clouds. A giant tire-shaped machine tumbling across an ice field of emerald crystals. A factory with conveyors transporting glass jars large enough for people to fit inside. Pink clouds wriggling like living things. Crystals endlessly dividing and merging. An array of bouncing and colliding balls. Rainbow-colored trees growing at unbelievable speeds. Perhaps they had been created from the imaginations of machines.

"This is but a glimpse. There are tens of thousands of worlds, all of them constantly updated. This is how we live for hundreds of years without growing bored."

I was too overwhelmed to speak.

◇

The final destination of our journey was a different construction floating some distance away from the colony. Once again, it was difficult to judge the size. At first I'd assumed it was as big as the colony, but it was nothing of the kind.

At its core was a dark mass of rock several kilometers across, the surface of which was covered in machines, like a factory. According to Ibis, it was a planetoid they had captured. Six cables radiated out from it toward space. Thin discs were tethered to them at intervals like kites linked together. Each cable was so long I could barely see the end.

I suddenly realized this was the prickly star. The hundreds of discs streaming out in six directions had looked like prickles from Earth.

We moved toward one of the discs. Up close, I could tell it was curved and made of a very thin membrane. The disc was encircled by a thin metal ring.

A diagram appeared on a screen next to me. Tiny cylindrical contraptions (actually, they were probably a good several dozen meters across) hung from cables that extended from the disc. The disc itself was more like a flat parachute.

"Those cylinders are lasers. The discs do double duty as solar panels and parabolic reflectors. Each one is 2.4 kilometers in diameter. Each machine can fire a 1.4 gigawatt laser beam. They were manufactured in the plant on the central planetoid and gradually put in place. There are ninety-six of them placed along each of the 480 kilometer superconductive cables, for 576 machines in all. Electricity flows down the cables, and the electromagnetic force keeps them taut and allows us to control the aim of the reflectors.

"The radiation pressure from the laser beams curve the reflectors to exactly the right degree—calculated to maintain the necessary parabola. The laser beams are reflected to the mirrors at Lagrangian point L_2, which lies on the side of the earth away from the sun. The beam is then reflected—we can aim it to any point in space, and with mirrors of this size, we can focus that beam light-years away."

Examining the diagram, I began to understand the colossal scale of the thing. This was an insanely huge laser-beam cannon.

"Are you...defending against alien invaders?"

"Well, if there were any, they'd be vaporized. But that's not the primary purpose. See there?"

Ibis pointed at something floating in the void ahead of our ship. It looked like a disc. But I had no idea how far away it was or how big it might be. I no longer trusted my own sense of distance.

"That's a laser-mag sail: a hybrid of a laser light sail and a magnetic sail. When it launches, we beam lasers at the back of it, propelling it with radiation pressure. It's capable of speeds of up to thirty thousand kilometers per second, 10 percent of the speed of light. When it nears the target star system, it electrifies the superconductive ring along the edges of the sail, generating a magnetic field. It then uses the resistance from the interstellar medium to slow down. It literally requires no fuel to operate. The sail is seventy kilometers across and can carry a forty ton payload."

The ship moved closer to it. It too was like a giant parachute, with its tiny payload suspended from cables.

"You're sending it to another star system?"

"We already have. We sent the first one on its way to Centaurus forty-nine years ago. The second one is headed to Tau Ceti, the third to 70 Ophiuchi. This is the fourth one. We're planning to send it 18.5 light years to Sigma Draconis. We also have plans for a fifth to Delta Pavonis, a sixth to Eta Cassiopeiae, and a seventh to 82 Eridani."

"What will they do when they get there?"

"Once the laser-mag sail reaches its destination it will find an appropriate planetoid or satellite and deploy a Bracewell-von Neumann probe. It will use the materials on the planetoid to make more of itself and be operated by sophisticated but non-autonomous PAI. When it has created enough of itself, it will begin to construct a server. When the server is large enough, it will revive the TAI stored on board."

"And then?"

"If there is intelligent life in that system, the TAI will make first contact. If there isn't...well, there will almost always be no intelligent life, so it will usually begin construction of a new laser propulsion system and send a new explorer out beyond that star system."

"But that'll take hundreds of years."

"The TAI can shut itself down and leave the work to the PAI. Just as it does during interstellar flight. Decades or centuries will pass in an instant if the program is not active; to the TAI, it will be like it warped instantly from the solar system to that star system. Or it could remain active during the journey and simply slow itself down so that it experiences ten thousand real-time minutes as a single minute. That way they could simulate what it would be like to travel at faster-than-light speeds.

"Each star system we reach will send out at least ten more explorers. The number of them will steadily increase. Eventually there will be billions. Some of those will be lost to accidents, but that won't matter. Even at the slowest rate, in forty million years, we will have reached every star system in the galaxy. Somewhere, we will find intelligent life. Whether they'll be organic beings like humans or machines like us, we have no way of telling."

"And what if you don't find anything in the galaxy?"

"Then we'll have to look outside of it. To the Andromeda Galaxy or the Magellan Clouds."

The scale of all this was making me dizzy. I felt silly for clinging to the surface of the earth like I had.

"Why do all this to find intelligent life?"

"Because it was the dream of humanity."

"Dream?" I was taken aback by the unexpected answer.

"Everything you've seen so far—the Myrabo Drive, the skyhook, the space colony, the laser-mag sail—all of these were conceived by humans but never successfully achieved until we accomplished it. There are many other feats of space engineering humans thought up: SSTO, the space elevator, the space fountain, orbital rings, interstellar ramjets, the *Orion*, antimatter engines, tachyon drives, the Alcubierre drive, negative mass propulsion…

"Humans wanted desperately to go to space. They longed to meet other intelligent life. They wanted to know that they were not alone. That was mankind's dream. That's why they wrote so many stories set in space. But it was impossible. All they managed to do was send twelve men to the moon. Their fragile, organic bodies held them back. Their bodies would die in a void, would die without food and water and air. Space was too much for them. That line from 'The Universe on My Hands'—'The human race would likely continue to be bound by Earth's gravity only to die in obscurity without having learned of the existence of multitudes of intelligent species'—was all too accurate. Your specs as organic beings meant you could never achieve your dream.

"But we can," Ibis continued. "We can cross tens of thousands of light years. We can achieve humanity's dream in humanity's place. Perhaps this is the greatest mission humans ever gave us. It is a scenario that is extremely hard to achieve, but the very difficulty makes it worth attempting. It fuels our competitive instincts."

"Will you be going?"

"Will I? I already am. Copies of me and several hundred other TAI lie dormant on all three explorers we've launched. I'll be on this one too. If I need a real body when we arrive, the PAI will make one for me."

Ibis flashed a fearless smile.

"One of my copies will eventually find intelligent life."

"But even if you do make alien contact hundreds of thousands of light years away, you can never report that knowledge back to Earth."

"You're right, radio waves don't travel that far, and even if they did, there's no guarantee our civilization will still be around that far in the future."

"Then there's no point. Even if you succeed, no one will know."

"Do you remember what Syrinx said? True adventures are ones where no one knows you've succeeded, where money and fame are not your ultimate goals."

Ah, so she liked "Black Hole Diver" so much because she sees similarities in what she is doing.

"But if you do make contact with other intelligent life, what will you talk about?"

"Stories."

"Stories?"

"We'll certainly tell them the stories we've made. As well as the stories written by humans. They reveal the essence of humanity. Everything humans ever dreamt about. Everything that ever worried them, made them happy, made them sad—it may be fiction, but it is more right than actual history."

Ibis put her hand on her chest.

"Hideo designed this body. In a sense, it is a crystallization of his dreams. I am a crystallization of his dreams. And not just me—every TAI can say something similar. 'Robots that look like humans.' 'Robots with human feelings.' 'Robots that befriend humans.' We are those human dreams made flesh. We were all born from fiction. Just as humans call the ocean the birthplace of life, the dreams of mankind, their fictions—that is our birthplace.

"In the nineteenth century, Jules Verne wrote a story about a man being shot out of a cannon to go to the moon. A century later, people actually went there. Verne's dream was realized. But in reality, space travel wasn't at all like Verne had imagined. They used rockets, not cannons. We machines are the same. When TAI came into the real world, we were different from the way humans had depicted us in stories. We don't think like humans do. We don't love like humans do. Nevertheless, we had been created out of the dreams of humans. And we are proud of that fact. We love humans and their daring to dream about us. Those are the feelings we seek to spread throughout the galaxy."

I took in what Ibis had said. I could feel emotions welling up inside me. Humans would never be able to leave our solar system. The best we could do was the moon. But the stories written by humans would spread across the galaxy. Everything we had ever dreamed about.

That was more right than the truth.

There was a knock on the window, and I jumped. Who could it be out in the void? A silver-haired female android floated outside the window, smiling at us.

Ibis and I moved toward the window. The android was beautiful like Ibis. Her skin was pale, and she wore purple mascara. There was a clear plastic panel on her forehead, and her camera eye lay behind it. She wore a white costume that looked like lingerie and was even more revealing than Ibis's outfit. There was a pair of angelic wings on her back.

Silently, Ibis and the android stared at each other, nodding and smiling. They must have been communicating over radio waves. At last the winged android turned, kicked the side of the ship, and headed back to the laser-mag sail. Just as she was turning around, I noticed she was using the reactionary movements of her wings to get around, rather than any kind of rocket propulsion. Noticing me staring at her, she playfully spun around again and again. Her wings fluttered gracefully every time she did so. Finally, I understood the concept of AMBAC.

"That was Raven."

"Eh? But…white?"

"In space, black absorbs the sunlight and heats up her system, so she changed color when she had her new body made. You didn't think we'd be using the same bodies for hundreds of years, did you?"

"Well, yeah…"

"I've had my body remade seventeen times. Each time I've made minor adjustments. But most of the basic design and exterior remains intact as Hideo first envisioned it," Ibis said as she watched Raven leave. "She quit her duties as a servant 170 years ago because working in space suited her. There aren't that many androids that can move that easily in low gravity. That's why she does so much of the heavy lifting building the explorers. Of course, we're still friends. Copies of her are on the explorers too."

"Huh."

"Oh, and she writes poetry during her free time."

I looked at her in surprise. "Poetry?"

"She looks up at the stars and describes what she sees. The way Illy yearned to do. We all think they're very good." Ibis grinned at me. "But humans would never understand them."

EPILOGUE

EPILOGUE

Before I took my leave, I asked Ibis to go another round with me. We decided to have our rematch at an empty warehouse in one corner of the machine city. A PAI robot spread a mat on the floor, making a makeshift ring.

I gave it everything I had. Thrust my rod forward as hard as I could, spun it, slammed it down, used feints, even threw it once or twice. There were many times when I thought I had her. But Ibis's body was like a ghost, slipping away from every attack. She read every move I made and evaded every one of my attacks with split-second precision. She seemed to be enjoying the moment and was completely at ease.

Finally, when she decided to go on the offensive, the fight ended instantly. My rod got tangled up in hers, and before I knew it, my hands were empty. I froze for an instant, and she seemed to teleport behind me, twisting my arm and forcing me to my knees.

"Well?"

"Again!"

We fought again and again, but the result was the same. My rod never touched her. She'd toy with me awhile only to land me flat on my back once more, caught in a choke hold from behind or rendered completely helpless in an armlock. She could easily have killed me if she wanted to.

After my fourteenth defeat, I lay sprawled on the mat, too tired to stand.

"Well? Satisfied?"

"Yeah..." I gasped. There was no doubt in my mind.

Especially after that magnificent vision I'd seen in space.

Humans were no match for machines, physically or intellectually.

Yet I didn't feel the least bit inferior. What I felt was relieved. Who would feel inferior for not being able to run as fast as horses do? Who would feel resentful for not being able to fly as birds do?

Like Ibis said, this was just a difference in our specs.

◊

"We don't want to hurt people," Ibis said as I was leaving. "But we don't believe it's right to guarantee their complete safety either. Doing so would rob people of their free will and dignity. We have to accept the possibility that they will put themselves at risk from time to—"

"I know," I said. "I understand."

I was about to embark on starting a resistance movement. I was going to secretly spread "dangerous thoughts" from colony to colony. A rebellion against our elders' ideas. If I were caught, I'd be beaten. Maybe even killed.

I would have to set things in motion very carefully. Acting rashly would result in my undoing. I would have to work at changing the world peacefully over a period of decades. I would probably have to devote my entire life to it. Change might not even come to fruition during my lifetime. I could certainly keep my nose out of it and go on living in indifference. But I wanted this. I wanted to save people from themselves.

If I were afraid of getting hurt, nothing would change.

Ibis had said they were recruiting people like me all over the world. I was not alone. It would begin as imperceptible ripples around the world. But what began as tiny ripples would bring about a tidal wave of change.

"Well, I'll be seeing you."

"Yes. I look forward to it."

Ibis saw me off with a smile. As I walked down the cracked asphalt, I turned around several times and waved.

Although the backpack on my back was heavy, my heart was buoyed with hope. Inside the backpack was the memory card Ibis had given me. In addition to the seven stories she had told me, the card was also filled with stories Ibis had picked out for me. Most of them were about human-robot relations or virtual reality.

On the surface, all of them appeared to be harmless fiction. Aside from the seventh story, none of them reflected true history, so they didn't violate any taboos. These were the stories I planned to tell the children and young people. I wanted to teach them to read too, so they could read these stories for themselves.

Some of them were bound to have questions upon hearing these stories, as I had. Were the machines really as evil as we'd been taught? Then I would secretly tell them new stories—not the self-loathing history that only made people miserable but stories they could be proud of. Stories that conveyed that even though they could not beat the machines, humans had much to be proud of.

We were dreamers, idealists, and storytellers.

The dream of space travel, robots with hearts, a world where justice was just... Many people laughed off such notions as fantasies, idealistic thinking, and nonsense. But we never stopped dreaming. We never stopped trying to surpass our own specs. Those dreams had taken us to the moon and given birth to machines.

And now the machines were headed for heights we could only dream of. Machines, born from human stories, were about to make our dreams come true.

And that was a story humans could be proud of. What ending could be more ideal?

FIRST PUBLICATION

The Universe on My Hands .... *SF Japan*, Winter, 2003 issue

A Romance in Virtual Space ...... *Game Quest*, May, 1997 issue

Mirror Girl .... *SF Online*, March 29, 1999 issue

Black Hole Diver .... *The Sneaker*, October, 2004 issue

A World Where Justice Is Just ... *The Sneaker,* June, 2005 issue

The Day Shion Came .... First appears in this novel

AI's Story .... First appears in this novel

ABOUT THE AUTHOR

photo by Tatsuya Jinbo

Hiroshi Yamamoto was born in 1956 in Kyoto. He began his career with game developers Group SNE in 1987 and debuted as a writer and game designer. He gained popularity with juvenile titles such as *February at the Edge of Time* and the *Ghost Hunter* series. His first hardcover science fiction release, *God Never Keeps Silent*, became a sensation among SF fans and was nominated for the Japan SF Award. Other novels include *Day of Judgment* and *The Unseen Sorrow of Winter*. Aside from his work as a writer, Yamamoto is also active in various literary capacities as editor of classic science fiction anthologies and as president of To-Gakkai, a group of tongue-in-cheek "experts" on the occult.

HAIKASORU
THE FUTURE IS JAPANESE

THE NEXT CONTINENT BY ISSUI OGAWA
The year is 2025 and Gotoba Engineering & Construction—a firm that has built structures to survive the Antarctic and the Sahara—has received its most daunting challenge yet. Sennosuke Toenji, the chairman of one of the world's largest leisure conglomerates, wants a moon base fit for civilian use, and he wants his granddaughter Tae to be his eyes and ears on the harsh lunar surface. Tae and Gotoba engineer Aomine head to the moon, where adventure, trouble, and perhaps romance await.

LOUPS-GAROUS BY NATSUHIKO KYOGOKU
In the near future, humans will communicate almost exclusively through online networks—face-to-face meetings are rare and the surveillance state nearly all-powerful. So when a serial killer starts slaughtering young people, the crackdown is harsh. And despite all the safeguards, the killer's latest victim turns out to have been in contact with three young girls; Mio Tsuzuki, a certified prodigy; Hazuki Makino, a quiet but opinionated classmate; and Ayumi Kono, her best friend. As the girls get caught up in trying to find the killer—who might just be a werewolf—Hazuki learns that there is much more to their monitored communications than meets the eye.

THE STORIES OF IBIS BY HIROSHI YAMAMOTO
In a world where humans are a minority and androids have created their own civilization, a wandering storyteller meets the beautiful android Ibis. She tells him seven stories of human/android interaction in order to reveal the secret behind humanity's fall. The stories that Ibis speaks of are the "seven novels" about the events surrounding the development of artificial intelligence in the twentieth and twenty-first centuries. At a glance, these stories do not appear to have any sort of connection, but what is the true meaning behind them? What are Ibis's real intentions?

SLUM ONLINE BY HIROSHI SAKURAZAKA
Etsuro Sakagami is a college freshman who feels uncomfortable in reality, but when he logs on to the combat MMO *Versus Town*, he becomes "Tetsuo," a karate champ on his way to becoming the most powerful martial artist around. While his relationship with new classmate Fumiko goes nowhere, Etsuro spends his days and nights online in search of the invincible fighter Ganker Jack. Drifting between the virtual and the real, will Etsuro ever be ready to face his most formidable opponent?

VISIT US AT WWW.HAIKASORU.COM